Dazzling betrayals.
Dangerous success.
Only love could turn it
all to gold . . .

## PRAISE FOR
## *THE LAST PRINCESS*
## BY CYNTHIA FREEMAN . . .

"FREEMAN HAS THE ABILITY TO TRANSPORT YOU . . . an ability to make you care about her characters and want to see their stories through to the end. I CAN'T IMAGINE ANYONE PUTTING THIS BOOK DOWN!" —*Houston Home Journal*

"FREEMAN'S LATEST IS MESMERIZING . . . She succeeds in holding her reader's attention from page one . . . I thoroughly enjoyed the book and predict it will delight Mrs. Freeman's fans."

—*Chattanooga News-Free Press*

"GLAMOROUS . . . Passion, infidelity, glittering locales . . ." —*Star News*

"RICHLY SATISFYING . . . Freeman creates characters with which most of us can identify and carries their stories from beginning to end. *The Last Princess* is one of her most enjoyable!" —*Rockdale Citizen*

"A GOOD STORY DESIGNED TO KEEP THE READER TURNING PAGES!" —*Dayton Daily News*

*Also by Cynthia Freeman*

SEASONS OF THE HEART
ILLUSIONS OF LOVE
A WORLD FULL OF STRANGERS
FAIRYTALES
THE DAYS OF WINTER
PORTRAITS
COME POUR THE WINE
NO TIME FOR TEARS

# CYNTHIA FREEMAN

# THE LAST PRINCESS

B

BERKLEY BOOKS, NEW YORK

This Berkley book contains the complete text of the original hard-cover edition. It has been completely reset in a typeface designed for easy reading and was printed from new film.

THE LAST PRINCESS

A Berkley Book/published by arrangement with the author

PRINTING HISTORY
G. P. Putnam's Sons edition/April 1988
Berkley edition/March 1989



ISBN: 0-425-11601-8

A BERKLEY BOOK® TM 757,375
Berkley Books are published by The Berkley Publishing Group, 200 Madison Avenue, New York, NY 10016.
The name "BERKLEY" and the "B" logo are trademarks belonging to Berkley Publishing Corporation.

PRINTED IN THE UNITED STATES OF AMERICA

10 9 8 7 6 5 4 3 2 1

*To Shelly, Carole, and Kimberly*

# Chapter 1

NOT since Gloria Morgan's engagement to Reginald Vanderbilt had New York society seen such a frenzy of excitement as was aroused by the announcement of the impending nuptials of Lily Goodhue and Roger Humphreys. Although few events elicited more than a yawn from New York society, as soon as the embossed, cream-colored invitations were received, the ladies of the Four Hundred promptly beat a path to their favorite couturiers. It was to be the marriage of the decade, a match—if one were inclined to embrace God—made in heaven; the coming together of two distinguished families who came as close to being aristocracy as was possible in America.

On the evening of the engagement party, the limousines lined the sweeping, tree-lined driveway to the Goodhues' Long Island mansion. Lily stood alongside Roger and her parents in the vast marble-floored hall, greeting their guests. Even among that galaxy of bejeweled society, her beauty was dazzling. It went beyond the fact that her hair was the burnished red of an autumn sunset, or that her eyes were the color of the huge emerald she wore on her ring finger, or that the features of her heart-shaped face were sheer perfection. She had an air, an inner radiance that few who saw her that evening would ever forget. It even outshone the expensive pink Chanel dress her mother had ordered from Paris.

As they stood posing for pictures which would appear in the next day's *New York Times* and *Herald-Tribune,* there could have been no doubt as to her parents' joy. Diminutive, southern-born Violet looked as youthful and lovely as the day when she had burst onto the New York social scene as the bride of the tall, handsome rubber magnate Charles Goodhue.

The guests moved into the house, which was decorated with extravagant urns of azaleas, roses, and lilacs arranged to exquisite perfection. Beyond the open French doors of the ballroom the terrace and grounds were softly lighted, and the fountains at the far end of the pavilion played under dim yellow lights. Blood-red rhododendrons lined the path down to Long Island Sound.

Just then the band struck up "Lily of the Valley" and Lily circled the room in Roger's arms. There seemed no question that she was in love. It was evidenced by the smile on her face and the lyrical note in her voice as she greeted her friends. Roger, too, appeared delighted. Despite his unmistakably Brahmin reserve, he seemed unable to take his eyes off Lily. Yet as the evening wore on, Lily knew she had to get away for a few minutes, to escape the hundreds of eyes, so many of which were jealously hoping to find some flaw in this perfect evening. As Roger turned to ask a cousin to dance, Lily slipped quietly from the room, ran across the terrace, down the broad stone stairs, and along the path toward the conservatory. The glass doors closed behind her, leaving her in a silent world of exotic blooms.

Idly she let her gaze wander to the glass ceiling. The dazzling sight of a million stars in the midnight-blue vastness suddenly made her wonder how she had come to this moment. If she was shocked to find herself the focus of this evening's party, she supposed, she would—literally—have to go back to the cradle to trace the roots of her sense of unworth. . . .

# Chapter 2

LILY had always felt herself to be an outsider in her own home. She had never really belonged and it seemed that she had been paying for the sin of her birth from the moment she had first seen the light of day. Was any of it her fault? That was something she had been trying to decide for almost twenty-one years.

Violet and Charles Goodhue had been childless for ten years of their marriage and had almost abandoned hope that they would have a child, an heir to the Goodhue fortune. It had been a dynasty hard won, a dynasty which had been established three generations before by ignorant Dutch immigrants, and by dint of fraud and corruption and ruthlessness it had flourished.

With the first generation's ill-gotten wealth, the second generation of Goodhues had bought respectability. At the same time, they saw that wealth quadrupled. Charles's grandfather, riding the crest of the new age of industry, had transformed a modest fortune into a staggering one in the rubber trade in the Amazon. The slaves who worked those South American fields were too far removed from the States to taint the Goodhues' ever luminous reputation.

So, by his day, Charles Goodhue felt confident that when the biographies were written, his antecedents would appear merely as swashbuckling cavaliers.

The roots of Violet's wealth were strikingly similar. She had come from a long line of rumrunners and slave owners. Her grandfather had made a small fortune into a great one during the War Between the States selling bootleg liquor to both sides. Afterward, when other former slave owners found themselves dispossessed, Henri DuPres had emerged on the scene the triumphant master of the greatest and richest plantation in Louisiana.

Despite their combined inherited fortunes, and Charles's sharp business acumen which continued to make those fortunes more vast, he and Violet seemed denied by heaven the very thing they so desired—a child.

The sore lack was unmitigated by any wealth or possession he could ever hope to attain. Adoption was socially unacceptable for their set, and the idea of having a child not of his blood was abhorrent to a man like Charles Goodhue. What he longed for most was his own heir. Violet had less desire than he, but she was chagrined to disappoint Charles in an area that mattered to him so. Yet her barrenness appeared to be fait accompli.

Then one morning in Baden-Baden, where they had gone to take the baths, Violet awoke with a strange nausea. Never having been ill, for all her diminutive, fragile build, Violet immediately sought the counsel of Herr Doktor Steinmetz, the resident physician at the watering place.

So when Dr. Steinmetz congratulated her with the news that she was to be a mother, she greeted it with speechless shock. Then, as the reality of it set in, she all but flew from the room. "Charles! Charles!" she cried out, entering their room. "We're going to have a son! The gift I've wanted to give you for so long."

Neither of them doubted for a moment that she would bear the son they so wanted. In early celebration, Charles treated her to a new ruby necklace and matching earrings which might have turned her neighbor, Alice Vanderbilt, ever so slightly green with envy if she had seen them.

From that moment on, Charles treated Violet with even more than his usual adoration. He catered to her every whim. She was, after all, thirty years old—well past the usual child-bearing years.

He had the nursery remodeled in blue and had the vast dressing room adjacent to Violet's boudoir equipped for her confinement.

Faster than they had anticipated, that final day of miracles was upon them. The house was still but for the frantic efforts going on in Violet's transformed boudoir. The only sounds that could be heard were the excruciating screams emanating from Violet herself. She had never known pain before and she could scarcely tolerate it. There was nothing fragile about the sounds coming out of her just then.

When at last the baby came, she cried out with relieved joy: "I gave you your son, Charles"—all the while thinking, *I will never, never, never go through this again.*

Motherhood was a joy she could easily have dispensed with. If it had not been for her strongly felt obligation to provide Charles with an heir, she would have taken every precaution against becoming pregnant. Now that her duty was done, she'd have no more of it.

Never again would she endure the nausea, the ungainly bulk, and worst of all, the isolation. In her day it was not fitting for an expectant mother to show herself in public. Violet and her lovely gowns remained closeted for two full social seasons.

The past nine months had proved sheer agony. Violet had spent most of that time in bed, out of sheer spite, and now she vowed that she would never, never subject herself to this again.

The infant was taken from her immediately following the birth. Violet was only too glad to have the child removed from her. She lay among her satin and lace pillows waiting for Charles's delighted praise. But it was grave eyes he turned upon her.

"What's wrong, dear? Is the child all right?"

He nodded. "Yes."

"What then?" she asked, extending her hand for him to come closer.

He could hardly form the words. "We do not have a son."

"What do you mean?" she cried.

"I mean, Violet, that you have given birth to a girl."

*Impossible—impossible! How could that have happened? It had to be a son. A son was all Charles wanted.* "I can't believe it!" she whispered.

Coldly he answered, "Believe it. It is a girl."

For the first time since their marriage, she heard censure in his voice, and she suddenly experienced an emotion quite foreign to her: overwhelming remorse.

Charles merely shook his head. "Yes, indeed, we have a girl and not even beautiful, like you, Violet. We have a red-headed, skinny little monster. I don't know where that flaming red hair could have come from. Not from my side of the family, certainly."

When the baby was placed in Violet's arms, she looked down at the child and began to weep. This was not the chubby precious son she had expected. The baby was scrawny and unattractive, and if Violet had dared, she would have given her away and forgotten the whole thing. Her capacity to love was very limited. Charles received what little affection she had to give and there was none left over for an infant of the wrong sex.

Both parents had been so unprepared for a girl that they had never considered any name but Charles Goodhue II. It wasn't until the day before the baptism that Violet was willing to make a decision. Having come from a long line of southern beauties, whose names had been inspired by the beauty of roses, pansies, and violets, she was hard-pressed to come up with one for this ugly baby girl.

Lily? She thought bitterly of the Biblical verse: "Remember the lilies of the field—they toil not, neither do they spin." Useless—like this child. So just before the infant lay in Violet's arms at the baptismal font to be anointed in the faith of that famous lineage of blooms, Lily Marie Goodhue was grudgingly given an identity in the world.

Watching from his pew, Charles could not refrain from staring enviously at his friend Henry Ford, as he stood with his young son at his side. How had he, Charles, offended God so much so as not to be allowed a son of his own? He felt his ancestors looking down at him with contempt. Without an heir, the fortune they had amassed had no meaning. Violet was so frail, he dared not let her risk another pregnancy; she had barely survived the trauma of this delivery. Much as he longed for a son, he couldn't face life without Violet. His love for her was the only thing on earth that exceeded his obsession for an heir.

Over the next few years, as Lily turned from infant to toddler to schoolgirl, she seldom saw her parents. She was enchanted by their elegance and glamour, but whenever she reached out to embrace them, they quickly withdrew, becoming remote, cold figures who never seemed to notice her existence. They spent their winters in the house on Fifth Avenue and traveled extensively through the continent while Lily was left on Long Island in the care of nursemaids and governesses, almost forgotten. In time she gave up her efforts to reach out to her parents, knowing from a very early age that any such attempts would be spurned. In spite of the incredible luxury of her Long Island home, she grew up with an overwhelming sense of deprivation.

It was impossible to mistake their indifference. She was unloved by her own parents, for which she felt a sense of shame, as if she was unworthy of their affection.

Had it not been for her cousin Randolph Goodhue, three years her senior, who was sent from Manhattan to visit from time to time, she would have had no friends at all. But even then, her sense of worthlessness increased when she was five and Violet, despite her vow never to have another child, unexpectedly became pregnant. Her memories of Lily's birth had faded and she was almost enthusiastic about the possibility of giving Charles a son. And this time, she swore, it *would* be a boy. She had just returned from a trip to Europe late in her sixth month when Lily first became aware of the change in her mother's figure.

"Mamma, why is your tummy so fat?" she asked that night at dinner.

Violet looked at her daughter reprovingly. "Children should be seen and not heard."

That night Lily asked Michelle, her French nursemaid, *"Pourquoi est-ce que Maman est si grosse maintenant?"*

*"Parce que ta maman va te donner un frère, mon petit chou."*

Lily squealed in excitement. *"C'est vrai? Un bébé!"*

She was ecstatic the day little Charles was born. He was so beautiful, like a little doll—her very own baby brother.

However, her joy was short-lived. She was chastened every time she tried to embrace him or make him smile. And as Charles began to walk and talk, she found herself standing silently by, watching, as her parents lavished love and affection on him. Seeing her mother and father play with Charles, Lily felt a sense of loss so strong, it was almost a physical pain. She decided the reason they never played with her was that she was so ugly. Everyone said so. She heard them whispering, even fat old Cook. And she would gaze into the mirror, comparing her thin childish form and unruly red hair, first with her mother's dainty perfection, and then with Charles's fat rosy limbs and curling dark hair, and be filled with self-loathing.

At night, she would cry into her pillow with unfulfilled longing. Michelle, fiercely loyal, would try to comfort her. "But you are beautiful, *chérie*—you are! And of course your parents love you."

"They don't love me!" Lily would sob. "I'm ugly. I wish I could die!" And sometimes her thoughts were darker still. If Charles would die, she would be all they had. Surely they would love her then. She knew such dreams were wicked, but no matter how she fought them, they came back, unbidden.

As little Charles grew, the children became a little closer. The Long Island house was a lonely place and even their affection for their son did not keep Violet and Charles from their extensive travels. Lily had almost overcome her resentment by the time she was eleven. She rather liked having someone to follow her around.

Then, one Indian summer day, glorious and warm, Lily rode her dappled mare into the field at the rear of the Long Island compound. Charles was on his fat little pony. It was a lazy, lovely afternoon as the sun filtered down through the trees. While the children rode, the elderly English governess gradually nodded off.

She was awakened by Lily's screams. "What is it?" she cried out, her heart pounding.

"It's Charles. He fell off the horse!" Lily screamed hysterically.

"The horse? You mean the pony!"

"No, no—I let him ride my horse for a minute, and he fell off!"

Tears pouring down her cheeks, she led the governess to where Charles lay on the ground. His face was covered with blood, and as the governess came closer, she saw with growing horror that his head was turned at an unnatural angle. Falling to her knees, she pressed her ear to his small chest, listening for a heartbeat. "Oh, dear Lord! He's dead!" she cried, grabbing his wrist and searching frantically for a pulse.

"You evil girl, you devil," she shouted at Lily. "How could you let Master Charles ride your big horse?" The woman knew that she had been at fault for dozing off. She dreaded the consequences. She would never be able to find another job. And all because of this wicked little red-haired monster!

Terrified by the insane look in the governess's eyes, Lily ran to her horse, leapt on, and galloped off into the nearby trees.

Blinded by tears, she almost didn't see the high stone wall looming up ahead, but she reined in just in time, slid from the saddle, and flung herself down in the high grass, weeping hysterically. She had committed the most horrendous crime imaginable in allowing Charles to ride her horse. It was no excuse that he had been begging her for weeks. His voice echoed in her ears, even as she covered them now with her hands. "Please let me ride Sugar, Lily. You have all the fun. It's not fair. I have to ride around on this slow old pony. Come on, please?"

"No, Charles. You're too little."

"How come you get to ride Sugar? You're mean," he pouted.

"No, I'm not mean, Charles. I'm eleven and you're only six. And just because you ask doesn't mean you get everything you want. Maybe with Mother and Daddy, but not with me."

Charles, lip trembling, had pleaded, "Please, Lily, please! I'll love you forever." He looked so sweet she had given in. She had been planning to mount behind him when Sugar reared at a garter snake and bolted.

Shrieking, "Hang on, Charles," Lily had leapt onto the small pony. She was desperately trying to catch up when the mare drew up short before the property fence, catapulting Charles over her head.

No wonder she was unworthy of love—she was unworthy even to exist. She *had* wished Charles would die—and now he had. Closing her eyes, she willed Charles back to life. Maybe this was only a dreadful nightmare and she would awake in the morning in Michelle's arms. But Michelle too was gone, dismissed for some minor infraction when Lily was eight.

Gradually the shadows lengthened and night descended. It was pitch-dark when she saw lights flashing in the distance. They had come for her. Maybe they would kill her too or lock her away in the cellars. Too frightened to run, she sobbed convulsively. The last thing she remembered was a dark figure looming over her as she lost consciousness.

When she woke up she was home in her own bed. But she was hardly safe. When she tiptoed into the hall she saw all the draperies had been drawn. The servants tended her needs in silence as if she were too evil for speech. From time to time she heard Violet weeping, but neither her mother nor her father came to see her.

Then, after so much silence and her mother's occasional weeping, came the sound of an automobile on the cobblestone driveway, the door opening, then the murmur of subdued voices. With trepidation, Lily slipped from her room and crept to the balustrade, looking out between the posts.

Below, in the vast hall, was a small black casket, and she saw Charles lying there on ruched satin. His mouth was delicately red, his cheeks pink, and his dark hair curled about his face. He looked so lifelike, she almost cried out, "Charles, you're not dead! You're just pretending!"

But he was, and the heavy scent of hundreds of white gardenias wafted upward, making her ill. She ran to the bathroom and vomited, then stood drenched in perspiration. She felt so dreadfully sick, she knew she must be dying.

But she had survived, and the next day she was ordered to dress for the funeral. She could scarcely bear it. At the gravesite, the smell of the gardenias almost made her sick again. Oh, why hadn't she died instead of Charles? She sobbed uncontrollably until the tiny casket was lowered into the grave, when once more she was rescued by merciful oblivion.

It wasn't until another week passed that her father spoke to her. Towering over her like the wrath of God, he spoke quietly and deliberately. "Even though you may have meant no harm, you are responsible for this terrible tragedy. Your mother is totally destroyed. She will recover faster perhaps if she doesn't have to face you. I think it would be best if we send you away to school." Then, as a fresh wave of grief washed over him, he added, "Right now I too would be glad never to lay eyes on you again."

Lily willed herself not to hear those devastating words, not to remember them. But they left a scar that never healed.

Enrolled at Madame Sauvier's, a school for girls in Lucerne, she was unable to forget the past. Although her room looked out on a vivid blue lake, surrounded by Alps, beneath which was a green pasture with yellow buttercups, she saw little of the beauty. Her eyes were always clouded by the past. There was no reprieve. Her nights were filled with anguish, and her days were spent in loneliness. She was too withdrawn to make friends. It was too painful for her to try to play with the other girls whose families loved them and cared about them. As children will, they whispered about her behind her back, and Lily shrank from them, knowing herself to be an outcast.

Her parents saw her twice a year. On her birthday, and at Christmas, but their visits were coldly formal and they never suggested she return home. Had it not been for Randolph, she would have been utterly friendless. He wrote regularly and after a year he actually came to see her. He was with his parents in France and took the train alone to come to Lucerne. It was the happiest day of her life when she met him at the station with the inevitable chaperone.

"Lily, Lily, Lily—I'm so happy to see you!" he said, lifting her up and twirling her around.

He tucked her hand in his as they ran to the village, the chaperone trailing behind them. Walking the narrow streets, Lily saw the real beauty of Switzerland for the first time.

As she sat across from him at the pâtisserie, sipping her hot chocolate, he observed her eyes above the rim of her cup. The brutality she had endured at her parents' hands was scored in their expression. She had been wounded, as surely as if she'd been struck. Randolph raged silently at the waste. Couldn't her parents see how beautiful and sensitive Lily was? He had always hated the way Uncle Charles and Aunt Violet had favored Charles, but it seemed incredible that they could blame her for the little boy's death. He resented his own parents for not intervening.

"Lily, how are you?" he said, taking her hand.

"Fine, Randolph, really. Fine." Lily smiled, but her eyes remained sad. She seemed so beaten.

"Have you made any friends yet?" he asked gently.

"No," she shrugged, a little hopelessly. "They don't seem to like me much. I guess it must be my fault."

"That's not true, Lily," he said softly. "You're the most lovable girl in the world."

"No one else seems to think so."

"You're wrong, Lily. Your parents do."

Lily looked at him incredulously.

"Well, even if they don't, Lily, I do. I've always loved you, ever since we were little."

Tears welled in her eyes, but she quickly brushed them

away. "Do you, Randolph? Even with these glasses, and the bands on my teeth, and my red hair?"

"Especially your red hair," he laughed.

Over the years, Randolph's visits and the knowledge that he loved her slowly repaired Lily's self-esteem. She began to do more things with the other girls and gradually made a few friends. By the time she finished Madame Sauvier's and went to the College of the Holy Sepulchre in Bern, she had come out of her shell. She even had a best friend, Colette Valois.

The two girls were totally different. Lily was five feet six, with pale skin and flaming red hair. Colette was four feet eleven, with olive skin and dark brown curls. Her parents referred to her as their *précieuse poupée.* She giggled and bubbled. Life had been good to her. She was the youngest of five, her four older brothers ranging from twenty to thirty, all tall and handsome.

"You are beautiful, Lily," said Colette. "When the braces come off your teeth, you will be *magnifique.*"

Lily laughed. "I don't think that getting rid of my overbite will bring about a miracle."

"You will see, *chérie*—Colette has plans for you."

She was right. When the bands Lily had worn for four years were removed, her mouth was perfectly sculptured, her teeth white and even. True to her word, Colette whisked her off to Paris, where her mother spent two days transforming the awkward schoolgirl into a swan. Her hair was styled, her face made up, her nails manicured, and even her eyebrows plucked. Then Colette took her to her favorite couturier and made her buy a wardrobe that really set off her slender height. That evening as Lily dressed for dinner, she saw herself as she really was, and not through her parents' eyes. And the girl who gazed back at her from the mirror was truly beautiful. She had a delicate heart-shaped face with provocative cheekbones, and the emerald eyes which had always been hidden behind glasses and bangs were large and luminous. Her body, which just last week had seemed gangling, was now slim and lovely in her new dress which showed just enough rounded bosom to make her desirably feminine.

When she went downstairs she flung her arms around Colette's mother, but she knew she would never be able to thank her enough.

# Chapter 3

UPON graduation, Lily asked permission to stay abroad with cousins who lived near the Valoises in Paris. It had taken little persuasion on her part for Charles and Violet to say yes. With their lack of blessings, she closed her eyes and found herself catapulted into a glamorous new world of excitement of holidays in Biarritz, skiing in Gstaad, and weekends in the country outside of Paris. She was no longer protected by the strict rules of a Catholic school, and men began to pursue her. Most were impoverished aristocracy and they weren't seduced just by Lily's beauty. One had to be smart to secure one's future these days and her money was worth more than their titles. Who cared about coronets anymore, except for their value in securing a wealthy American wife? Still, her dazzling looks made the chase all the more exciting and she was soon considered one of the most desirable American women in Paris.

For the next year or two, Lily was wined and dined in almost every European capital. She had more proposals than she could count—but her answer was always no. She had yet to fall in love. Each time a man aroused her feelings, she pulled away. She found she could not give herself, emotionally or physically. Had her parents' rejection permanently crippled her feelings? Having never been loved, was she incapable of loving? The thought frightened her. She wanted to be loved, to have a family, children of her own.

She was celebrating her twenty-first birthday at the Valoises' villa in Cannes. Corks were popping and the champagne flowed, but Lily felt somehow detached. Doubts about her ability to love and be loved continued to plague her as she wandered out onto the terrace, then into another pavilion.

The previous day she had received an unexpected letter—one from her parents, whom she hadn't heard from in months. After all these years, at last they had written for her to come back.

"It is time for you to return home, Lily. You must settle down. We have forgiven you. Your place is here, not roaming around in a foreign country. . . ."

Until she received the letter, Lily had thought of herself as being beyond shock, but her parents' letter had stunned her. Why *did* they want her back? For what reason? Had she unwittingly done something to redeem herself? They had been perfectly content not to see her for long periods of time. Had they suddenly come to realize now that she had not been responsible for the death of Charles? In the next week, Lily kept asking herself over and over: Was it possible—she was almost afraid to think it—that they regretted their treatment of her?

Lily had changed from the stumbling, unsure creature who had been sent away to school. She was now full of grace and, though she little realized it, beauty. For as much as she thrived abroad, she was gradually becoming aware of a feeling that she didn't belong there either. Europe had always somehow been a strange and foreign world—one that she never truly felt a part of. Now, with this missive from home calling her back, Lily found herself only too glad to go. She was filled with an overwhelming sense of longing to return to her home.

It made no sense, perhaps, to go back to a home where she had been so miserably unwanted and lonely, and yet, for reasons she could not articulate, Lily knew that was where she wanted to be.

She had always hungered for her parents to love and forgive her. Perhaps the time had come when it would happen—at last.

As she got up and walked back into the villa, she had made her decision—she would leave for home as soon as she could book passage.

Yet as she stood at the rail of the *Ile de France* and waved down to Colette standing below, the moment was bittersweet. Europe, after all, had been the only home she'd known for years and years. Tears streamed down her cheeks unchecked as she bid her dearest friend and the land of her youth adieu.

At home the reunion with her parents was strained and awkward. Years of brief visits had forged little common ground. After a couple of strained dinners with their daughter the elder Goodhues resumed their social life, leaving Lily to amuse herself as best she could at home. It seemed any hopes for a real relationship with her parents were not about to materialize.

Lily wandered through the house as though seeing it for the first time. Outside Charles's old room she hesitated. Then, taking a deep breath, she opened the door. Her parents had kept everything exactly as it had been the day he died. They had even hung his small jodhpurs over the end of the bed. *Dear Charles,* she thought. *I loved you too much to ever have hurt you.* She walked back into the corridor and closed the door.

Two weeks later she received the first hint of what had prompted her father's decision to bring her home. She was at a dinner party seated next to Roger Humphreys, the son of one of her father's best friends. Glancing down the table she saw that she was finally earning her parents' approval. Not because of her sweetness of character, but because she exuded glamour and beauty. Colette would have been proud. Lily was a beauty. The candlelight played upon the delicate bloom of her cheeks, and her faintly accented English enchanted not just Roger but the whole table. Suddenly it dawned on Lily that she had been brought home to make a good match and provide her father with an heir to the family fortune. Strangely enough, Lily found herself not resenting that. It seemed only fitting that she, as their daughter, should marry well.

After that first dinner her social success was assured. She was immediately in a whirl of activity.

Weekends were spent visiting neighbors in Southampton, playing tennis at Forest Hills, or sailing off Cape Cod. But wherever she went, Roger Humphreys seemed to be present. His all-American good looks were the antithesis of the fine, drawn Europeans who had courted her in France, his blunt manner the opposite of their suave flattery. She found him refreshing and was intrigued by his Boston accent, his Harvard degree, and his athletic prowess. He never tried to make love to her, but although she was surprised, she assumed that it was an American kind of restraint, a trait which she rather admired. So she was completely unprepared for Roger's embrace one day when they were forced to seek shelter in the boathouse. "Lily," he blurted out, "I'm in love with you. I want you to be my wife."

She caught her breath. She had never thought of Roger in terms of romance. He was a pleasant companion, charming and good-looking to be sure, but she had felt no stirring of emotion when she was with him.

For a second she was shocked into silence. Then she stammered, "Roger, you've caught me by surprise. I'll have to think about it."

"I wish you would, Lily," he said, squeezing her hand. "We would make such a good team."

Team? My goodness, they could play touch football or row together to Hyannis Port. Her trepidation was almost replaced by laughter.

Of course, Lily had no way of knowing that her destiny had already been determined. Even while she was still in Paris, Charles Goodhue had invited Roger's father, Jason, to lunch at the Harvard Club. Before Lily had even sailed for home, Charles and Jason had laid their plans for a merger between "the children." Both fathers had agreed to press for an engagement—and then marriage—as soon as possible. A week later, while Lily was still on the Atlantic, Jason Humphreys invited his son to lunch with the same purpose in mind.

After ordering, Jason took a sip of his drink and began: "You know, Roger, you are twenty-six years old, and it's time you settled down. I have a lovely young girl that I'd like you to meet."

"Look, Father, I'm sure that she's a lovely girl, but I'm not ready to get married."

"Now Roger, I want you to listen. You know, I had lunch with Charles Goodhue last week, and he tells me that his daughter, Lily, is returning from Europe. From everything Charles tells me, she would make a perfect wife."

"But Father . . ."

Jason held up his hand. "I'm not interested in your protests, Roger. Let's face it. This girl is the Goodhues' only child, and you know how much the Goodhue Rubber Company is worth. Someday she'll inherit it all."

"But Father, I haven't even met her, and you're planning a wedding already."

"That's correct, Roger. Every young woman your mother and I have suggested you have rejected. Now it's time to grow up."

"Why don't you just let us meet and see if we even like one another?"

"I'm not going to let Lily Goodhue slip through your fingers. There are going to be a hundred men after her fortune the second she reaches New York. You're our only son and you have an obligation to the family to marry well."

Roger sat in silent rebellion. Why was he cursed with four sisters, so that the burden of carrying on the family name fell to him? *I'm not ready to be tied down,* he thought. *I'm only twenty-six!*

But as he stared across the table at his father, he realized that he no longer had any choice. People were already beginning to wonder why he never had a steady girl. He knew he would have to marry soon, like it or not, and the unknown Lily certainly had the right qualifications. Later, after he met her, he decided he was probably a very lucky man. Lily was very beautiful, and he found himself actually liking her; she was unaffected and easygoing and when he was with her she was almost like one of the boys. But seeing how the other men hovered about her, he knew he couldn't delay and he took advantage of the time alone in the boathouse to blurt out his proposal.

Lily went home perplexed. Although she was grateful that Roger had not demonstrated any great passion for her, she thought it odd that he did no more than peck her on the cheek. Even if it was America, she didn't think men were all that different. Despite his clear blue eyes and thick sandy hair and strong, even features, she knew she was not in love with him, and she would have no trouble deciding about his proposal.

# Chapter 4

THE next morning Lily went down to breakfast with a light heart. At last she felt she was the child her parents wanted and she was expecting to entertain them with the scene in the boathouse. She gave them a laughing account, concluding: "Of course, I wouldn't think of accepting him."

Charles brought his spoon to his lips and took a bite of soft-boiled egg. Dabbing his lips with his napkin, he said, "And why not, my dear?"

She wasn't sure she had heard him correctly. "Did you ask me why not?"

Coldly he enunciated, "I did, indeed."

In less than a second, Lily was again the terrified eleven-year-old Charles had sent away. Gone entirely was the confident woman.

"Because I don't love him," she stammered.

"Lily, darling," said her mother warningly, "love comes with marriage and children."

Lily stared blindly at her plate. How could she have been so foolish? It was obvious her parents didn't care about her feelings. But even so, why were they rushing her? There were plenty of young men, and she was just twenty-one. . . .

"Your mother is quite right, Lily," said Charles. "There is plenty of time for you to learn to love after the wedding. The point is, he will be an excellent husband. His family is as wealthy as ours, and he would be a careful steward of the fortune you will inherit."

In a voice that brooked no argument, Violet added, "Be sensible, Lily dear. You may be very pretty, but looks can fade fast. If you are to marry and have children you must do it soon, and men as eligible as Roger do not grow on trees."

"But I'm not in love with him!" Lily cried. "Not the least bit!"

Violet was becoming exasperated. "You're being ridiculous! Is there anyone else you fancy yourself in love with?"

"No, but perhaps that's because Roger has been by my side ever since I've returned. We seem to have become an 'item' without my even realizing it."

"Look, Lily," said Violet. "Roger will be an ideal husband. You should take it as a compliment that he wishes to take you as his wife."

Devastated, Lily tried to hold back her tears. Why Roger Humphreys? Of all the men she had met, why him? He was wealthy, but there were other wealthy men. Suddenly, a startling thought came to her: Her parents had planned this all along. That was why they had called her back from Europe, to arrange this marriage. It seemed incredible, but she couldn't shake the suspicion.

Lily went through the day feeling once again a stranger in her own home. The thought of saying yes to Roger was unthinkable but as the days passed she knew she could not live with her parents' cold disapproval either. Charles totally ignored her, while Violet bombarded her with ceaseless arguments.

It didn't occur to Lily to leave home. No young woman from her social circle took her own apartment, and she wasn't trained for a career. As the weeks since Roger's proposal became a month, she began to feel she had no choice but to marry him. He was attractive and devoted and he would be a reliable husband and a good father. In the end she couldn't bear her parents' anger any longer. All the time she had been in Europe she had built defenses against this lack of affection. Now at home she found their cruelty had once again reduced her to a timid child. The more she thought about it, she decided that an early marriage was the only solution. It would give her a home of her own, and above all, children. So without really analyzing her feelings, she made her commitment.

Perhaps Violet was right, she would develop a deeper affection for Roger after they were married, and perhaps love was not the integral ingredient in marriage anyway. After all,

Europeans usually married for practical reasons, and their marriages appeared eminently satisfactory. But the main reason behind her decision was the deep-seated feeling that because of what had happened to little Charles, she *owed* it to her parents. It was with these thoughts that Lily finally accepted Roger's proposal and, ironically, from that moment on she became happy with her decision. She began to fall in love, if not with Roger, with the idea of getting married. She became so caught up in the excitement of buying her trousseau and planning the wedding that she ignored the reality of what she was doing until the day of her engagement party. It was then that she walked out into the garden to have a few moments to herself to consider what she had done. And it was there on the bench that Roger, having missed her on the dance floor, came to find her.

"Where have you been, Lily?" he asked as they walked back toward the house.

She answered laughingly. "Why? Did you miss me?"

He hesitated before saying, "Yes, yes, of course."

She took his hand and turned to him, longing for him to crush her in his arms. Winding her arms around his neck, she said, "Roger, darling—kiss me."

She tilted up her face, her eyes closed. His lips pressed hers briefly, almost casually, and she was conscious of a painful disappointment. It had seemed so important that she elicit a passionate response from him and she had been sure that this was the moment.

But Roger was already signaling a waiter for another glass of champagne. "You know, tomorrow I'm going to be away for the Cup races," he said. "Of course, you're more than welcome to come, if you like."

Trying to hide her frustration, she said evenly, "I don't think so. You'll be busy and won't need me to distract you."

"Yes, it's going to be quite a race," he said, "and I'm not letting Kennedy get away with the Cup—not this year."

"I hope so, for your sake," she said sadly as they went back in to dance. They didn't have a chance to talk again until the large double doors closed on their last guest.

"It was a great party, Lily," Roger said as her parents went upstairs. "And you looked beautiful."

"Thank you. That's sweet of you to say, Roger."

"Well, I mean it. Now what are you going to do with yourself while I'm away?"

"Well, Mother and Father are leaving for Paris in the morning, and I'm driving down to see them off. Then I'm staying at Aunt Margaret's. Randolph wants me to go to the opera."

Roger kissed her good-bye, promising to call if he had time. After he left she stood alone in the echoing hall, feeling utterly deflated. Her parents were leaving, Roger was leaving, once again she felt abandoned.

Sighing, she went up to bed. At least there was tomorrow with Randolph to look forward to, she thought, and suddenly some of the sadness lifted.

# Chapter 5

THE next day at noon, Violet and Charles's luggage was stowed in the back of the black Duesenberg; the steamer trunks had already been sent. Having spent the morning in bed, prostrate from smiling at all her friends at the party, Violet came downstairs in good spirits. She was looking forward to ordering Lily's trousseau from her own dressmaker in the Rue de la Paix. As they rolled along toward Manhattan, she indulged herself in a happy little daydream. It would be the most lavish wedding in the history of New York City.

St. Patrick's would be filled with flowers—exotic orchids flown in from Brazil, roses from France, and of course lilies. The sanctuary would be filled with everybody who was anybody in society. The bridesmaids—twelve of them, just as in her own wedding—would wear peau de soie in the latest French style and the Fanchon bridal gown would be a vision in Alençon lace and seed pearls. And in the dream the bride was no longer a tall, willowy redhead, but a petite feminine Southern belle. . . . Violet closed her eyes and smiled.

When the whistle blew for visitors to go ashore from the *Berengaria,* Violet kissed her daughter with real affection. Lily had provided a way for Violet to relive her own girlhood. And Charles seemed so much happier these days. Roger would be a perfect son-in-law and, with God's blessings, there would be many grandsons.

Lily stood beside Randolph and his mother as the huge ship pulled away from the dock. For some reason seeing her parents leave for two months made her sad.

"Cheer up, cousin," Randolph said, giving her a comforting

hug. "This evening you and I are going to paint the town red!"

As they drove through the streets of Manhattan, Lily felt the emerald weighing heavily on her finger. Impulsively, she slipped it off and put it into her handbag. Somehow, tonight, she didn't want to be engaged. She wanted to be free, and carefree, and unencumbered. As Randolph had said, they would paint the town red.

Opening night at the Metropolitan was the gala initiation of the social season, and nothing could have been more exciting than seeing the dazzling array of New York's privileged social set emerging from their polished limousines and chauffeur-driven Rolls.

The ladies had outdone themselves in obeisance to the latest fashion word. Slender and not-so-slender bodies were wrapped and tied and bowed in chiffons, silks, and brocades. Enormous gems sparkled on fingers and dangled from wrists. Furs were draped casually across bare arms. The men were correctly and uniformly attired in white tie and tails. They served as mere foils for the couturiered birds of paradise.

Lily peered through the window of the Rolls-Royce as the chauffeur pulled up in front of the marquee. She felt as if she were floating up the grand staircase on Randolph's arm, so mesmerized was she by the spectacle. Although she had frequented the Opéra in Paris, the Met seemed even more opulent than that. There was a special kind of magic, as the operagoers promenaded back and forth and milled around. Lily wondered with a smile if this weren't the real show.

That night there was a stellar cast—Pinza, Tibbett, and Müller—and the electricity in the air, the excitement engendered, permeated the crowd and the very stratosphere. As Lily mounted the staircase to Randolph's box she glimpsed a tall, extraordinarily handsome young man, but what captured her attention even more than his startling good looks was his exasperated expression. What, she wondered, was there in this happy scene to annoy him so?

In fact, it was the lengthy absence of his date. *Where in the hell was Claudia? What did women do in a powder room, aside from the obvious?*

Heaving a sigh, he turned and caught Lily's eye. He had never seen anything quite so exquisite as this auburn-haired woman in the black dress.

Although Harry Kohle had known a thousand beautiful women, he was mesmerized by her vivid green eyes and the luminous skin set off by double strands of pearls. He was still staring when Randolph, who had been checking their coats, came up and took her arm. My God, he thought, this gorgeous creature was with none other than his old classmate.

"Randolph!" Harry cheerfully greeted his friend, his eyes on Lily.

"Harry Kohle! By God, it's good to see you! What were you up to all summer?"

"Doing a little writing of my own." His eyes still on Lily, Harry asked, "Aren't you planning to introduce me?"

"I'm sorry," Randolph laughed. "Of course, you don't know each other. Lily, this is my good friend, Harry Kohle, from Columbia. Harry, this is my cousin, Lily Goodhue, recently returned from Paris."

"Your cousin!" Harry echoed incredulously. That meant she was fair game. Before he could begin his pitch, Claudia finally materialized. She was dressed in a crimson satin gown which both emphasized and revealed her full curves.

"Harry, where were you?" she said in an exasperated tone. "I thought you said to meet you over there."

Harry didn't bother to correct her. Turning back to Lily, he made the introductions as the lights dimmed twice, indicating they should find their seats.

"We're off," said Randolph. "I'll be seeing you, Harry. Nice to meet you, Miss Sawyer."

Harry Kohle nodded briefly, but his eyes were again on Lily as he said, "Good to see you, Randolph. Miss Goodhue, a pleasure."

Ezio Pinza was in top form and at the end of the first act the applause was thunderous.

While Randolph was still deciding if they should brave the crowds for something to drink, Harry appeared at the entrance to their box holding three glasses.

"Anyone for a drink?"

Lily laughed. He must have dashed downstairs and back up again as the curtain fell, but his gaiety and enthusiasm were appealing.

Randolph was not surprised, knowing Harry Kohle to be a very resourceful fellow, the life of any party. "Brilliant,

Harry! I was quailing at the thought of the mob around the bar. What do you have there?"

"Ginger ale," he said, passing around the glasses.

Then, producing from his pocket a silver flask, he said, "Bourbon?"

Lily laughed. Harry Kohle obviously had no intention of letting Prohibition cramp his style.

"You son of a gun!" Randolph said. "I forgot the booze because I was out with my cousin."

"Oh, really?" said Harry, his eyes never wavering from Lily's face.

Randolph started to reply, then stopped short. This was no longer amusing. In fact, he was downright annoyed at the way Harry was looking at Lily . . . and worse, the way Lily was looking at him! She was so entranced it was only when the lights dimmed for the next act that she remembered Harry's date.

"Couldn't Claudia join us?"

Harry looked slightly abashed. "I believe she has gone to the powder room."

After Harry left, Randolph commented acidly, "Did you buy that story?"

"Randolph!" Lily said.

"You don't know him the way I do. I'll bet he arranged to have a row with her."

"Why?"

"Do I have to tell you, Lily?"

"Ssh!" she said as the conductor picked up his baton.

Maria Müller sang with such clarity and force the audience almost didn't let her continue her performance. When the act finally came to a close, Harry was back at their box before they even rose from their seats.

"It's so warm in here. Would you care to take a little air on the balcony?" he asked.

This time, Randolph was frankly unfriendly. Harry Kohle had more cheek than anyone else he knew. Wasn't Lily offended by his brashness? But shockingly, she was replying, "I'd love that." She knew she was being more flirtatious with Harry than she had ever been with Roger, but she felt this was her last chance to have fun as a single girl. Besides, Harry was terribly amusing and she was going to enjoy herself tonight. Outside she shivered a little and Harry quickly drew her stole around her bare shoulders. His hands felt warm against her skin as they brushed the nape of her neck. Lily didn't want to analyze the sensation, the implications were too disturbing. But it was impossible to deny he roused sensations that Roger never stirred.

As he and Lily seated themselves again, Randolph muttered furiously, "What was that all about?"

"What do you mean?" Lily said innocently.

Randolph didn't bother to reply, but sulked for the rest of the performance, even when the cast finally took the last bow as the audience shouted and tossed bouquets.

Lily had to admit a feeling of disappointment when Harry Kohle failed to appear at their box.

Outside, Randolph's Rolls was waiting, but just as he started to open the door for her, Harry came up beside her.

Noticing that Claudia was nowhere in sight, Randolph said angrily, "Did someone shanghai your girlfriend?"

"Well, she wasn't feeling well all evening. I've sent her home in a cab." Harry spoke casually but actually his behavior during the intermission had caused Claudia to make an ugly scene. He had taken advantage of her fury to pack her off.

Now, smiling debonairly at Lily, he said, "I'd like to take you both to a late supper. I know a fabulous place."

It was not surprising that Harry was attracted to Lily, thought Randolph. If she weren't his own cousin, he would have been madly in love with her himself. But he knew Harry's reputation. He was the love-them-and-leave-them type. And he wasn't going to let Lily get hurt. Unfortunately, he was trained not to make a public scene and he couldn't seem to get Lily's attention, not even to tell her to put her ring back on.

First they went to Ginger's, on the corner of Forty-second and Lexington, where they dined on oysters and steak, then uptown to a Harlem speakeasy.

They descended the narrow staircase of a room filled with lots of smoke. Four girls wearing scanty sequined costumes belted out "Bill Bailey, Won't You Please Come Home?" Then there was a hush and the lights dimmed. The music grew soft. Then a spot hit the far corner of the stage and there appeared a rising young singer predicted to be the next Ethel Waters.

Her voice was soft, low, and sultry. Then, much like the

hush after the fall of the curtain at the opera, there was a full minute of silence before the applause broke out. Several encores later the audience finally let her go and the band struck up a Charleston.

Harry took Lily's hand and guided her onto the dance floor while Randolph watched angrily. His frown deepened when the music slowed to a fox trot and he saw Lily rest her cheek on Harry's shoulder. When they returned to the table, Lily asked gaily, "Are we going to have champagne?"

"Of course," replied Harry, signaling the waiter.

"Lily, I don't think you should," Randolph said authoritatively.

"Oh, don't be an old stick-in-the-mud! Let's have some fun!" Smiling, Lily took his hand. "What could possibly happen with you here to protect me?" Her words made him feel like Methuselah. Harry had taken over.

"Cheeky devil," Randolph muttered to himself as Harry slipped the waiter a bill, but he was speechless when the man returned with a magnum. *Next thing, Harry will be drinking it from her slipper!* Randolph had seen Harry in action before. He hoped he wasn't overreacting to his cousin's interest in his friend, but all the time he had seen her with Roger he'd never sensed such electricity. In fact, he had never seen Lily so alive, so spontaneous, so . . . happy as she seemed tonight.

When he heard of her engagement, he had heartily approved. Lily had been so desperately lonely and unloved in her childhood—she needed marriage and family. And Roger came from a good family, seemed a decent enough fellow. But tonight it was clear that there was something lacking in the relationship. Of course, propriety prevented their being demonstrative in public, but still, a couple engaged to be married usually had a way of looking at each other, a way of touching hands when they thought that no one else was looking. Lily and Roger did none of that, and for the first time Randolph wondered if Roger himself were in love. That was beside the point, though. Whatever her feelings for Roger, Harry was not the man for her. He was not looking for marriage. All through college he'd had girls falling at his feet. He'd go out with them for a while, usually sleep with them, and then toss them aside. Randolph wasn't about to see Lily hurt by a cad like him. But as Harry guided her about the dance floor to "The Man I Love," Randolph noticed a look on Harry's face he'd never seen before.

As for Lily, she was in such a state of euphoria that she thought of nothing beyond the moment. All she knew as she swayed in Harry's arms was that she had never felt this way before.

But the enchanting evening came to an end, much as Lily knew it would. The Rolls stopped before Harry's apartment. He got out and stuck his head back in the car window. Ignoring Randolph, he asked, "May I call you tomorrow?"

Lily came back down to earth with a thud. Finding her voice, she said haltingly, "Harry, I—I can't."

"Why not?" he asked softly. "I want to see you again—you must know that."

"Because I'm engaged," she whispered. Randolph signaled the driver to proceed, but not before she had seen the shock on Harry's face.

"Lily, I have to talk to you," Randolph said on the way home. She had been so wrapped up in her own thoughts that she scarcely heard him. "I have to talk to you about Harry Kohle," he said more loudly.

"What about him?" she asked defensively.

"He's not for you, Lily."

"What makes you think I care?" she retorted.

"I was with you tonight—you seem to forget—and I saw the way you looked at him."

"I really don't think that's any of your business. I had a wonderful time tonight."

"That's just the point—"

Interrupting him, she said deliberately, "There was nothing wrong with anything I did so don't try to make me feel guilty about it!"

Lily was so adamant that Randolph subsided into injured silence. She was obviously in no mood to listen to reason, but tomorrow he would warn her in no uncertain terms. For there was another obstacle to any further involvement with Harry Kohle, something far more important than his reputation as a womanizer. Harry Kohle was a Jew and Charles Goodhue was a vehement anti-Semite. The reason for his prejudice had puzzled Randolph until his father had told him the story.

Apparently, Charles Goodhue, in his first independent venture, had bought a copper mine in Montana from a Morris Birnbaum. The surveyors' reports had been glowing, and it had seemed that young Charles was going to score a monumental coup. Then several months later he discovered that the reports were faked, the mine worthless—and that he had been a naive victim of Birnbaum's chicanery. Charles's father excoriated him with fierce contempt for taking any man's word on a business deal without investigating. Deeply humiliated, Charles couldn't bear to admit his own foolish error and rash judgment. As a result, he came to despise not only Birnbaum but all Jews. Even now, years later, he was known as one of the most virulent anti-Semitic men in the country, ranking with his good friend Henry Ford.

Randolph was sure that Lily knew nothing of her father's prejudice, but that made no difference. It was impossible for Lily Goodhue even to have the most casual relationship with a Jewish man. Randolph vowed to tell this to Lily tomorrow morning before she got some crazy idea about falling in love with Harry Kohle.

Lying awake in her own bed, Lily cautioned herself to be sensible. Yet it seemed Harry had introduced her to a whole new world she didn't know existed. It wasn't just the champagne. She'd drunk it before without this heady sense of release. Tonight she had felt a total release from the stress of the last few months. Dancing in Harry's arms she had felt as if she were floating on air. Then she remembered the look on Harry's face when she had told him that she was engaged. . . .

*Engaged,* she thought with a shudder. Soon she would be Roger's wife and that would put an end to evenings like tonight. But she wanted to get married. Not for the first time, she tried to imagine how it would feel to be in bed with Roger. Would he take her to heights beyond her wildest imaginings, fulfill her deepest yearnings? Instinctively, Lily knew that she possessed a capacity for sexuality. But for all her look of sophistication, she had never before experienced that mysterious sensation of sensual awakening—until tonight. Still she rejected the idea that it had anything to do with Harry Kohle. It was the champagne, the music, or simply a reaction to the idea of settling down, a last fling of sorts. If only Roger were not so restrained in his lovemaking. Suddenly it seemed as if her engagement were on very shaky ground. It was dangerous to romanticize her feelings for Harry. She didn't need Randolph to tell her this was no more than an evening's diversion.

# Chapter 6

IN Manhattan, there was at least one other person who wrestled with disturbing, conflicted thoughts.

Beneath his happy-go-lucky countenance, Harry Kohle was a man of extraordinary perceptiveness. Lying on his back, staring at the ceiling, he realized his attraction to Lily went far beyond her extraordinary beauty. He sensed her intelligence, her warmth, her utter lack of pretense. Harry knew after just a few hours that Lily was the woman he wanted for his wife.

But that realization was like opening a Pandora's box. Convincing her to break her engagement was the least of his problems. He knew from the way she had responded to him tonight that if he put his mind to it she would. But that led to the fact that he had no way to support her. Here he was, twenty-four years old, with no reliable source of income, and obviously not in a position to marry. Even his future was muddied by the turbulent currents of his own desires, in conflict with his father's wishes. As sure as he felt about Lily, she couldn't have come into his life at a worse time.

The Kohles were an old banking family; they had established themselves in New York Jewish society over one hundred years before. Anton Kohle had been the first of his name to come to America, arriving from Bavaria in 1776, just as the Declaration of Independence was being framed. In Europe, the Kohles had been petty moneylenders, but the first generation in America had moved into merchant banking. The family business grew into one of the most prestigious international firms in the country. In the present generation, there were three sons who had followed their father into the lucrative field of banking—and one who so far would not: Harry, the youngest, the thorn in all their sides.

Temperamentally, Harry knew himself to be utterly unsuited to sit behind a desk and pore over figures. From earliest youth, he had hated the musty smell of the Wall Street bank with its correct atmosphere. His father's stiff white collar became a symbol of everything Harry was rebelling against. The world of commerce bored him; his only interests were art and music and, most of all, literature.

Although the Kohles were patrons of the arts—they collected prodigiously—it was not for the love of beauty. To them, art was an investment. The Kohles' fondness for collecting had nothing to do with appreciation; it stemmed from the pure pleasure of possessing priceless works in as vast a quantity as possible. The thought of one of their own becoming a writer or painter was appalling. In fact, they held artists and other "creative" people in something like contempt.

Harry's embrace of the aesthetic for its own sake was something that his father, Benjamin Kohle, could neither understand nor condone. He wanted no dreamers in the family; his children were to be shrewd businessmen—and the two qualities were mutually exclusive. He could little fathom Harry's love for pure aesthetics; his youngest son had long been the least pragmatic of the Kohle fold.

All his life, Harry had been troublesome, rebelling at school and at home—and Benjamin had been baffled by the unexpected strength of will he had discovered in the boy. It had taken severe discipline to keep him in line—or God knows what kind of wastrel he would have become.

He didn't realize how much his attitude hurt Harry, who had always wanted to please his father, but in his own way. As a little boy, he had secretly wept when told he would never live up to his three older brothers' achievements. Over the years, though, he developed a deep resentment at being forced to live up to their standards, but even then, under a guise of bravado, he remained bitterly unhappy that his father held him in such low regard. It was as though he had no choice in his life, no voice in his future. When the time came for him to go to Harvard like his brothers, he wanted to skip college and embark on a writing career. As a child, he had read voraciously—Tolstoy, Flaubert, and Dostoyevsky. They were his idols and he began to feel that he, too, had the ability to create if he were allowed to pursue that talent.

But the combined weight of opposition from his family had been too much for him. In the end he agreed to a compromise—he stayed in New York but only to enroll in Columbia. His triumph was illusory: Benjamin Kohle promptly insisted that Harry study business at Columbia, not creative writing.

Unenthusiastically, he waded through his courses in management and market economics, loathing every minute of it.

"This is a disgrace to the family!" Benjamin Kohle thundered at the end of Harry's first semester, when he barely made Cs. "I'm amazed that you dare to show your face around here with marks like these!" He would have been angrier still if he had known that in his free time Harry had begun to write a novel.

At first, he had been doing little more than playing with words, but then ideas had come. His was to be a novel about death and destruction—and rebirth. As the first few chapters began to take shape, he started to think that he might be creating something of worth, perhaps even something of long-lasting significance. But Harry spoke of it to no one, especially not to his father. He knew that becoming an author was not a "practical" goal. The publishing world was fiercely competitive and his kind of serious work was often rejected in favor of cheap popular fiction, but for many months he worked late into the night while his friends slept or studied. Then the demands of his own courses caught up with him. Although he hated the business courses, his own pride kept him from continuing to get such low grades and he was forced to spend more time with his texts. His social life became pretty demanding too. Harry had always been popular, and now at nineteen he was discovering a whole new world of debutantes, college girls from Poughkeepsie and Bryn Mawr, even a few bored wives who were only too eager to share the bed of the darkly handsome Columbia student.

Still, the manuscript was always in the back of his mind; finally, in the middle of his senior year, he went to Benjamin and said, "Father, would you consider my taking a few years off after college and trying my hand at writing?"

Benjamin Kohle could hardly contain his rage. "That is

the most boneheaded idea I have ever heard! I've been too tolerant with you already. I hope you will have finished your business degree by the end of the next term."

Harry stared back angrily. "I can't promise you that," he said tightly. "I've signed up for several English courses this semester."

Benjamin Kohle said menacingly, "I see you've been fooling around in your usual self-indulgent fashion, and as a result you'll not finish on time."

Harry exploded. "Good God, Father! I've done everything you want so far! Why can't I take a little creative writing? What difference does it make if I finish six months later?"

"God damn it, Harry! This is the last straw. I have no intention of subsidizing this ridiculous venture. I'll pay for one more semester at Columbia and after that you're on your own. And let me tell you, if you persist with this ridiculous idea of becoming a novelist, you'll starve. You'll be begging me to take you back into the bank."

Later, Benjamin relented and paid another full year's tuition. He'd agreed to give Harry a small allowance after graduation, but he restricted his youngest son's spending severely. "Since you're thinking of becoming an artist, you'd better learn now how to live on a pittance."

Harry was disconcerted to discover just how much he missed his formerly generous funds. He had become fond of his social life, and it was a rude shock not to be able to take his girlfriends to the best nightclubs and restaurants.

Still, he would not abandon his hope to become a writer. Secretly he harbored the hope of going to Paris after he was graduated from Columbia—if only for a year. His father would no doubt drive a hard bargain, make him promise to enter the family business in exchange for a year's worth of garret rent. *But it would be worth it,* thought Harry. *It would give me the time I need to prove myself as a writer.* And after all, wasn't Paris the place where writers like Hemingway, Fitzgerald, and Stein had begun? He had already rehearsed the speech he planned to use on his father. There was a good chance that if he struck a bargain like the one he envisioned, the old man might relent.

But now, lying in his small apartment and thinking about Lily, he realized that if he really wanted to pursue her he would have to give up his writing ambitions, at least for the time being. He knew that once he put it aside he might never return to the novel, but if he went to work in the bank there would be no financial problems.

The idea of postponing his career as a writer—much less abandoning it—still gnawed at him. If only Lily could have come along two years later, when he could have had his dreams fulfilled by having written his novel, maybe even to see it published. But time was not on Harry's side. He well knew it. If Lily were engaged, she would be married in a matter of months, maybe weeks. He had to pursue her now or lose her forever. And that he was not prepared to do. Suddenly the bank, which had long loomed in his mind as the worst alternative, took on a benign cast.

He would not be admitted to full partnership immediately, but right from the start he would be paid enough to support a wife and family, just as his brothers had been. With that question settled, the only real obstacle was Lily herself. Suddenly he realized how crazy he was being. Here he'd been up half the night trying to figure out how to support her, when he didn't know if she would even see him again. He twisted restlessly on the bed, willing it to be time to call her.

By eight o'clock the next morning, he couldn't wait any longer.

"Randolph, I'm sorry to be calling you this early, but this couldn't wait. Now don't hang up. I know Lily's engaged, but I must speak to her. Insane as it may seem, I've fallen in love with her, and whoever her fiancé is, I don't believe she's in love with him."

Randolph's instincts hadn't been wrong. "Look, Lily is going to be married soon. She's very happy. I want you to stay away from her."

"I just want to talk to her, Randolph, that's all. There's no harm in that, is there?"

"I know you, Harry. I've seen you in action and I've watched a lot of girls get hurt. I don't intend my cousin to be one of them."

"I don't blame you for feeling that way. But you must believe me. I fell madly in love with Lily last night."

"Harry, if I had a dime for every girl you've thought you'd loved, I could retire. Go get some sleep. You'll feel better." And with that Randolph slammed down the phone.

Harry took out a cigarette, lit it, and watched as the smoke spiraled up to the ceiling. He obviously wasn't going to be able to reach Lily at her aunt's. He'd have to call her Monday at her parents' house on Long Island. He knew he'd have no trouble getting the number from one of her friends. And he was also certain she was not in love with her fiancé, no matter what Randolph said. Harry had enough experience with women to read the signs. No woman in love with one man responded to another the way she had to him.

He decided to give her a few days and try to see her the following weekend. He would use the time to find out a little about her fiancé.

# Chapter 7

ON Saturday morning Harry called the Long Island number. He wanted to make sure not only that Lily was home, but that Roger Humphreys was absent.

When the butler answered the phone, he said briskly, "I'm calling for Roger Humphreys. May I speak to him, please?"

"He is not here, sir. I understand he is on Cape Cod. Would you like me to ask Miss Goodhue for the number?"

"That won't be necessary, thank you. I believe I have it."

Harry put down the phone, exultant. Lily was at home, and Roger was safely absent. Seizing a topcoat, he left the apartment, ran down the three flights of stairs, and jumped into his Stutz Bearcat. An hour and a half later, he drove up the long cobblestoned driveway, parked the car, and ran up the steps. He rang the bell without stopping to think what he would say to her. When the butler answered he could only stammer, "I'm . . . here to see Miss Goodhue. The name is Harry Kohle."

Taking Harry's hat, the butler left him in the foyer and disappeared.

Lily had just come in from playing tennis when the butler found her. "Miss Goodhue, you have a visitor. A Mr. Harry Kohle."

*Good God, what was he doing here?* she wondered, waving the butler away. "I'll be down directly."

After he had left, she gripped the banister tightly to keep from falling. During the last week, she had thought about Harry constantly. Why hadn't she just told Graves to say she was out?

But deep down, she knew. She had to see him once more. She had to know. She had begun to think her feelings were more than just the product of the champagne and music.

Taking a deep breath, she walked slowly down the stairs to the foyer. "What are you doing here?" she asked, trying to control her quivering voice.

"I had to see you. I'm in love with you."

Lily was staggered. This was far different from her fantasy. It was frightening—threatening. . . . My God, he was real. She found herself trembling again as she had the first night she'd seen him. She prayed it didn't show. In that instant, she wanted to cry out, "Why are you doing this to me? Why can't you leave me in peace?" But instead, she asked bitingly, "What are you doing here?"

"I had to see you."

"Why?"

Harry wasted no time in pretense. "Because I'm in love with you."

Lily could not believe the simple declaration.

"I told you I'm engaged. To Roger Humphreys."

"But you're not in love with him," he said, challenging her.

"Of course I am!"

"If that's true, then why did you only mention your fiancé at the end of the evening?"

She lowered her eyes.

"And why didn't you wear the ring I see you have on your finger now?"

Lily finally found her voice. "I don't owe you any explanations, Mr. Kohle. And I don't want you to ever try to see me again. Not ever!"

Harry's voice was very calm as he replied. "I don't give up that easily."

"If you have any decency, you will leave now." She went to the door, held it open, and waited. She refused to look up. All she remembered was that as the door closed behind him, she leaned against it and sobbed.

Harry gunned the motor as he drove away. He hadn't expected Lily to greet him with open arms, but neither had he expected total rejection. He decided he would test the strength of his own feelings by seeing if he could forget her. For the next few weeks, he did everything in his power to erase her image. He spent his evenings carousing, starting in the fanciest restaurants or hottest new Broadway shows and ending at the speakeasies up in Harlem, drinking more than was good for him. He was the life of every party—and only the most perceptive observer would have noted that his eyes were curiously lifeless, his smiles forced and mechanical.

If only he had known Lily's own troubled thoughts stirred by his unexpected visit. Little could he suspect how greatly his very presence had affected her.

Lily's cold reception had been the result of an intense battle between her heart and her head. She must at all costs protect the bulwark which blinded her to all the things that were wrong in her impending marriage—and Harry Kohle threatened to breach that defense. The ironic result of his visit was to intensify her determination to reaffirm her relationship with Roger. So while Harry painted the town, Lily clung to Roger's arm, gave him loving smiles, and laughed at his jokes.

The weekend they were houseguests at Jill Robinson's country estate Lily determined to force Roger to try to make love to her. On Saturday night, Lily floated downstairs in white chiffon and sparkled like the ring on her finger. She drank a good deal of wine at dinner and was gay and talkative. Later, when Roger was dancing with Jill, as befitted his obligation to his hostess, Lily cut in and led him into the library. Turning down the lights, Lily caught her breath, overcome with a sense of her own sexuality. Whether it was stimulated by Roger or her own sense of need, Lily knew only that she wanted Roger to sweep her off her feet. Deliberately, she lifted her lips to his, winding her arms around his neck.

"I love you, Roger. I love you," she whispered fervently.

"I love you, too," he said, and in that moment he almost believed it.

Slowly they sank onto the brown velvet sofa, intertwined. . . .

But then suddenly there was a knock on the door. Roger leapt up, looking disheveled and feeling ridiculous.

"Oh, my God," he muttered. "What are we doing?"

"Out the French doors," she said, trying not to giggle. "I don't want you compromised."

As he stepped into the garden, Lily opened the door.

"I hope I haven't disturbed you," said Bert Hamilton. "I

just wanted something to read before I go to bed." He walked over to the first case, took down a book at random, and fled with an apologetic smile.

Lily checked her hair in the mirror, then went back out to the drawing room.

"What have you been up to?" asked Jill. "You and Roger were certainly gone a long time together."

Lily flushed guiltily. "What do you mean?"

"Oh Lily, don't pretend! You two are engaged, after all."

"Nothing happened," Lily said. She saw the look of pity in her friend's eyes. Oblivious to the fact that most of her crowd considered Roger a cold fish, Lily felt the moment in the study confirmed his passion. Her doubts had been quieted and she could look forward to her wedding day with no further qualms.

In Manhattan, Harry Kohle had also made up his mind. His attempts to drown Lily's image in an orgy of other beds had failed dismally. As he walked down Madison Avenue all he saw in the huge plate-glass windows was Lily's face—that magnificent, beautiful face. In that moment, he made up his mind. She was mistaken if she thought he was going to give up this easily.

Impulsively, he stopped in front of Ratto's Florist and went inside.

# Chapter 8

AT the French desk in her bedroom, Lily was writing a letter to her parents. She was about to say, *Roger and I are so happy these days . . .* when there was a light knock on the door.

"Come in," Lily called.

Her maid, Marie, entered, almost hidden by the most enormous basket of flowers Lily had ever seen. Lily of the valley, white orchids, and palest pink *rubrum* lilies. She was overwhelmed. She couldn't believe Roger had done something so romantic. But when she opened the little envelope, the bold black scrawl read, "To the most beautiful woman in the world. With all my love—Harry."

Heart pounding, she threw the card into the wastebasket. How could he do this to her? Just when she had begun to feel a sense of peace. Harry Kohle was callously upsetting her again.

"Where do you want the flowers, ma'am?" said Marie for the second time.

"I don't want them. Throw them away."

After the door closed behind Marie, Lily burst into tears. She wept for a long time, only gradually beginning to recover her composure. There was only one thing to do, she determined. And that was to pretend Harry Kohle never existed.

But if Lily thought that strategy would work, she was entirely mistaken. Harry Kohle was only beginning to make himself known to her. That same afternoon, the phone calls began. Then came the boxes of candy and then more flowers.

Lily refused to take the calls, gave the candy to the servants.

threw the flowers away, but as the bombardment continued, she grew increasingly frantic. What would happen if Roger learned about this—or, worse yet, her parents? She was at her wits' end. She first thought of calling Randolph, then decided her best chance was to confront Harry himself. She had no trouble finding his number, but her bravado faded rapidly as she waited for the ring.

"Mr. Kohle?" she said when he answered. "I'm calling to ask you to stop your nonsense and leave me alone."

"Did you get my flowers today?" he asked pleasantly.

At his bland response, her calm shattered. Almost in tears, she asked, "Why? Why are you harassing me?"

"I love you, Lily," he answered with sudden intensity. "This is the only way I know to get your attention. I honestly believe your engagement is a horrible mistake. You don't love Roger."

"What makes you so damned smart, Harry Kohle? Why do you think you know everything?" she cried, her voice trembling.

"Not everything, Lily—just you. If you were really in love with this Humphreys, you wouldn't have acted the way you did with me. And you would not have been so angry when I came to see you. For some reason, you're trying to convince yourself to go through with the wedding, but you're not doing a very good job of it. Why don't you admit it?"

"Stop, stop! I don't want to listen." She put down the receiver with shaking fingers. Oh God, she thought, Harry was right. Every word he said seemed to come from her own heart. She didn't love Roger. The marriage would never work. Sinking onto the couch, she buried her face in her hands and wept. How could she go back to Roger, feeling this way? But she must. Harry presented no alternative. And in any case, it was impossible to break her engagement. She was bound now by her words and deeds as well as by her parents' wishes. There was no turning back now.

After a sleepless night, Lily arose wearily, refused breakfast, and went out to the rose garden. She began pulling weeds and cultivating around the bases of the luxuriant bushes, soothed by the rhythmic, repetitive motions. The sun rose higher and higher while she knelt trying to think only of the soil beneath her palms.

It was well into the afternoon when Harry turned into the

drive and stopped in front of the house. About to ascend the broad stone steps, he suddenly noticed Lily's figure in the garden. To his worshipful eyes, she looked as exquisite in a simple cotton smock and a straw hat as she had that night at the opera. He stood for a long time, his heart beating irregularly. Then he quietly made his way up the path. It wasn't until his shadow fell over her that she looked up, startled.

Gently, he reached down and helped her to her feet. She tried to pull away from his hands, but somehow found it impossible. When they stood face to face, she whispered, "I wish you hadn't come."

"I had to. Do you think I could just let you go?"

"It would have been better because nothing has changed."

"That's not true. Everything has changed."

"I'm still going to marry Roger."

"All right, you're going to marry him. But if you're so certain of your future, you shouldn't be afraid of spending an evening with me. Let me take you to dinner just once—tonight?"

"No!"

"I promise that you'll have nothing to fear; I know a little place where no one will see us."

If only he knew that she was more frightened of herself than she was of him.

"I just can't! It wouldn't be right."

"Lily, you'll have a lifetime with Roger. Can't you just give me a few hours?"

Nervously pulling a rose from the bush at her side, Lily rubbed the petals until they shredded between her fingertips. "If I spend the evening with you, will you promise to go away afterward and leave me in peace?"

"I promise," he lied, knowing he would never leave her in peace.

Without another word exchanged, they turned and walked to the terrace and through the French doors to the library. Leaving him there, Lily went upstairs, slipped into a silk blouse and a tweed skirt and jacket. She twisted her luxuriant hair into a severe knot at the nape of her neck, added a dab of lipstick, and descended to the library again.

They drove in silence up the coast. Lily sat with her hands folded in her lap, feeling as though she were being hurtled into the unknown. She could have said no to Harry, but from the moment she had first seen him at the opera, her life had been out of control.

After an hour and a half, Harry turned off onto a winding dirt road and came to a halt in front of an old inn. It was a beautiful setting. The light of the setting sun filtered down through the sycamores, casting a lacy shadow upon the ground, while nearby a small brook cascaded over the boulders. The water was so crystal clear, Lily could see the flash of fish gliding by with balletic grace.

Even in the chill air, Lily felt an inner glow at the sight of the old-fashioned structure. The sign overhead read "Creekside Inn—Est. 1839." The patina on the clapboard siding was silvery with age. Smoke puffed gently from the stone chimney, only to dissipate in the treetops.

After they were seated in the pine-paneled dining room, Lily did her best to pretend that this was just a casual dinner with a friend, but she was uncontrollably aware of Harry's disturbing good looks and the current of electricity that seemed to spark between them. Lily suddenly felt ill at ease. This was not right, her being there. It wasn't a question of propriety or convention, it was her own sense of honor Lily felt she was violating. She had been trying to fight his mysterious attraction ever since the night they met. She was sure it was love, but whatever it might be, it frightened her.

"Do you come here often?" she asked, to break the awkward silence.

"As often as possible. I love this place."

Lily wondered if he had brought his other women to the inn and felt a pang of jealousy at the thought he might have spent the night.

The waiter provided a welcome interruption as he came up and asked, "Are you ready to order, sir?"

"Lily, have you looked at the menu?"

She hesitated. "What do you recommend?"

"They do wonderful game here—especially the quail."

"Is that what you're having?"

At his nod, she said, "I'll have that, too."

Although she had expected to be too nervous even to swallow, she finished every bite of the wild mushroom soup, *caille en croûte,* and flaming cherries jubilee, all accompanied by a wonderful Château La Rose served to Lily's amusement in heavy china coffee cups. Perhaps it was the effect of the full-bodied wine or the seductive smell of herbs and wildflowers, but as had happened the evening of the opera, she was filled with romantic yearning.

As they lingered over their coffee, Harry said, "They have the most fascinating wine cellar here—pre-Prohibition, of course. Would you care to see it?"

As they descended the wooden staircase to the cellar, the smell of old oak casks brought from Spain a hundred years before assailed them. Harry held the candle as they walked up and down the dark aisles. As they moved farther back into the cavernous room, Lily shrank closer to him. The dark pools of shadow were forbidding and she had to suppress a desire to reach out for Harry's hand. At the end of one of the rows, he lifted the candle to read a label, but as he turned, the flame lit up Lily's face and he stopped, mesmerized by her incredible beauty. Their eyes met and locked.

Gently, he took her in his arms. The touch of his lips on hers brought her as close to heaven as she would ever be on this earth.

"Lily, darling, I love you. You know that this is only the beginning."

Tears filled her eyes.

It wasn't until several hours later as they drove through the gates of the Long Island estate that Lily came back down to earth. Harry kissed her over and over before letting her out of the car.

"This has been the most wonderful evening of my life, Lily," he said. "Will you come to Manhattan next weekend?"

Lily knew in that moment that she was in love with Harry, but almost instantly came the harsh realization there was nothing she could do about it. How could she disrupt her parents' hopes and plans—not to mention Roger's? In her world, people honored their pledges and Lily knew that she could not bear the guilt and shame.

"Lily, will you come down to Manhattan next weekend?"

Lily was silent for a long moment, so Harry added, "Please?"

"I can't, Harry—I really can't."

"Why, darling?"

"Because I can't just walk away from my engagement to Roger. Can't you see that?"

"Lily, I believe in loyalty and duty as much as you, but it's also dishonorable to marry a man you don't love."

Lily pulled away from him and got out of the car. "You know I'm right," he said, following her.

"Harry, I just can't think when you're around. I'm frightened of you and your effect on me!"

"It's not me you're frightened of, Lily, it's yourself. Come to the city next weekend, just for two days. Afterward, if you still want to marry Roger, I swear to you, by all that I hold holy, I will never try to see you again."

"I can't give you an answer now," she said. "Let me think about it."

Standing in the moonlight, Harry longed to kiss Lily again, plead with her once more, but he walked away, without a backward glance. Lily had to come to him of her own free will. He had begged her for the last time.

Lily did not sleep all night, but by morning she admitted that nothing could keep her from going to Manhattan. Her decision had been made weeks ago, the first night she had met Harry Kohle. She would not break her engagement or disappoint her parents, but she could not turn her back on one last magical weekend. She knew that Roger would never take her to the heights of joy Harry could. She had known it all along. So for once in her life, she wanted to be completely fulfilled as a woman—to be loved as only Harry Kohle could love her. It would be a golden memory to treasure in the long arid years to come.

The one thing Lily could not come to terms with was the deception she was about to perpetrate on Roger. As the week wore on, she found herself increasingly uncomfortable in his presence.

Fortunately Roger had another sailing race that weekend, so Lily was not forced to lie to him. She was just vague, saying she would visit friends in New York, and then she called Jill Robinson to ask if she could stay for the weekend. Jill was delighted. Then, nervously, she placed the call to Harry.

When he heard the ring, Harry lunged for the phone. For the last week he had remained by it longingly, wondering when—and if—she would call. Breathlessly he said, "Hello?"

"Harry, this is Lily. I'm coming to New York."

Harry's eyes filled with tears at the news. In that moment he realized that this was the first time in his life he had gotten something that he had wanted with all his heart and soul.

"When will you be here?" he asked urgently.

"Tomorrow. I'll be on the five-o'clock train."

"I'll be waiting."

# Chapter 9

THE next day Lily packed her bags. Before she could give way to indecision, she hurried downstairs to be driven to the train. It was five forty-five when she arrived at Pennsylvania Station. Harry met her on the platform. They did not embrace, but when Lily smiled up at him Harry felt as though his heart would burst.

"Lily, I'm so glad you're here." He picked up her suitcase and escorted her outside. As he helped her into his car, he asked, "Where are you staying?"

"With a friend of mine, Jill Robinson. It's on the East Side."

Unspoken was the question of whether she would come to his apartment. They said little as Harry maneuvered the Stutz through the heavy traffic to the Robinson brownstone in the East Sixties.

"Is seven too early, Lily?"

"No, I'll be ready."

She watched as Harry's car disappeared from view, and a moment later she was hugging Jill, who quickly took her by the hand and led her up to a guest bedroom. After closing the door, Jill perched on a slipper chair and said, "So do tell! You sounded so mysterious on the phone, my dear."

"Well, I . . . I came into town to see someone," Lily stammered.

"I take it, someone other than Roger."

"Yes."

"Frankly, I'm not surprised. I've watched you, Lily, and if this is supposed to be the happiest time of a girl's life you certainly haven't been walking around with stars in your eyes."

"Is it that obvious?"

"To me it is. And if you looked in a mirror right now you'd see the difference. You're positively glowing. Who is he? Where did you meet him?"

When Lily told her, Jill gasped. "Harry Kohle? Why, I know him—he's gorgeous! Are you going to go to bed with him?"

Lily was too shocked to speak. Secretly thinking about it was one thing. Hearing the idea voiced aloud was another.

"Well, I've thought about it," she said finally.

"Come on, Lily! Isn't that really what you came down for? Do you think you're going to kiss and say good night? It doesn't work that way."

"I suppose not."

"What's the matter, an attack of conscience? You're entitled to a fling or two."

"It's not a fling, Jill. I really think I'm in love."

"Are you going to break your engagement to Roger?"

"No."

"But if you're in love with Harry, why marry Roger?"

"Oh, you just don't understand. I have so many obligations."

"Lily, don't let your parents force you into this marriage. I've known your father all my life. He isn't concerned with your happiness—just the merger of two great fortunes."

"You may be right, but I just can't fight them. I can't face the thought of total estrangement. . . . Besides, Roger is a decent man; he'll make a good husband. What if I don't have stars in my eyes—nobody has everything, and I feel that I could be content with him."

"What about Harry?"

"What about him? He hasn't mentioned marriage."

"So this *is* going to be a fling? Do you think you're going to be able to walk away from it?"

"I guess I'll have to."

"I wonder. Things have a way of becoming complicated when you're in love. Maybe you should just kiss Harry good night."

"I want to know what it feels like to be with someone I'm crazy about. Even if it's just for a night. Does any of that make sense?"

"You bet it does. As far as I'm concerned, it's essential women in our set have a little romance in our lives. Our marriages can become so limited."

"So you don't think I'm dreadful for doing this?"

"You have my blessings, dear."

"Jill, you're such a good friend, and I need one so desperately right now. I've really needed someone to talk to."

"I'll always be here. I promise."

As they sat across from one another at dinner that night in the dimly lit restaurant, neither Lily nor Harry could believe they were there.

It doesn't make any difference what happens after this, thought Lily. She was going to hold on to this memory. It would be her most cherished gift. No one in this world had ever been able to make her as happy as Harry had. Whatever the chemistry was between them, she would not try to fathom it. For tonight—if only tonight—she would just enjoy.

Harry felt even more in love with Lily now that she was before him. She was worth giving up any dream for—even one he held as dearly as writing. As Lily was silently vowing to become satisfied with memory, Harry resolved more than ever to make her his.

"What's your pleasure tonight, sir?" the waiter asked.

"Lily—champagne?" he asked.

Shyly she smiled back at him. "Yes, I'd love some."

If Lily's life had depended on it, she could not have recalled afterward what they ate or, in fact, if they had eaten at all. As the champagne flowed and the soft jazz music played in the darkly elegant club, she sat mesmerized by the man across from her.

Harry held her very close while they danced, and at that moment both felt only the magic of one another. When they finally stopped moving to the rhythm they both felt, they realized that it was just the two of them standing in the center of the floor. The musicians were already packing up and the waiters were beginning to turn the chairs upside down.

Harry summoned the waiter and paid the check. Then he helped Lily with her wrap. Without a word between them, Harry took her hand. They stepped out into the cool night and began to walk, though not in any particular direction.

When they came to the East River, they stood and looked out. A thousand lights twinkled in the midnight-blue sky.

Turning, Harry put his arms around her and drew her close. "Lily, you're the loveliest thing I've ever seen in my life."

"Am I?" she murmured softly.

"Oh, yes," he whispered as his lips covered hers.

They clung to one another hungrily before Lily drew back.

With his arms still around her, Harry said, "Lily, I love you. I'm happier tonight, with you, than I've ever been in my life."

His words were magic to Lily's ears. It felt so right for her to say, "I love you too," but she found she could not reply.

Taking her face in his hands, he looked at her searchingly. Slowly he said, "Stay, Lily. Stay with me tonight."

She could scarcely catch her breath as a sense of inevitability came over her. This had been fated. She knew she was powerless to resist—not that she even wanted to.

"Will you stay?" he whispered again.

"Yes, Harry."

Silently turning from the river, they walked back the way they had come. Lily could scarcely feel her feet hit the pavement. She felt that high. It was as in a dream: the ride through the cool, misty night, the creak of the old-fashioned elevator, his arm around her, warm and strong, and then, at last, they were alone. . . .

As Harry closed the door behind them, she glanced around without curiosity. It was surely the shabbiest room she had ever been in, and perhaps under different circumstances she might have been taken aback. But at this moment, she was aware of nothing but Harry.

They stood in silence, facing one another. Then, tenderly, Harry drew her into his arms and gazed at her before he lowered his lips gently to touch hers again.

As the kiss deepened, Lily quivered with desire and, sensing her response, he parted her lips with his tongue.

His hands caressed her body until he found the buttons at the back of her dress. He undid them and the gown slid slowly from her shoulders and dropped to the ground. Gently, he released the delicate silk undergarments. Harry stood back to admire her body. Then he cupped her breasts, rubbing the nipples and sliding his hands with aching deliberateness over her hips and thighs. If Lily had ever doubted herself capable of love, those doubts were forever erased. And if she had questioned the rightness of her love for Harry, she now knew the answer. When she felt his naked body pressed against hers, she knew the full meaning of love. He lay her gently on the bed, gazing down at her perfection for a long moment before covering her body with his own. Instinctively, she sensed his need and reached down, feeling him grow hard. When he entered her at last, her urgency was as great as his. As he moved slowly to ensure her pleasure, she was overcome with indescribable joy.

Afterward, as they lay in each other's arms, he said, "You know what tonight means, don't you, Lily? I can't give you up—not for anyone or anything. I want to marry you."

A wave of joy swept over her, but it was quickly replaced by despair. "Harry, I'd love to marry you—but I can't."

"We've been through this, Lily. I know all your arguments and they don't amount to a damned thing. You're not going to sacrifice yourself to please your family. I won't let you."

"It's not just my family—there's Roger, too."

"You don't owe anyone your life, Lily. In any case, would you be doing him a favor by marrying him when you love me?"

"But I feel so guilty. . . ."

"It's your parents who should feel guilty, forcing you into a marriage to satisfy their own wishes. Besides, what are they going to do to you if you defy them? Beat you? This isn't the Victorian age."

Lily found it too painful to explain the relationship between herself and her parents. Instead she said, "I'm an only child. They're very protective of me."

"I'm not exactly penniless, Lily. My family owns the Kohle Mercantile Bank, and they will be happy to give me a well-paying job. Won't your father accept that? Why does it have to be Roger Humphreys?"

Lily felt a sudden hope. If it was a good match her father was after, wouldn't the Kohles' wealth and prominence satisfy him as much as Roger's family's? And wouldn't her love for Harry, her passion for him, soften her father's judgment? Lily sighed. "Oh Harry, do you really think so?"

"Of course!"

"But what about Roger?"

"Is he really going to be heartbroken? Or is it just possible that he has been pushed into this engagement as much as you have? I'll tell you something, if I were in love with a woman like you, I'd never leave you alone the way Roger has. Good God, he's off in Hyannis Port every weekend."

"Oh Harry, you make it sound so simple."

"It is, Lily—if you have the courage."

She was silent for a long moment. "Do you really think it could work?"

"I know it can," he said. Taking her into his arms again, he made her believe that it could, and also made her stop thinking about the ordeal that lay ahead. Soon she had no thought for anything but the unbelievable joy she felt.

The next morning Harry begged to go with her to face her parents, but she refused, terrified to let him witness the scene she expected.

Lily had had a sample of her father's cruelty the morning she told them of Roger's offer of marriage. She had been as frightened of him then as she had been as a child. The thought of Harry seeing how little her parents loved her was too humiliating to bear. Remembering the terrible stigma of being unwanted, she could never reveal the dreadful events of her childhood, even to Harry.

"Please let me go alone," she said.

"All right. But if you need me, I'll come immediately."

# Chapter 10

IT was early evening when Lily arrived home, grateful that her parents would not return until the next day. She would at least be alone with Roger when she told him. She picked up the phone, half terrified and half relieved when he answered.

"Roger, I'm so glad you're back. Do you think you could come over for tonight? I know it's last minute, but . . ." Her voice trailed off.

It was odd to be wondering if her fiancé wanted to see her, but from the beginning their courtship had been odd. . . .

"I'd like that, Lily, I really would. In fact, I've got to say that I've missed you a whole lot. I want to tell you about the race."

"At seven, then."

Looking at herself in the mirror, Lily was shocked at her pallor. Even the extra rouge didn't help. Her face was paler still when Roger took her father's place in the dining room an hour later, and she hardly understood a word he was saying as he rambled on about reefing and heeling and jibbing. All she heard was the echo of Harry's voice saying, "I love you, darling, more than words can say."

Suddenly Roger touched her arm and asked, "How do you feel about *that?*"

"Pardon me?" she mumbled. "I'm sorry, I—"

"I know you're not keen on boating, but Sunday is the last day of the season. I haven't pressed you before, but you ought to give it a chance. Married to me, you're going to have to learn to crew."

Lily's courage almost faltered. How could she do this? Roger really sounded as though he'd missed her. *Fidelity, honor, loyalty,* those words were difficult to ignore. For the first time in forty-eight hours, she was ashamed of what she was about to do.

"How about it, Lily?" Roger was saying. "Are you going to be my skipper?"

Toying with the small spoon, she said gently, "I don't think I can."

"You mean you don't want to?"

"No, Roger. I mean, I really cannot."

Something in her tone startled him. "I don't quite understand."

Lily took a deep breath. "I don't know how to tell you this, Roger, but the truth is that I have fallen deeply in love with someone else."

Without a word, he got up and walked to the French doors.

Lily sat devastated. Nothing could have been worse than his silence. It would have been easier if he had screamed at her. What he was feeling she could only guess, but he must have cared more than she had realized.

The truth, if Lily had known it, was very different. The only emotion Roger experienced was relief. He had never loved Lily more than the moment she gave him back his freedom.

The past five years had been sheer torment, having to keep his love affair with Christopher closeted. The only thing that had brought him to resign himself to the marriage was that Lily would have provided a cover. It would have been in no way remarkable for Chris to have visited as a houseguest or even to become a member of their household.

And he liked Lily very much as a person. If he had to marry, he was happy that it was she.

But now that she had released him, he knew he was going to stop living the lie. He would take Chris to Paris, where such liaisons were accepted. He had tried one last time to please his parents. He would not consider marriage again.

Lily sat trembling, waiting for him to say something—but when he finally turned back to her, the look on his face was one of infinite kindness.

Taking her hand, he said, "You are the finest woman I have ever known, Lily. I'm not going to stand in your way. I only hope this other man deserves you."

When the tears subsided, she said, "I can't thank you enough for your understanding. I hope that you will meet someone you'll really be happy with."

Smiling, he said, "I hope so too."

That night Lily slept peacefully, but she knew that her ordeal was only beginning.

The next day she looked out of her window and watched her parents' trunks being brought into the house. Roger had been so reasonable, she hoped her father might be the same. She decided to wait until after lunch to confront him.

It was almost three o'clock when she knocked on his door. Praying her courage wouldn't fail her, she said, "Welcome back, Father."

"Thank you. How have you been?"

"Fine. We've had lovely weather the past few weeks." She hesitated. "Father, I have something very important to talk to you about."

He recognized the apprehensive expression on Lily's face. She'd had that look ever since babyhood. He despised people who always knuckled under to him and now he said coldly, "What is it, Lily?"

"I . . . wonder if I might have a brandy, Father."

"Help yourself, Lily. This is your home."

After she had taken a sip, she felt slightly better.

She said haltingly, "Father, I . . . don't quite know how to begin."

Impatiently he said, "Lily, I've just gotten back from a long trip, and I'm tired. Please just say what you have to say."

She swallowed the rest of the brandy, took a deep breath, and blurted, "I don't want to marry Roger."

"Really? When did you come to that conclusion?"

"The truth is, Father, I didn't from the beginning."

He bent over Lily menacingly and said, "You've made a commitment, young lady, and by God, you're going to stick to it."

"But I didn't make the commitment, Father! You and Mother put a great deal of pressure on me to accept him."

"In any event, you're going to marry Roger."

"No! I'm not in love with him, and he's not in love with me. He never was."

"Love? I suggest, Lily, that you forget all about this foolishness. I don't want you upsetting your mother. I wouldn't worry so much about being in love with Roger, as about making him a suitable wife."

"I've already told Roger, Father, and he's accepted it."

"You've what?" Charles Goodhue stared incredulously at his daughter. "What's brought this on? There's another man involved, isn't there?"

"You're right, Father," Lily said, trembling. "I'm in love with someone else. Is that a sin?"

He had known there was another man involved, otherwise she never would have found the courage to defy him.

"How did you meet him? What's his name?" he barked angrily.

"He is a friend of Randolph's; his name is Harry Kohle."

Charles Goodhue was, for once in his life, speechless. His face reddened and the cords in his neck stood out like twisted ropes.

"I will see you dead, Lily, before I will allow you to marry a Jew."

Lily was terrified. With all his faults she had never realized her father was anti-Semitic.

With blind rage, Charles shouted, "Do you realize your children will never be accepted?"

"By whom?"

"By society. By me! Your sons were supposed to carry on the Goodhue banner, but I will never allow one of them behind my desk. Do I make myself clear?"

"Yes. That's why you wanted me home, isn't it? To make sure you had the proper grandson to carry on your name. You picked Roger to merge the two fortunes. You weren't thinking about me—just money."

"Why do you think Harry Kohle wants to marry you?" he spat.

"Because he loves me—he doesn't need my money!"

Contemptuously he said, "You're a fool. He wants you for two reasons only: your inheritance and your social standing. But let me tell you, if you marry this Jew, you are no longer my daughter and you'll never have a penny of my money!"

Perhaps it was the thought of Harry's love, or maybe it was her father's blunt avowal he didn't love her, but Lily no longer felt afraid. She understood that Charles's threat was real; but what difference would it make? She had never been his daughter in the real sense of the word. And before leaving his house for the last time she wanted him to know how terribly he had abused her.

"Father, you've taken your frustrations out on me since the day I was born. First you hated me because I was a girl, and then because I lived and little Charles died. You know as well as I that his death was just a terrible accident, but for years you made me believe I killed him. Then when you called me home I was foolish enough to think that you had forgiven me. I even deluded myself into believing that you loved me. But I was just a tool to augment your wealth and carry on the family name. You're cruel, Father, and I no longer feel I owe you anything. I'm going to marry Harry Kohle with or without your blessing. You can do whatever you like with your money."

With that, she turned and went up to her room, where the tears she had been holding back finally burst forth uncontrollably. It was almost dark before she felt sufficiently composed to call Harry. All she told him was that she'd had an unpleasant scene with her father and that she was leaving.

"Oh, Lily darling, I feel terrible that I've been the cause of such trouble."

"Don't say that, Harry!" she cried. "You're the best thing that has ever happened to me!"

"When can I pick you up, darling?"

"Can you be here by seven-thirty?"

Lily packed what she could in one large suitcase; the rest she would have sent. Then she walked down the hall to say good-bye to her mother.

Violet, who had become hysterical when Charles told her the news, was resting now against her satin and lace pillows, still occasionally touching her eyes with her handkerchief.

"Mother," Lily started to say.

But Violet interrupted. "I'll never forgive you for what you have done, Lily. You've brought us nothing but unhappiness from the day you were born—and now this. No, I will never forgive you."

Covering her face, she wept. "What can I say? What will I tell everyone?"

"Tell them, Mother, that Lily is going to marry the man she loves. I am sorry that I have brought you such heartache—but I won't any longer. I will be leaving in just a few minutes."

"You don't care about anyone but yourself. You're ruthless," Violet wailed.

Her hand poised over the doorknob, Lily turned and looked back at her mother. In that moment she felt terribly sorry for her. She was so superficial, so childish. Neither she nor Charles had ever once considered that Lily had a right to some happiness. If there was a debt to be paid, it was theirs. She had already spent years trying to expiate whatever sins she might have committed.

At one time she would have given anything to win their love. But now she had found love in Harry, and it had given her a coat of armor to protect her against the rest of the world.

Just now Lily felt wise and calm and charitable.

"Mother, I hope in time you will be able to forgive and forget. I do love you, and I am sorry that I am causing you pain."

Letting herself out of the room, Lily closed the door softly behind her and went downstairs.

It was precisely seven-thirty when Harry drove through the wrought-iron gates and stopped in front of the house. Before he could ring, Lily flung open the door and ran into his arms.

"I am so grateful that you're here."

"I am too," he said, holding her tightly. Then he put her suitcase into the trunk, helped her into the car, and drove away.

Lily never once looked back.

# Chapter 11

THEY spent the night in each other's arms. Harry kept consoling her about her parents' reaction and telling her a little about his own family.

"It won't be so bad, darling, you'll see," Harry assured her. "They'll love you."

In truth, he was not nearly so sure as he sounded. Lily was Christian and the Kohles married only Jews.

His mother had had endless discussions with her cousins and other relations about who would be the perfect wife for Theodore, Anton, and Sidney, and his brothers had dutifully acquiesced in her choices. How would his parents react tomorrow, when he presented a woman not only not of their choosing but also not of their faith?

On the plus side, he would be giving up his dreams of writing and going into the bank, which should make his father happy. Then there was Lily herself. She was so lovely, so charming, and she was a Goodhue—not that he was in the slightest awe of her family, but it was a name to be reckoned with.

The next morning, in spite of Harry's assurances, Lily somehow sensed his apprehension, and a feeling of foreboding settled upon her as they mounted the stairs to the Kohles' town house.

"Darling, if you don't mind," Harry said, "I think that I had better speak to my parents alone first."

Lily waited nervously in the drawing room while Harry went up to his father's study. His parents had been surprised by Harry's unexpected call, but when he announced his intention of marrying Lily Goodhue, his mother almost fainted with shock.

After her successful efforts with her three older sons, she had lately turned her energies to choosing an appropriate bride for Harry. Aware that he had already been entangled with a number of inappropriate young women, she had determined it was time he settled down.

Now she realized that, as with everything else in his life, Harry intended to go his own way. No Kohle had ever married a non-Jew. "Goodhue" utterly stunned her.

Then, recovering herself slightly, she began to marshal her arguments. They knew absolutely nothing about this girl. She wasn't of their religion, and even if she were to convert, she still would not be one of "their own." And what would the children be brought up as?

No, this marriage was totally reprehensible. . . . It could not be allowed to take place!

Harry had always been so much more difficult than their other sons . . . but this was outrageous, even for him. His marriage to Lily Goodhue would create a chasm within the family which could never be bridged.

Benjamin Kohle now spoke with a stern calm which was more intimidating than any thunder, because it was like the calm before the storm.

"Harry, how long have you known this young woman?"

"Close to two months."

"I might have expected something like this from you, Harry. I've allowed you a lot of latitude in the last few years, hoping it would help you grow up—but now I see my folly. This marriage is far more serious than any of your other escapades. Just a few months ago, you were obsessed with taking a year off to finish your novel. What happened to that grand plan?"

"Father, writing is no longer important to me. Lily is!"

"Harry, you stood here and swore that nothing in the world was more important to you than that book. And now you're ready to drop the idea entirely. Is that evidence of maturity?"

Harry was trying very hard to control his anger. He took a deep breath and said, "Father, things change. When the right woman comes along, she becomes more important than any dream. I'm serious about Lily."

"But you were just as vehement about your book," said Benjamin scornfully. "What guarantee do I have that your plans for marriage won't cool in a few months?"

"Father, you don't understand. Writing was my dream, Lily is real. I want to go into the bank as soon as possible and start to earn my own way."

"I don't think you understand, Harry," Benjamin said. "Your mother and I can't possibly give our blessings to a son who marries outside our faith." In all fairness, Kohle's prejudice was nothing like that of Charles Goodhue. Benjamin counted many Christians among his friends and colleagues. He just wanted to make sure his children stayed in the fold. Suddenly he narrowed his eyes and asked, "Do you have to marry this young woman?"

"Of course not," Harry nearly shouted. "How dare you insult Lily!"

His father replied cynically, "It's a natural inference, my boy. One usually does not announce impending nuptials in so hasty a fashion."

Pacing angrily about the room, Harry searched in vain for words to make his parents understand. His greatest frustration was that they were rejecting Lily sight unseen. They wouldn't even give him the opportunity to show them what an extraordinary woman she was.

He tried again. "Father, I don't want to defy you. Please, at least meet Lily, give her a chance."

"We don't need to see her, Harry. It's not her personal qualities that are at issue, it's your responsibility to the family, and to our traditions."

Harry threw up his hands in despair. "Father, I love you and Mother. I don't want to hurt you, but you can't rule my life. I'm going to marry Lily."

Benjamin's voice was cold and remote. "I am sure that you have no idea of the blow you are striking against our family. There is no way that your mother and I can condone this act of folly."

"So you will not give my marriage your blessings?"

"No. If you persist in marrying this girl, forget your idea of working at the bank. You will no longer be a member of this family."

Harry was stunned at the implications of his father's words. "You can't mean that!"

"You have no idea how painful this is to me," said Benjamin. "All my hopes for you . . ." His voice trailed off. Then he added, "I hope you will come to your senses because there will be no place in my will either for you or for any children you may have outside our faith."

"Fine. Keep your money. I don't want any of it on those terms."

"Am I to infer from your bravado that you're planning to live on Miss Goodhue's money?"

"I'd starve before I'd live off my wife's money!" Harry blazed, stung by his father's contempt.

"You might just end up doing that. After all, what kind of work are you prepared for? Driving around in your Stutz and being a ladies' man?"

Harry stopped his angry pacing and faced his father defiantly. "God, I've learned a lot today—not only how prejudiced and unjust you are, but also how low an opinion you hold of me. Well, I don't need your help to succeed in this world, and I'll prove it!"

Benjamin felt an overwhelming sense of grief as he watched his son turn to his mother, hesitate as if to bid her good-bye, and then turn and leave the room.

Lily stood up trembling when she saw Harry's ashen face. Obviously the scene must have been much the same as the one she had endured with her parents.

"I'm going upstairs to pack my things," was all he said. His voice was full of hurt and she followed him up to his room and helped him fill two suitcases. When they were done, he took a last look at the room he had known from his earliest childhood. He glanced at the pictures in the silver frames on the mahogany dresser. There was one of himself with his three brothers in Nice, the summer he'd turned thirteen—the year he was bar mitzvahed. He couldn't bear to look anymore.

Not until they were back in Harry's shabby rooms could they shut out the world and let their passion obliterate their problems. Afterward Lily drifted happily to sleep. They were young, they had their lives ahead of them, and they had infinite faith in each other. But as Lily lay curled up against him, Harry realized how dependent she was, and his fears for the future overwhelmed him. How could he take care of her? He had a business degree, that was true. But aside from his aspirations as a writer, the only other career he'd even considered was in his family's bank. Now that future was forever closed to him.

Harry sat up late into the night, making plans and discarding them, growing more and more frantic with worry. He knew he could not burden Lily with these dark thoughts or allow her to feel that he was less than her beacon of strength. But when she woke and saw him silhouetted against the window there was no way he could hide his heart.

"Darling, what's wrong?" she asked. "Are you having second thoughts about us?"

"No, no. It's just that our lives are so complicated. The truth is that my father, like yours, said he'll disown me if we get married."

Her breath caught in her throat. "Oh Harry, I'm so sorry! I don't want to be the cause of this—"

"Lily, darling, that's not the issue. Our immediate problem is how I'm going to support you. Where do I go to get a job? The truth is I'm not suited for anything."

"Harry, if you could do anything you wanted, what would you do?"

"I'd be a writer—that's what I've always wanted to be."

"Well, what's to prevent you?"

"I don't think I can make a living at it."

"Harry, there are an awful lot of books out there. Those authors must be making a living. And you're much smarter than all of them."

Harry smiled. Her faith in him was so touching. "I can't do that to you, Lily. It's too uncertain."

"Well, nothing is for sure, and besides, what else can you do?"

He sighed. "I can get a job in a brokerage house, I guess."

"Will you like that?"

"That's not the point. I want to support you in the style to which you are accustomed."

"Harry, listen to me. Until I met you, I may have been wealthy, but I was the unhappiest girl in the world. The important thing to me is that we are together, and that you are happy. So if you want to be a writer, that's what I want too. Tell me, have you ever published anything?"

"Just in the college paper, but I started a novel almost five years ago. It would take months to finish and then there are no guarantees it would ever be sold. In the meantime, we could starve."

"But what if you had time to finish? Do you really believe in it? You think it could be published someday?"

Harry hesitated. Then, with quiet conviction, he said, "I believe in it with all my heart. But it's a question of time, Lily—time we don't have!"

There was a sudden light in Lily's eyes. "That's where you're wrong. My grandmother left me some money. There wasn't any need to touch it until now, but it's there for us."

Harry flinched. His father had predicted this. God, he was not only a pariah, but a gigolo.

"Damn it, Lily, I can't live on your money. What kind of man would I be if I did that?"

"Once we're married, it's *our* money." She slipped her arms around him. "Darling, don't you know that whatever I have is yours? In any case, it would only be temporary. You'll be published soon. I'm simply investing in our future."

When he turned to face her, there were tears in his eyes. "Oh God, Lily—how did I ever get so lucky as to find you?"

A week later they had their license. As radiant as if she were walking down the aisle with twelve bridesmaids, Lily put on an ivory Fanchon suit. Above her burnished hair sat a small Lilly Daché hat sewn with diminutive pink forget-me-nots. The short veil that framed her eyes made her seem extraordinarily ethereal.

Today was their wedding day and they almost ran like children to get the car. But as they rounded the corner, Harry stopped short at a flower stand.

Pinning a bunch of pink baby roses on Lily's shoulder, he kissed her tenderly, then belatedly handed the vendor a quarter for the flowers.

When the justice of the peace pronounced them man and wife, Harry slipped the gold wedding band on Lily's finger.

In that moment of union, all the anger, all the recriminations they had endured from their parents were forgotten. They knew only that they were husband and wife, and that now they would have each other for the rest of their lives—the two of them against the world.

After the short ceremony, Harry turned to Lily and said, "Do you promise that I'll always wake up to such a vision as this?"

"I'll try." She smiled shyly.

At that moment all their troubles were forgotten. But what they did not know was that Lily was already pregnant.

She had felt queasy the very day of her wedding. She chalked it up to prenuptial jitters. But when the nausea continued to plague her morning after morning, she finally heeded Harry's counsel and took herself to her doctor.

When the doctor called the next day with the news, Lily's joy knew no bounds. At first she was anxious about telling Harry. He'd fretted so about how he'd support the two of them, let alone a little one. Harry just didn't seem ready for a family. But when her eyes met Harry's after she told him, she knew his joy matched her own.

In 1917, Grandmother Goodhue, in a burst of patriotism, had bought $25,000 in Liberty Bonds for each of her grandchildren. At the time, that had been an insignificant amount, a mere pittance. Little did she know what an astronomical sum that would be to Lily. Without it, she and Harry would have been penniless. With it, they had the means to launch his writing career. Lily wondered if it were fate.

With Christian Raines, her father's attorney for years, sitting across from her, Lily had already cashed the bonds in anticipation of her wedding. With a baby on the way, she knew that she and Harry would put it to good use. After an intimate dinner in Harry's apartment, she decided to outline her plan.

"Harry," she began timidly, "I think we ought to buy a small farm."

"A farm!" Harry exclaimed, startled. "Why?"

"It has a lot of advantages. Just think of what fun it would be to have a cow and chickens. Fresh eggs—our own vegetable garden."

"Lily, I don't know one end of a cow from another!"

"We could learn. I'm sure it's not all that difficult. But the most important thing is that you would be free to write. And if we paid cash, we'd have no monthly payments."

Although on the surface it seemed a crazy scheme, after a few days he began to think the idea had merit. He had been plagued with worry about how they could stretch her money to cover the expense of living in New York City until he got something published. Perhaps a farm was the answer.

Lily contacted a rural real estate agent, but in the weeks that ensued, she almost despaired of finding the place of their dreams. There were plenty of small farms, but few that they could afford. The agent almost gave up on them, but then he discovered a New York State homestead that was going for four thousand dollars.

They drove up the next weekend. Standing in front of the broken fence, they viewed the property through different eyes. Lily saw only the beauty of the landscape, with the house sitting nestled in the shelter of the sycamores and the little creek gurgling nearby. She was blind to its deficiencies. To her, the barn had already been painted red, the wood-frame house white, and the front lawn was neatly weeded and mowed.

"What do you think, Harry?" she asked eagerly. "Shall we buy it?"

"Gee, darling," said Harry, "it's all so rundown." Originally the farm had been over one hundred acres, but the last owners had subdivided it and sold off parcels until only five remained.

"You and I can fix it up," Lily said, excited by the challenge. "Can't you just see it?"

Again, Harry hesitated. "I don't know, Lily. That house is listing like the Leaning Tower of Pisa."

"Oh, no—it just needs a coat of paint. And just look at the property."

The trees and fields were lovely, he had to admit. But the house needed an enormous amount of work. Gradually, though, he found her enthusiasm contagious. It would be the perfect place to write.

"You've fallen in love with it, haven't you, Lily?"

"Well, sort of—but not unless you want it as much as I do."

Putting his arms around her, he said, "I think we're going to be very, very happy here."

Harry sat down to work in the city while Lily took the train upstate to explore her new world.

In the general store ten miles from the farm, she found a source of inexpensive calicos, ginghams, and quilts. Visiting attic sales she discovered Blue Willow china and old pressed glass. Best of all, the roadside antique stores offered affordable highboys, four-poster beds, a tall maple rocker, and a hundred-year-old oak cradle. Her most exciting buy, though, was a Singer sewing machine with an old-fashioned treadle. She had never sewn a stitch in her life—but then, she thought, she had never done anything worthwhile. One of her neighbors gave her lessons and soon she was putting up ruffled curtains and pulling up a bedspread of her own making.

But while Lily rejoiced in her newfound abilities, the days Harry left his typewriter he was not much help getting the place in order; he found hammer and nails alien implements. Whatever their high hopes, the house was still far from being ready to move into. But they decided that in spite of the unfinished repair they had to make their move. Ignoring the house's exterior, they quickly painted the interior walls, scrubbed the floors, laid the rag rugs, and moved in.

On their first night there, Lily walked from room to room happier than she had ever been. The thought of seeing the small bedrooms crowded with children made her heart fill to bursting.

When she placed the rocker alongside the cradle in her newly-painted yellow bedroom, Lily's heart beat in happy anticipation. Soon enough she would be rocking their child. Harry watched from the doorway at the miracle Lily had wrought with the house. He wouldn't have given a plugged nickel for it; his aesthetics did not extend to interior decorating, and when Lily had dragged home the various antiques and had raved about patinas, he had been frankly dubious. But today he saw the house with fresh eyes. The living room was mellow and warm. The patina on the mahogany table *was* magnificent, and an old red leather chair by the fireplace encouraged one to curl up with a book. The walls were covered in a small cheerful mustard-yellow print which set off the richness of the wood tones, and in the center of the room lay a faded blue oval rug.

Sitting at his new desk, Harry touched his old green student lamp and Royal typewriter, vintage 1920, both ready for action.

Just before nightfall, they had carried the last of their possessions from the car and slept for the first time under their new roof. Suddenly, at three in the morning, they were wakened by water dripping on their heads. There were leaks in the roof, and as they ran from room to room, Harry shouted, "Here's another one, Lily—bring me a pot."

Then, as quickly as the rain had come, it subsided—but there were ugly stains on the bedroom floor and on two of the beautiful walls in her living room.

"Everything's ruined!" she sobbed, while Harry rocked her back and forth in his arms as though she were a child.

Looking down at her red, callused hands, she cried even harder. As if things weren't bad enough, the rain started up again in the morning and continued for two solid days. Lily felt it was the wrath of God visited on her for defying her parents. But when the sun came out again she cheered up. A neighboring farmer patched the roof and helped her re-paper the walls and sand the floors. As the days passed, Lily never gave a thought to her work-roughened hands. At the first hint of spring she paid the neighbor and his son to paint the outside of the house and barn; by early March, the white wicker furniture with new cretonne cushions was set out on the porch, the hammock was up, and Lily was content.

One evening at sunset, she and Harry strolled down to the creek. "Everything's so perfect, Harry," said Lily, taking his arm. "Don't you think so?"

Looking down at her he smiled. "I don't know if everything's perfect, but you are."

Harry had settled into a routine in which he wrote at least four or five hours every day. He was satisfied by his daily efforts, but the highlight of his day was the time he shared with Lily. Despite the work and the rustic setting, day after day seemed a honeymoon to him.

He had decided that for the time being he would set aside the novel and try to establish himself by publishing articles. Despite Lily's nest egg, he felt that he must begin to earn a living for them, and he hoped that after a while he could do well enough to take up the novel again. But at least it was writing.

His first article was on "Life Amongst Chappaquites in Upstate New York." When Lily proofread it, she could hardly keep from laughing. The title alone . . . Well, this was hardly the literary masterwork she had envisioned, but still—it could be a couple hundred dollars if he sold it.

When Harry caught her smile, he asked, "What's so funny?"

"It's not supposed to be funny?"

"Of course not! Let me have it back. If you don't see the point of my work, I'm not going to show it to you anymore."

"Gee," she teased, "I think I've already had my baby."

"What do you mean by that?"

"You're acting a little childish, don't you think, Harry?"

"Because I take my work seriously? I did a lot of research for that article."

Seeing that Harry was really upset, Lily quickly became serious. Obviously he did not have a sense of humor where his work was concerned.

"I'm sorry, I didn't understand. It was my error."

But Lily didn't realize how destructive her gentle teasing had been to Harry's self-confidence. He was terribly unsure of himself and his writing abilities. He needed someone to reinforce his belief in himself. So it was with increased trepidation he mailed the article to *Collier's*. In writing, the only test of quality was acceptance, and the three-week wait was agony. When the letter finally came, he stood stunned by the mailbox, looking down at the check. He raced into the house and waved it under Lily's nose. "What do you think of them apples, Lily?"

"I knew it was going to happen," she replied calmly.

"No, you didn't, but I love you anyway."

In spite of her now huge size, he picked her up and twirled her around and said, "I could very well get the Pulitzer Prize."

"If not for this one, then for the next," Lily responded proudly.

# Chapter 12

LILY was in the beginning of her ninth month. With the increased size of her belly, almost everything had become difficult, even the trip into town each week to see Dr. Hansen. As her pregnancy entered its last few weeks, Harry became terribly nervous. The idea of a country doctor and a midwife delivering a child at home seemed both primitive and foolhardy.

One night he said, "Lily, I think we should take a cheap apartment in New York until the baby is born. I want you to see a doctor there. I should have insisted on it before."

Amused by his concern, Lily assured him, "Darling, there's nothing to worry about. The doctor says I'm built like Guinevere. Besides, he delivers babies at home all the time. Please don't worry." She kissed him again but, weary as he was, he couldn't sleep. If anything happened to Lily, he would simply die.

When Lily's water broke at four in the morning, Harry knew he should have insisted they go back to the city.

Jumping out of the drenched bed, he cried, "Lily, are you all right?"

"Of course I am. Now be an angel and get me a new nightie out of the second drawer in the dresser."

"Are you having any pain?"

"It's a little early for that, darling. Let's get some fresh sheets on the bed."

Harry obeyed and asked, "Is it dangerous losing all that fluid?"

"No, it's normal. Please give me a hand with this gown."

He helped her change, then stripped the bed, turned the mattress, and remade the bed. Once he had finished, he began to fuss. "Are you sure you're all right?"

"I couldn't be better."

"Let me get you something."

"Not a thing, thank you."

To divert him, she added, "Why don't you call the doctor?"

Frantically, Harry cranked the wall phone in the hall and waited, feeling the sweat pour down his back. "God damn it," he muttered when there was no answer.

"Get me Dr. Hansen immediately. It's an emergency."

He waited and waited and at last heard the receiver lift.

"This is Harry Kohle, Dr. Hansen. Lily's in labor. You have to come right away."

"I'll be there as soon as I pick up the nurse."

Returning to Lily's side, Harry asked, "Are you in pain now, Lily?"

"No, I'm not. Darling, why don't you just calm down?"

"I am calm. Now, can't I get you something?"

"No, no, nothing. But I'll tell you what. Why don't you boil some water and fix a pot of coffee. Maybe you could also start the fire."

"A fire? Are you cold?"

"Er . . . just a little."

After tucking the blanket in for her he left, and she heaved a sigh of relief.

As he pumped the water into the pot, he looked out the window. A gray dawn shot through with lightning was breaking. Noticing the heavy clouds on the horizon, he shivered; he hoped they weren't in for a storm. His fears were interrupted by the coffee boiling over. The forecast was for clear weather. Harry chided himself for letting his imagination run away with him.

He poured coffee for Lily and took the cup back to their room, then kindled a fire in the grate.

"It tastes awfully good, Harry," she said.

Suddenly he heard a clap of thunder, followed almost immediately by a torrent of hail. He had been right about those thunderclouds! How would the doctor ever get through? The storm raged on, and as the minutes became hours, Harry became increasingly frightened as Lily's contractions grew closer together. Her quiet reassurance ceased as the pain became excruciating. All he could do was pray as he watched her digging her nails into her palms.

"Squeeze my hand, Lily. No, harder."

Eight hours had passed since Lily's water had broken, and there was still no sign of Dr. Hansen. He lived twenty-five miles away, and Harry knew that in a storm like this the roads were probably impassable. He tried calling again; the line was dead, and he hung up cursing himself for not insisting that Lily have this baby in New York City.

As for Lily, she no longer cared about being valiant or courageous; she only prayed for the agony to end.

As Harry wiped her forehead with a damp cloth, she finally screamed, "It's coming! It's coming!"

More terrified than he'd ever been in his life, Harry guided the infant into the world with shaking hands. Hearing its first cry he looked with awe at the tiny creature he and Lily had created. Lily reached out her arms and he gently gave her the baby. She had dreamed of this moment for so long, and now it was a reality.

"How are you, Lily?"

Smiling up at her husband, she murmured, "Happy, so happy."

The phone rang, making them both jump. When Harry picked up, Dr. Hansen was on the line. "I've been trapped in a ditch for hours. They just pulled us out. Tell me, how is Lily?"

"Thank God, she's fine. We had a little boy about a half-hour ago."

"Well, congratulations! It seems you didn't need me after all."

"You were needed. In fact, it's a miracle everything's okay. How soon can you get here to check up on Lily?"

"I'll start right now."

Later Harry called Randolph. "We have a son," he bragged.

"Oh my God! Beautiful Lily is a mother. Have you decided on a name?"

"Jeremy Anton Kohle."

"Well, give Lily my love, and tell her that I'll be there to see her tomorrow. That's not too soon, is it?"

"No, please come. We'd love to see you."

Bright and early the next morning, Randolph arrived, carrying a huge box four times Jeremy's size, and loads of other gifts as well.

Lily told him, "If it weren't for you, I would never have known this joy—my wonderful husband and my beautiful child."

"You deserve all the happiness in the world, Lily dear. I have to confess that I had my doubts about your marriage, but it obviously suits you. I just want you to know that if there's ever anything I can do for you, financially or otherwise . . ."

Quickly Lily said, "Oh, no. Harry and I are getting along just fine."

"How is the writing coming?"

"Marvelously. He just sold an article to *Redbook*."

"Why, that's great!" Randolph said, a shade too heartily. "What's it about?"

Lily was suddenly vague. "Oh, you wouldn't be interested."

"Yes, I would."

"Well . . . ," she said haltingly, "he wrote it under a pseudonym."

"Come on, give."

She started to laugh. "I think it's Daisy Keller."

Following the Jewish tradition Harry had Dr. Hansen circumcise his son, but it wasn't a religious ceremony and Harry felt bad both for his child and for his parents.

Ever since Jeremy's birth he had been thinking about his mother and father. He had had no contact with them since the fateful morning in his father's study, and over the months he had secretly mourned their loss. What purpose did religion serve if it made people lack compassion? But apparently nothing was of greater importance to Benjamin and Elise Kohle than their beliefs.

Even though Harry expected that it would be an exercise in futility, his joy in his son was so great that he felt he had to share it with his parents, or at least try to.

Seated at his desk one night after Lily was asleep, he wrote to tell them about the baby.

Dear Mother and Father,

Seven days ago, Lily and I became the proud parents of Jeremy Anton Kohle. He is the loveliest little boy in the world.

In light of this joyous event, I wonder if we might not find it in our hearts to lay aside our anger. I understand your beliefs and I respect them. But the happiness we could have together as a family seems so much more important at this time.

I want so much for our son to see his grandparents. It would mean a very great deal to Lily and to me, and to our child.

I have missed you greatly, and thought about you so often. I regret that I have not lived up to your expectations, but I am terribly happy with Lily and now with our son.

Please let me share our joy with you.

With all my love,
Harry

After reading it over carefully, Harry posted the letter with mingled feelings of pessimism and hope. Almost three weeks passed before they replied. Harry tore open the envelope, almost dreading to read the contents.

Dear Harry,

Please forgive our delay; when your letter arrived we were abroad and we have just returned.

Like you, we know that our last meeting was very difficult and the memory of it is still painful. With no intent to denigrate your wife, we still would not feel comfortable visiting in your home.

However, since this child is our grandchild, and is in no way at fault, we would love you to bring him to visit us in Manhattan. We would, of course, expect Lily too.

Despite its condescending tone, Harry was delighted. He had never stopped loving his mother and father and had only wanted them to be proud of him. He bounded into the kitchen where Lily was nursing Jeremy.

"You look happy, darling."

"I am, Lily. Look, a letter from my parents."

Frowning, she asked, "Why, after all this time?"

"Well, actually, I sent them a note telling them about the baby."

"What did they say?"

Quickly, he improvised. "Oh, they're anxious for us to bring the baby to see them."

"That's wonderful! I can hardly believe it."

"I don't know, Lily, maybe they were waiting for a gesture from me. You know, perhaps you should think of contacting your parents."

"Maybe," said Lily. "Maybe." But she was still afraid of being rejected.

Early one Sunday morning, Harry drove his family to Manhattan in the secondhand Model T Ford they had bought after selling the Stutz. The two thousand dollars meant much more to them than a sports car at this point.

When they arrived at the town house, Harry's parents at first seemed quite formal. But when they looked at the infant, their faces miraculously softened, and as Lily gently placed Jeremy in Elise's arms, she couldn't help but smile. In that moment, Harry knew he'd done the right thing.

Later at lunch, Elise covertly eyed Lily. She had visualized the Goodhue heiress as a spoiled, petulant debutante. But it was clear that she had been mistaken; Lily was not only beautiful, but sweet and gracious. And somehow, in spite of her prejudices, Elise had immediately warmed to her.

Benjamin, on the other hand, felt less magnanimous. He believed that Harry had written because he needed help. It was common knowledge that Lily had been disinherited, so that they couldn't be living on her dowry, and now that they had a child, it seemed obvious that Harry was desperate to get a job in the bank.

Benjamin had heard that Harry had written several articles here and there, but good Lord, that certainly was not enough to support a family. After lunch, Benjamin decided to make it easy on his son. He took him into the study for coffee, smiled, and said, "Well, Harry? When would you like to start at the bank?"

Harry stared at his father in disbelief, realizing at last why Benjamin had been so welcoming. He thought he had won; that Harry had come to ask for work, not because he loved his family.

"Is that why you think I'm here, Father?" said Harry with a short laugh. "I'm a writer and I have no intention of changing my profession. What I wanted today was for us to be reconciled as a family—nothing more."

Angry as much at having been wrong as at learning Harry would not be joining the family business, Benjamin exploded with rage.

"You are throwing away the opportunity of a lifetime. Well, you've been an idler all your life and now I see that you're never going to change. You're always going to be a good-for-nothing. I hope you realize it's not just your heritage you're throwing away, but your son's."

"My son will have his own legacy!" Harry shot back.

"His father the author? Tell me, what great strides have you made in the literary world?"

Harry was so hurt he could barely answer. "Don't worry about us, Father, we're getting along fine."

But Benjamin was too shrewd to be taken in. "How much money have you made in the last year?"

"That's none of your business. The point is, I haven't had to ask for your help."

"Now that you're living out in the country, I sincerely hope that it's not a hovel like the one you had when you were at Columbia."

"God, there's no end to your cruelty."

"Well, you don't need to put up with any more of it," said Benjamin, "because I wash my hands of you."

Harry cringed as his father's brutal, merciless words ripped away at the last vestiges of self-esteem, but he could not give his father the satisfaction of knowing how much he'd been wounded.

"Even if we never see you again," Harry shouted, "I'll tell you for once what I really think of you. You're a bully. The moment someone refuses to do things your way, you explode. My brothers knuckled under but I won't. And that's what you can't forgive!" Harry walked out of the study and slammed the door.

When he appeared in the living room, Lily and Elise, who were chatting about the baby, looked up in surprise.

"Lily, it's time we were leaving," was all he said.

Realizing he must have fought with his father, both women exchanged sad glances, but all Lily said was, "Of course, darling."

Face remote and set, Harry went over to his mother, took her hands and kissed her cheek. "It was wonderful to see you, Mother."

Elise followed them to the door. "We had such a nice visit, my dear," she said to Lily. "You'll come again soon and bring the baby?"

Harry answered for her. "I don't think so, Mother. Not for a while." They left her standing on the front stoop, waving forlornly.

On the drive home, Lily longed to ask what had happened, but seeing Harry grimly pressing the gas pedal to the floor, she remained silent. It was only when they lay alongside each other in bed that Harry gave her a brief sketch of the scene. He couldn't bring himself to repeat his father's scathing assessment of his future. Instead, he just said, "It was the same old thing, Lily. He wants me to come work in the bank, and I told him that I wouldn't do it."

"Oh," she said slowly. "That was all?"

"Yes," he lied.

"Well, it's too bad that that had to spoil the day for you, sweetheart. Your mother was so charming to me."

"I knew they would love you, Lily," he said, drawing her into his arms, finally finding solace in her embrace.

Over the next few days Lily decided it was time to pocket her own pride and write her mother and father. After several attempts, she penned a short note telling them about the baby and asking them to visit. Several weeks passed with no answer. Then, almost one month to the day, Lily received a phone call burying all hopes of eventual reunion.

It was from Christian Raines, her father's attorney. "Lily, I have some very sad news," he said gently. "Your parents' sailboat capsized in Long Island Sound and I'm afraid their bodies have just been identified."

Lily began to weep.

"I'm afraid I can't even ask you to the funeral," Christian went on. "Your father's will not only disinherited you, leaving his fortune to charity, but specifically requested you not be present. My dear, I know he would have forgiven you in time. He even had a letter from you in his desk. Perhaps he would have answered . . ."

There were a few more kind words uttered, but Lily was no longer listening. Remembering her years of exile in Europe, she found little comfort in the probability of being reunited with her parents had they lived.

# Chapter 13

IT seemed that the adage "Time heals all wounds" did not apply in the case of Harry's relationship with his father. As the months passed, Harry's memory of his father's words continued to plague him. Deep down, he feared that his father was right: He would fail as a writer as he had at school. If it had not been for Lily, he might have given up, but she constantly bolstered his ego.

"Darling, I know how bad you feel about your parents, but you have to believe in yourself. I know that you're going to be famous."

Between Lily's faith on the one hand and his own pride on the other, he threw himself into his work with a vengeance. Writing furiously, he submitted one article after another. They ranged from the philosophical to the humorous to the literary—whatever he thought might find a market.

He totally abandoned the idea of finishing the novel. Potentially, of course, it could make a great deal more money than any article, but he just didn't have the luxury of devoting the year he now felt it would take to complete it.

He worked so hard that Lily almost had to pry him away from the pine desk for meals. One night she woke up at two in the morning to find Harry's side of the bed empty and hear the clatter of the typewriter coming from downstairs. She put on her robe and went to his study. "Harry, do you realize that it's two in the morning? Come to bed, darling."

Wearily, he rubbed his eyes. "I want to finish this, Lily," he said, sighing.

"Can't it wait until tomorrow?"

"Lily, I don't want to talk about it! I set my own deadlines, and this is going in the mail today."

Pityingly, she saw his lined face, his red-rimmed eyes.

"Darling, what are you trying to prove?"

Remembering his father's words, he snapped, "I'm not trying to prove a goddamn thing. I'm just trying to keep bread on the table and a roof over our heads."

Lily was dumbfounded. This was the first time Harry had ever lashed out at her. And why was he so upset about money? After all, they had over twenty thousand dollars in the bank, they owned their own house, and their expenses were almost negligible.

"Harry, I'm sorry," she said reasonably. "I'm not trying to interfere, but you just look so tired."

Slamming his fist on the table, he shouted, "Damn it, Lily! I'm going to finish this, now!"

After a moment's shocked silence, she turned away, tears welling up in her eyes. She was halfway upstairs before Harry came to his senses. Running after her, he said huskily, "Please, darling, forgive me. I didn't mean to yell."

"I'm sorry I interrupted you," Lily said through her tears. "I didn't realize how you felt. Of course, if you want to finish your article, you have a right to."

Kissing her he said, "I'll just be another twenty minutes, darling."

So Lily fast learned lesson number one in her marriage: Harry did not want to be disturbed when he was writing. Determined to be the perfect wife, she became scrupulous about not intruding on his privacy, no matter how she might worry about his physical well-being.

Yet secretly Lily did not quite understand why Harry pushed himself this hard. There were days when she barely saw him, and then lovemaking became rare. Since he'd never confided in her, she didn't understand that in addition to wanting to prove his family wrong, he was torn between the need to sell his work and taking the time to finish his novel. Therefore, between those two obsessions, Harry found himself with a feeling of total impotence.

Finally, one day he stopped in disgust, staring at a silly

humorous piece about trout fishing. With a single motion, he ripped out the sheet, crumpled it, and threw it in the wastebasket.

Rolling in another sheet of paper, he took a deep breath and began writing. *The responsibility of a man to his conscience . . .* For the next day and a half, the words flowed like molten lava. God, it felt good, he thought. He had forgotten that writing could give him this sense of fulfillment, but then, he hadn't worked on anything meaningful since he got married.

Finally he typed, *The End.* It wasn't a particularly commercial piece, unless by some lucky chance *Harper's* or *The Atlantic Monthly* was interested, but it was something he could be proud of.

Breathlessly, he rushed to Lily, who was sitting in the bedroom nursing Jeremy. He simply had to share this with her.

"You've got to hear this!" he said, ignoring the baby.

Lily put her finger to her lips. "Sssh, darling! You'll wake Jeremy!"

Staring at her as though she had struck him, he whirled and walked out of the room. At that moment he almost hated his own child. What if Jeremy did wake up? Was that the end of the world? Harry fumed. He didn't ask much of Lily, but when he needed her, dammit, she should at least listen to him!

He left so rapidly Lily didn't even realize he was upset. She cradled Jeremy in her arms and lay down alongside him in her own bed. He was so precious, so very precious.

Awakened by his whimper, she looked at the clock and realized with surprise that she had slept for two hours.

Quickly, she changed his diaper and put him on his stomach in the playpen. Leaving him cooing at a stuffed animal, she hurried down to the kitchen, where she started to make dinner. In the midst of frying chicken, she suddenly realized that she hadn't spoken to Harry all day. Her conscience bothered her a little. Had he even had lunch?

After putting a pan of biscuits in the oven, she went down the hall. For a moment, she hesitated. Then, not hearing the typewriter, she walked over and put her hand on his shoulder.

"Would you like some dinner, Harry? The chicken will be ready soon."

"Chicken?" he replied with exaggerated surprise. "Why, what a treat!"

Lily stood dumbfounded. "What's wrong, Harry?"

"Wrong? You've noticed that something is wrong?"

"Harry, why are you acting like this? Is the work going poorly?"

He stared at her incredulously and thought, She doesn't even remember. All she cares about is the baby.

"I'm sorry I didn't bring lunch, darling," she was saying.

"Your concern is a little too late. You didn't even look up when I wanted to read you my article."

Suddenly Lily remembered Harry's brief appearance in the bedroom. "I'm sorry, darling," she said. "I didn't realize what you wanted. Please read it to me now."

"No. It's too late," Harry said, sulking.

"Oh, Harry, please don't be like that. Jeremy is only six months old—babies have a lot of needs."

"And so do husbands!" he retorted angrily.

Lily stared at him in consternation. This was the first indication she had that Harry was unhappy. But she hadn't neglected him! He was locked up with his work most of the time—she would have loved it if he spent more time with her and the baby. Still, she didn't want to fight, and soothingly she said, "I'm sorry, darling. Maybe I have neglected you. Will you forgive me?"

Looking at her for a long moment, he softened. He never could be angry with her for long. She did look tired, and she had been working hard . . . and he was acting like a spoiled child.

That night they slept in each other's arms.

Unhappily, after their brief moment of reconciliation they both reverted to their former habits. Harry resumed his total absorption in his work while Lily, adapting to his isolation, became more and more fascinated with Jeremy. Neither husband nor wife admitted that they were drifting apart.

As Jeremy began to crawl and get into mischief, Lily found it impossible to discipline him. Occasionally it occurred to her that she really ought to be a little firmer with him, but he was such an adorable baby, and when he looked up at her with those big blue eyes, she couldn't find it in her heart to chastise him.

Harry too adored him, but unfortunately spent little time with him. When Jeremy got up in the morning, Harry was sleeping, and Jeremy was asleep again by the time Harry stopped working in the evening. So the little boy got almost none of a father's much-needed discipline. Harry wasn't about when the toddler washed his rubber duck in the toilet or painted the walls with lipstick. And Lily only laughed at his antics. On the days when he helped her plant seeds, he somehow got more into his mouth than into the ground, but by the time she could say, "Jeremy, spit those out!" he had already swallowed them.

One morning in November as she sat feeding him breakfast, she was suddenly overcome by a feeling of nausea. Although it wore off rather quickly, the same thing happened again the next morning, and without having seen Dr. Hansen Lily knew that she was pregnant.

Nothing could have thrilled her more.

But nothing could have thrilled Harry less.

"Lily, we just can't afford another baby right now! You know I've been working my tail off, night and day, and I still haven't been able to make any real money."

"For heaven's sake, how much does it cost to feed a little tiny baby?"

"It isn't just the money. Lily, until I get on my feet, we shouldn't be taking on any more responsibilities."

"But I'm already pregnant."

Harry sat silent for a moment. Maybe he should give up his attempts at writing. Call his father and go to work in the bank. If only the timing in his life hadn't been so bad. If only he had become established as an author before he met Lily, everything would have been so different. Instead, his lack of success had eroded his confidence and now with a second child he feared he would never be able to take the time off to finish that novel. It was like a conspiracy against him.

As if she knew what he was thinking, Lily impulsively put her arms around him, whispering, "Be happy, Harry. It's the greatest gift I could give you."

And it was, dammit! He would never forget how he had felt, holding Jeremy in his arms at that moment of birth.

"I am, darling—truly, I am."

Suddenly they were aware of Jeremy's presence as he

tugged at his mother's skirt. Looking down at him, Harry smiled.

Andrew Kohle was born at Mount Sinai Hospital on June 18, 1935. A late spring rain pelted heavily against the windows. That was another omen, Harry thought. His children always seemed to be born when it was raining. But this time he'd insisted on bringing Lily to New York City to stay with Randolph the week before the baby was due. He wasn't chancing any more home deliveries. He and Randolph were sitting in the waiting room when the nurse announced, "Mr. Kohle? It's a boy."

"Isn't he wonderful?" Lily said when Harry was allowed into her room.

"Yes, of course, darling. But let me tell you, Lily, this has got to be the last for a while. We can't afford any more children."

Having a second child made Harry feel his deficiencies as a provider even more keenly, and he wrote feverishly, submitting one article after another.

But something was wrong. Half of the articles he submitted now were rejected. Was he slipping or was he writing the wrong kind of material? He didn't realize that in his drive to sell his work, his style had become forced and mechanical. Instead of sharing his worries with Lily, he became cross and withdrawn. After every fight he begged her forgiveness, but the tension in the house kept mounting.

But there were other storm clouds on their horizon. In spite of Lily's care, she became pregnant again. In no uncertain terms, Harry made his feelings clear. She had no right at all to have more children, knowing how he felt. Harry was furious at first, but he knew, on reflection, the responsibility was as much his as hers. Over the next months, his attitude softened. When he saw his new son, named after Randolph, Lily's favorite cousin, Harry was again filled with love for his offspring. "Oh, Lily, he's just wonderful."

"You mean it, don't you?"

"Oh, yes."

Randolph himself handed out the cigars proudly, as though he were the father. Secretly he thought the child looked just like him, and when he cradled little Randy in his arms, he almost felt that this was his own baby. Randolph lavished gifts on the child and sent Lily a luxurious full-length mink coat.

Even she didn't know that he could never have any children of his own. His diabetes had left him impotent and until now he had channeled all his energies and dreams into the Goodhue Rubber Company, of which he was president and principal shareholder. With little Randolph's birth, he found another outlet for his love and he determined to do everything in his power to see that the child had a happy life.

Although Harry had accepted the baby with love, his obsession with making a living became frenzied. Night after night he sat at his desk until the early hours of the morning. There were now five people to be fed and provided for, and the expenses seemed enormous, no matter how frugal Harry and Lily tried to be. Harry found it hard to be philosophical when unpaid bills were staring him in the face. And the worst thing was that Lily didn't understand his anxiety at all.

She kept repeating, "We have our little nest egg."

But Harry knew that the nest egg was inexorably dwindling. One didn't have to be a Wall Street banker to understand that if more went out than came in, eventually there would be nothing left. Sometimes when he watched her from his window, as she frolicked with the boys, he felt his stomach churn with anger. How could she be so carefree? He decided she could enjoy her family because he had the burden of responsibility for them. They didn't even share that. And his most crushing realization was that he would never be able to finish his novel; with three children, it was a ridiculous dream. The most he could hope for in terms of a writing career was a steady income from his articles.

Gradually his sales picked up and the terrifying pile of bills began to diminish. But his newfound peace of mind was short-lived. Perhaps it was God's will, but in spite of her care, Lily found herself pregnant again, scarcely a year and a half after Randy's birth.

This time there was no controlling Harry's rage. "God damn it, Lily! How could you have allowed this to happen?"

"It wasn't my fault, Harry. I was careful! You can't blame me if it didn't work."

"Who am I supposed to blame? I know you, Lily," he said

in an accusing tone. "You weren't willing to wait a few years, were you?"

"Willing? I didn't plan this!"

"The hell you didn't! You'd like to have a dozen kids. Well, I'm not a stud, and I don't want to be a father anymore! I don't want this baby."

"But it's ours, Harry!"

"I don't want it." Fists clenched, he stalked out of the room.

Hearing the door slam, Lily sat on the bed and gave way to tears. When he finally returned, Lily was in bed, pretending to be asleep. She heard him undressing in the dark and hoped that he would take her in his arms, but he eased onto his side of the mattress and turned his back on her.

The next eight months witnessed a growing rift between the Kohles. Since all the precautions Lily claimed to have taken had failed, Harry made up his mind that he was going to abstain from sex altogether. At this point, it was a little like locking the barn door after the horse had been stolen, but Harry was angry enough to carry out his threat. His fury abated only after the baby was born: a beautiful little girl they named Melissa. When they took her back to the farm he did his best to pretend she'd been a happy surprise; but even though he and Lily tried to act as if nothing had changed, there was a rift in the marriage neither could deny.

Lily was absorbed in the new baby, who bore an uncanny resemblance to her violet-eyed grandmother. In a burst of sentimentality, Lily asked Harry if she could take the children to see his parents. To make up for his unreasonable behavior during her pregnancy he acquiesced. Thus began a pattern of visits during which Harry stayed home and worked while Lily took the children in to see Elise and Benjamin. The adults maintained a formal chatter, all three careful never to touch upon Harry's writing or the fact he never came. Still, Lily felt she was doing the right thing, and she noticed that on her return Harry did his best to spend more time with the children.

There was no question he was enchanted by his daughter, whose smiles could cheer him out of the darkest moods. Unfortunately for Harry, children do not always remain chubby, adorable, vulnerable little creatures who make a parent feel strong and protective. By the time Melissa began to walk, it seemed to Harry that the boys were becoming unruly hooligans. Jeremy was relatively docile, but Drew was a hellion, and Randy was almost as bad. Even dainty little Melissa had terrible tantrums. And whenever he attempted to discipline them, Lily protected them like a lioness defending her cubs.

Harry found it harder and harder to concentrate on his writing. For the third time in as many months they were forced to dip into the nest egg to pay bills. As the bills mounted up, Harry grew increasingly tense. Jeremy, who was starting school in the fall, needed clothes and shoes, and Harry knew it was only the beginning.

There were the constant doctor bills—Lily ran to the pediatrician at the first sneeze, and if one child came down with something, they all caught it.

Harry believed a man's success was measured by the way he provided for his family, and each birthday became one more reminder that his chances of success were growing dimmer. Luxury be damned! He wasn't even able to take out an insurance policy for his family. What would happen to them if he died? He shuddered to think about it. And he couldn't forget that he had cost Lily her inheritance.

With all his anxieties, it was impossible for him to be the understanding, patient father he wanted to be. In the summer, when the children were out of doors most of the time, it was fairly tolerable. But in the winter the constant noise made it impossible to work at all. One day he reached the breaking point. He unlocked his door, jerked it open, and yelled at the top of his lungs, "God damn it, go to your rooms if you can't be quiet!"

Lily quickly gathered the children up and took them into the kitchen. "Now children, Daddy needs a little peace and quiet. He can't work with you screaming like that."

Unused to being chastised, they started to protest. "We didn't do anything, Mommy!"

As usual, Lily smiled and said, "I know you didn't. How about if you play hide-and-seek in the attic? But first I'll make you some hot chocolate."

It worked for that day, but in spite of Lily's best efforts, the scenes became daily occurrences. The children were simply not used to minding her, and their games invariably erupted into the hall outside Harry's study.

What aggravated him most was that he was the one who always came off looking like the ogre.

One night he paced the floor till five in the morning, then lay down on the sofa in the study. Waking after a bare two hours' sleep, he sat at the desk once again with a mug of strong black coffee. He had just begun a particularly important paragraph when Jeremy opened the door.

"Daddy, can you get my kite out of the tree now?" he asked hopefully.

Harry started, then, in a burst of fury, he caught the little boy by the arms and shook him so hard that his teeth rattled. At the sound of his cries, Lily leapt from her bed and rushed downstairs.

"Harry, what on earth do you think you're doing?"

Suddenly Harry stopped. Good God, was he losing his mind? Jeremy had done nothing and now he was weeping, terrified, the red, angry marks on his upper arms beginning to show.

Lily picked up her son and rushed from the room. For the rest of the day, the house was unnaturally silent. Lily read to the children and played with them in the attic, bringing them homemade fudge, cookies, and milk to help keep them quiet.

Harry sat in his study, beset by guilt. His failures weighed him down. He was a bad father, an inadequate provider, and a man given to self-indulgent tantrums. He couldn't forget the look on Lily's face as she had taken Jeremy away. Here she was, struggling to create a home in this godforsaken place while he did nothing but complain. She said she loved him—but how long would she be able to live with him under these circumstances? His father's words came back to haunt him: "You'll see, Harry, how long love lasts without money."

He felt as if his marriage was indeed bankrupt. He had already taken Lily's chance at a brilliant marriage, her inheritance, her lovely youth. She had paid for their house, borne his children, worked like a charwoman, and he couldn't even keep a civil tongue in his head. The time had come for him to face reality.

Harry rolled a blank sheet of paper into the Royal and typed, *Dear Father*, then sat wondering how to phrase his capitulation.

• • •

After the children had been put to bed, Lily came quietly into the study and seated herself in the worn leather chair. Life had not been easy, and just because she refrained from complaining didn't mean she was immune to the hardships. Yet somehow it didn't seem all that grim to Lily. She had taken their troubles in stride, happy with the life she had chosen. As long as she had Harry and her children, the rest of the world could go hang. But she no longer could bear to see Harry so unhappy. She, too, had decided the time had come to face reality.

"Lily," Harry said, "I cannot tell you how dreadful I—"

"Please," she interrupted. "I think what we have to talk about is far more important than this morning's scene. You may think that I'm oblivious to your frustrations, but I'm not. The truth is that this house is not quite the haven that I thought it was going to be for your writing. I hadn't considered the effect of four active children."

"Even so, I know I should be more patient. Still, it's hard when you feel like a total failure. Is that honest enough, Lily?"

"You're not a failure, Harry. I don't want to hear you say that."

"Yes, I am," he returned grimly. "I just don't have what it takes, or I wouldn't be in this position."

Gesturing at the paper in the typewriter, he said, "I've been sitting here thinking about what I'm going to say to my father. I'm giving in, Lily. I can't go on letting my family suffer because of my arrogance."

"You mean that you would abandon your writing?"

"Writing? What writing?" With a cynical laugh, he got up and paced the floor. "That was a child's dream. This is the real world, Lily. I'll never be able to write that book."

"How do you know you won't?"

"What do you think I've been doing for the past six years? Sitting here, beating the hell out of this typewriter, and what do I earn? Five hundred dollars a month. As for the novel, when am I ever going to get to it?"

"Harry, please sit down and listen to me," Lily said.

Reluctantly, he did as she asked.

"Darling, I've thought about this very carefully. I feel that the only way for you to get out of this trap is to be free to write your novel." Harry began to protest, but Lily interrupted him. "No. Please hear me out. The only way we are going to be a happy family again is for you to finish that manuscript. That's what's creating the wall between you and me, and between you and the children."

"Look, nobody has to tell me what I've turned into, and I'm terribly ashamed of it."

"Forget about that. What's holding you back are the pressures of having to support us."

Harry rubbed his eyes. What alternative was there—he was the breadwinner. What good did it do to discuss it?

"I know that you worry about our finances," Lily continued. "But worrying isn't going to solve our problems. Let me ask you something: How long do you think it would take you to finish your novel if you were able to work on it constantly, without interruptions?"

"I don't know, Lily. Maybe a year. I'll never be able to do that."

"That's not true, Harry! I have a plan. I want you to go to New York, rent a room at the YMCA, and do nothing but write until that novel is finished."

"Really? And what's going to happen to you and the children in the meantime? How do you plan to eat? Or pay the taxes here, and feed the cow? The roof needs repairing again, and the car needs a new set of tires. There are a million expenses you're probably not even aware of."

There was a sting in his words, but Lily realized that this was a moment for truth.

"Darling, I don't want to hurt your feelings, but can you forget your ego for once?" she said gently. "The answer is for me to earn some money while you're gone."

"No—" he began, but Lily silenced him again.

"Will you just hear me out?"

"No, I won't, Lily. Even if I did accept the idea that you were going to support me, what would you do? You don't have a profession."

"Strangely enough, Harry, I do."

"And what is that, pray tell?"

"I've made every curtain in this house, and you've seen Melissa's pinafores and dresses, and her rag dolls. And look at the pants and jackets I make for the boys. Do you realize that I made their entire wardrobes? We haven't bought a thing. And wherever I go, people compliment me on their clothes."

"So who do you think you are going to sell these clothes to, Lily? Bloomingdale's?"

"There are all kinds of little shops that sell handmade things. And that's what I plan to do—all I have to do is manage for a year until you finish that book. Don't you see?"

Her faith in him was so touching that Harry was at a loss for words.

Finally, with tears in his eyes, he whispered, "Lily, how did I ever get so lucky?"

It was a last-minute reprieve. Here he had been ready to crawl back to his father when Lily offered him freedom to pursue his dream. His gratitude to her was inexpressible. Once again he realized that in spite of her fragile beauty she really was a woman of enormous strength.

# Chapter 14

AT Lily's insistence, Harry made his preparations quickly. No delays, no procrastinations. Yet when the morning came for his departure, he couldn't bear the thought of leaving his family. The memory of his cruelty to Jeremy and harshness with the other children tortured him. He prayed that his intolerance would leave no lasting scars. If he did nothing else in his life, he promised himself, from now on he was going to be a loving, patient, and doting father.

He was brought out of his reverie when Jeremy said, "Daddy, can I carry your suitcases out to the car?"

He looked down at the small handsome face. "Sure—come on, kids. We'll do it together."

It was painful to kiss them good-bye and then watch them wave from the platform, Lily standing like a fortress while the children clung to her.

"Take off those frowns and smile at Daddy, boys," she directed, "and Melissa, throw Daddy a kiss."

She started wailing, "Dada, Dada!" and stretched her hands toward the train.

The boys tried valiantly to smile. Daddy was going away for a long time, Mama had said so.

A tear rolled down Jeremy's cheek and Lily put her arm around him. He was the sensitive one. "Darling, Daddy's coming back. Throw him a kiss."

He did so, and Harry saw it through gathering tears. Now, as the train rolled out into the distance and picked up speed, they grew smaller and then were lost from sight.

An enormous stab of loneliness assailed Harry; he felt as though he were abandoning them.

Yet this period of exile was so important. It was his last chance to become a writer. So much was riding on it. The only comfort he had was knowing that Lily did have the remainder of the little nest egg to draw on. But what it meant was that they were putting all their eggs in one basket—in Harry. If he didn't make it, then what? He shuddered to think.

In spite of his guilty feelings and fear of inadequacy, he felt a strange sense of rising excitement at the prospect of New York. As the train neared Grand Central Terminal, another feeling superseded all his conflicting thoughts. He was a stranger, alone and alien in the very place where he had been born. After having been all but disowned by his family, he no longer felt that he had a home or roots.

He had seen his parents only a few times in the last six years. Once for the naming ceremony of each of the four children. But it was always stiff, formal, and awkward. Had it not been for the children, he doubted that they would have even met.

He allowed no hint of his longing to be revealed, but in his heart of hearts he kept hoping that they would embrace him as their son. Wouldn't one think that they would admire him, if for no other reason than that he had never turned to them for any kind of financial assistance?

Hearing the screech of brakes as the train came to a halt, he came back to the moment. But it wasn't until he walked off the train and into the swirling crowds that his spirits rose.

He picked up his suitcase and strode buoyantly out of the station into the July sun. He had planned to save the money and walk to the Y, but the noonday heat and the distance led him to the extravagance of hailing a cab.

Arriving at the 92nd Street Y, he looked around in dismay. Although the aroma of chlorine and Lysol permeated the atmosphere, the place certainly did not give one the impression of being anything but moderately sanitary. He missed the homey charm of Lily's antiques and bright chintzes. And the heat. God, it was stifling! He had forgotten how humid and sticky July in New York City could be. His shirt clung to him like a second skin. He willed himself to remember those winters on the farm when the snow spread out like a soft fleecy blanket. . . .

That night he had dinner at a small café on the corner of 87th and Lexington, which he remembered from his student days. How strange it was—he had been richer then than he was now as a grown man. He had had a generous allowance; his Stutz Bearcat was always parked in front of Delmonico's, where Benjamin Kohle's son was always given a good table.

"What will you have, sir?" asked the waitress.

Harry was grateful to her for interrupting his train of thought.

A half-hour later he stood on the curb outside, feeling the hot night embrace him. He turned and began walking. After a while, he realized that he was on Fifth Avenue, aware of an urgent desire to see his old home, just to touch something real and familiar out of his past. It was strange, he was a grown man with a family of his own, yet he still had a great longing for the roots of his own childhood, to feel a sense of belonging.

His steps slowed as he came to the Frick mansion and he stopped in front of the wrought-iron railing enclosing the gardens. Smiling slightly, he recalled how more than once as a small boy he had been chased out of those gardens.

Then he walked up the broad stone stairs to the Kohles' and rang the bell. Life was a barter, he thought. The day he had first brought Lily here, he had forfeited his right to a privileged life. The door was opened by the butler, Collins, who had been with the family for more years than anyone could remember.

"Mr. Harry," he said formally, without visible surprise. "Good evening."

"Thank you, Collins. You look as spry as ever."

The butler's face remained impassive. He was well aware of Benjamin Kohle's attitude toward his youngest son. "Your parents are out for the evening, Mr. Harry. I will inform them that you called."

Harry had no intention of stopping if everyone was out, but he was taken aback by Collins's attitude. The butler had no intention of inviting him in. Was it so clear, even to the servants, that he was persona non grata?

Looking past Collins through the door, he glimpsed the

wide circular staircase. It looked exactly the same and suddenly he remembered long-forgotten images of the past. One day he had slid all the way down, only to be reprimanded by Elise as she watched him with fright.

"No message," he said curtly. "Good night."

Standing in the doorway of his tiny room at the Y, Harry took a look around. Then, suddenly, he slammed his fist against the door frame. God damn it, he would succeed! By the time his novel was published, not only Lily but all the Kohles would be proud of him.

The next morning, Harry awoke galvanized with a new strength. Wasting no time, he dressed quickly, went to the cafeteria and wolfed down a roll and a cup of coffee. His eagerness spurring him on, he hurried over to Third Avenue to buy a secondhand typewriter. He had left the old black Royal at the farm. Not only was it cumbersome to transport, but after years of pounding, it was on its last legs. He and Lily had agreed that Harry needed a new machine.

The first pawnshop he passed sported a Royal in the window. It looked to be in pretty good condition and Harry tried the door, but it was still locked. He had to wait until nine when the proprietor, Mr. Garfinkel, arrived to open up. "What can I do for you, young man?" he asked.

"How much is the black Royal in the window?"

"For you, I'll make it thirty."

Harry smiled. Garfinkel would have sold it to anyone for that price. "I'll give you fifteen."

"Eighteen I wouldn't take."

"Eighteen and that's it, Mr. Garfinkel."

He thought he had driven a hard bargain, but when he peeled off the precious bills from the small roll in his pocket, he wasn't quite so amused. That two hundred dollars had to last until Christmas. He wasn't going to ask Lily for a dime more, even if it meant starving. He hated the idea of her picking fruit for hours in the hot sun and then standing over a steaming kettle in the little kitchen, making jelly to sell to Swanson's general store down the road.

Fueled with resolve to get to work, he went back to the Y to set up his typewriter, and pulled his partially finished manuscript out of his suitcase. He suspected that most of what was written would have to be redone, but for the time being he was going to push on with the story.

He rolled the first piece of paper into the machine, nervously feeling his sweaty palms. The prospect was so overwhelming that his breathing became labored. He had never felt quite like this before, but unmistakably he felt that at last he was about to come face to face with his destiny.

Swallowing hard, he poised his index fingers over the "f" and the "j." Next to him lay the yellowed manuscript that had lived in his mind and haunted his thoughts for so many years.

He thought he knew his story, understood his characters so well, but suddenly in this instant, for the first time, he realized that he was not at all the same person as the boy who had started this novel as a freshman at Columbia years before. No longer was he a callow youth, but a man greatly matured by life. He looked down at the first page, where the date read "February 27, 1926" . . . such a long time ago. His fingers trembled as he experienced mingled feelings of trepidation and daring.

Harry felt it was like the pause at the crest of the roller coaster just before it begins to gather speed for the long plunge. His breathing was staccato as he struck the keys.

July 22,1939 Second Draft

THE WARS OF ARCHIE SANGER

by
Harry Kohle

*Chapter One*

Archie lay looking up at the cloudless sky, aware of an immense silence after the screaming fury of the cannons, the acrid scent of smoke still burning his nostrils. Then, somewhere in the distance, he heard a single mournful dove . . . or was it the sound of God weeping?

Taking a deep breath, Harry plunged himself into the nineteenth century. His fingers touched the keys, images of tired, hungry men in blue trudging down hot southern roads materialized before his eyes. Soon he was with them, breathing the choking red dust.

He had begun. The conflicts that tore Archie Sanger's soul were the same that had plagued man since Cain and Abel, the same that raged in the Kohle household. As a writer and as a man, Harry Kohle understood that. He was writing about a different time, a war fought on the battlefield rather than in a peaceful New York brownstone, but Harry realized the new passion he brought to his work was fueled by the strife in his own family.

It wasn't until the moonlight touched a corner of his desk that he knew that he had worked without stopping for twelve straight hours. He got up and stretched. In spite of the stiffness in his joints he felt exhilarated. He had written forty pages, pages he really believed in. He would have liked to share his elation with Lily, but they had agreed that there would be no unnecessary phone calls.

As the weeks passed, Harry developed a hardworking routine which was mirrored by Lily's own hectic schedule at the farm. Missing Harry as she did, Lily was happy her days were so busy, because at night, lying alone on her bed, she was filled with longings. She remembered only the good times, when she and Harry had been newly married, before the children were born, before all of the misunderstandings. When Harry had gotten on that train, she had felt not just the sadness of parting, but the misery from her youth, of being deserted—even though she knew that Harry, unlike her parents, really loved her. But despite her bravery, the responsibility of providing for the family proved an incredibly heavy burden. The physical strain of working and caring for the children was bearable; she was young and strong. But many times she feared that she had taken on more financial responsibility than she was capable of handling. For the first time, she realized the extent of the pressures Harry felt. Since he had always paid the bills, she had had no idea how quickly the money flowed out the door. Her complacent reliance on their nest egg now seemed ludicrous. If her jams, jellies, and handiwork didn't sell, they would soon be penniless. Once, when she had failed to add enough pectin to the raspberry jelly and it had boiled down into a rubbery mess, she had actually sat down on the kitchen floor and cried.

Even more worrisome than the money situation was her increasing inability to control the children. Jeremy was a good little boy, but Randy was stubborn as a mule, and Drew was a wild Indian, always into mischief. Melissa was the worst of all, for she was given to loud tantrums when she didn't get her own way. Vainly, Lily tried to reason with them, not realizing that they simply needed a firm "No!"

Terrified of repeating her parents' mistakes, Lily had decided early on that the only thing children needed was unconditional love. In time, everything would fall in line; they would obey, she thought vaguely, because they loved her.

But in Harry's absence she realized that there might be more to raising children than that. As they ran rings around her, she found herself longing for a firm hand.

One evening when Randolph called from the city she was so pleased at the prospect of his company she almost burst into tears.

"Can you come up for the weekend?" she asked eagerly.

"I'd love to. How is my little godson?"

"Just fine—he'll be so thrilled to hear that you're coming. And the others, too, of course."

When the big Packard pulled up in front of the farmhouse, the back seat was filled with the gifts Randolph's secretary had selected at F.A.O. Schwartz—teddy bears, roller skates, and best of all, a new football.

As the children ran out into the field to toss it around, Randolph went into the house with Lily, where they sat down over freshly squeezed orange juice and coffee cake.

"Did you make this?" he asked in surprise. "It's fabulous."

"Of course I made it."

"You never cease to amaze me," he commented, shaking his head. "Isn't Harry going to have a piece? Or is he sleeping in today? I don't hear the usual clatter of typewriter keys."

"Well." She drew a deep breath. "Harry's not here."

"Oh?"

"I guess I didn't tell you. He's in New York, working."

"Working? At what?"

"He's going to stay at the Y for a few months while he finishes his novel."

Looking at her searchingly, he asked, "Lily, is there something you're not telling me? Have you and Harry separated?"

"Of course not!" she answered indignantly.

"Come on, Lily—since when does a married man with four kids move out? Can't he do his writing here?"

"It's the kids. They just make so much noise he can't concentrate. It's not the right atmosphere."

"And he's getting it at the Y? That's a lovely atmosphere, I'm sure. Pardon my asking, but what are you and he using for money while he's gone?"

"I'm working, Randolph."

By the time she had finished describing her various projects, Randolph was open-mouthed with astonishment. "Good Lord, Lily, you have got to be joking!"

"No, I'm not—I've been making a good profit. In fact, I've already started taking orders for Christmas aprons and pinafores."

"I'm not going to stand by and see you struggle this way. How much do you figure it takes to support you and the kids for a year?"

"I don't care to talk about it, Randolph."

"Lily, this is ridiculous. I have more money than I'm ever going to be able to spend, and I'm a bachelor with no obligations. Can't you let me help you out? Call it a loan, if you will."

"We prefer to make our own way, Randolph. Harry's pride would never allow him to accept help—why, he will barely accept mine."

"Don't tell him, then."

"That's out of the question."

Sighing, he gave up. "All right, if that's the way you really feel. But I want you to know that if you ever need anything for any reason, I'll be there."

"Thank you," she said softly, covering his hand with her own. "You're such a good friend, Randolph. Just about the only one I have. I don't know what I would have done without you all these years."

Randolph smiled and kissed her. In the beginning, he had been terribly hurt that Lily had gotten married without so much as a telephone call. He had really felt that Harry was the wrong husband for her, but when he had seen how happy she was, how much they loved one another, he had forgiven her. Loving his cousin as he did, he felt that she was entitled to the man of her choice.

Over the years, his friendship for Harry and Lily had

grown, but there was an even stronger motive for his visits: little Randy. Resigned to the fact that he could never have children, he believed this nephew had been sent by God as a kind of compensation. This was the son he would never have—and to his secret joy, Randy adored him. The little boy even resembled the Goodhues, in both looks and stature. If Randolph had fathered him, Randy could not have looked more like him. Before the boy was two years old, Randolph had told Lily of his intention to make the boy his heir. If Charles Goodhue had known, he would have spun in his grave. He had disowned Lily for marrying a Jew. And now her son would one day inherit the entire fortune.

As for Lily, she had never cared about the money. She had always adored Randolph and was grateful he cared so much for her and her children.

# Chapter 15

THE farm and the 92nd Street Y were just an hour and a half apart by train, but Harry and Lily might have been separated by hundreds of miles, they saw each other so rarely. Though Harry tried to go home at least one weekend a month, the train was expensive and every minute away from the manuscript kept him that much longer from reaching the end.

As summer turned to fall, his urgency to get on with his work compelled him to sit at the desk for hours on end, immersing himself so completely that he almost forgot what day it was. Since he rarely remembered to eat, he lost fifteen pounds. The only thing that kept him going was gallons of black coffee from the Thermos always at his elbow. He smoked constantly, which cast a hovering gray pall over the room. His sleep was erratic, never more than four hours at a time, for even his nights were consumed by his ever-present obsession with the book.

He had just seated himself at the desk one morning when he heard a knock on his door. At first he thought he was imagining it. Who would be coming to visit? But there it was again, that knocking sound! Irritated, he stood up and abruptly flung it open.

There was Lily, surrounded by the children, who were smiling and chorusing, "Hello, Daddy!"

Suddenly, he was aware of an unmistakable feeling of resentment at their intrusion. Just as quickly, he attempted to smother it. What was wrong with him? This was his family! He looked at the five of them and forced a smile.

Then Melissa was in his arms, touching his cheek with her

chubby fingers, and any remaining annoyance at the interruption vanished.

"God, I'm glad to see you, Lily!" he whispered, taking her in his arms.

Then Jeremy piped up. "Daddy, can we go skating in Central Park?"

Before he could respond, Randy interrupted. "No! I want to go see Cousin Randolph's cars."

"Cars! Who wants to see stupid old cars? I want to go skating." Drew, as always, stubbornly supported Jeremy.

Lily quickly quieted them. "Randy, you know that we agreed to go skating."

And skating they went, but not without vociferous complaints from Randy. He and Drew argued all the way to Central Park.

Harry had a throbbing headache as he led them into the rink. Good God, they had been here only ten minutes, and already they were grating on him. Had he and his brothers squabbled like this when they were little? He was sure they had not. His father and mother would never have stood for it. Why didn't Lily do something? All she said was a gentle, "Children, children, behave. Be good." To which the children paid absolutely no attention.

Randy skated next to Harry, but he felt a strange irritation to see Jeremy hanging back, clinging to Lily's hand—she held Melissa on her free arm—while Drew skated confidently by.

But quickly he admonished himself. For God's sake, they were only little boys.

Even on the ice, the boys remained irritable and unmanageable, and after an hour Harry had had enough. Perhaps lunch at the Automat would quiet them. Lily sat them down at a table and went to get a dollar's worth of nickels. The mistake she made was to ask, "What would you like?"

"Peanut butter and jelly!" they chorused.

"They don't have that, dears. How about ham, or cheese?"

"I don't like ham," Drew announced.

Randy added, "I don't like cheese, either."

Annoyed, Harry broke in, "Why don't you just bring them whatever sandwiches there are?" He turned to the children. "You have to make do with what there is."

Melissa stuck out her lower lip defiantly. "Won't."

Feeling as though things were degenerating, Harry turned

and took away the catsup bottles she was playing with. "You'll do as I say, Melissa!"

Pouting, the little girl cried, "Mama! Want Mama!"

"Harry, please don't upset them."

"Upset them?" Harry expostulated. "For God's sake, Lily—can't you exercise a little discipline?"

But the little gladiators had numbers on their side, and after a while Harry gave up. It was easier simply to tune out the cacophony.

After spending twenty-five dollars to have them all stay at the Lido Hotel overnight, he felt almost a sense of shame at his relief when he saw them off on Sunday. He couldn't wait to get back to his script. Archie Sanger now brought more solace to him than did his family.

After that one weekend, Lily planned no more surprise visits. She realized it was easier to wait for Harry's rare weekends at home. Her business was doing better and better and she spent most of the long winter evenings bent over her sewing machine. The first thaw had arrived by the time Harry called to tell her the novel was done.

Spring had come and gone and Harry hadn't even noticed the buds on the trees. Gentle rains had given way to summer heat, and then to autumn chill. The first winter snow had fallen by the time he wrote, *Finis*. Harry bent over his typewriter and wept.

It was finished. Finished at last! Two thousand pages of it. He held it close to him, cradling it as though it were a living child. All that was missing now was Lily. Harry needed her to share this moment.

After drying his eyes, Harry fished in his pants pocket for a coin. He ran to the phone down the hall to call her. He didn't pause for a second, even though it was four in the morning.

"Lily!" he all but screamed as he heard the receiver lift. "It's finished! Can you believe it?"

"Oh my God!" she cried, instantly awake. Tears of joy streamed down her cheeks. "Harry, darling—that's wonderful!"

"I'm coming home this morning on the first train. I can hardly wait."

"Oh, Harry, neither can I."

"And Lily—I love you. I don't think you'll ever know how much."

After she hung up, she raised her eyes to heaven. It had been worth it. Every little hardship had been worth it, if only to hear the joy in Harry's voice. He would be home by noon. His arrival was all she could think of. She couldn't go back to sleep; instead, she dressed and began to straighten the house for his homecoming.

After breakfast she bundled the children up and sent them out to pick armloads of pine and holly.

Finally it was time to meet Daddy. Lily looked on as they assembled, their hair combed into place, their faces shining, wool caps over their ears and mufflers around their necks. Yesterday's transgressions were forgotten. She turned to them, her heart bursting with joy and love.

"Now, I'm going to ask you to do me a big favor. When Daddy comes home, I want you to be very sweet and very polite—let him have a little time to get used to us again. He is going to work at home now, and during the day you will have to be as quiet as possible. We're all going to have to cooperate. Is that a deal?"

They nodded their heads.

With the buckles on their galoshes jangling, they raced out and piled into the Model T, then drove away in a cloud of glory on the icy road. Lily thought her heart would stop as she saw Harry step down from the train. Even the children were forgotten for the moment as Lily and Harry ran to each other.

Harry dropped his suitcase and held her in his arms, kissing her passionately.

"It seems like an eternity," he whispered huskily. "You don't know how much I've missed you."

"It *has* been an eternity—I don't want you to go away ever again."

"I won't ever leave you."

It had been so many months since Harry had seen the children. God, how tall they had grown!

Gathering them to him, hugging them, he said, "I'm so happy to see you."

They didn't respond with quite the enthusiasm he had expected. Hadn't they missed him? It bothered him for a moment, but then he thought, Well, you can't have it both ways. You can't go away from children for a year and a half and expect a rousing welcome when you come back.

Picking up Melissa, he kissed her. "You look beautiful, baby."

"I'm not a baby," she announced, frowning.

"You're my baby."

"No! I'm Mommy's baby."

He was slightly taken aback. Dammit, the children saw him as a stranger, an outsider. Could he ever make up for this lost time?

As they drove down the dirt road to the farm, snow began to drift down gently. The trees already seemed an enchanted forest. Harry saw the beauty of it all so clearly today, as he never had before.

Once they had slowed and halted before the house, Jeremy struggled with his father's bag while Harry carried Melissa.

Looking up at the house, Harry stopped short, then broke into gales of laughter. Above the porch, the children had hung a large sign in multicolored block letters reading "WELCOME HOME DADDY." They'd attached crepe-paper streamers for a festive touch. What a homecoming!

Blinking back the tears, he smiled at his sons, then at Melissa in his arms. He had almost forgotten how adorable she was. He could have taken a bite out of her rosy red-apple cheeks. How precious she looked with the snowflakes tangled in her eyelashes.

Later he sat in the living room while Lily went to get dinner on the table. The two older boys were looking at him expectantly.

Determined to be the father he had vowed to be, he asked Jeremy, "Tell me about school, son. You must be a fine reader by now."

Jeremy looked at his father with mingled guilt and fear. He hated being asked that question. No matter how hard he tried, he was simply awful.

"I don't read very well!" he said desperately.

"Oh, I don't believe it. Why don't you get your book and show me?"

Jeremy hesitated for a moment. Then, with dragging steps, he went into his bedroom and brought back his school primer.

"Come on, hop up in my lap," urged Harry.

Haltingly Jeremy began, "S-s-"

"Oh, come on," Harry prompted. "You must know that. See . . ."

Obediently, Jeremy repeated, "See. D-d—"

Impatiently, Harry finally said, "See Dick. Jeremy, that's the first page, for goodness sake. Don't you know that? What have they been teaching you in school?"

But the more he prodded Jeremy, the more nervous the little boy became. Even the words he recognized suddenly looked like gibberish to him, and he was acutely aware of his father's exasperation.

"I just can't do it, Daddy," he finally said, bursting into tears.

"Of course you can—you're in the second grade! You should be able to read this whole book by now. What's wrong with you? Don't you study?"

Wailing, Jeremy ran into his bedroom and slammed the door. Harry was dumbfounded. Jeremy was a bright boy. It was quite obvious that Lily had allowed him to drift into bad habits, but now that he was home, that was all going to change.

Harry marched to the bedroom and knocked briefly on the door, then went in to find his son facedown on the bed, weeping.

"Come on, Jeremy," Harry said softly, sitting on the edge of the bed. "Stop that—you're a big boy."

Turning, Jeremy put his arms around his father and sobbed. "I'm sorry, Daddy. I do try hard."

Homecoming was not a time for discipline. "Okay, son. But now that I'm home, we're going to work on that reading of yours, and you'll soon be going like a house afire. How about a piggyback ride?"

Jeremy managed a weak smile, but when they returned to the living room, the other children were very quiet. Secretly, Randy gloated at Jeremy's discomfiture. Jeremy had always gotten most of the attention from Mommy—unless Drew was getting into trouble or Melissa was screaming—and now he felt that things were being evened up. With a child's clarity, Randy realized that he was somehow overlooked, and he resented it furiously. Jeremy was a dummy—he'd heard the other kids calling him that. Why, he himself was already learning to read, and Drew had known how for a long time.

Drew, on the other hand, was angry and upset with his father for chastising Jeremy. Didn't he know that his brother didn't like to be yelled at? Jeremy did try to read. Drew wanted to punch his father and tell him, "Go back to New York."

Meanwhile, as soon as Jeremy had begun to cry, Melissa had gone running to her mother, crying that she didn't "yike" Daddy at all.

Harry was mystified. What had gone wrong? Lily came in now, saying, "Children, go wash your hands. Dinner is ready." It was rather like a reprieve.

Harry carved the roast leg of lamb, and Drew passed the glazed carrots in the Blue Willow dish. Whatever unpleasantness had just transpired was past. The meal was the best Harry had had since he'd left for New York. No wonder Lily had been able to sell her wares. Her pickled watermelon and her mint jelly were ambrosia, the jam on the homemade bread heavenly.

The *pièce de résistance* was peach cobbler, accompanied by aromatic black coffee, which somehow tasted so much better than the bitter brew from his Thermos. As he finished the last bite, he commented, "Lily, a perfect meal. It's hard to believe that once you didn't know how to boil an egg."

It wasn't until later that he realized that the meal had been a rather silent affair. God, Jeremy was sensitive! But all of them seemed so subdued.

As soon as they had eaten, Drew asked, "Mommy, can we play in the attic?"

But Lily had replied, "No—we've had a big day, and now it's time for bed. Kiss Daddy good night, and I'll come to tuck you in in a few minutes."

There was a shuffling of feet as the children looked at each other, wondering who had to go first. Then Jeremy timidly reached up and brushed his lips against Harry's cheek, and Randy dutifully followed suit.

But when Drew came to stand by him, Harry saw an unexpected look of belligerence on the little face. And Melissa unequivocally refused, shrinking away and yelling "No!" as she wriggled out of his grasp.

After she had tucked in the children, Lily put on an apron and began to rinse the dishes. Watching her, Harry saw her as if for the first time. The children forgotten, he put his arms around her.

"How did I ever get along without you?"

He untied her apron, picked her up, and carried her down the hall to their room, then kicked the door shut. He unbuttoned her dress and kissed her with searching intensity. Their enormous need was so great they made love with a hunger neither had ever felt before. It was their most incredible coming together yet, and nothing existed outside their room. . . .

In the morning, as Lily and he sat alone at breakfast, drinking the last of their coffee, Harry said, "You know, actually, Lily, I felt a little bad yesterday."

"Why, darling?"

"Well, I just didn't realize that Jeremy was so sensitive about not being able to read."

"How do you know about that?"

"Oh, there was a bit of a fuss when I asked him to read to me, and he couldn't. You know, Lily, he should be reading at his age. He's in second grade."

"Oh, Harry, I wish you hadn't said anything to him. He's coming along, but he's just a little slow."

Forgotten were the vows of patience and understanding that Harry had made so fervently. As though there had been no interruption in their marriage, he quickly shot back: "Slow? That's ridiculous, Lily! Drew was reading even before I left for New York."

"Yes, but Jeremy isn't Drew. He doesn't catch on as quickly as Drew—can't you realize that?"

"That's not true! You've just coddled him, and the net result is that he hasn't achieved up to his abilities."

"He's just an average child."

"Who told you that? His teachers? Then they're no good."

"You've been away and you don't know. I've spent time with his teacher, and she's very good."

"Well, darling, then the problem is he won't work."

This wasn't the way to begin their reunion, Harry knew, but dammit, he was upset about Jeremy. Lily insisted that the children had different needs and abilities, but he didn't think the issue was as complicated as she made out. Finally, Harry conceded that Lily had seen more of the children than he had for the past year and a half, and that he would wait and see.

For the next few weeks, Harry made a great effort to observe the children through Lily's eyes. Drew was doing fine in school and so was Randy, but Jeremy was at the bottom of his class, and Harry was baffled. Either he wasn't motivated or, as Harry suspected, he had simply become a mama's boy. Because of his worry, Harry found himself becoming a stern disciplinarian. If he had to be tough to force Jeremy to achieve, that was what he would be. He had come home ready to assume his place as head of the house.

# Chapter 16

HARRY refused even to consider Lily's proposal to continue with her sewing and canning. She had done nobly, but now that *The Wars of Archie Sanger* was finished, he was not about to live off his wife. He started writing articles again, but uppermost in his mind was *Archie Sanger*. Finishing the novel had seemed like the biggest hurdle, but now he realized that a far greater one was finding a publisher. He knew that the first stage was finding the right agent. With little publishing experience, he felt as if he were looking for a needle in a haystack. Here he had written a 2,000-page manuscript and had no idea what to do with it.

However much he might delude himself in other areas of life, he was harshly critical of his own work and he knew he had written a good book.

The problem was that he needed to sell the book fast to support his family. He decided the only way to choose an agent was to contact several at once.

Harry drove into the city early one morning and went straight to the public library, where he asked for a copy of *Literary Market Place*. Going down the list, he felt as if he were picking horses without a racing form, but he copied down twenty-five names and addresses at random. That night, back at the farm, he sat down and tried to frame a letter.

His instinct told him that he should not give away too much of the story; just enough to whet their appetites. Finally, after several tries, he came up with a draft that seemed to satisfy all the requirements. Then he laboriously copied it over twenty-five times, addressed the envelopes, and drove down to the village to post them. His mouth was dry and his confidence wavered as he stood in front of the box. Then, before he could change his mind, he opened the lid and dropped the sealed envelopes inside. Would anyone respond? Or would they all take his carefully framed letter and file it in the closest wastepaper basket?

He drove back to the farm, walked up the gray wooden stairs and then down the hall to his study. He couldn't even share his fear with Lily; it was imperative that he appear positive, and he was relieved that she and the children were still out.

He had half an hour to himself before he heard Lily call out, "We're back!"

He got up and went into the kitchen. Smiling broadly, he said, "How was your walk?"

"See what I found?" Melissa chirped, holding up a small spray of pine cones.

"That's beautiful," he replied, lifting her up in the air. "But not half as beautiful as you are."

"Okay, children," Lily said. "Now scat. Go play while I make dinner."

Seating himself at the table, Harry watched as she began to prepare their meal. She worked so hard. He prayed to God that the book would sell so he could give her the break she deserved.

Shortly thereafter, the aroma of frying chicken and baking cornbread wafted from the stove.

As they seated themselves, Lily smiled and asked, "How did your day go, dear?"

"Fine—just great," he answered. "I sent off twenty-five letters to what are, I hope, the best agents in New York. So now all I have to do is sit back and wait for the offers to pour in."

"Hip, hip, hooray!"

Melissa liked the sound of that and chimed in, "Hip, hip, hooray, Daddy!"

"That's right, Melissa. That's what they'll say the minute they read Daddy's book."

After four weeks of waiting, he finally received a response. Ripping the envelope open, he read,

Dear Mr. Kohle:

If you will submit an outline or the first hundred pages of the manuscript, we will be happy to read your work.

Best,
Ellis Knox

Wasting no time, Harry bundled up the first hundred pages of his precious manuscript and mailed them. Then he steeled himself for another long wait while he forced himself to churn out popular articles. Enough editors knew him as a reliable source of well-written filler that he knew he could support his family for the time being. But after six weeks of silence, he decided to write again to Ellis Knox, stating that since he had received no response, perhaps Mr. Knox had been unable to reach a decision on the first hundred pages. Consequently, he was enclosing the rest of the novel. Harry knew it was insanity to send the whole. It was foolish to risk offending one so lofty as Ellis Knox. Then again, what did he have to lose?

Again, he went to the post office in a state of high anxiety. If he had only known what had been happening at Ellis Knox, Literary Agents, his fears would have been allayed.

Harry had been extraordinarily lucky in his choice of agent. Ellis Knox was unusual in that he looked at every piece of work that passed his assistants' initial screening. In the final analysis, he wanted to make the decisions. But that meant that there was often a considerable backlog on his desk, and the first hundred pages of Harry's manuscript had gathered dust for almost four weeks. However, as soon as he had read the first pages, he realized that he had found a unique new voice. He had been at the point of dictating a letter to Harry Kohle when his secretary had staggered in with the rest of the script. Ellis felt a curious thrill when he saw the entire manuscript. Picking up the next hundred pages, he read with an increased sense of reverence. "Judy, hold my calls for the rest of the day," he shouted into the intercom.

Early the next morning he finally laid the manuscript aside and rang Jerry Schwartz. Jerry was the associate whose judgment he trusted most. Now Ellis wanted some confirmation that he wasn't dreaming.

"Could you come in here?" Ellis asked. "I have something I want you to see."

The younger man was shocked when he saw the size of the script. "What in the world is *that*?"

"I want you to read it, Jerry."

"You've got to be kidding. It's bigger than the Old Testament."

"Be that as it may, I need your opinion."

With a wry smile, Jerry said, "There go my evenings for the next week."

But the following morning he knocked on Ellis's door at nine. "You're not going to believe this," he admitted sheepishly, "but I read two-thirds of that script last night. I don't think I turned out the light until four-thirty. I just couldn't put the damned thing down. You were right—it's a phenomenon."

Ellis wasn't surprised. He was as sure of the quality of this book as he had been about anything in his life.

"Sold to the right publisher, it could be one of the biggest books of the year," he declared.

"The man's an absolute genius," Jerry said flatly. "As for sales, we'll be at war in another year, and while I hate to be cynical, you can bet the public will want war stories by the time this is published."

That was all Ellis needed to hear. "Judy, get that fellow Harry Kohle on the phone."

When Lily answered, instinct told her this was it. Harry had been very silent, but Lily knew how he had pinned his hopes on Ellis Knox, though lately his name had been accompanied by none-too-endearing adjectives.

With a nervous stammer, she said, "I'm sorry, Mr. Knox, but he's out at the moment. May I have him call you back?"

"Yes, if you please. I'll be in my office until five. Otherwise, he can reach me tomorrow morning."

When Harry returned from the village, where he had gone to buy a paper, Lily cried breathlessly, "Do you know who you just missed?"

"Franklin Roosevelt?"

She could hardly get the words out. "Ellis Knox!"

Harry's mouth fell open. He grabbed the phone and gave the operator the number.

A moment later, a voice was saying, "Mr. Kohle? I'm delighted you called. We're very interested in your work and would like you to come into the office to discuss it further. How about tomorrow at two-thirty?"

Harry couldn't believe his ears, but somehow he managed to stammer, "That will be fine." Then, impulsively, he blurted out, "I don't know how to thank you, Mr. Knox."

"The name is Ellis. And there's no need to thank me; you know, without the author, we agents have nothing to sell."

Harry felt as though he had died and gone to heaven. It wasn't until the next morning that Jeremy reminded Harry that he was supposed to attend the boy's school play that afternoon.

He looked at Jeremy as he ate his oatmeal. The child had talked of nothing else for the last week. Harry swallowed his coffee, cleared his throat, and said, "Jeremy, I'm sorry but I have to go into New York today. An agent called, and he wants to talk to me about publishing my book. I'm afraid I won't be back in time for your play."

Jeremy's mouth dropped in dismay. He had been so thrilled when he was chosen to play Christopher Columbus. He wanted his daddy to see him in a starring role. Numbly he stirred his oatmeal. The other children chorused, "Oh, Daddy, please, can't you go?"

Lily spoke quickly. "Now, I know you're disappointed that Daddy can't be there, but there is nothing more important than your father's work. There will be other plays, and he will be there for them. Now get your schoolbooks. The bus will be here any minute."

As Jeremy got up from his chair he mumbled, "It's okay about the play, Daddy. It doesn't matter. I understand."

Harry rose and hugged his son, silently blessing him for offering absolution. But on the train into New York he kept wondering if there was something else he could have done.

His doubts vanished the moment he entered Ellis Knox's office. Harry didn't know what he had expected, but the name was so dignified that he had pictured Ellis to be in his sixties. Instead, Harry was disconcerted to see a handsome man of about forty, with a square jaw, riveting gray eyes, and dark hair just touched with silver at the temples, who towered over the writer by a good four inches. His clothes were Savile Row, and he had the unmistakable appearance of a man with a table permanently reserved for him at "21."

"I must tell you that yours was the most powerful manuscript I've read in years," Ellis began as soon as Harry was seated. "Everyone else here agrees. How long did it take you to complete?"

Harry almost pinched himself to make sure he wasn't dreaming. Even though he'd been confident *Archie Sanger* was good, he had been desperate for outside confirmation of its impact.

"How long did it take me?" he repeated. "Well, I started it while I was at Columbia. But then I got married, had a family, and was forced to put it aside. Still, *Archie* burned in my head. Luckily for me, my wife helped me to survive while I wrote the book."

"Lucky for us, too," said Ellis, pleased to find that Harry Kohle was not only an extraordinary writer, but an articulate, handsome man. "Now I understand that you are a writer by profession. Where have you been published?"

"*Esquire, Harper's, The Atlantic Monthly.*" Harry ran quickly down the list, omitting *McCall's* and *Redbook.*

"I think I have read some of your pieces. I knew your name sounded familiar."

With the preliminary amenities out of the way, Ellis moved quickly. He drew up an agency contract which Harry scarcely read before scribbling his signature at the bottom. Then the two men stood up and shook hands once again.

"I hope that this will be the beginning of a long and fruitful relationship," Ellis said. "I have every confidence in your book."

Harry left the building walking on air. He couldn't wait to get home to tell Lily.

In the agency, Ellis knew he had his work cut out for him. He knew he had a major novel to sell, but it was so long that several of his closest editorial contacts rejected the script without, Ellis suspected, even reading it.

Finally, one afternoon he lunched with Charlie Blair of Farnsworth and Barnes, an old friend and virtually his last hope. "Just read it, for Christ's sake," Ellis insisted. "Would I be pushing this if I didn't think it was something truly out of the ordinary? Haven't I given you enough winners to ask you to look yourself?"

Blair wearily acquiesced. "Okay, Ellis, you win. Leave the first hundred pages and I'll get back to you."

When he read the portion of the novel that night, he became as excited as Ellis had. The book was extraordinary.

The next morning he called Ellis and said tersely, "Bring that monster over right away."

Closeting himself in his office, he did nothing all day until he reached the last page. What a book! he thought as he sat back to ponder its commercial possibilities.

The following Monday morning over coffee and Danish at the conference table, he tried to ignite his colleagues' enthusiasm. Everyone trusted Blair's judgment, but the other editors saw no way they could publish such a long book.

"For God's sake, Charlie," said his publisher. "It's not a book, it's a goddamn tome."

Upset and angry, Blair went back to his office. As one of the owners, he knew he could take on any project he wanted, but he also knew the danger of publishing a book without full house support. After a while he picked up the phone and called Ellis.

"The book is great," he said to the agent, "but everyone has problems with the length. It's several hundred pages more than *Gone With the Wind*. Your writer is simply going to have to face some severe cutting if he ever wants his book published at a popular price."

"I'm not sure how Kohle will react. He's very protective of his work."

"Tell him we don't want to change anything, just shorten it. Look what Perkins did on Thomas Wolfe. Many major writers get cut and if I promise to do it myself, you know you'll be in good hands. Tell him if we can reduce the book by a third, we'll pay three thousand dollars."

"Let me try," said Ellis. "But I can't guarantee success."

"What's Kohle like?" asked Blair. "I'm curious, after reading his book."

"Intense, dedicated, believes passionately in his work. The whole world could cave in, so long as it doesn't touch his typewriter. Lives on a farm in upstate New York with a wife and four children. Incidentally, she's the former Lily Goodhue, and he's from the Kohle banking clan."

Charlie snorted. "Guy probably doesn't even need the dough. Well, speak to him and let me know."

• • •

At first Harry exploded when Ellis suggested cutting a third of the book.

"Forget it," he shouted. "How dare they, those Philistines! The answer is definitely no."

Ellis let Harry fume until he'd run out of steam. Then he said, "Come on, Harry, you've got to be reasonable. Several other publishing houses have refused even to read the book on account of its length. Charlie Blair has promised to work very closely with you, and he's a hell of an editor. I know how you feel, but sometimes you've got to compromise."

"When they're done it will be theirs and not mine. I can't do it, Ellis; I've struggled too hard."

"Well," Ellis said, "don't make any hasty decisions. I think something can be worked out. Why don't you sleep on it."

After hanging up, Harry sat in his study for a long time. He knew the length of the book was a problem, and not only did he want *Archie* published, he wanted it to sell. He wasn't so naive to believe the public would pay twice as much for an unknown writer than they did for Theodore Dreiser. So while it would kill him to do it—he loved every paragraph, sentence, and word in *Archie Sanger*, he decided he would have to give in. He only hoped that Charlie Blair was half as good an editor as Ellis said he was.

That night, he held Lily close, needing the comfort of her warmth and strength. "Lily, I've come to a decision about Charlie Blair's offer; I'm going along with him."

"But I thought you told Ellis you wouldn't even consider it. We're not that desperate for money. Why don't you wait and try a few more publishing houses?"

"Because I want the book out. By the time it's printed, America may well be at war. The timing will be perfect. Just because I'm a stubborn bastard doesn't mean I'm unrealistic. After all, I don't have Kohle blood in my veins for nothing."

Hugging him, Lily knew how much he wanted his book to be a success. How much he needed to regain his father's respect.

Harry slept restlessly, trying to think of a way to cut the book without losing its strength. Finally, at four in the morning, he had an inspiration. Barely able to contain his excitement, he called Ellis at home at eight.

"I've got it," he shouted. "The perfect solution. The way the book is structured, we can publish it as two separate novels. The first would be *The Wars of Archie Sanger*, and the second *The Redemption*. It will just mean writing a couple of new chapters at the end of one and at the beginning of the other."

"My God, that's brilliant!" said Ellis. "And you're supposed to be a novice at this game?"

"Do you think Blair will agree?"

"Hell, yes! Do you realize what this means? We'll have two books to sell. I'll call Charlie as soon as the office opens."

"You'll let me know how it goes?" Harry asked anxiously.

"The second I hear."

Harry hung over the phone all morning, but it didn't ring until almost lunchtime.

"I won't keep you in suspense," Ellis said. "Farnsworth and Barnes agree to the idea of two books and are offering five thousand dollars."

Harry's heart leapt up in his chest. God, how he and Lily had struggled to arrive at this day! His dream had come true.

"I'll be damned," he finally stammered. "There's no way for them to back out?"

Ellis smiled. "Not a chance."

There was a long silence before Harry said, "I don't know how to thank you."

"You don't have to. This is only the beginning."

"Listen, Ellis. I know that it's a hell of a long way, but could you drive up this evening? Lily has heard so much about you; she'd love to meet you. I want you here to share our celebration."

Ellis was only too happy to oblige.

"Ellis Knox coming for dinner—oh my God, Harry! How am I going to entertain him, an important New York agent?"

"Just as you always do, darling. Perfectly."

Lily piled the children into the car and dashed into the village, where for once she bought lavishly. This was no time for thrift.

By the time she returned home, her menu was set. First she made her silky homemade chicken-liver pâté which tasted almost like foie gras, then began preparing stuffed mushrooms and melba toast. Turning to the main course, she lovingly readied veal Cordon Bleu. She was most confident of her dessert: a spectacular lemon meringue pie.

She wanted everything to be absolutely perfect. Ellis was,

amazingly, the first guest they had ever had to dinner—except, of course, her cousin Randolph, who was always happy to take potluck. But the heavy oak kitchen table wouldn't do for tonight, and they didn't have a dining room.

Finally she decided she would serve them in the living room. She dragged a round corner table in front of the fireplace and covered it with her one beautiful tablecloth. Then she put out her nicest china, an antique flowered Limoges she had found at a Fourth of July fair. Only she would know that her own dinner plate had a crack in it and that Harry's saucer was chipped underneath. A huge bouquet of roses brightened the center of the table, and Lily looked at her handiwork with satisfaction.

She fed the children early, then put them to bed, quelling their protests with lavish bribes about taking them to the carnival the following week.

After that, she spent a little time in front of the old-fashioned pier glass, trying on her long-unused collection of Parisian frocks. She supposed that they had formed part of her trousseau; her life had certainly provided little opportunity to flaunt them. After a long day hoeing potatoes, it had seemed incongruous to dress for dinner.

Realizing that time was getting short, she chose a lettuce-green chiffon and brushed her hair into a loose pageboy. As the bell rang, she called downstairs for Harry to put out a couple of bottles of the magnificent French Bordeaux Randolph had given them at Christmas.

Ellis entered the small house to the crackling glow of the fire and the sweet smell of roses. He glanced about the cozy room with pleasure, turning just in time to see the loveliest woman he had ever laid eyes on walk into the room.

Noticing the Paris gown, he reminded himself she was a Goodhue, but what really took his breath was her creamy complexion, the tumble of curling red hair, and her brilliant green eyes.

"Mrs. Kohle?" he murmured. "I'm so pleased to meet you." He was so entranced by her appearance he almost forgot to give Harry the champagne he'd bought to celebrate the sale of *Archie Sanger*.

The evening was marvelous, enchanted. The food was delicious, the wine fit for the gods. There was a special air about Lily when she asked her husband, "What do you think?" or

"How do you feel about it, darling?" Ellis had never met a woman who made a man feel that important. Shockingly he realized that he was half in love with her himself and, quite frankly, he didn't know what he would do about it.

Ellis was one of the most charming men Lily had ever met, though where her husband was lively, Ellis was reserved. But he had a twinkle in his eyes and a humorous turn to his mouth. Drifting from one topic to another, they discovered a great deal about each other and realized they were becoming friends. At the end of the evening, they drank a toast to *Archie Sanger* and their great hopes for the book.

As Ellis rose to leave, Lily found herself clasping his hand and saying warmly, "Be sure to come out and visit us again, won't you? We'd love to have you."

"You can count on it," he smiled. "And next time, I'm determined to come early enough to meet your charming children."

"Just be sure you come on one of their charming days," Harry said, laughing.

On the drive home, all Ellis could think of was Lily Kohle. It wasn't just her incredible looks. She was the most extraordinary woman he'd ever met, so different from all the New York women with whom he'd been involved since his bitter divorce ten years before. He couldn't get over the gourmet meal she'd cooked without help. Or her obvious belief in Harry's work. That's right, he berated himself, Harry, *her husband. She's married to your newest client, and plainly, she's very much in love with him.* But try as he would, he couldn't stop thinking of Lily Kohle.

Ellis had found out a lot about the Kohles that evening. Although they were both from wealthy families, neither of them had any money of their own. Scuttlebutt had it that Lily Goodhue had been disinherited for marrying a Jew, and Ellis had inferred that Harry Kohle had not fared much better. Old Benjamin Kohle had not taken kindly to the idea of his son becoming a writer.

Apparently, they had survived on Lily's small inheritance from her grandmother and Harry's articles—and Ellis knew just how much that kind of writing brought in. Lily had pitched in, selling homemade preserves and handmade clothes to let Harry finish his novel. And yet, in spite of their poverty, Lily seemed a happy woman.

# Chapter 17

HARRY'S ultimate dream was to have *The Wars of Archie Sanger* published. He had never thought beyond that day or how it would change the rest of his life. In the weeks after the publication of the book, "Harry Kohle" became a household name. As it was published at the height of the Battle of Bataan, all America discovered universal truths in this depiction of the horrors of war.

The novel was displayed in bookstore windows in every city and reviewed on the front page of *The New York Times Book Review*, and within a month of publication, it hit the bestseller list.

Harry watched with happy disbelief. Ellis kept him informed, but the reality of Harry's fame hadn't yet penetrated his consciousness. The only tangible aspect of the whole phenomenon was the fan letters which had begun to arrive in huge packets in his mailbox. At first Harry attempted to read them, charmed by their praise, but after a while he became overwhelmed by the sheer volume and gave up.

Several months after the book went to number one a check arrived from the agency which finally brought home his huge success. Ellis had forwarded a royalty statement giving Harry an unbelievable profit of $40,000 on the first five months of his book's sales.

Strangely, instead of making him feel reassured, the money filled Harry with all kinds of new anxieties. Having labored so long in poverty and obscurity, he was afraid his talent would be seduced by success. He'd become used to his new affluence—and, worse yet, believed his own reviews. Then what if it all collapsed? If instead of being a major new talent he turned out to be nothing more than a one-book author? If his creative abilities simply dried up?

It was so tempting to use this new financial freedom to relax. Get to know the children again. Spend some time with Lily—even take the honeymoon they had never had. But Harry still felt he had to prove himself first. He had thought that the success of *Archie Sanger* would do it, but paradoxically, it seemed to have intensified his drive to succeed. He refused to acknowledge that a large part of his insecurity came from his parents' refusal to acknowledge his achievement. They came to his publication party, and condescendingly mentioned his reviews. But at least in Harry's mind, they never gave him the same respect accorded his brothers, who worked at the bank. Harry never stopped to think that this was their limitation. When his father said, "Nice job, *Archie Sanger*. Bit long though," he would have said the same to Tolstoy.

Whatever the reason, Harry knew no peace. In the ensuing months, even before the publication of *The Redemption of Archie Sanger*, Harry threw himself into a new work, tentatively entitled *The Mountains Roared*, which would be the third part of the trilogy. He paid little attention to the bombing of Pearl Harbor and America's entry into the war. He was just pleased his eyesight was now weak enough to keep him from being drafted, but not so weak that he couldn't write.

Lily scarcely saw her husband. Unable to divine his deep-seated feelings of anger because of the perceived rejection by his family, it was impossible for her to understand his urgency. Did he still feel that he had something to prove to her? Well, she would have to reassure him, make him realize that in her eyes as well as in the world's, he was a major success. She reached out the only way she knew.

"Darling, you really should get some fresh air. It's lovely today—how about a picnic?"

"Lily, please, I'm in the middle of a chapter."

"When do you think you might be through with it?"

"I don't know," he returned irritably. "A day or two, maybe."

Gently she touched his shoulder. "Harry, I understand what it means when the creative urge hits you, but couldn't you try to sandwich your family in between strikes? We all miss you—you haven't even had dinner with us in two weeks. Don't you feel that you owe it to the children?"

"Look, Lily, I'm not a train. I don't run on a schedule."

For a moment she felt like slapping him. But just as she resisted the urge with her children, she resisted it with her husband, saying mildly, "Harry, I know that, but can't you take it a little easier? There's no rush for you to finish. We have enough money from *Archie Sanger* to last us for years, and Ellis says that *Redemption* will bring in at least as much, and probably more."

" 'Ellis says, Ellis says'! He's not God, Lily!"

Instantly she dropped her hand and stepped back. "All right," she said tightly. "I'm sorry for disturbing you."

As soon as she had left, Harry felt tremendous remorse; the hurt in her voice had penetrated even his self-absorption. He knew he was neglecting his family and he could no longer use financial need as an excuse. But no matter how he tried to analyze his compulsion to keep writing, he couldn't change his behavior. He knew that it was absurd to drive himself so hard now, yet every minute he spent away from his typewriter made him feel intolerably guilty. Worst of all, he couldn't seem to accept Lily's constant attempt to reassure him that time away from work was not just idle and self-indulgent. Still, he would have to try. He ripped the sheet from the machine, balled it up, and flung it into the wastebasket. He walked down the hall and entered the kitchen.

"I'm sorry, darling. Please forgive me."

She did, but the barrier remained. A little while later he went back to his office and, as always, she sought comfort in the children, gratefully taking them outside to play.

Still, that evening she was able to forget the hurts and embrace Harry with genuine warmth. For a day or two Harry seemed to make a genuine effort to spend time with her. But it wasn't long before he slipped back into his old habits. The muffled clattering of his typewriter formed a haunting background to her intense loneliness. She had never dreamed it would be like this once Harry had become a success. This was worse than the old days with the pressure to publish enough articles to pay the bills—and infinitely worse than the months he had spent in New York. Then she had hope for the future, the future she was now living in despair.

The children were now all in school all day and she no longer even had Melissa to share her time with. She had never prepared herself for this departure. Why, only yesterday they had been chubby babes in arms, and now they marched off happily to hop onto a big yellow bus, while she was left behind with tears in her eyes. Perhaps Harry shared her loss, but he just saw their leaving as a natural growth which happily gave him a good eight hours of peace and quiet in which to work. For Lily, the children represented all she had. It seemed to take hours every morning to recover from her sense of loss. The children were not just a part of her life—they *were* her life. The shortages caused by the war curtailed her elaborate meals and Harry opposed her doing any more for the war effort than rolling bandages at the local Red Cross. Suddenly she glimpsed her existence ten years from now, when the children would be leaving home for good. Since Harry wouldn't hear of her returning to work, she didn't even have that to anticipate to help fill the coming void. Lily was merely an appendage of the other five people in the house. And when the children were gone, what would her role be? It was a frightening thought.

But though she knew she should try to talk through her feelings with Harry, she kept putting it off. Someday, she kept telling herself. In the meantime, she did her best to keep her household calm and happy, and over the next few years she did succeed.

# Chapter 18

IN some ways she and Harry seemed to have come to terms with each other. She no longer chastised him for his remoteness and he, in turn, felt a guilty relief at no longer having to apologize constantly. But she never told him how lonely she'd become and Harry never confessed his feelings of failure in the midst of his success.

He finished *Mountains*; Ellis predicted it would sell even more strongly than the previous books. Lily occupied herself with the PTA and all the children's after-school activities. In fact, the children were the only area where she and Harry still openly disagreed. And it seemed that Jeremy was the focus of their differences, for Harry persisted in his belief that the reason for the poor performance in school was sheer laziness.

If Harry had centered his efforts on his second son rather than his first, Lily felt it would have been far more appropriate, for Drew was obviously brilliant. Even methodical Randy was a far better student than Jeremy. But Harry somehow never worried about them, nor imperious little Melissa.

Once in a while, Lily wondered if Harry was unconsciously repeating his father's error of singling out one child to bear the brunt of his own frustrations. In any event, what concerned her was the effect on little Jeremy.

With *Mountains* finished, Harry seemed, for a brief period at least, more relaxed. One evening he sat next to Lily before the fire and said, "I'd almost forgotten how wonderful it is to not be at the typewriter."

"Oh, darling, you have no idea how much it means to all of us. The children just love having you at dinner."

"Speaking of the children, Lily, I don't want to rake over old coals, but we really must talk about Jeremy."

"What about him?"

"He's just not doing well in school."

"He's doing just fine."

"Fine! I saw his last report card, and it was abysmal."

"It wasn't abysmal. He got two Cs and the rest Bs."

"And you're satisfied with that?"

"Yes, I am!"

Harry got up and began pacing the floor. "That's absurd, Lily. He's much smarter than that. I don't think the local school is right for him."

"There's nothing wrong with the school. Look how the other boys are doing."

"Exactly. You keep telling me that the boys are different—well, I think Jeremy needs more discipline than the others. I think we should send him to a military school."

"Over my dead body!" Lily almost shouted.

"Why are you being so blind? Don't you realize that one day Jeremy will have to make his own way in the world? He'll never survive if you don't stop protecting him. I want him to be able to compete, to win. That's what it's all about, Lily, winning!"

Lily felt tremendous anger, anger she hadn't realized she was capable of, toward Harry. "The answer is no! You will not send Jeremy to a military academy. I was sent away for years and it was terrible. I want you to leave Jeremy alone—let him grow up to be a happy person, for God's sake."

Lily jumped up, ran into her bedroom, and slammed the door.

After a moment's shocked silence, Harry got up and went into the bedroom, where Lily lay facedown on the bed, crying into her pillow.

Kneeling beside her, he said, "Lily, I'm sorry—I just thought it might be best for the boy."

"It's not best for him," she sobbed. "It's not best for him to be sent away from his home and his mother."

"Okay, okay! Have it your way," he exploded. "But if Jeremy's marks this next term don't show a big improvement, he's going to some kind of prep school."

Harry spent a cold night on the sofa and was up very early the next morning. After dressing quickly, he dialed Ellis's number and asked without preamble, "Are you free for lunch?"

"Sure. Say, one o'clock?"

He could hardly wait to get out of the house. Usually his and Lily's grievances were short-lived, but for some reason, the subject of Jeremy stuck in his craw. He hoped lunch with Ellis would restore his good humor and perhaps his sense of proportion. One reason Harry was so furious with Lily was that even though her own method of raising Jeremy might be flawed, Harry knew his was equally at fault.

After ordering, Ellis and Harry talked a while about the current sales figures for *Mountains*. "It's doing even better than the others." Ellis smiled. "You're going to make a mint."

Harry shrugged. "The review in the *Times* wasn't so good."

"Come on, all they said was that the central character wasn't as sharply etched as Archie Sanger. Other than that, it was quite favorable. Don't take it all so much to heart."

"I suppose you're right."

Ellis laughed. "Your problem is that you're never satisfied. The *Atlantic* loved it. You can't please everyone." Then, looking at him more closely, Ellis asked, "Harry, what else is bothering you?"

"It's Lily," said Harry, realizing the reason he'd come in for lunch was to share his problem. "She and I . . . well, the fact of the matter is we've been going round and round about Jeremy. I think that the boy should go away to school, and she is vehemently opposed to having any of the children leave home. It's the only thing we ever fight about."

"Well, she's terribly devoted to those children."

"That's all fine, but I think she wants to keep them tied to her apron strings forever, and she mollycoddles Jeremy to death."

"How old is the boy? Eleven? Maybe she thinks he's a little young to go away."

Stubbing out his cigarette viciously, Harry frowned. "Yes, but dammit, he just isn't doing well at the school he's going to. Lily's a wonderful mother—and a wonderful wife, the best—but she just doesn't crack the whip. They run the house, not she."

"From what I've seen, Jeremy seems like a rather quiet, tractable kid," Ellis said quietly. "Perhaps Lily doesn't feel he would benefit from more discipline."

Barely hearing the other man's words, Harry continued. "He's a smart boy. And by God, he's going to make it, or else!"

"Like his father," Ellis said ironically.

But the gentle sarcasm was lost on Harry. "I don't mean to bore you with my problems, Ellis. It's just that Lily and I so rarely argue. I don't want to make her unhappy, but I just don't feel I can give in on this issue. What the hell should I do?"

Ellis paused reflectively. "Well, you probably won't change her mind by arguing, but maybe you can alter her point of view. Isolated out there on the farm, she's gotten so close to the children that she may have lost her sense of proportion. Perhaps you all need a change."

"Like what, a vacation?"

"Have you ever thought of moving? The war in Europe is almost over and when it ends in the Pacific there's going to be an enormous housing shortage. Now is a perfect time to make an investment."

"Leave the farm?"

"Is that such a radical idea? The farmhouse is charming, and I know how happy you've been there—but one of these days, now that there isn't any financial imperative, you might like to scale back on your writing schedule and move a little closer to the city. I think that perhaps what Lily needs is some new interests."

Harry looked at him with dawning interest. "A new house? You know, it's incredible, but I've never thought of it. We've lived on the farm for so long."

"You've had such tunnel vision, Harry. You've worked like a demon. Not that as your agent I want to discourage you, but as your friend I think that both you and Lily could benefit from being less isolated."

As they ate their lunch, Harry mused. "I don't want to live in Manhattan, I know that much. I can't write when there are so many temptations and distractions." A sudden vision of his parents' brownstone loomed before him.

Thoughtfully, Ellis said, "You know, I saw a property in Greenwich not too long ago that was the most magnificent piece of real estate. If I were married with children, I would have bought it on the spot." Continuing, he rhapsodized, "Ten of the most verdant, beautiful acres on God's green earth. A low, rolling meadowland which gradually sweeps up to the crest of a hill and at the summit, the panorama is indescribable, bluish-purple mountains to the west, a lake to the east which is so clear and calm that it reflects the sky and the trees like a mirror, and when the sun rises over it in a blaze of pinks and golds, well, you just have to see it."

Forgetting that Ellis too had been a writer, Harry was startled to hear him so lyrical about a country property.

"And you think it might be right for Lily and me?"

"I can't imagine a more beautiful setting." Ellis choked back the next words: "for Lily." He could picture her in a lovely white frame house, with roses rioting over the veranda and smooth lawns stretching down to the beach. She would give it the same warmth and graciousness she had the farm, he thought enviously, little dreaming of the imposing modern house that had leapt into Harry's mind.

"By God, I'm going to go see it this afternoon," Harry exclaimed. "Who's handling the property?"

As he bid Ellis good-bye, his head was awhirl with his new idea. Damned if Ellis wasn't right! He and Lily deserved to enjoy the fruits of his success. Until the publication of *The Mountains Roared,* Harry himself had been afraid to accept his financial worth, but now, with the final novel of the trilogy firmly perched atop the bestseller list, he could admit that he was not only a famous author but also a very wealthy man. He had once promised Lily he'd buy her the moon. Well, he could start by getting her an estate like the one where she'd lived as a child.

Strangely, as he drove through Westchester, the image of Lily faded, to be replaced by a picture of his father. And the house of his dreams was nothing like the warm, happy home Lily would have wanted but was instead a stark, modern showplace that would convince Benjamin Kohle that his youngest son had made it big without any help from his father. He began to dream of a glass palace, perhaps designed by Mies van der Rohe. And when it was finished, he would have a party that would set Manhattan on its ear. It would be the social event of the year.

It was late in the afternoon when he finally stood at the

top of the hill and surveyed the panorama, even more magnificent than Ellis had said. The vista left him awestruck.

Taking one last look, he ran down the rolling slope through the meadow with a sense of freedom he had never felt before and jumped into his car. This was his—and he had to secure it before someone else discovered it. He didn't even flinch when the agent told him, "The price is three hundred thousand dollars."

Without a moment's hesitation, he wrote out a check for fifty thousand as a deposit. This would be a total surprise for Lily, a wonderful surprise.

When Harry arrived home in a state of euphoria, all the discord was completely forgotten. He and Lily embraced and forgave each other, and made love that night.

The next day, as soon as the bus had disappeared, Harry said gaily, "Lily, darling, I'm not going to work today. I just feel like going for a drive. I want to celebrate."

"What are we celebrating?" Lily asked, bemused.

"You and me."

Laughingly, she said, "Okay. Shall I bring a picnic with champagne?"

"Absolutely."

"Where are we going?"

"It's a surprise."

As they drove along, Lily's spirits rose even higher. Harry was as charming as the night they met. They talked about a multitude of inconsequential things, for the first time in a long time. It was as though they were getting to know each other once again, and Lily was so happy that she paid no attention to where they were going until Harry pulled off a country road, saying, "This looks like a good place for a picnic."

They set off down the narrow lane hand in hand. The meadow, facing Long Island Sound, was the color of ripe wheat and scores of sailboats dotted the water.

As they stood in rapt silence admiring the view, Lily became aware of a feeling of expectancy. It was as if Harry were waiting for her approval. "Have you been here before?" she asked.

When he didn't answer, her suspicion grew. "Harry, what is going on?"

He turned to her and she saw that his eyes were alight with

excitement. "Darling, I wanted it to be a surprise. I bought this property yesterday, Lily. Don't you love it?"

"For us—to live on?" she asked incredulously.

"Can you think of a more magnificent site to build our dream house?"

"That's not the point. You bought this property without even asking me? Harry, how could you? Doesn't my opinion count for anything with you anymore? Suppose I hated this place?"

"I thought you would be thrilled," he shot back defensively. "I only wanted to surprise you!"

"You might have asked me what I thought would make me happy. Have you ever heard me express a desire for a dream house?"

For a moment they stared at each other angrily. Then Harry said, "Lily, if you don't want this place, I'll simply cancel my offer and stop my check. I'm not going to argue with you about a goddamn house. I only did it for you."

In reality, their argument was not about real estate. However, neither could tell the other what was in his heart.

It wasn't that Lily disliked the property, it was that in buying it without consulting her, Harry had reinforced her lack of self-esteem. Harry, on the other hand, felt she was being unreasonable, just as she was when they discussed Jeremy. The two issues somehow merged in his mind.

He stood staring stonily at the water. Lily turned to continue arguing, but seeing his bleak expression she softened. For the first time since the publication of *Archie Sanger,* he seemed hurt and vulnerable. Suddenly she felt utterly ungrateful. Of course he had done this as a wonderful surprise, not to demean her.

Slowly she reached out, touched his arm. "It *is* beautiful, Harry."

He turned and searched her face. Was she merely acquiescing, or did she truly understand?

"Do you really like it? Because if you don't, I'll just tell the realtor we've changed our minds."

"No, Harry, keep it," she said softly. "We'll build our dream house."

As they celebrated over champagne, neither realized just how different their respective dream houses could be.

# Chapter 19

HARRY hired Mies van der Rohe, the most prestigious architect in America. When Lily first saw the plans she almost fainted. The preliminary drawings were so stark, so austere, she found it difficult to imagine herself living in such a house. She had visualized a charming farmhouse, like those she had admired so in Provence, but having made the commitment to the property, she didn't want to upset Harry now. It seemed so important to him. So what he loved was a house of chrome, marble, and glass—then she would learn to love it too. After all, she was married not to a house but to a man.

After the groundbreaking, they drove out to the site frequently, even though no real work would begin until the spring. Even that would be delayed by the difficulty in buying materials. All winter Harry was as impatient as a small boy and for the first time in years he was happy to be called out of his study to join the family. It was as if his obsession with the house had eroded his devotion to work.

Lily was happier than she'd been in years, until one day at the end of May Jeremy came home from his next-to-last day of school, went into his room, and locked the door. At five o'clock, Lily, busy with dinner, realized that she hadn't seen him since he had gotten home.

She went to the door, tried the handle, and found it locked. "Jeremy?"

Rattling the handle, she suddenly felt panicky. "Jeremy, open the door!"

Finally the knob turned and she saw a wan, red-eyed boy.

"Darling, what's wrong?" she cried, drawing him into her arms. "What—"

Then her eyes fell on the small rectangle lying facedown on the bed, and she knew. "Jeremy, is that your report card?"

He watched in silence as she read with a sinking heart the solid line of Cs—with a single A in art.

"Oh, Jeremy," she cried softly. "Oh, sweetheart—"

"I'm sorry, Mom," he mumbled, tears beginning to roll down his face again. "I tried—I really did."

"I know, darling," she said, drawing him onto her lap and stroking his head gently. "Don't cry now."

"But Daddy will be so angry!" he wailed.

"We'll tell him together. Please, don't cry."

In truth, Lily had always been perplexed by Jeremy's inability to master reading. He might not be brilliant, but he was certainly as intelligent as most children. But he had never seemed to grasp the difference between a "b" and a "d," and had always confused "dog" and "god." All year she had drilled him, but it seemed to do no good.

It was baffling, but at the moment Lily's main concern was how they were going to face Harry.

That night, after the children had gone to their rooms, Harry sat at the kitchen table while Lily asked, "More pie?"

"No, thank you, dear. Just a little more coffee."

Pouring a cup for him, she took a deep breath.

"Darling, Jeremy got his report card today, and frankly, I don't think you'll be pleased."

Harry scanned the proffered card and his face grew livid. Slamming his hand down on the table, he shouted, "This is it, Lily. I'm not going to settle for this! Jeremy is going to boarding school next fall. Whether you like it or not." He jumped up and stalked down the hall to his study with Lily at his heels.

"Harry, he did the best he was capable of."

"That's what you say, but I don't buy it. The issue is closed, Lily."

For once, Lily refused to capitulate. The arguments raged all through June and July, invariably ending with Harry's shouts and her tears. The tension in the house grew unbearable. The dinner hour was strained, the children silent, asking to be excused as soon as they had finished. Even their celebration of VJ Day, when all America was welcoming a new era of peace, was marred by their quarrels.

Lily ached as she watched Jeremy grow increasingly tense and unhappy. Why couldn't Harry be content to let him develop at his own pace? He wasn't a Drew or a Randy, but he would eventually find his own niche in life. But it seemed that was impossible for Harry. Nothing she could say would convince him that Jeremy was not simply lazy.

Finally, as she sat in the kitchen alone after another stormy session with Harry, Lily suddenly knew that it was hopeless. Even if she won she knew that Harry would never allow Jeremy to be happy at home again. Every report card would bring another battle, and her son's wavering self-confidence would eventually be battered again. She had always been convinced that staying at home was best for any child. Now she was not so sure. One evening after dinner, she said, "All right, Harry. I give up. Pick out a school for Jeremy."

Startled, Harry said, "Well, there are several we should consider—"

Lily interrupted curtly. "It was your idea, Harry; you pick it."

"You're not happy about this, are you." It was a statement, not a question.

"No."

"But you do agree with me that it is for Jeremy's own good?"

"No, Harry!" She suddenly blazed. "It's to keep you from destroying the rest of your family."

When they told him that he would be going away, Jeremy's face was expressionless, but Lily caught the flash of anguish in his eyes. In the next month, she watched him with deepening apprehension. He had always been open with her, but now he retreated to his room, where he sat for hours staring into space. All Lily's efforts couldn't draw him out; he simply would not talk about his feelings.

If Lily had known the truth, her torment would have been as great as his. The prospect of leaving home for the unknown terrors of boarding school petrified him. His self-control finally broke on the September morning they left the house to drive to Deerbrook Academy. Through tears which threatened to spill over onto his cheeks, he choked out, "You'll come to visit me, won't you, Mom?"

"As much as I can, darling," Lily said.

When they reached the school, Jeremy got out of the car without speaking.

"Good-bye, son," Harry said gently, holding out his arms for a hug. Jeremy looked so small and lost on the huge stone steps, that even though he was convinced this was for the boy's own good, at that moment Harry felt terribly guilty. And that guilt was heightened when Jeremy turned away, ignoring his father's proffered embrace.

Lily was silent the whole way home. When they reached the farm, she went straight to her bedroom, leaving Harry to cope with dinner. It was the first time he'd ever had to fix a meal for himself and his offspring.

The hamburgers were raw inside, the buns were cold, and the beans were burnt.

Melissa waved her burger in the air. "Warm this up a little, Daddy."

"It's warm, Melissa. Eat it."

"But it's raw, Dad," Drew complained.

"No, it's not. Eat it."

"They are too raw!" the children chorused defiantly.

He took a closer look, then gave an exasperated sigh. The meat was clearly inedible.

Abruptly he grabbed the plates and tipped the contents into the garbage, then took down a jar of peanut butter and slathered some on slabs of bread.

Melissa frowned at him defiantly. "I'm not going to eat this! Mommy doesn't make us sandwiches for dinner."

"Mommy's not feeling well. Now I don't want to hear another word from you, Melissa."

Staring back at him with injured dignity, Melissa crossed her arms and refused to touch her sandwich.

Harry sank into a chair. Were they always this bad? How did Lily put up with this, day after day?

"Drink your milk," he ordered curtly.

Melissa began to storm. "I want Mommy!"

She slipped from her chair and ran toward Lily's room, but Harry caught her before she could leave the room. As he lifted her into his arms, his heart softened, despite the stormy look in her violet eyes.

"You're not my friend!"

"Of course I'm your friend, sweetheart. Please don't bother Mommy. Listen, I'll make a bargain with you."

Lip quivering, Melissa demanded, "What will you give me?"

"I'll take you all to Neilsen's tomorrow, and you can have hot dogs and chocolate milkshakes."

She sniffed and said, "And I want Randy's harmonica."

Suiting action to words, she abruptly leaned over and made a swipe at it, but Randy quickly held it away out of her reach and Melissa began to wail.

Feeling more harassed than ever, Harry ordered, "Randy, give it to her."

"But it's mine," Randy said resentfully. "Why should I?"

"I said, give it to her!" Harry exploded. "You're a big boy, and she's only a baby."

Without further ado, he plucked the toy from Randy's hand and poked it at Melissa. "Here. Now stop crying."

It was like a miracle. Melissa demurely climbed back onto her chair, picked up her sandwich, and took a dainty bite. Finally they were all in bed. After years of telling Lily she was too soft with the children, no sooner was he in charge than he was resorting to bribery to keep the peace. But it was somehow different when the ball was in his court.

He walked into the living room, poured himself a double Scotch, and sank into a chair. When he had finished his drink he felt a little better. He realized there had been no sound from the bedroom for hours. Lily must be hungry. Perhaps he should fix a tray for her. There was a piece of cold roast chicken in the refrigerator, and some tomatoes and lettuce freshly picked from the garden. After adding bread and pale pink quince jelly, he took the tray down the hall.

"Are you awake, sweetheart?"

"Yes," she answered tonelessly.

"Would it bother you if I turn on the light?"

"No."

When he looked at her, he was shocked. Her eyes were red and her face distorted from weeping.

"I've brought you something to eat," he said uncertainly.

Glancing at the tray, she shook her head. Obviously, she blamed him for sending Jeremy away, but Lily had to learn to cut the umbilical cord sooner or later. Watching her as she lay motionless with her eyes focused on the pastoral print on the opposite wall, he urged her again, "Lily, you really should eat something."

"No, thank you."

"At least have some milk."

"Later, Harry."

He removed the tray, pulled up a chair, and sat down near the bedside.

"You're upset with me, aren't you, Lily?"

"Yes," she said flatly.

"Look, Lily, I know that you're feeling terribly bad today, and it's perfectly understandable, but children have to grow up."

"That's easy enough for you to say, Harry. You weren't abandoned as I was as a child. And now you've made me do the same thing to my son. Jeremy would have done just fine at the local school, and he and I would both have been so much happier."

"Lily, the local schools were no good, or he wouldn't have done so poorly. Obviously they weren't teaching him properly."

"Jeremy is no genius, Harry. Aren't you ever going to accept him for what he is?"

"I didn't say he had to be a genius; he just has to work up to his potential. And as for leaving home, I went away to school when I was Jeremy's age, and it didn't do me any harm. As a matter of fact, I loved it."

"I found it detestable," Lily flared.

Harry gave up. "I'll leave the tray for you," he said curtly. "Call if you need anything else."

He fully expected that Lily would resume her usual routine the next morning, but that day passed, and then the next, and she showed no inclination to get out of bed. He was left to cope with the task of getting Drew, Randy, and Melissa off to school in the morning, and fed and bathed at night. Worse than that was his concern over Lily. She seemed to have entered a sort of decline. He had always thought of her as a tower of strength upon which he could depend unquestioningly. But now her strength seemed to have disappeared, and he was beside himself with worry. It was impossible to comfort her—she still seemed to blame him for exiling Jeremy, even though she hadn't alluded to it after that first day.

Occasionally in the afternoon she would get up, put on a wrap, and walk out to her garden, but instead of working she would simply stand and stare at it, tears gathering slowly in the corners of her eyes.

At those times, Lily was remembering Jeremy as a small boy, helping her plant seeds and popping them in his mouth when her back was turned.

"Spit those out!" she could hear herself saying.

When she went back into the house to lie on the bed once again, the images that came to her mind were even more tortured. How was Jeremy doing at school? He was one of the younger boys; and she hoped and prayed that the older children weren't teasing him. She remembered only too acutely the misery of her own days at boarding school.

His first letter was far from encouraging. Lily seized it with a trembling hand and rapidly read the lines, then reread them, tears welling up in her eyes. There was not a word of complaint. Dutifully he listed his classes and his sports. But he didn't mention a single friend or teacher that he liked. She could hardly sleep that night for worry.

The next day she would have driven up to see him, but Deerbrook discouraged visits from parents, and Harry flatly forbade it.

"You'll make him a laughingstock if you hover over him, Lily," he said. "Schoolboys have a very rigid code about these things. You know, you're already preventing him from adjusting, with your constant phone calls. I'd like to talk to him too, but I know it's not good for him."

So Jeremy was now denied even the comfort of his mother's voice. The only things that kept him going were the letters and calls from Drew, which Harry allowed, though if he had known the emotions the calls produced he might not have been so generous. Each time the brothers hung up, Jeremy was in tears while Drew slammed down the receiver, filled with resentment against his father.

Meanwhile, Lily still spent most of the time in her room, leaving the house untended and the children to run wild. By the end of a month, Harry was at his wits' end. For the thousandth time Harry tried to understand why her reaction to Jeremy's leaving was so extreme. He finally decided it was the result of being sent to Switzerland after her brother's death. Lily couldn't separate her parents' banishment of her with their sending Jeremy away. Elated with his new insight, he got up early the next morning and fixed her a breakfast tray. Noting her pallor and the dark shadows under her eyes, he said gently, "Good morning, darling. How did you sleep?"

With a listless shrug, she replied, "Oh, the same as usual."

He handed her a cup of tea and said, "Lily, dear, we need to do some talking."

"There's nothing to talk about," she replied expressionlessly. But Harry persevered.

"Please hear me out, darling. I've been very concerned about you. All month I thought you were being stubborn about sending Jeremy away to school, but last night I realized that his leaving must remind you of when you went to boarding school after little Charles died."

"That has nothing to do with my reaction now—"

"Lily, I think it does. At least subconsciously. You've created a false parallel. Your parents sent you away because they wanted to get rid of you. We're sending Jeremy so he can get a good education. He'll be home every summer, and for all holidays. Please, darling, don't let the ghosts of the past poison what we have together."

For a moment Lily wanted to deny Harry's words, but she could not ignore their undeniable truth. Suddenly she felt a surge of love and warmth toward him; she had been terribly unjust. He loved their son as much as she did. Why should she assume that she was the only one who cared about him?

Seeing the change in her expression, he said quickly, "Darling, the children are at school and we have the whole day to ourselves. Why don't we drive over and see what progress they've made on the house?"

Nodding, she reached out her arms to him. "I love you, Harry."

# Chapter 20

DURING the following month, they drove to Greenwich almost every day. By the end of October, the construction was sufficiently advanced that for the first time they could walk through the rooms and visualize how they would look when the workmen were done.

Secretly, Lily was dismayed. The living room was even worse than she had feared—huge, austere, cold. Standing in the vast octagonal foyer, she looked up at the vaulted cantilevered ceiling and shuddered. She supposed that the bold stained-glass clerestories were striking, but they were suited to a cathedral, not a home.

With a sinking heart, she knew that she was going to hate this house. But she determined not to say one word to Harry. Nothing could be allowed to jeopardize the new harmony between them. What did a house really matter, anyway? The important thing was that it made Harry happy. He seemed much less driven and had drawn closer to the younger children, obviously trying hard to be a better father. She was not about to do anything to rock his new equanimity.

Lily even went along with Mies van der Rohe's recommendation of Douglas James as interior designer, biting her lip when she saw the uninviting functional built-ins of teak and birch. Perhaps the furniture wouldn't seem so alien when it was in place.

But when Mies van der Rohe's chosen landscape architect unveiled his plan for flat terraced lawns punctuated by ultramodern sculpture by the likes of Henry Moore and Marino Marini, she didn't even try to hide her dismay.

Harry intervened firmly. "The garden is my wife's domain, and I don't believe that this is quite what she had in mind. Perhaps you can work with her and come up with something more to her taste."

Knowing how important the garden was to Lily, he wanted it to be just the way she liked it. After all, he wanted her to love the Greenwich place as much as he did. Luckily, he thought, she seemed to be thrilled with the house.

Construction resumed early the next spring, and Harry began to talk about selling the farm, but Lily demurred. "Jeremy was born here. The children have grown up here. I just can't bear to let it go."

Smiling at his wife's sentimentality, Harry said, "If you feel that way about it, we needn't sell. But we can't just let it lie vacant. It will deteriorate."

"I'll find someone to live in it," Lily announced confidently, and two weeks later she had a tenant. The Gallaghers were an older couple who had sold their own farm and retired, but then found themselves unhappy guests in their children's homes. They were almost pathetically grateful for Lily's offer of the house rent-free in return for their acting as caretakers.

With that matter settled, Lily no longer dreaded moving day. It was set for the first of May; the wildflower seeds Lily had scattered in the meadow behind the Greenwich house, now called The Meadows, had burst into full bloom. Even she was entranced by the effect. But the moment they were settled she realized that the small housewarming she had planned was nowhere near what Harry had in mind. He intended an extravaganza comparable to her engagement party to Roger so many years ago. Well, if that's what he wanted, that's what she would do. With Jeremy home from school, subdued but apparently surviving, she was feeling particularly loving. Harry had earned the right to flaunt his success.

The gala was set for early June. Under her direction, the florists had outdone themselves. The profusion of arrangements had managed to soften Douglas James's stark interiors into gentle beauty. The caterers had arranged a magnificent buffet, both indoors and out on the veranda, while a small army of maids and waiters scurried about readying the house.

At five o'clock, Lily got out of her bath, donned the satin slip and silk stockings lying ready on the chaise, then saw with a thrill of excitement the gown she had bought in New York the week before.

It had been a memorable occasion. When she got off the train at Grand Central, she kept picturing the twenty-one-year-old bride Harry had greeted in Manhattan so many years before.

The postwar Manhattan crowds came as a shock. Buffeted and out of breath, Lily managed to hail a cab to take her to the Plaza, where she planned to lunch. Heavens, had the city always been so noisy and dirty? The truth was, she supposed, that she wasn't a city girl at all. Her childhood had been spent on Long Island and in the Swiss countryside, her married life on a remote farm. There had been only that brief time in Paris, and Paris was a far cry from New York.

Still, luncheon in the elegant Palm Court revived her spirits. As she sipped her coffee, she found herself taking a keen interest in the other guests. The women all seemed so chic, so beautifully dressed. She loved the long, full skirts and fitted bodices, the close-brimmed hats. This was apparently the "New Look" she had read about in *Vogue*. She determined to pick a dress that would make Harry proud.

After finishing her coffee, she crossed the street to Bergdorf's. When she had found the designer salon, she mustered her nerve and approached a saleswoman and said, "I'd like to see some long gowns . . . Dior, perhaps?"

After that, Lily enjoyed every minute, suffering only a moment's shock when she learned the price of the dress she liked was five hundred dollars. Heavens, the Schiaparelli she had bought in Paris years before had cost no more than a hundred. On the other hand, this was a special occasion, and they could afford it. Harry had told her to spare no expense.

"I'll take it," she said firmly.

"Very good, madam. And shall I arrange for evening slippers tinted to match?"

In the end, there were shoes, and lingerie, and luxurious elbow-length white kid gloves. Lily went home in a state of euphoria.

Now, as she slipped into the shimmering gown of the most delicate tea-rose yellow, she felt as if she were floating on a cloud. The top was a dramatic halter style and the full skirt billowed out from a tiny waist, almost grazing the floor.

Lily heard the door open, and saw Harry come up and stand behind her. As she started to turn around, he said in a queer voice, "No, don't move. You look magnificent, absolutely magnificent."

"Do you really like it?" she asked, almost shyly.

"Like it?" He seemed at a loss for words. "Lily, darling, you look exquisite."

Then he reached into his pocket and withdrew a slender velvet box. Inside, there were the most priceless diamond necklace and earrings Lily had ever seen.

"Harry! . . . I don't know what to say. . . . " Lily remembered her mother glittering with jewels as she made an entrance, but she had never dreamed of, or even desired, such things for herself. "Oh, Harry—I'm not sure I deserve these."

Very softly he said against her ear, "You deserve them. I always promised that I'd buy you the moon. These are just to tide you over till then."

As she turned to face him, he saw tears sparkling in her eyes. Taking out his handkerchief, he gently wiped them, then stepped back and said, "You're the most beautiful woman I've ever seen."

Downstairs their guests were beginning to arrive. Although Lily felt as if her social skills were rusty with disuse, she smiled graciously, hoping that the trembling of her knees was not apparent.

Since Ellis had had a hand in the guest list, there were many writers and people from the media whom Lily didn't recognize. When she spotted Ellis's familiar face she greeted him with more than her usual warmth.

"You look lovely, my dear," he said before he was swept aside by a new group of guests.

As Lily shook what seemed like the thousandth hand, she thought with a curious kind of detachment that this was the social world her parents had planned for her. She recalled for a fleeting moment the Long Island estate and Roger Humphreys.

Glancing at Harry, who was the center of attention, she realized for the first time just how famous he was. He was reveling in the adulation tonight—and why not? If anyone had worked for his success, it was he.

By eight o'clock most of the guests had arrived, but Harry was inexplicably loath to leave his position in the foyer. He wanted to be there when his parents and brothers arrived. Although he had seen them regularly over the last few years, it had always been at Benjamin's house or the farm. Well, tonight they would see just how far he'd come. At eight-fifteen Benjamin and Elise Kohle arrived, followed by Theodore, Anton, and Sidney with their wives.

Their first glimpse of Harry's house as they turned in the drive had been a rude shock to them all. Ablaze with lights, the glass-and-steel pile had proclaimed Harry's success. Now, as they crossed the threshold and beheld the costly decor, the sisters-in-law exchanged identical looks of dismay.

Seeing their faces, Harry admitted to himself how much he had wanted this triumph. His brothers had simply gone into the family business. His fortune was his own.

"Mother," he said, kissing her, "I'm so happy that you could come."

"Oh, my dear," she cried, "we are so delighted to be here. The house is simply lovely."

Then, as she greeted Lily, Harry turned to his father and said evenly, "I'm glad that you are here, Father."

But to his shock, as the old man's eyes met his, they seemed to hold nothing but genuine pride and pleasure.

Clasping Harry's hand warmly, Benjamin said, "This is quite a place you have built for yourself."

Harry turned to his brothers and realized that they too seemed genuinely pleased for him. "Congratulations, Harry," Theodore said. "Before we join the other guests do you think you and Lily could show us the house? It looks like Mies van der Rohe. Am I right?"

Overwhelmed by their warmth, Harry took them upstairs, trying to conceal his pride as he pointed out the marble which had taken six months to come from Florence, the onyx in the bathrooms, the his and hers dressing rooms.

Lily trailed along behind Harry, listening in growing dismay. He had never been one to show off his possessions, let alone be impressed by his own celebrity. All that mattered to him was the writing itself. But tonight she found him shockingly arrogant. It was painfully apparent that he was determined to ram his success down his family's throats.

Meanwhile, the Kohles could do nothing but nod and murmur. It wasn't so much the house, for they themselves had been born into the greatest of luxury. But to think that Harry had achieved this on his own. They had lived so long with the image of Harry as a dreamer, they had trouble reconciling that long-held picture and the reality of this material wealth.

As they descended to the main floor again, Elise said to Lily, "We must get together again for lunch soon. I always love seeing the children."

Lily scarcely heard her. All she knew was that she didn't recognize Harry tonight. He was acting like a stranger, and one she didn't like much at all. As his family joined the other guests in the living room, Harry cried exuberantly, "I've arrived, Lily! I made them eat crow!" He signaled a passing waiter and took two glasses of champagne. As he turned back to her, she saw a look of triumph on his face. "I've waited for this moment for so long. You know, without my hatred of them to inspire me, I would have given up long ago."

Raising his glass, he proposed, "Let's drink to success."

Then, without waiting for her, he drained the champagne and strode out of the hall. Her own glass untouched, Lily found all her happiness turned to ashes. Tonight Harry had told her why this house had been built, and for whom. She suddenly wanted to tear the diamond necklace from around her neck and say to Harry, "This wasn't to show your love for me, but to flaunt your success in front of your parents."

Hurrying blindly through the crowd, she found herself face to face with Ellis.

"Well, Lily," he said, smiling, "what do you think of this extravaganza?" Bending to kiss her, he was startled to see tears glittering in her eyes.

"Lily, what's wrong?"

The concern in his voice evoked a feeling of such vulnerability that she found it hard to reply calmly. "Everything's fine, Ellis."

"Why don't we get away from the crowd for a moment?"

In the quiet library, Lily sank wearily into the sofa.

"What will you have to drink?"

She shrugged slightly. "Anything."

"I really fix a very mean martini."

"Yes . . . I'd like that."

He poured the liquid into the glass from the shaker. "Here's to your happiness, my dear."

The somber look on her face showed that word was clearly

a long way from her thoughts. "Why don't you tell me about it?"

"There's nothing to tell."

"You don't have to pretend with me, Lily. I'm your friend."

"I wouldn't even know where to begin. I just feel like a stranger in my own home." As she said the words, she remembered sitting in that pavilion on Long Island so long ago. She had been a stranger then, in the place where she had been born.

"Well, I can understand that. You have a house full of people whom you've never met before tonight."

That's true, she thought, my husband among them, but all she said was, "May I have another?"

He refilled the glass, saying, "I have a feeling there's something you'd like to tell me."

Lily ached to confide in him, yet she couldn't admit to this new side of Harry she was just beginning to see, and how hurt she was by his failure to acknowledge her role in the completion of his novel. How could he think he'd written it out of hatred, not through her love?

"It's hard to explain, Ellis. I guess I'm just having a difficult time keeping up with Harry's success."

Ellis sensed she wasn't telling the truth, but tactfully forbore to press her. Instead he said gently, "Maybe there have simply been too many changes in your life all at once. Jeremy going to school, your leaving the farm. I know how much you loved the place."

Lily nodded. Uncannily, Ellis had put his finger on the major reason for her sorrow. This house was not her home; it was Harry's monument to himself. Touching Ellis's hand, she said, "I guess that's it. I do miss the past."

"Well, you have good memories and when Harry simmers down you'll enjoy your life here too."

His gentle words gave her hope. "Perhaps you're right, Ellis. You have no idea how much it means to me to have you as a friend." She got up and kissed him lightly on the cheek. "Thank you."

Lily went back to the living room and for the rest of the evening played the part of the perfect hostess and proud wife. After the last guest had left and Lily and he went upstairs, Harry was still in an expansive mood.

"It was the party of the year, Lily, don't you agree?" Without waiting for a reply, he continued, "You did an absolutely spectacular job, pulling it all together."

"I'm glad it pleased you," she replied quietly.

"At long last," he said, "I think my family is going to treat me with the respect I deserve. They were knocked out by this place—"

She could bear to hear no more. "Harry, if you don't mind, I'm awfully tired, and I'd like to get some sleep."

But when the lights were off, Lily lay awake for a long time, brooding over Harry's earlier words. Although in the weeks and months to come she would do her best to be a dutiful wife, she would never entirely forget his casual dismissal of her contribution to getting *Archie Sanger* published.

# Chapter 21

As predicted, *The Mountains Roared* met with the same success as the other two volumes of the trilogy, but there was a greater price to pay. As Lily had feared, Harry's life became infinitely more complicated. The public was already clamoring for his next work and his publishers were trying to sign him for two more books.

More disturbing to Lily was a Hollywood offer to adapt *Archie Sanger* for the screen. The studio hoped it had another blockbuster on its hands, on the scale of *Gone With the Wind.*

Luckily, Lily had recently hired a wonderful couple who were utterly trustworthy, and whom the children liked, so she felt she could go with Harry, but she was afraid the atmosphere in Los Angeles would make him more self-important. Her only consolation was the hope that the change of scene would bring renewed life to their marriage.

Unfortunately, despite the glorious California weather, the first couple of days Harry was almost as obsessed and unavailable as he had been when trying to finish his first novel. Sitting alongside the pool at the Beverly Hills Hotel, Lily soon began to regret that she had come. Harry had to attend endless conferences at the studio, where debates raged hot and heavy, with constant changes demanded by the director which had to be written at once. Harry was infuriated by the need to cater to the various temperaments involved, and being the perfectionist he was, he lost all track of time. Night after night he forgot to call to tell Lily that he wouldn't be back in time for dinner.

The first few times she understood, but after a while she

could no longer excuse his selfishness and one evening she found herself in tears. She ordered a steak sandwich and a double Scotch from room service and when Harry finally came home she feigned sleep.

The next morning, sitting across from Lily at the breakfast table on their little patio, Harry said sheepishly, "I'm sorry about last night."

"The least you could have done was call."

"Darling, you have no idea how involved those sessions get. You lose all track of time."

"Don't you eat?"

"Well, we sent out for sandwiches."

"Couldn't you have called then?"

"I'm really sorry, Lily."

*Dammit!* she wanted to scream. *Am I so unimportant that you can simply forget I exist?*

But a little voice inside her whispered that if she pushed him too far, he might respond, "If you don't like it, you can . . . ," and suddenly she didn't want to put it to the test.

"I understand, darling," she forced herself to say. "But I'm beginning to realize that you're just so busy I might as well go home. After all, you came out here to work, not for a holiday. I think perhaps the sensible thing would be for me to go home. Maybe you'll make more progress without having me here to worry about."

Harry wasn't sure how to respond. He had deluded himself that writing for the screen would be far less demanding than working on a novel—a few hours a day and he and Lily would be free to play. But it hadn't turned out that way. And it was certainly better that she go home than stay and feel neglected.

Reluctantly he said, "You're probably right, Lily. I don't see that the situation is going to improve."

At the station he hugged her tightly. "I'm going to miss you terribly, darling. I'll be home the second the script is finished."

She felt a wrenching loss as the train pulled out, but by the time she was crossing the Rockies, she found herself thinking not of Harry but of the children. How desperately she longed for them.

She had hoped that they would be home when she arrived, and would run to her with open arms, crying, "Mommy, Mommy! We missed you." But instead the house was empty and silent. Randy was at Boy Scouts, Drew at baseball, Melissa at her ballet lesson. They didn't come home until shortly before dinner. They kissed her perfunctorily and retreated to their bedrooms. Melissa promptly got on the phone with her girlfriends, Randy busied himself with his homework, and Drew was in the middle of a project. It seemed they needed her as little as Harry had, but at least at home she had more to do to fill the empty days.

Life settled into a reasonably settled routine until the morning two weeks later when she was sitting in bed having coffee and reading the morning paper. Turning to Hedda Hopper's column, she read: *The newest man in town, who has all the ladies agog, is Handsome Harry, who was seen dining in the shadows with Jennifer Quinn at Chasen's last night. From the look of things, it was like bringing Kohles to Newcastle.*

Lily thought that she would die. Jennifer Quinn, that young, blonde, voluptuous starlet, newly cast in the screen version of *Archie Sanger,* and Harry? But Lily had just spoken to him last night! Even if the two of them had been spotted together, surely they could have been dining to discuss some aspect of the ongoing production. Or so Lily tried to reason. Then again, she thought, Hollywood was a seductive place, where infidelities were merely winked at. And just what was Harry doing wining and dining—for business or pleasure—when so recently he had had time only to send out for sandwiches?

In the end, Lily's doubts and fears overcame her. She seized the phone and called the Beverly Hills Hotel. It was nine o'clock her time, six in the morning on the coast, she'd better find Harry snug in his own bed.

When she heard his sleepy voice, she could barely find strength to speak. Relief began to wash over her, but then she remembered what had prompted her call. "Harry?" she began uncertainly.

"Lily! Is something wrong?"

"I should say there is," she said sternly, in spite of herself. "Have you seen today's paper?"

"Of course not. I'm sleeping."

"I think you should take a look at Hedda Hopper's column."

"What for? Can't you just tell me?"

Lily sighed wearily and read him the piece.

Harry snorted a laugh. "And that's what's bothering you? That I had dinner with one of the actresses in our movie?"

"Yes," she said, bitter that he refused to acknowledge this was reason to be upset.

"I'm really surprised at you, Lily. It's just idle gossip, grist for the mill—didn't that occur to you?"

"Frankly, no."

"Oh, for God's sake, Lily! She's just a little actress."

"And I'm just your wife. When I was out there in Tinseltown, you never had time to call me, let alone take me to dinner."

Harry's tone was grim. "I took her out because the director asked me to."

"So if I want to have dinner with my husband, I'm to speak to him?"

"Lily, this doesn't sound like you. You've never been a jealous, suspicious wife."

Lily sighed. Harry was right. But she was determined to see this through. "Well, I've never had my husband linked with a starlet in a gossip column before."

There was a silence. Then Harry said quietly, "Lily, I'm coming home."

Lily tried to control herself, but already she'd been pushed to her emotional limit. "You must be feeling terribly guilty to come as far as that."

"Lily, I love you. And if I have to come to New York to tell you in person, dammit, I will!"

No sooner had she hung up than she regretted having called. Harry had never given her cause for worry. If only she'd never seen that gossip column.

Lily was still mulling all this over when Harry called back. His voice sounded conciliatory. He seemed genuinely glad to be coming home. Lily's eyes brimmed with tears as he told her when his plane would arrive. He asked haltingly if she would meet him.

"Darling," she said, nearly breathless, "you know I will."

Harry couldn't get there soon enough for Lily's taste. She ached for him from the moment they hung up the second time to the moment his arms were flung around her.

Feeling like honeymooners, they took a suite at the Waldorf. They each felt an urgency to reaffirm their love, with no questions asked, no problems posed.

For one blissful week, they reveled in each other's company. Harry showered Lily with attention reminiscent of their first days of courtship yet now more resplendent thanks to his hard-earned wealth. They danced until dawn, went to the theater, strolled through the city by moonlight.

But from Hollywood, the desperate telegrams and phone calls were unending. Harry was holding up production.

Lily was the one to return to reality. "Darling, I love you. And these past few days have been my happiest yet. But I know you've got to complete the picture. You have to go back." Even as she said this, Lily cherished the hope that Harry could somehow complete the rest of the script at home.

They toyed with the idea of Lily returning to Hollywood with him, but Lily knew this would not be for the best. She made the excuse of the children. Harry was sorry she wouldn't be coming, but he did understand. Lily smiled to herself ruefully. If Harry only knew: The children barely needed her.

Standing at the terminal windows, Lily felt desolate as she watched the plane become airborne. After this wonderful interlude, she could barely stand the thought of being parted from him. She finally turned away sighing, walked outside, and found her car. She sat behind the steering wheel and stared ahead of her. What was she going to do today? She could go home, but the glow of those few days had left her feeling for the first time in many years less like a mother, more like a woman.

Lily felt a sudden urge to book the first flight out, but that was impossible.

She found herself turning off on Fifty-ninth Street and veering toward Fifth Avenue. Back at the Waldorf, she gave the keys to the attendant and re-registered, asking for the same suite as before. She needed desperately to hold on to the feeling she had had here with Harry.

After the bellboy left, she looked around the sitting room, then through the open door to the bedroom, trying to recapture the events that had taken place there. But that was impossible; only Harry's presence could do that.

She grabbed her purse and all but ran down the hall, but once out on the street her steps slowed. Aimlessly, she walked down Park, then over to Fifth, and then turned back to Madison. The shops were magnificent, and the mannequins in the window seemed to beckon to her.

Two days later, she drove back to The Meadows, with a trunk full of boxes and bags, hardly able to remember what she had bought. It was all so ridiculous, as was the total pampering of herself at Elizabeth Arden.

There was nothing wrong with a woman's wanting to look beautiful, but this compulsive shopping spree had happened for all the wrong reasons. None of it was a substitute for a husband.

The moment Harry opened the door to his bungalow at the Beverly Hills Hotel, the phone was ringing. Thinking that it might be Lily, he ran quickly to answer.

"Hello?"

It was Percy Levine, *Archie Sanger*'s director. "Harry? It's about time you got back."

"I'm sorry. As I told you, I had some personal business back East."

"Well, at least you're back now. I want you to come to dinner this evening. We've been having a little trouble with Jennifer. She simply refuses to work unless you're here to write every word that comes out of her mouth. I'm going to put you next to her at the table tonight and I want you to charm her into a more reasonable frame of mind."

"Charm her? I can't stand her. The woman's totally brainless."

"Maybe, but she's the hottest thing in britches right now, and the boss insists we use her. Since you're the only person who will satisfy her, you're the one to see she cooperates with us a little more than she has been."

"The sacrifices I have to make," he said in mock exasperation.

After spending the evening with her, he had to admit that, dim as she was, she was one of the sexiest girls he'd ever been near. And however shallow Jennifer Quinn was in person, she could project incredible depth on the screen. When Harry saw the daily rushes, he was stunned by the emotions she could evoke in her role as a southern blonde harlot: the vulnerability, the hidden sweetness, the sense of being a helpless victim. But he almost laughed at the irony of Lily's being jealous of her—that dinner with Jennifer had been one of the most boring he had ever had.

Tonight again, as they sat together, he was struck by how utterly vacuous she was. Did she ever think about anything other than herself? The truth was that Jennifer was secretly convinced that if she could ensnare Harry, he would build up her part so that she could eclipse Ingrid Bergman. This movie could secure her place in the Hollywood pantheon.

But as they dined, her fluttering eyelashes, heaving bosom, and breathless voice had no effect on Harry; when she suggested Ciro's, he excused himself, saying, "You'll have to excuse me. I'm really tired from my flight."

Jennifer was taken aback. Usually her ploys had more effect than this. She had thought Harry would jump at the chance to see more of her.

Still, she was clever enough to control her pique. Smiling sweetly, she said, "I hope we'll get together again soon, Harry."

He said politely, "I hope so too."

God, was he glad to be back in his bungalow! The last thing he had wanted was to spend more time in a nightclub with Jennifer Quinn. His mind dwelt on the week he had just spent with Lily. With her was where he longed to be.

But Lily was three thousand miles away. It was no use torturing himself. To help console himself, Harry poured himself a Scotch. He took off his shirt and pants, all the while taking long swallows of his drink.

With the water running, he almost didn't hear the knock. But then there it was again, louder. Harry slipped on a robe and pulled the sash tight around his waist and then answered the door. There stood Jennifer Quinn, wrapped in a Black Diamond mink coat, with a bottle of champagne and two glasses.

She smiled her Scarlett O'Hara smile.

Harry just stared at her. She was the last thing he'd expected to see.

He hesitated for so long that she finally laughed. "Aren't you going to invite me in?"

She handed him the bottle with a coy smile. "It's already chilled," she purred.

Harry cleared his throat and said abruptly, "Jennifer, this is a lovely idea—but as I told you earlier, I'm really very tired tonight. I was just getting into a hot tub. Now, if you'll just let me . . . "

Jennifer smiled again. "I understand. But how about just a sip of champagne? It's sure to relax you."

Harry tried to be diplomatic. He didn't want to offend his head star. "Okay—maybe one glass. Just let me turn off the water before the tub overflows."

When Harry returned to the room, he stopped short. Jennifer stood before him totally nude, except for a black, rhinestone-studded garter belt, sheer black nylons, and black high-heeled pumps.

Harry didn't know what to say, what to do, where to look. Jennifer walked toward him seductively, wrapped her arms around him, and held him close.

In spite of himself, he felt himself harden. Then, before he knew it, Jennifer had pushed him to the bed. She kissed him all over with desperate passion.

Harry couldn't restrain himself. Few men, at that moment, could have resisted Jennifer's wily charms.

When their gymnastics had finally subsided, Jennifer straddled Harry. "You're going to make me a star, aren't you, Harry?"

Harry smiled weakly. "I'm not sure I'm going to be able to do anything after tonight."

"Oh, yes you are," she said, stroking him gently. "Come on, roll over."

But the magnitude of his folly was beginning to sink in. Harry got out of bed and put on his robe. He lit a cigarette and walked to the window, filled with deep self-loathing, as well as disgust. How could he do this to Lily? Lily, whom he loved and had so recently left.

He looked back at Jennifer, lying suggestively on the bed. The tempting blonde-bombshell starlet. The successful novelist and Hollywood novice. God, even the cigarette was cliché. Yet here he was, living the whole thing.

Jennifer broke his reverie. "Well, what will it be tomorrow? My place or yours?"

The suggestion riled Harry. "Look, Jennifer. You're a very lovely, desirable young woman. But I am a married man. Anything between us, aside from work on the movie, ends here."

"Married man—ha!" she laughed. She got out of bed and tried to wrap herself around him.

"No." The vehemence in Harry's tone was directed more toward himself than at her. "No, I mean it. I am a married man. I don't play around."

Jennifer eyed him quizzically. "You really mean it, don't you?"

He nodded silently.

Shrugging, she smiled insouciantly. "Well—it's been fun. See you at the studio."

After she had gone, Harry drained the cold bathwater. He turned on the shower, as hot as he could stand, and stood under it, scrubbing himself as though he could wash Jennifer's touch away.

# Chapter 22

AT long last the script was done. The studio was ecstatic with the first rushes which had been shot even as Harry was completing the script. He had adeptly transferred the impact of his prose to the screen. The moguls planned to have the film ready by December. It would be their biggest release. The buzz in the industry was that the studio had a blockbuster in the making. All the signs—stars, script, direction—pointed to a record success.

At long last Harry returned to The Meadows. The day after he came home, he sat at breakfast with Lily. It was a beautiful morning and he felt at peace with the world. The recollection of the night with Jennifer had faded to a benign memory. He assuaged his guilt by telling himself that her advances had been utterly unsolicited. She had seduced him, and after that night he was as good as his word: The only relationship he had with her was a professional one.

Retreating from the memory of that fateful evening, Harry embraced his family all the more. "Darling, it's wonderful to be home," he told Lily. "I want you to cancel the kids' summer camps. I don't want them to go away. And I especially want Jeremy home."

"But Harry, you said that he needed to go to summer school."

"Well, forget it. I want him home this summer. I haven't seen the kids in six months and I want to try to make it up to them a little."

But when Lily called Jeremy, she was startled to hear him say, "No, Mom, I really need this extra tutoring."

"Oh, no you don't, honey! As far as I'm concerned, you're doing just fine in school. And your father is very anxious that you come home."

"Dad wants me home?"

"Of course he does, darling. He hasn't seen you for months and he misses you."

After struggling through a few years at Deerbrook, Jeremy had managed to get into Exeter. He well knew he needed summer school to give him a head start. And although deep down he still loved his father and craved his approval, the long years of striving in vain to meet Harry's expectations had chastened his feelings. Since going to Deerbrook, Jeremy had retreated into himself. He had turned from an open, confiding child, to a quiet, withdrawn boy who kept all confidences to himself, not even sharing his fears with his mother or with Drew.

Drew, for his part, was extremely unhappy at having his plans for summer camp scotched. He had been headed for a special baseball camp and was hoping that with the extra practice he might make pitcher.

But of the three of them, Randy was the most disgruntled. Cousin Randolph had invited him to spend the entire summer with him, and now Harry's insistence that they spend the summer as a family had dashed his hopes and plans.

Melissa was almost as upset as Randy.

Pouting, she complained, "All my friends will be at camp, having loads of fun. I'm going to miss everything."

Lily tried to soften the blow. "We'll have a lot of fun here, too, Melissa. It's not too often that we have Daddy around."

At that, Melissa brightened a bit, a plan beginning to form in her mind. "Will he take me to New York for lunch at Delmonico's, and buy me a doll house as big as Amy's?"

"I'm sure he will if you ask him, darling." Lily smiled. She was so thrilled at the prospect of having Harry and the children all together at home for the summer that she would have promised anybody anything at this moment. At last her dreams were coming to fruition and the family life she had dreamed of for so long was becoming a reality. But as the summer began, Harry and Jeremy started things off on the wrong foot by arguing about his grades from Deerbrook.

"You say I'm right," Harry shouted, "but you don't ever seem to do anything about it!"

Lily put a cautioning hand on Harry's arm. "Don't badger him, Harry."

Impatiently he shook it off. "Lily, this is between me and Jeremy. All right, son, what do you have to say for yourself?"

By the time the evening was over, the tone of the summer was set.

Drew was livid over Jeremy's distress, while Randy retreated to his room and Melissa was in a sulk because Daddy hadn't yet promised to take her to Delmonico's.

Harry had been full of plans for excursions and outings, but the sullen atmosphere dimmed his own enthusiasm and the children's as well. They didn't want to go on any family picnics, or even out to Coney Island. And they rebelled against every other suggestion Harry made.

Still, remembering Lily's admonition, Harry persevered. He held his tongue even at the times he was sorely tempted. Come July, the family set off in the big Chrysler station wagon for two weeks in Nantucket, full of high hopes.

But the trip fast turned to fiasco. After two days of constant bickering, Harry exploded. "This is it! We're going home; pack your bags." The moment they arrived home, he went straight to his round tower study, and closed and locked the door.

Lily was sick with disappointment. What would it take to get this family together? After wrestling with the subject for days, resisting the urge to face Harry with recriminations, she could hold back no more.

"Harry, I want to talk to you about the situation between you and the children."

"What about it?"

"You were the one to disrupt their plans, just so that you could see them—but after a few tries at being Daddy, you shut them out and went back into your ivory tower—all because you couldn't stand the stresses and strains of fatherhood."

"You're blaming me for the fact that they answer back to me and argue?"

"Harry, you're half the problem."

"How so?" he asked angrily.

"You have to try to interact with the children. They're not just to be ordered about and controlled. You have to show a little understanding."

"When have I not been understanding, for God's sake?"

"Well, you weren't very kind to Jeremy."

"Oh, so we're back to that again."

"You must have noticed how withdrawn he's become."

"Because of me? Lily, you have a problem—you don't understand that your children are growing up. You've indulged them so much that they expect the world to cater to them!"

"Harry, you're far too hard on Jeremy. You always have been."

"Jeremy's starting to become a man. He's quiet because there are things he doesn't care to share with us."

"Doesn't that trouble you?"

"Not at all. I didn't run home with every little thing to Mom and Dad when I was that age."

"You and he are different people, Harry!"

"Lily, you've always had this idea that children need constant love and attention. Well, maybe what they need is a little more discipline and a little less coddling!"

"It doesn't help to criticize them constantly."

"Dammit, I try to be the best father I know how. And if that doesn't suit you, Lily, then that's just too damn bad!"

Abruptly he switched off his bedside lamp, pulled up the covers, and shut his eyes.

By the time Lily woke up the next day, Harry was in his study, working with a feverish compulsion, and the door remained closed for virtually the rest of the summer.

After Labor Day, Drew and Randy were off for Deerbrook Academy. It came as no surprise to Lily that, unlike poor Jeremy, the younger boys were actually eager to leave home.

Lily was apprehensive about the coming departures but she comforted herself with the thought that Melissa would still be hers. But to her utter shock, her daughter had other plans. "Amy is going to Miss Parker's, and I want to go, too!"

"But Melissa, darling, you don't want to leave Daddy and me, do you?"

Melissa was defiant. "The boys get to go to boarding school. I should too."

Lily was saddened to the point of depression by the prospect of losing all her children at once, but the three younger ones headed off to their new schools without so much as a backward glance. Only Jeremy seemed to share his mother's unhappiness. His somber face haunted her as he stood on the steps at Exeter, his arm forlornly upraised in what she took to be his wave farewell.

Inwardly Lily wept. This should have been the most memorable summer of his life—the last of his childhood—and he had spent it knowing himself to be a failure in his father's eyes.

No, Lily could not forgive Harry, and there was cold silence in the car as they drove back from New Hampshire.

# Chapter 23

As the fall turned to winter, Lily gradually fell into a state of resignation. Harry remained his sometimes cantankerous self; life with him was the way it had always been. Lily resolved to make the best of it. At least the children weren't around for Lily and Harry to quarrel about.

Harry began a new novel, one that obsessed him with the same passion he'd given the Archie Sanger trilogy. The plot was complex because of its generational and geographical sweep, but for Harry the key to its appeal was its Israeli setting. He had never overcome his guilt for marrying outside his religion, and the idea of describing the birth of the new Jewish state haunted him day and night. It was all he thought about from the moment he woke up to the moment he fell asleep. The deeper he became involved in developing the plot, the more he realized that he would never succeed without help. Until now, though he had occasionally tried hiring researchers, he had never been satisfied with their work, or so he said. In truth, researching was a feature of his writing that he cherished, and he never trusted anyone to do as thorough a job as himself. But this new project was of such epic proportions, he was forced to concede that he could not do it alone. Reluctantly he hired Gloria Williams, a middle-aged woman, to serve as his typist, and Rafi Jacobs and Anthony Bart as researchers. These two had worked on De Mille's *Cleopatra,* as well as the film version of *Archie Sanger.*

With the children gone, Harry found the peace and tranquillity he had so often longed for. He looked forward to diving into his work and relished the thought of a quiet house.

But Lily found the silence oppressive. With no career and no real hobbies of her own, she had little to occupy her time. And with Harry locked up with his new novel, she found herself lonelier than ever. She began to wonder if she'd made a mistake in devoting herself exclusively to her family for so many years.

One evening, when Harry asked if they might invite Ellis up for the weekend, she was thrilled at the prospect of a guest. The next Friday afternoon found her waiting in the driveway for Ellis's Bentley.

"Oh, Ellis! I'm so glad to see you!" she cried when at last he arrived.

Ellis beamed. "God, Lily, it's been too long. I've been so busy, I haven't seen you all summer. How have you been?"

"Just fine, Ellis," she said, mustering a smile.

"The boys got off all right, I presume. I understand that Melissa put up a fuss to get to go away to school, too."

"How did you know?"

"Harry told me."

"I wasn't sure he'd noticed," she said, stopping herself before she said something she'd regret. "Just leave your bags and I'll have Joe come out and get them. Let's sit on the terrace and have a drink."

Cocktails in hand, they watched the lengthening shadows in silence. Now that Ellis had a chance to look at her more closely, he was a little concerned.

Lily seemed to have lost a good deal of weight, but more than that, her enthusiasm seemed to have vanished, the light in her eyes had dimmed. She was still beautiful, still charming and gracious—but some of her old spark, that electricity he'd felt the first time he'd met her, was gone.

Ever since that night of the housewarming, he had suspected that there were problems. But whenever she spoke of Harry, she never hinted at what the trouble might be.

Ellis decided to broach the subject. "You miss the children, don't you?"

"Terribly," she sighed.

"But it's more than that. I can tell."

"Oh . . . I hate to burden you with my problems."

"Lily, I told you a long time ago that if you need a friend, I'm always here. Now what's troubling you?"

"Well, Ellis . . . I don't know. It's just that Harry works so hard. He's so consumed by what he's doing—"

At that moment, Harry came through the French doors. "Do I hear my name being taken in vain?" he said, clapping Ellis on the back. "I could sure do with one of your famous martinis."

Lily and Ellis didn't have a chance to resume their interrupted conversation until Sunday morning after breakfast, when Harry had gone up to his study to work. Ellis came upon Lily as she was working in her rose garden. For a moment, he just watched her in silence while she didn't know she was being observed. She was utterly enchanting. Ellis knew then that if he could have chosen any woman in the world, it would be she.

This was the first time he had allowed himself to spend a weekend with her and Harry in a long while, but his long absence had failed to dim his affection. If anything, he found himself more drawn than ever.

Finally Lily sensed his presence. She looked up and smiled. Ellis took her hand and helped her to her feet. "You look wonderful, Lily." Then, slightly embarrassed, he continued. "I love that straw hat."

Lily laughed aloud. "This old thing? I've had it for almost twenty years!"

"It's still lovely. As you are."

A long silence ensued. Finally, Ellis broke it, saying gently, "Lily . . . I'm concerned. Is there anything bothering you?"

Half smiling, Lily shook her head but avoided his probing gaze. "Not really . . . How about some coffee under the tree? I'm ready for a little shade at this point."

"I'd like that."

Lily went and brought back a tray. They walked down the path to the shade of the linden tree. As Lily set out the china, Ellis looked up at the sky. It was so peaceful, so lovely. Even as it was happening, he knew this was a moment to be cherished.

Lily poured him a cup of coffee and added two teaspoons of sugar. How like her to remember how he took it, he thought. But even as she passed it to him in silence, Ellis detected a mournful note in her graceful manner. The reason for her despair seemed clear. Harry neglected her. It was as simple as that.

Sure he was not mistaken, Ellis persisted in his questioning. "Lily," he said simply, "are you happy?"

Lily averted her eyes. "No one has everything they want," she said uncertainly.

"And what is it you'd wish for if your wish could come true?"

"Oh, Ellis, not any one thing. It's just that I miss the children. And I miss Harry. I think the thing that hurts most is that however much I miss them all, none of them seems to miss me."

Lily stopped abruptly. She had said more than she'd wanted to. But somehow she could no longer pretend, either to herself or to Ellis.

Ellis looked deep into her eyes. "You can tell me anything, Lily. Everything. You need someone to talk to." He paused, then ventured, "And isn't there more to it than just your children going off to school?"

Lily sighed. "Oh, Ellis, it's more than that. Harry is obsessed with this new book. I scarcely see him. Tell me, are all authors so unapproachable?"

"Some are, some aren't. Some are terribly intense and. many are recluses. I have to admit that there are pretty few who have happy homes and marriages."

"But Harry is married, and I want us to be happy. So what I need to know is, what drives him so?"

"To be honest, Lily, I think he's still trying to prove that he's a success—to you, to himself, but mainly to his family, the Kohles. And I'm sorry to say that he may never get over that need. I really think an abiding lack of faith in himself is what makes Harry tick."

She laughed incredulously. "But he already has proved himself to his family. And certainly to me. He has enormous celebrity. We have more money than we'll ever be able to use. Can't he see that?"

"I see it, and you do, but I think Harry still has his doubts."

Lily shook her head sadly. "Isn't it a shame? He's missing so much when it's all right in front of him."

Ellis probed further. "Have you ever told him how you

feel about his neglecting you? Asked him to spend more time with you?"

"Not in so many words. I guess deep down I feel he can't change. And I don't really want to change him; I love him. It just seems that life has gotten in the way."

Ellis was torn. Lily was so vulnerable just now. If he wanted to, he could easily influence her against Harry. But his conscience would not allow him to take advantage of her doubts and loneliness. Still, in good conscience he couldn't say, "It's going to be all right, Lily," when he knew it wasn't true. What she needed was honesty, not easy platitudes. Ellis chose his words carefully.

"It's very tough to live in the shadow of someone like Harry. Someone as devoted as he is to his craft. Lily, maybe you can't do anything to lessen Harry's compulsion, but you can do something about your own life."

"What, Ellis? What can I do?"

"Look, Lily. I know that I suggested this place. I was all for the move from the farm. But now I know it's wrong for you. When I told Harry that it would be perfect for your family, I had no idea that all the children would be going to boarding school. This is no place for you to live alone."

Lily winced. Living with Harry was like living alone.

Ellis continued. "Why don't you consider moving to Manhattan?"

"Move—away from The Meadows? Ellis, we're just now settling in! Why, Harry would never hear of it. He loves this place."

"I'm not saying sell it; you could make it your weekend home. Come up here for the whole summer, if you'd like. At this point he could write anywhere. I'm thinking of you. You need the stimulation of a wider world, an outlet for all your talents and energies. You're a remarkable woman. You don't give yourself nearly enough credit."

Lily was deeply flattered by the compliment. But move to the city? Her mind reeled.

"What could I do in Manhattan? I'm not qualified for anything in particular, and Harry wouldn't want me to work, I'm sure."

"I'm not suggesting you work in the strictest sense. You could do any number of things: volunteer work, charity organizations. You've been so isolated out in the country, you don't realize that there is a world out there that would welcome you—and your talents."

"Ellis, you're always so full of praise. I don't deserve half of it."

Ellis raised his right hand and smiled. "The whole truth and nothing but the truth. I swear." He paused, then continued. "I've known it from the first time I saw you, that night I came out to the farm, how special you are."

Lily flushed with pleasure. In that moment, she realized how long it had been since Harry had given her any kind of compliment.

"You just don't know your own worth, Lily. Why, you're the last princess in town."

Laughing, she asked, "What does that mean?"

"You're the last of a rare breed," he said thoughtfully. "Loyal and courageous and loving. You've stayed with Harry through thick and thin, with no word of complaint. And I'm sure you've had your moments of despair. But just now I think it's time you thought of yourself for a change."

Lily just shook her head. "You don't balance the books in a marriage, Ellis. It's a process of give and take."

"Fine. I just think you've been doing most of the giving."

Lily didn't say a word. What could she say? Ellis was right. Suddenly the prospect of Manhattan no longer seemed outrageous.

"Ellis," she said at last, "I know I've said this to you before, but you're such a dear friend. What would I ever do without you?"

"I only want you to be happy, Lily." Secretly he thought, *If only you would agree to be happy with me . . .*

That evening after Ellis left, Lily could scarcely wait to speak to Harry. If it had not been for Ellis, she might have continued to live in near exile. But Ellis had opened her eyes. Her needs had to be considered as well as Harry's. If only she could make him see.

That night, Lily looked at herself closely in the mirror in a way that she hadn't for a long time. She suddenly saw how pale and weary she looked. She was withering away, no doubt about it, and all in consequence of her mental state.

Lily took a deep breath, stood straight, and went upstairs

to Harry's study. As he pulled the black hood over the typewriter, she asked, "Darling, would you like a drink?"

"Sure, I'd love one."

She went to the bar and poured them each a jigger of Scotch, added ice and soda, then handed Harry his glass.

There were days when the blank paper stared back at him and he wanted to take the typewriter and throw it out the window, and other times when for the want of a single word he would have sold his soul. But today the work had simply flowed without effort. God was in his heaven, all was right with the world. Harry sipped his drink contentedly.

Lily nursed her drink for some minutes before broaching the subject that bore so heavily on her mind.

"Harry," she finally began, "I've been thinking."

"That's pretty obvious. What's on your mind?"

She cleared her throat and continued. "I think that you and I need a change."

"Change?" He gestured expansively. "Why, I wouldn't trade places with the King of Siam. I have everything I want—more than I ever expected to have. I love my wife, I love my home, I love my children—I love my life just as it is."

He wasn't making it easy for her. She took another sip, drew a deep breath, and tried again.

"Harry, the truth is that *I* need a change."

He frowned briefly, puzzled. "Lily, we just had a change—we moved here. And you know I can't get away just now. Rafi and Tony and I are thrashing out a lot of preliminary work, and I can't just up and leave. But if you'd like to take a little trip, darling . . . "

Again there was that nagging reminder of how superfluous she was. But the echo of Ellis's words fortified her. Boldly, she went on.

"No, Harry, what I'm talking about is on a larger scale. I don't know if you've noticed, but I've been floundering lately, not really knowing what to do with myself."

"I know that it has been hard on you, having the children away at school, but you'll get used to it, darling."

"No, I don't think I will, Harry. Let me try to explain. The truth is that I never really prepared myself for this time in my life, and now I think I need to do something different."

"So what do you want to do? Study to be a brain surgeon? You don't need to work; I make plenty of money."

"It's not money, Harry. I want to do something where I feel useful."

"You don't feel useful now?"

"It's just that I feel so isolated. . . ."

"Isolated?" Harry was genuinely surprised. "You have a car, Lily. Are the responsibilities of the house so onerous that you can't leave? Have I ever objected to anything you've wanted to do? I don't keep you in shackles."

Lily looked at him for a long moment; he didn't understand at all. "I'm not talking about a shopping spree or lunch in the city. I'm talking about a life, Harry. A life I haven't made."

Harry shook his head. "I don't understand women. Here you are, you live in the finest suburb in Fairfield County, you have servants, you have money. You can buy and do anything you want. Meanwhile, I work day and night—and you're complaining."

"All of that is true, I'm not denying it. But I feel useless, Harry, and while you're sequestered in your ivory tower, I have to find something to fill the void in my life."

None of this was the least bit comprehensible to Harry; Lily was no career woman. She never had been. Harry frowned. "Could I have another drink, please?" He accepted his glass and took a deep swallow. "So what exactly is it you want from me? What am I supposed to do?"

"I want to move to Manhattan."

Harry looked at his wife in disbelief. "Manhattan! Are you out of your mind? We've just spent a fortune on building this house. Now you're proposing we leave it? Lily—are you going through the change of life?"

"No, of course not. But I need a change in my life."

"But you've always loved the country!"

"That was when we had children at home, Harry. I loved it when we were at the farm. There was so much to do. . . . " Her voice trailed off.

"You sound terribly deprived, Lily."

"Harry, would you please stop being sarcastic? I'm trying hard to explain. If I keep busy with something, I won't always be jealous of your world."

"You're jealous of my writing?"

"Not of your writing, but of the fact that it takes you away from me. It consumes your every waking moment. I guess I just want something to consume me."

He got up and walked to the window, his hands shoved deep into his pockets. "But I love this house. I feel so inspired here."

"But don't you see that this is only a house? It hasn't become a real home."

Finally he began to understand what Lily was driving at. He began to see what a lonely place The Meadows was for her, especially with the children gone and with him locked up with his book. More important, he realized with a rush that he was as in love with her then as he had been that first night at the opera. He had neglected her in pursuit of his own interests, his career. Now he would make it his business to make it up to her. Slowly, he took Lily in his arms and held her close. "I haven't done this in a long time, have I, Lily? Told you how important you are to me."

"No, you haven't," she said. "And I've missed you terribly. This has been the worst time of my life—worse even than when you lived away from us in New York."

Kissing her gently, he said, "We'll drive into the city tomorrow to look for an apartment—that is, if it's an apartment you want."

"Oh, Harry, I'd love it."

At this moment, she loved Harry perhaps more than at any other time in their marriage. Harry was willing to leave the home he cherished—for her. The very next day, when she and Harry drove to the city and picked out a charming pied-à-terre on Sutton Place, her happiness knew no bounds.

Little did Lily know a simple change of scenery would not change her life. If anything, Manhattan was as overwhelming as she'd always found it to be. Harry, on the other hand, fast began to thrive. Though Rafi and Tony, his researchers, were happy to return to New York, he had a new secretary, twenty-three-year-old Valerie Kirk. Lily felt herself floundering, but was loath to let Harry know. Wasn't this move his great concession to her? How could she complain to him again, and so soon? Over and over she was reminded of the old saying: "Take care what you wish; you just might get it."

Lily tried to make the best of it. She kept to herself. Mainly, she kept out of the apartment. She didn't want Harry to know she still had so little to do. Some days she'd go on little shopping sprees, just to have something to show for her day. But early on she found herself counting the weeks until the whole family would be together again for the Christmas holidays. She and Harry had agreed to celebrate the reunion back at The Meadows. Harry was looking forward to it too, as he told her one night at dinner.

"I have to tell you, Lily, that I love being back in the city, but there's nothing quite like Christmas in the country."

"I'm so glad. I feel exactly that way. And this Christmas is going to be our best one ever. But there is one thing I want to talk to you about. I want you to try to be patient with Jeremy."

"Lily, why do you always say that to me? I think I'm patient enough as it is."

"Not always, darling," she said softly, then stopped. She did not want to quarrel. But Harry was already angry. He pushed his dessert plate away and took a long swallow of coffee. Damned if *his* father had treated him with kid gloves! He was easy on Jeremy by comparison. But at least his mother had always backed his father up. That was a hell of a lot more than Lily had ever done. They had never agreed when it came to the rearing of their children. In the end, Lily usually had her way. And Jeremy was already the worse for it. Why fight about it now?

"Okay," he said finally. "Have it your way. When Jeremy comes home, I'll treat him with kid gloves."

"You don't have to go that far, Harry. Just be understanding."

For Lily, the remaining weeks seemed to drag, but at long last it was mid-December.

# Chapter 24

CHRISTMAS of 1949 was a joyous reunion for Lily. She had never been so happy to be at The Meadows as then, and as the family trimmed the tree together—without a single quarrel—Lily couldn't help but feel this was the way it was always meant to be.

With a pang, Lily thought to herself how tall the children were getting to be. They grew up so fast. And that was the trouble with having had her children so close together: They all grew up at once. Lately she'd been thinking of asking Harry if they might have another, but every time she came close to asking, she couldn't find the words. She knew Harry didn't want to be a father again; he barely liked being a father to the four he had.

And so, instead, she hovered over Jeremy and Drew, Randy and Melissa, as though they were in danger of disappearing right then. Finally the tree was decorated from top to bottom. It seemed out of a winter fairyland.

Turning to Harry, Lily beamed. "I'm so happy here. You know, I have to tell you that I really love this house."

"Lily, you don't know how happy you've made me by saying that. You know I really wanted this house for you."

Christmas dinner was superb. As usual, Ellis joined them, as did Randolph, who for once defied his mother to spend the day with Lily and his godson. Not an unkind word was uttered as they laughed and talked and ate. The boys rattled on and on about football and Melissa was on her best behavior.

After dinner everyone clustered around the grand piano

and Lily seated herself at the keyboard. As they started on Christmas carols, Harry gestured to Jeremy, led him into his study, and closed the door. For a moment he said nothing as he looked at his son, thinking only, God, he was growing up into a handsome boy! He even was beginning to show a little stubble of beard.

"Would you like a little brandy, son?"

"No thanks, Dad."

It was a sign of acceptance into the adult world, but Jeremy's heart was pounding so much that he could barely stand, and the thought of liquor was repugnant to him.

"Have a little port, then," Harry said, pouring the liquid into two snifters.

Jeremy took the glass but simply held it in his hand, not touching it.

"So tell me, how is school treating you these days?"

Looking at the painting on the wall, Jeremy noticed that it was a Modigliani. The colors were a fabulous crimson and blue. He thought ruefully, If only he could have been a painter—but then, he probably wouldn't have been any good at it anyway. . . .

"Fine," he finally replied woodenly.

"You know, you've got fine opportunities at Exeter, and you'll have even greater ones next September at Harvard. You know, your great-great-grandfather . . . "

"I know, Dad, I know." He almost couldn't bear to hear it.

Of course he knew. His ancestors and their illustrious careers seemed to dog him in the very halls of these institutions.

"There have been many times," Harry continued, "when I regretted not having gone to Harvard in the family tradition. You know, kids never understand their parents' motives. My father had the best intentions in wanting me to go there; I see that now."

Suddenly Harry stopped himself. *Don't pontificate,* he thought.

"Well, son, all I wanted to say is that I'm proud of you, and proud that you're planning to go to Harvard. You have gotten your application in, haven't you? When do you hear?"

"They don't make a decision until after the first semester's grades are in," he said, trying to hide the tremulous note in his voice. If his father only knew how close it was, how much depended on those grades.

"Well, I have every confidence in you. Speaking for your mother as well as myself, we both think you're exceptional."

Twirling his glass between his sweating palms, Jeremy felt the back of his shirt cling to him. Chilled, he walked over to stand by the fire. Would his father feel the same way if he didn't get in? Being accepted at Harvard had weighed so heavily on his mind that he had barely been able to sleep for months. Not only was there the burden of his father's expectations, but also those of his grandfather, Benjamin Kohle. Jeremy had become his grandfather's protégé and Benjamin was as ambitious for him as Harry was.

All too vividly, he remembered sitting across from him at the Harvard Club over lunch. "Jeremy, I have every hope that you will follow in my footsteps and enter the bank. I'm pleased to see that you're not at all like your father, who was a renegade—though, mind you, I'm not entirely displeased with him nowadays—but it is my fondest wish that you enter the family business. We can't let the heritage of our forefathers die; I know that you cherish that responsibility."

There was only one possible answer. "Of course I do, Grandfather."

"It will be a great day when we can add another Kohle to the letterhead, just as soon as you graduate from Harvard."

Jeremy shuddered at his tremendous sense of responsibility. How could he ever measure up?

Meanwhile, Harry moved closer to his son and put his arm around him. He felt he had finally gotten through to the boy. "Son, I'm glad we've had this little talk. Now we'd better go back and join the others."

They could hear "Jingle Bells" resounding as they crossed the vast foyer and entered the living room, where everyone was still clustered around the piano.

The holiday had come and gone in an aura of joy; it had been everything Lily could have hoped for. It seemed to have erased the memory of the bitterness of the previous summer.

Another week would bring a new year. It seemed to Lily her family was at last on the verge of becoming everything she'd always hoped it would. Even Harry and Jeremy seemed to be getting along. But soon the blissful respite was coming to an end. On the second of January, Lily and Harry waved good-bye to each of their four children. The spring semester was beginning; she and Harry would be heading back to Manhattan.

As they walked back into the house and closed the door behind them, it wasn't merely a door they closed—it was an era in their lives.

Henceforth the children would be only visitors. Jeremy was now on the threshold of adulthood; the others would soon follow, and one phase of their lives had come to an end.

A bittersweet feeling came over her. Here they were, just the two of them, as it had been in the beginning. Yet this was the natural progression of lives and family and marriage. And as people grew older, who remained most important in one's life? She almost whispered aloud, Harry, Harry.

If she had ever needed him, it was now. As they looked simultaneously at each other, a wave of love for him enveloped her. She had seen a new dimension in him during this holiday; he had taken her concerns over Jeremy seriously—and she loved him for restraining himself.

When they settled into their apartment, Lily felt far more reconciled to their new life than she had been before the holidays.

Harry was happy and productive here and she was becoming used to the children's absence. Finally she felt ready to embark upon the odyssey of self-discovery Ellis had encouraged her to investigate.

Lily volunteered to serve as a docent at the Metropolitan Museum of Art. She was accepted into the program and fast became immersed in her studies. Between the training sessions by day and the books she had to pore over by night, Lily found herself mooning over her children's absence less and less.

She was so caught up in her own work, she nearly forgot Jeremy, studying for his finals up at Exeter, but she arranged to have a large basket of goodies from Chadwick's delivered to his dorm room as a special surprise.

That evening she called to make sure he'd received it. "Hello, darling. Did your basket arrive?"

"Yes, it did. Thank you very much."

Jeremy's tone was so lifeless, Lily became concerned. "What's the matter, darling? You sound tired."

"I've been studying a lot."

"Well, don't push yourself too hard, sweetheart."

"No, Mother. I won't."

But Lily was not at all convinced, and that night, as Harry got into bed, she said, "Darling, why don't you give Jeremy a call tomorrow? I think he needs a little moral support. He sounded so depressed when I spoke to him today. But please don't mention the finals. I just think you should let him know you care."

"Of course. I had every intention of calling him."

The next day, Lily listened to Harry's end of the conversation. "Hello, Jeremy, it's Dad. . . . No, nothing special, just called to say hello . . . Studying? Yes, that's what your mother said. . . . Listen, all I want to say is that I have a lot of faith in you. . . . I know you'll make me very proud, and I don't have a single doubt that Harvard will accept you. . . . Yes, of course, I'll let you go now."

After Jeremy had hung up, he buried his face in his hands. The words *I know you'll make me very proud* rang mockingly through his head. If his father only knew! No matter how hard he struggled, he seemed to turn up nothing better than Cs and an occasional B.

Grandfather Kohle's words flashed through his mind: *We can't let the heritage of our forefathers die. . . .*

Was he going to be the one to let it perish?

Just then, Laird Phillips, his roommate, entered the room. "Jeremy, old buddy, what's the deal? Have you fallen asleep sitting up?"

"No," Jeremy answered, lifting his head dully.

"Well, I wouldn't be surprised if you did. I saw the light on in the study when I got up this morning. Were you up all night again?"

Jeremy nodded. He seemed about to faint.

"Listen, Jeremy," said Laird, his voice full of concern. "You've got to knock it off. You're killing yourself. You must be prepared by now."

"The best I can hope for is a C in math. I'm afraid physics will be even worse."

"So what's the worst that can happen? So you get a D—

big deal. You are a shoo-in at Brown. Maybe you can transfer to Harvard later."

"You don't understand. If I don't get into Harvard, it will kill my father."

"Jesus Christ, what does he expect? Perfection?"

"Yes," Jeremy replied tonelessly. "That's exactly what he has always expected from me."

"Well that's just tough luck for him. You can't study any more than you do, Jeremy. You haven't had one date this year, or been to a single party."

Jeremy just shrugged, then buried his head in his hands. He was miserably unhappy. In spite of himself, he suddenly became racked with sobs.

Laird was embarrassed by this show of emotion, but it made him all the more concerned for his roommate. Clearly, Jeremy was pushed to his limit. "Come on, Jeremy," he said, patting him on the shoulder. "It's not as bad as you think. Don't take it so hard."

Gradually Jeremy regained control of himself. Laird insisted he have something to eat, then lie down. Meekly Jeremy did as Laird said. He ate a little and then, exhausted, collapsed on the bed. Laird pulled the blanket up over him, turned off the light, and closed the door. His emotions spent, Jeremy was asleep by the time his friend tiptoed down the hall.

Laird was soon caught up in studying for his own exams. He barely saw his roommate. It was finals week when he got a few minutes to spend with Jeremy and was astonished to find him so gaunt and pale.

On the last day of exams, Laird went off to celebrate with a bunch of his friends. The party was wild and carefree, but somehow he couldn't put the thought of Jeremy out of his mind. What he needed was a little fun. After all, by now the die—for better or worse—was cast.

"Jeremy," Laird called out as he opened the door to their room.

The silent figure hung from the crossbeam, so horribly still Laird knew as soon as he saw him that it was too late. Even so, Laird pulled the Swiss Army knife from his pocket and desperately sliced through the rope. Jeremy fell limply into his arms.

Laird gingerly carried him to the bed. He ran to the hall

phone and dialed frantically. "Operator," he shouted. "I need an ambulance. Right away. Exeter. Room twenty-four. Hurry!" But even as Laird shouted, he knew that Jeremy was beyond help. Still, he would make the effort.

Darting back into the room, he began with mouth-to-mouth resuscitation. But Jeremy's lips were cold. Already his face had taken on a bluish cast. Nonetheless, Laird continued his hopeless maneuverings, even as the ambulance's whirring siren blended eerily with the boisterous shouts of the campus revelers still downing beers by the keg in the courtyard.

# Chapter 25

LILY was snug in the cozy living room of the Sutton Place apartment, bent over her needlepoint—a Metropolitan reproduction. A smile came to her lips as she reminisced about their happy Christmas vacation. She resolved that her children would have to come home for the summer vacation as well. And she had a feeling, given the Yuletide success, that no one—not Drew, not Randy, not Melissa, and certainly not Harry—would balk at the thought.

Just then the phone rang. Lily set aside her needlepoint and picked up the receiver. A voice greeted her before she had a chance to say hello.

"Mrs. Kohle? This is Dean Whittaker."

"Dean Whittaker! Why, hello." With a thrill, she thought, Could Jeremy have made the Dean's list? How proud Harry would be!

"Mrs. Kohle," said Dean Whittaker, "I'm afraid I have some bad news for you."

"Bad news?" she repeated inquiringly. She couldn't imagine any trouble Jeremy could be in.

"Mrs. Kohle, I'm afraid we've—lost Jeremy."

"Lost him? Why, what do you mean?"

"I'm so sorry. . . . There's no other way to tell you this. Jeremy committed suicide this morning."

Lily dropped the phone and sat for a moment in stunned silence. Then she let out an anguished, horrified shriek. The door of Harry's study flung open and he came racing out with Valerie Kirk on his heels.

"Lily! Lily, what is it?" he cried, seizing her by the shoulders. But Lily was sobbing too hysterically to speak. When she finally recovered enough for words, all she could utter was, "No, no, no!"

"Lily, please," Harry begged her. "Please, tell me what it is."

"Jeremy," she gasped at long last. "Our Jeremy is—dead!"

"Lily, what are you saying?"

"He—he's taken his life." She sobbed again at hearing the awful truth coming from her own lips.

"Oh my God."

"Oh, Harry. I want to see my baby."

It was Valerie who finally noticed the dangling phone and replaced the receiver. Later it was she who made all the necessary calls and drove Harry and Lily up to New Hampshire to bring back the body. The parents remained in shock. Neither was eating. They barely slept; they didn't talk.

As the car rolled along the scenic highway, Lily pondered again the unanswerable question that had plagued her every waking moment ever since the dean's fateful call: Why? What had driven her firstborn to such a point of despair? Somehow, she could not turn to Harry for comfort. He was totally wrapped up in his own grief. If she had, she might not have counted on him for much solace.

Laird Phillips was the one to shed light on the events that led up to and surrounded Jeremy's death.

"He was just terrified of failing, Mr. Kohle. You've never seen anyone study the way he did. He cracked the books constantly—had no social life at all. I tried to tell him to relax a little, but he'd never listen. He felt such tremendous pressure from you."

Harry couldn't let him go on. "At Christmas I told him that I would be proud of him, no matter what."

"Well, that's not the sense he came back with after the break. He was frantic, wanted to make you proud of him. He said it was what you expected, but he also knew he just wasn't up to it; he felt defeated from the start. Jeremy was a good student, but he had a terrible time reading. I know. I saw him go at it. He said the words got confused for him; I can't explain it better than that. Neither could he. But he said that he would just die if he failed to live up to your expectations." Laird broke off. He could see the Kohles were grief-stricken. Perhaps he was telling them too much.

Lily could hardly take in what this boy was saying. Why, if what he said was true, then Harry was to blame. She should never have trusted him alone with her Jeremy. After all these years, how could she expect him to change? Harry had remained as demanding of Jeremy as he'd always been. She was a fool for ever having thought otherwise.

Unable to bear the thought of it anymore, Lily burst into tears. Her sobs ended the conversation with young Phillips.

Randolph couldn't have been more stunned by the news of Jeremy's death. Right away his thoughts went to Lily. She had already endured so much. Knowing that neither she nor Harry was in any shape to make funeral arrangements, he took over the grim task. He also took it upon himself to notify relatives. Benjamin Kohle was the first person Randolph contacted, going in person to the Kohle town house.

They were not complete strangers, since they had met at the children's naming ceremonies. Now Randolph's heart went out to him as the old man sat staring blindly out the window.

Gently, he said, "Mr. Kohle, I haven't talked to Lily and Harry yet about where Jeremy should be buried, but I know that, as a Catholic, he cannot be buried in consecrated ground because of the way he died. Do you have any wishes?"

There was an uncomfortable pause. Finally, Benjamin said huskily, "I would like Jeremy to be put to rest in the Kohle family mausoleum if Lily and Harry agree."

"I'm sure they will," Randolph said gently.

After Randolph had taken his leave, Benjamin once again turned his eyes bleakly to the window, but he saw nothing, his mind crowded with wrenchingly painful thoughts.

Why, oh why had he let all those years go by without seeing Harry's children? Why had he wasted the opportunity to know them? Stubbornness and arrogance were surely a disease of the heart.

He had had twelve grandchildren, but strangely only in Jeremy had he experienced that mysterious feeling of lineage. Harry's child—Harry was the only one of his sons made in his image—and he had thought that Jeremy, too, seemed made in his image.

He had hoped that the circle of the family, broken by Harry's defection, would be magically repaired. So why had God dealt him this great blow?

Tears rose in the faded blue eyes. No man should live beyond his time. No man should ever have to live to bury his son, or his son's son. It was contrary to the natural order of things . . . and it was almost more than he could bear.

Sitting alone in the high-ceilinged study, he wept unabashedly.

It had been impossible to keep the manner of Jeremy's death from the press. The news reports represented sensationalism at its worst, and while none of the accounts openly speculated as to the reason for the Kohle child's suicide, they proffered a range of possible if not probable motives for it.

Ellis had been the first to catch wind of these reports. He contacted Harry in hopes of keeping the papers—and reporters—away from Lily. Harry was enraged at the thought of such muckraking. He did his best to shelter Lily, but come the day of the funeral there was little he could do to keep her from the prying eyes of the media.

But Lily hardly noticed them, so deep was her grief. What did she know about Jeremy? She was his mother! She was the one who had brought him into the world almost seventeen years before on a wild, wet, stormy day inside a little farmhouse.

That precious baby, that sweet little boy, who had knelt with her, planting seeds in the moist black earth.

"Spit those out, Jeremy."

"I made a picture for you, Mommy—you, me, and Daddy."

"Don't you want to put in your brothers and Melissa?"

"No, Mommy—just you, me, and Daddy, okay, and Drew."

And again, she cried out in her inner soul, Where did I fail you, Jeremy? What were your last thoughts? Were you in so much pain? Why wasn't I there to reassure you?

Only Randolph's arm saved Lily from collapsing as the huge bronze doors of the mausoleum swung open to receive her child's body. While she presented a stony face to the proceedings, she felt as if her heart had broken. When at last it came time to entomb her darling, when the heavy bronze doors were swung shut with an ominous clang, Lily's knees buckled.

She had no recollection of the following hour, but somehow she found herself back at The Meadows, with crowds of mourners beginning to arrive. As a steady stream of cars rolled up to the doors, she stood in her place in the foyer, her natural breeding giving her the appearance of iron composure.

But after the guests had all moved on into the living room, she stood in the foyer for a long moment grieving.

Fragments of conversation drifted in from the other room, and there was the clink of ice in glasses as highballs were passed. She caught sight of a sumptuous buffet—arranged for, no doubt, by the efficient Valerie. Suddenly the numb feeling was replaced by a surge of bitterness. Lily turned away and mounted the stairs. She hated them for their conversation, for the occasional bursts of subdued laughter, even for their appetites for food and drink. How could they act so normal when her son was lying in a cold mausoleum, shut away from life and love and laughter forever?

She walked slowly down the hall to Jeremy's room, entered, and shut the door behind her. Suddenly she remembered another moment, many, many years before, when she had stood in another child's bedroom—that of her brother, Charles. She had thought merciful time had erased the agony of that memory, but now the veil had lifted and revealed it as vividly and terribly as ever.

After a long time she finally went to her own bedroom and lay down. It was Melissa who first came to check on her after the last of the mourners had driven away.

"Are you all right, Mommy?" At her age, she was little able to understand the meaning of her brother's death.

"I'm all right," Lily told her. She began to realize she would have to be strong for the other children's sake. She forced herself to get up and let her daughter help her downstairs. They were at the landing when they heard raised voices. Lily ran down to the living room in time to hear Drew shout angrily, "I hate you, you son of a bitch. You drove Jeremy to this! It's your fault. All these years, you pushed him and prodded him. And for what? Harvard, Harvard, Harvard! The place even you—brilliant, big-shot writer you—didn't get in."

If Lily could scarcely believe what she was hearing, Harry was stunned. Such damning words—and from his own son. At first Harry said nothing, he was so shocked by Drew's cruel speech. Then, abruptly, anger wiped out grief. He wasn't going to take this from anyone, let alone his own son!

"How dare you, you miserable little bastard! Who the hell do you think you are?"

Drew was angry enough to stand his ground. "What's the matter, Father? Does the truth hurt? You killed Jeremy as surely as if you'd tied the noose around his neck and kicked the chair away."

Harry began a harsh retort but it was Lily who ended the confrontation. She took five brisk steps toward Drew, raised her hand, and slapped him across the face as hard as she could. With tears welling in her eyes, she said, "I will not stand for that kind of talk in this house. You are never to speak to your father that way." The tears streamed down her cheeks as she said the words. "Do you understand me?"

Not once in his life had Drew known his mother to raise a hand against one of her children. That fact made a stronger impact on him than the slap itself.

"Now I want you to apologize to your father—this instant!"

Drew knew in his heart he would never forgive his father for driving Jeremy to his death. But at the same time, he could not bear to cause his mother any more grief than she'd already suffered.

Without looking at his father, Drew muttered, "Sorry."

Later, when the children were about to leave to return to their boarding schools, Drew took his mother aside. "I'm sorry," he told her. "But not for what I said. I'm only sorry to have hurt you."

Lily nodded sadly. "I know, dear. And I know how much you loved Jeremy. But you must know that your father loved him, too. He only wanted the best for your brother." Drew said nothing, and even as she said the words, Lily couldn't help but feel that they sounded hollow and, worse still, untrue.

For days after the children had gone, Lily nursed her grief like a strong drink. Drew's accusations washed over her like a curse. For as much as she tried to deny it, she couldn't shake the ever-growing conviction that Drew was right: Harry was responsible for Jeremy's death as surely as if he'd hanged him. Lily couldn't shake the thought. After a week of living in gloomy silence with Harry, she could bear it no more. She resolved to spare him another scene like the one with Drew, but she also resolved that they should part for a while.

One evening the following week, Lily determined to broach

the subject over drinks. Before she could speak, Harry said, "Lily, why don't you talk to me? Why are you shutting me out?"

Fighting to maintain her resolve, Lily clenched her fists by her sides.

"God, Lily. Do you think I didn't love that boy with all my heart? I would have done anything to keep him alive! Everything I ever did or said to him was for his own good!"

He bent over and pulled her to her feet. "Lily, say that you believe me!"

In a voice devoid of all emotion, she finally answered, "Harry, the only thing I know is that our son is dead. He committed suicide because he didn't feel he could live up to what was expected of him."

"And you blame me." Harry let go of her, picked up his glass, and downed the rest of his Scotch.

Then, turning back to her, he asked abruptly, "When do you want to start back to the city?"

It was as though someone else had taken over and was speaking for her. "I'm not going back to the city at all, Harry."

"What do you mean? Do you intend to stay here?"

"Harry," she said with slow deliberation, "I'm moving back to the farm."

Harry was dumbfounded. "The farm?" he echoed. Then, his eyes narrowing, he said, "With or without me?"

"I'm sorry, Harry." She could hardly believe it had come to this.

Harry was quick to pick up the silent accusation in this parting. "You're just like Drew," he said quietly. "You think I'm responsible."

Lily could not deny it. "I just think we need some time apart for a while. We certainly don't seem to be doing each other any good."

A part of Lily knew how much her decision was hurting him, but she was even more certain that if she went back to the city with him, sooner or later she would voice the terrible accusation burning within her—and that would mean the end for them. Their only hope was that a few weeks apart would soften the pain.

The next day, despite her protests, Harry insisted on driving her up to the farm.

Mrs. Gallagher greeted them, her face lined with grief and

concern. "I'm so sorry, Mrs. Kohle, Mr. Kohle. Such a tragedy."

Harry carried Lily's bags up the stairs to their old bedroom. Memories of their first days together there, and of their children, came back to him in a rush as he made his way through the halls. After they had coffee and crumb cake, which Mrs. Gallagher insisted on serving, there was nothing for him to do but leave. On the ride up he'd decided he would stay only if Lily asked him to. But Lily was wrestling with her own grief, trying hard not to let her sadness harden into bitterness. Harry kissed her quickly on the cheek, and when he walked to the car, she didn't so much as wave.

"Come home soon, Lily," Harry called to her from the car window. And then he was gone. Lily gazed into the distance long after the car had disappeared. With a pang of relief, she realized that she did still love him. But it would take time—perhaps a lifetime—for her to forgive him for Jeremy's death.

# Chapter 26

HARRY brooded all the way back to New York. He knew for certain that Lily blamed him for Jeremy's death, as surely as Drew did. Didn't they realize how much he'd loved his firstborn son? If he'd pushed him, wasn't it only because he wanted the best for him? If only Lily knew how guilty he felt, how responsible. He never would have encouraged or scolded the boy had he known it could come to this.

The first thing Harry did upon returning to Sutton Place was start a fire in the fireplace. He hoped to shake the chill that had gone straight through his bones. Even as he poked the kindling, he feared that the iciness he felt within him was caused only partially by the cold. Jeremy's suicide would linger in him like a perpetual frost. Harry made himself a stiff drink and sat before the fire, staring hard into the flames. Hours later, when he heard the front door open, he bolted from his chair.

"Lily?" he cried hopefully. "Is that you?"

"No. It's me. Valerie."

Harry tried to hide his disappointment. "Oh, I thought maybe you were my wife."

"I tried you up at The Meadows, and they said you were taking Lily to the farm, then coming up here this evening. I thought you might want to discuss getting back to work."

"Oh, Valerie, I don't think I want to go back to that quite yet."

"Of course," said Valerie. "I understand." She turned to go but then paused. "You look like you could use some company. Someone to talk to . . ."

It was Lily Harry hoped for, but really he needed someone—anyone—to listen. He'd been penned up with his grief for too long. Gratefully, he accepted Valerie's offer. She was so good to him.

For the next hour, Harry poured out his feelings. His guilt about Jeremy, his grief, his anger at Drew's blaming him and at Lily's abandonment. He said far more than he'd intended to say, yet somehow—was it the fire, the Scotch, or Valerie's kind, encouraging eyes turned upon him—he couldn't help but go on.

When he had finished, Valerie sighed sympathetically and put her hand on his. "Oh, Harry, this isn't the kind of treatment you deserve." She moved to the bar and poured them each another drink. She then gave voice to all the bitterness that Harry was feeling. She decried Drew's outburst and nodded disapprovingly over Lily's decision to go to the farm. Little did Harry realize how she was playing up to his emotions, taking full advantage of him when he was so vulnerable.

Valerie's words fell on receptive ears. Harry had always valued her as a competent, efficient secretary. But now, suddenly, he began to see her for the charming and seductively beautiful woman she was.

Handing him his drink, she said, "Oh, Harry, a man of your genius shouldn't have to put up with all this."

In a swift move, Harry drew her to him. He kissed her with a passion that was returned equally in her own ferocious embrace. Without a second thought, Harry carried her to the bedroom he and Lily shared. He made love to her and lost himself in the sheer ecstasy of their pleasure. For the first time since Jeremy's death, he was numb to his burden of guilt and grief.

For a long while they lay in the dark, not speaking. Then Valerie ventured to ask, "You're not sorry?" The magnitude of what he had done so impetuously began to hit him. Still, he could not honestly say he regretted what had passed between them. Pulling Valerie close, Harry murmured words of reassurance. "No, of course not."

At the same time, Harry knew that he must make it clear to Valerie that he did not intend to embark on a full-fledged affair. For all their current troubles, he knew he was meant to be with Lily.

"You're very lovely, Valerie," he began, choosing his words with care. "In every way. But you know, I've been married to Lily a long, long time. Tonight . . . I'll always treasure this. I want you to know how much this means to me. God, this is the first relief I've felt in two weeks. But Valerie, it has to end here."

This was less than what Valerie had hoped for. While she listened to Harry in what he took to be accepting silence, in her heart she began to plot how best to take advantage of Lily's absence. She hoped Mrs. Kohle would stay away in the country a very long time. If she did, Harry would be facing a lot of lonely nights, and for all his good intentions, she had already discovered that his resistance to temptation was weak.

Harry, on the other hand, hoped that Lily would miss him and return to New York City after only a few days. He called her every day, and while they conversed pleasantly, Lily never mentioned when she might return. After a while Harry became afraid to ask.

Although Harry had put Valerie off when she'd inquired about returning to work, he came to see that *The Genesis* would prove his only source of solace. He called Valerie, whom he had not seen or spoken to since the night of her visit, and asked if she might be able to start work again the next morning.

Her voice sounded pleasingly agreeable. "I'll be there at nine."

If Harry was apprehensive at the thought of seeing Valerie again, his fears were allayed the minute she arrived at his door.

Her demeanor was professional yet friendly. It was as though nothing beyond amicable work on *The Genesis* had ever passed between them. Within a week, the two of them were in full swing, immersed in the creation of the novel Harry felt would be his biggest success to date. And the whole time Valerie seemed content to maintain the sense of decorum which had characterized their relationship to date. Harry was surprised and relieved to be met with such uncomplaining competence.

After three weeks of separation, Harry finally broke down. "Lily," he said, "we can't go on like this. I'm coming to see you this weekend."

But Lily demurred. "No, Harry, don't. I think that for a while we shouldn't see each other."

Harry was chilled by the icy determination in her voice. He knew it was no use pressing, but he felt desperate and depressed at the prospect of remaining apart indefinitely. "Lily," he said hoarsely, "please come home. I need you. It's important we stay together—now more than ever."

But Lily remained firm. "There's a lot I need to work out on my own now," she told him.

The next day Harry threw himself into his writing with renewed intensity. Valerie sensed the vigor of his efforts. She suspected his fervor wasn't stimulated by the material alone.

At the close of the day's work, Harry asked if she would want to dine with him that evening. "Look, I've kept you so late—why don't you stay?"

She did her best to sound casual. "Sounds great."

Mary, the maid, had left a meal ready for Harry. There was plenty for two. Harry opened a bottle of red wine to go with it.

He found it comforting to have someone to dine with for a change. He had truly put their recent tryst out of his mind. What gave him special pleasure was the newfound companionship Valerie offered him. But by the time they sat over their cognac, Harry was just tipsy enough to begin admiring Valerie for virtues other than conversational ones. Lily suddenly came to mind—like a warning—but Harry angrily banished her from his thoughts. Where was Lily now? he asked himself. She didn't care enough about him to come back, why should he care at all about her?

After they'd drained their snifters, it was Harry who walked to her end of the table, reached down, and gently turned her face up to his. Their first kiss was warm and sensual, but somehow tentative. Then, once again, Harry swept her up in his arms and carried her into the bedroom. Accidents may happen once, but with this second incident, Harry could pretend no longer.

After that night, it was somehow understood that they would be lovers. For a time Harry had neither the will nor the desire to draw back. He didn't call Lily for several weeks, and though he was somehow surprised when she didn't call him, he spent his time—round the clock—with Valerie. By day, they pored over his work; by night they were in each other's arms.

It was impossible for Harry to block Lily out of his mind. As time passed, he began to understand that he was using Valerie as a distraction from his troubles with Lily and a balm for his guilt over Jeremy's death. Deep down, he knew it was still Lily he longed for. To continue this affair would only put off and perhaps jeopardize their eventual reconciliation. Harry also felt a pang of guilt for Valerie's sake. He could offer her no future. Was it fair for him to lead her on? Harry resolved to end the affair for good. He would let Valerie down gently, try to make her see how this relationship wasn't good for either of them.

Harry chose to break the news to her in a little Italian restaurant in the Village. That way he wouldn't risk the temptation of the proximity of his own bedroom.

As they sat drinking Chianti at the candlelit table with its cheery checkered tablecloth, Valerie looked so genuinely happy he was reluctant to broach the subject of why he had brought her there. But he had taken her to this place with a purpose in mind. He was determined to carry it out.

"Valerie," he began, "there's something I have to say to you. I've been thinking a great deal lately about the two of us. I feel that perhaps the time has come to call this whole thing off."

"Oh, Harry." She tried to stop him from speaking further, but Harry held up his hand to silence her.

"The last thing I want is to hurt you. I care about you. There's no denying that. But ridiculous as it sounds, I'm not prepared to sacrifice my marriage. And I'm afraid if we keep this up much longer, that's exactly what I'll do."

Valerie was silent for a long moment. She was chagrined though not completely surprised by the news. Harry had long been devoted to his wife. But from her first day on the job, Valerie vowed to become the next Mrs. Kohle; she had fallen in love with Harry on sight and had loved him by reputation even before then. Though Harry seemed more determined now than he had been their first night together about ending the affair on the spot, Valerie felt this was nothing worse than another temporary setback. As before, it was a setback she would just wait out. There was no sense pushing Harry, no reason to turn nagging when his marriage to Lily was still so plainly on the skids. Valerie knew how little in touch the Kohles were. She was also well aware of her own native talents. Harry was not the first to fall under her spell, though he proved more recalcitrant than others she had charmed. She was by no means ready to give up. At the moment, she felt the best touch was a soft one. Follow Harry's lead. There was no sense fighting battles; Lily would capitulate without so much as a shrug.

"Harry," Valerie said, eyes brimming artfully with tears, "I won't ever be the one to make you unhappy. Not ever. I'll do whatever you say. But I'll tell you this much, you need someone to talk to. Someone to listen. And if Lily won't be the one to do it, then I think it might as well be me." She looked him straight in the eye, her lip trembling fetchingly.

"Valerie, you know how much I care about Lily. I love her so. But I just can't get through all this alone—Jeremy's death, her blaming me, makes it even worse. You're right—I crave another person's company. Just the solace of a sympathetic ear."

Valerie nodded and Harry continued, emboldened by her loving gaze. "If two people who love each other can't draw together in times of trouble, when can they? God, I need Lily so much now. . . ." His hoarse voice trailed off.

Valerie reached over and grasped his hand.

"Harry," she said, "I'm here now. All I want is to be with you. I understand how you feel about Lily. But I'm prepared to offer you what she won't. I'll listen to you. I'll be with you for as long as you'll let me. You call the shots. But don't turn me away before need be. Harry, you just can't . . ." Valerie's tears rolled down her cheeks.

Harry was overcome by her offer. How could he not be? Between Lily's neglect, Valerie's devotion, and the effects of the Chianti, he was a lost man.

Half-drunkenly, he shook his head. "She blames me," he told her. "I know it. She holds me responsible for his death."

"She should know how much you loved Jeremy. Even I know."

Harry held her trembling hands in his. "Valerie," he whispered. "Oh, Valerie. What did I do to deserve you?"

Valerie blushed. "I've been asking myself the same question with regard to you."

In the haze brought on by the wine, in the glow of her

seductive praise, Harry half forgot the reason he'd summoned her to the restaurant. He was suddenly as taken with her as he'd been on their first night. They continued as they had begun: working together by day, sleeping together at night. The whole while, Valerie plotted how to make this temporary arrangement a permanent state.

# Chapter 27

*I*F Lily seemed overly stern in dealing with Harry, she crumbled on her own. Her grief over Jeremy's death seemed insurmountable. Some days she felt it was a burden she wouldn't survive.

At night the Gallaghers could hear her crying through the thin walls. The unending sobs often went on until daybreak. By the end of the month of May, they feared that Lily's grief would never heal. For Lily's part, try though she would, she couldn't forgive Harry for pressuring her son. Drew's words rang in her thoughts much as she tried to banish them.

Meanwhile, unbeknownst to Lily, there was someone in addition to Harry who felt punished by her absence. While Harry found solace in Valerie's arms, Ellis wrestled with his unhappy dilemma alone.

Ellis had long been in love with his best friend's wife, yet he'd always managed to restrain his romantic impulses for Harry's sake and in deference to Lily herself. But now, with Lily away in the country and their marriage seemingly on the verge of collapse, Ellis found himself sorely torn—and sorely tempted.

Lily had just experienced a mother's worst nightmare. Ellis could hardly take advantage of her in her present vulnerable state. Yet how, in good conscience, could he abandon her at this crucial time? Without Harry by choice, Lily was all alone. Perhaps she was finally coming to realize what Ellis had known all along but had been loath to tell her: Harry was a decent man who loved his children and his wife, but his devotion to his writing, and to himself, would always top his list of priorities. Harry was driven by an insatiable need to achieve; as a result he neglected his home and his family.

For years Ellis had watched as Lily toughed it out, rarely saying a word against Harry. But he knew that she ached with loneliness, that life with Harry was as good as life alone. What Lily needed was a loving husband, an attentive one who would place her happiness above all else. What she needed, Ellis liked to think, was a man like himself. Ellis knew he couldn't offer Lily the thrill of being married to a literary celebrity, but he suspected that was one thrill Lily never particularly cherished. And he could offer her much. After all, he owned the most prestigious literary agency in New York City. He could provide for Lily—probably as well as Harry could—and, even more important, he would never neglect her. And he would never allow her to go into exile the way Harry seemed to permit. Ellis observed that Harry was little affected by his wife's absence. He was working harder than ever on *The Genesis,* and it seemed writing wasn't the only thing Harry was up to. One evening Ellis had dropped by the apartment unannounced, as was his custom. He had papers for Harry to sign. To his shock, Valerie answered the door, wrapped in Harry's dressing robe.

"Ellis! Hello," she had said sweetly. "We weren't expecting you."

"Well, obviously," he answered, coldly surveying her bare feet below the hem of the robe.

For whatever surprise Valerie feigned, she seemed genuinely pleased to be discovered.

"Harry's taking a shower—he'll be out in a minute. Why don't you come in and let me fix you a drink?"

"No, thanks. Please just give these to Harry."

Ellis never mentioned the incident to Harry, and Harry never raised it himself. But the meeting changed the way Ellis regarded his friend. The agent's thoughts ran straight to Lily. Did she know? Could she suspect? Ellis doubted it. For however comfortably ensconced Valerie seemed to be at Harry's, Ellis figured Lily was in the dark. Ellis would not be the one to tell her, but he would also no longer allow her tattered marriage to keep him at arm's length.

He might have gone straight to the farm that evening. He might not have denounced Harry for the philanderer he clearly was, but he would have declared his own heart. But as luck would have it, Ellis had to fly to London the next evening. He was scheduled to leave at seven.

If it hadn't been absolutely crucial, nothing could have held him back, but he was scheduled to meet with Colin Dempsey-Brewster, who had just finished his memoirs as head of the OSS, in order to sign a six-figure contract. There was no earthly way to put off that and a series of other appointments overseas. But the minute he came back the next week, Ellis resolved, he would visit Lily. He set off for Britain full of hope for returning to a new life with the woman of his dreams.

Although Harry never saw Ellis that evening, the fact of his friend's discovery weighed heavily on his mind.

It had been six months since Jeremy's death, and Harry hadn't seen Lily in all that time. If he didn't act soon, their marriage was doomed. That much Harry knew.

The very day after Valerie had opened the door to Ellis, while Ellis himself was London-bound, Harry drove up the highway in his Ferrari. When he opened the door he discovered Lily in the foyer. She had heard his car drive up. She paled at the sight of him. Harry ran to her and held her in his arms.

"Lily, I've missed you," he told her.

"Harry, I . . . I need more time."

"It's been six months already. Half a year!" Harry trembled with rage at the thought of being apart any longer. He realized then what a fool he'd been to spend any time with Valerie. How could he have settled for anything less than his beautiful, lovely wife?

"Oh, Harry." Lily sighed.

"You still want to stay away, don't you?" He paused. Lily said nothing. "You still blame me for Jeremy's death. You're trying to punish me. Haven't we both already suffered enough?"

Lily fell to the floor and began to sob. "Please go away, Harry—please!"

Harry just stared at her. This was a rejection he was never going to forgive—or forget. "Okay, I'll go. But Lily, if you don't come back soon, there will be nothing left to come back to. I won't wait around forever while you wallow in your own self-pity."

After he had driven away, Lily's tears gradually subsided. She was surprised at how numb she felt after the wrenching scene. At one time in her life, the mere hint of divorce would have horrified her, but today, with the prospect looming before her, she felt neither shock nor fear.

Since the loss of Jeremy, nothing seemed to matter to her. Harry little appreciated how much she needed the time to heal. If he couldn't spare her several months out of a lifetime, then maybe she would be better off without him after all.

Harry drove back to Manhattan in a frenzy of rage and despair, his speedometer registering ninety. In truth, his words had only been a threat. Harry could hardly contemplate life without Lily, a divorce was the last thing on earth he would pursue. But he didn't know how to get Lily back. Nothing seemed to move her, not even the week the children had spent at the farm at his urging. Not even his own pleadings would help. Now, having tried everything he could think of, he was at the end of his rope.

That night Harry sat by the window for a long while, staring out over the city, a drink in his hand. Finally he telephoned Valerie. Just from the way he said her name she knew that Lily had refused to return. Although Harry didn't suspect it, Valerie had worked on him subtly to insinuate the idea of giving Lily an ultimatum. She had been waiting all afternoon to hear the results.

"Harry, dear," she said, her voice oozing sympathy. "Tell me all about it."

But Harry would let her go no further. "Valerie, I just wanted to let you know about tomorrow. I don't want you to come in; I don't think I'll feel up to working."

"Are you feeling all right?"

"No . . . not really. And I'm not in the mood to go ahead with *Genesis*. At least not right now."

"How about if I come by? Maybe I can help somehow. . . ."

"No!" Harry almost shouted the words. "Thank you, Valerie, but I think I need to be alone."

"You know that I'm here if you need me."

"Thank you."

After hanging up the receiver, he stared down into his glass and swirled the melting ice. Then, slowly, he picked up the phone again and dialed Ellis's number.

He knew his friend would be disapproving of his extramarital escapades. Ellis's silence on the subject would remain a more stinging indictment than any words, however fierce, might convey. But he needed his friend's calm counsel and wisdom. And he also longed to redeem himself in Ellis's eyes.

The butler answered. "I'm sorry, Mr. Kohle, Mr. Knox is out of town."

"Where did he go, Edward? When will he be back?"

"I believe, sir, that he is in London until next week."

Sighing heavily, Harry said, "Well . . . just tell him I called."

Harry went to the bar, got the crystal decanter, and brought it back to the coffee table; he settled back against the sofa cushions, poured the Scotch, and drank deeply.

# Chapter 28

THE moment Ellis arrived home and saw Harry's message, he returned the call. The phone rang and rang. It seemed strange that no one would answer, if not Harry or Valerie, then one of the servants at least. Ellis tried later that evening but again got no reply. When he couldn't get an answer the following day, he figured Harry had gone back to The Meadows. But the maid told him, "No, Mr. Knox. He's not here. He sent us up last week and told us to do a little cleaning, and otherwise to consider it a little vacation. . . . No, as far as I know, he's at the apartment. . . ."

More than a little worried, Ellis put on his jacket and told his secretary, "I'm going out."

The thought of finding Harry and Valerie in a love nest once again didn't appeal to him. But the moment he walked into the foyer and saw the pile of papers and mail, he knew something was terribly wrong.

As he rang the bell imperatively he berated himself. He should have come over last night.

When no one answered after much ringing, he sought out the superintendent. "I need to get into the penthouse." Ellis looked so frenzied, the superintendent didn't even ask why. He just gave up the keys.

When Ellis strode into the room, he stopped short. A still figure lay on the sofa. For a brief, agonized moment, Ellis thought that Harry was dead. Rushing to his side, Ellis realized with a wave of relief that Harry was merely dead drunk. Still, finding him this way came as a shock. Harry had never been a heavy drinker. Ellis had rarely even seen him tipsy.

Without a word, he slung Harry over his shoulder, carried him into the bathroom, and propped him against the shower wall. He turned on the water: ice-cold and full force.

After a few insensible moments, Harry started to come to. Gasping for breath under the steady stream of water, Harry gasped, "What . . . what the hell is this? Ellis, get out of here—"

Ignoring him, Ellis ordered, "Get out of those clothes. Here's a robe. I'm going to make you some coffee."

As they sat at the kitchen table some twenty minutes later, Harry mumbled tiredly, "I'm glad to see you, Ellis."

"Well, I'm not glad to see you. Not like this. You look like hell. Have you been holed up here drinking all week?"

Harry nodded.

"What prompted this binge? You've never been a drinker."

Harry could barely speak. "I went up to see Lily the day after . . . the day after you dropped by. She refuses to come back to me."

Tears streamed down Harry's face, then he suddenly broke into sobs. "I love her so, I never wanted to hurt her. I know she blames me, but I didn't mean to hurt Jeremy either. And I need her so, Ellis. . . . I'm just lost without her. . . ." Raising his head, he cried, "I even threatened to divorce her, Ellis, but it didn't seem to mean anything to her. Of course, I would never divorce Lily. . . . It was wrong of me to have an affair with Valerie, and I'm never going to go near her again. I just don't know what to do, Ellis."

Ellis listened in grim silence. If Harry were serious about breaking off with Valerie, if he really meant to patch it up with Lily, where would it leave him? All week in London, Ellis had been floating on cloud nine, rehearsing what he would say to Lily. "Lily, I'm not going to pretend with you. I love you and I have ever since the start . . . and I want you to be my wife." God, how foolish it all seemed now.

If his heart wasn't breaking, he might even laugh. But Ellis hardly had a chance to consider his own position. Harry, his best friend, sat before him in sorry shape. And for all of Lily's aloofness, who could guess how she felt in her heart? Ellis knew what he'd have to do. This was the truest test of friendship he'd ever faced, and the truest test of his love for Lily.

"Harry," he forced himself to say, "this thing will work itself out. Just knock off the booze, will you? It won't help anything."

But as soon as Ellis was gone, Harry thought to himself, That's easy for you to say. It isn't your wife who is leaving you. . . . He planned to drink himself into oblivion today, and tomorrow, and probably the day after that.

But if Harry was in a somber mood, Ellis was gloomier still as he drove up to see Lily at the farm the next day. He knew he couldn't say the words he had planned. Just when he thought he'd have a chance to let Lily know how much he loved her, that chance was snatched away. But the instant he saw Lily, all his own anguish was lost in overwhelming concern for her. Since the last time he'd seen her, her physical state had visibly deteriorated.

"I just got back from London, Lily, and thought I wanted to spend a little time with you. How have you been?"

"Oh, I'm surviving."

Ellis didn't quite know how to proceed. For lack of anything better to say, he ventured, "Listen, why don't we go out into the garden? It's such a glorious day." Ellis volunteered to make some tea for them. He told Lily to go on out.

They sipped their tea contentedly, though Ellis remained disturbed by the distant look in her eyes. Lily seemed as bereft as she had the day of Jeremy's funeral. But Ellis sensed it was a new grief that troubled Lily: most likely Harry's visit, and his threat of divorce. Ellis was sure she'd taken it to heart.

After they had exchanged small niceties for longer than he could bear, Ellis took the initiative, careful to be gentle at first.

"Lily, I know something's wrong. What is it?"

"Wrong?" Lily sounded nearly hysterical. "What could be wrong, other than the fact that my son is dead? Oh, Ellis, every night I wish that I could go to sleep and never wake up! I just don't want to live in a world without Jeremy."

She began to shake and sob as he had never seen her in all the months since Jeremy's death. Ellis held her close, the way he'd longed to, patting her back and saying softly, "Please don't say that, Lily darling—don't say that. You have so much to live for."

Even after she regained control of herself, Ellis knew he couldn't run the risk of leaving her alone that night. He cleared his throat and asked, "Lily, could I impose upon you just this once? It's a long drive, and I don't feel like going back; I'm tired."

Lily nodded. She seemed too distracted to comprehend the degree of his concern.

Mrs. Gallagher let him know how relieved she was to have him there. "I'm sure glad you're staying. I'll get the room ready for you. I've been so worried about the missus I can't sleep nights."

After Lily was in bed, Ellis brought her a mug of warm milk with a healthy slug of brandy and honey, then tucked the eiderdown in about her gently. "Sleep well now."

But it was Ellis whose sleep was restless. Keeping a lonely vigil, he strained for the sound of weeping from her room next door, and twice tiptoed in to check on her.

But miraculously Lily slept through the night. At six o'clock, hearing Mrs. Gallagher in the kitchen, he got up and dressed. "I'm going down to New York and I'll be back in about five hours. Mrs. Kohle is sleeping right now, but could you please check on her every half-hour or so? And when she wakes up, don't leave her alone."

"I'll do that, Mr. Knox."

He arrived in New York at just nine o'clock. Chatwick's was not yet open, but he hammered on the door until they let him in.

The chefs bustled about in the kitchen, carting juicy roasts, savory pies, and newly baked bread back and forth. Ellis selected a succulent tarragon chicken, along with pâté, French bread, imported cheeses, several elegant fruit tarts, and chocolates and had them all packed in a willow hamper lined in blue-and-white-checked cloth along with cutlery, two crystal glasses, and a crisp '49 Chablis.

With the hamper stowed in the trunk of the car, he turned the key in the ignition and drove back up to the farm. He knew that it seemed quixotic to drive five hours for a picnic basket, but if the gesture pleased Lily and helped take her mind off her sorrows, it was well worth the effort.

At eleven he was driving down the dirt road again, and the dust had barely settled before he was inside the farmhouse, calling, "Lily, get your jacket. We're going for a drive."

She was in the kitchen. Mrs. Gallagher had actually gotten her to help knead some dough for bread. Lily balked at the suggestion of a picnic, but Ellis was firm. He feared that if he passively accepted her refusal, she would sink still deeper into her depression.

"Get your jacket, woman. We're going out."

Lily was angry as they drove down the front drive. "What right do you have to do this?" she demanded. "I told you I didn't want to go."

"That's too bad," Ellis said easily. "Since I'm in the driver's seat."

Ellis took secret delight in her fierce reaction; even anger was preferable to apathy.

Gaze averted, she maintained a cold silence as Ellis drove down the country lanes. Of all people, she had expected him to understand. And now, suddenly he had become a stranger, at once arrogant and domineering.

He pulled off the road and parked near a grassy clearing in the midst of a grove of maple trees. The sunlight glowed as the lightest of breezes rippled over the field, but Lily did not notice or appreciate the pleasant scene.

Ellis took a steamer blanket out of the trunk and walked to Lily's side of the car; he opened the door and offered her his hand. Lily frowned but let him lead her to the meadow and settle her on the blanket. As Ellis smoothed out the checked cloth, Lily surveyed the food in the hamper.

"Ellis," she cried, "you didn't go all the way to Chatwick's for these things, did you?"

Ellis grinned.

"I wish you hadn't. I'm really not worth all this trouble."

"I'm a better judge of that than you, don't you think?"

Pouring the wine, he continued. "Lily, I was terribly worried about you last night, you know."

"Why?"

"All this talk about wanting to go to sleep and never waking up. That frightened me."

"I'm sorry. That's the way I feel."

"Lily, will you please tell me what happened when I was in London?"

"I don't want to talk about it."

"But this time you *are* going to talk about it!"

"Ellis, can't you just leave me alone?"

Taking her shoulders, he forced her to look into his eyes, and when she tried to wrench away, he held her even more tightly. He was not going to allow her to escape—not this time.

But his gentle, caring touch had an effect on her. Ellis was such a good friend. Tears streamed down her cheeks. Choking back the sobs, she told Ellis everything that weighed so heavily on her mind.

"Oh God, Ellis!" she cried. "I can't help feeling as if Harry drove Jeremy to it. The thought tortures me, day and night. It's terrible, it's unfair, and I know it. But I just can't get it out of my mind, and I feel so guilty about even having those thoughts! After all, Jeremy was Harry's child, too, and I know in my heart that he would never have wished anything evil for him."

And with that she lost all control. She wept violently, but as Ellis cradled her head on his shoulder once again, he knew that this was a different kind of storm.

Her tears released a flood of revelations. The truth of it was, for however much she blamed Harry, she equally blamed herself. She was Jeremy's mother, after all. Shouldn't she have realized how pressured he felt, how despondent he'd become? If Jeremy had died of an accident or illness, she would have gone through that normal period of bereavement, but it was the way he had died that had tormented her. She felt she had failed him, that she could have done something to prevent what he had done. Hadn't she, in all honesty, projected her own guilt onto Harry because she couldn't bear it? She had made him the scapegoat in hopes of alleviating her pain. Oh, not deliberately, of course. But gradually, over the time she'd spent at the farm, she came to understand what—albeit subconsciously—she had done. But deep down she knew she was to blame. Drew's haunting indictment should have been directed at her too.

At long last, Ellis broke the silence. "You realize, don't you," he said quietly, "that you have a choice to make? And the only one who can make it is you. The point is, do you still love Harry? Because if you do, you have to forgive him."

Lily knew how much she had hurt Harry by staying away. But she'd been so fearful of the words she might use against him—in anger or in grief. She had stayed away in part to preserve what remnant of their marriage was still left. But now it was time for her to take positive action. If she still loved Harry, she must.

Even Ellis sensed the change in her emotion. She was at a crossroads and knew it. Ellis hoped against hope she would tell him, "No, I don't love Harry any longer." But Lily turned her green eyes upon him and said, "The point is, Ellis, do you think Harry still loves me?"

With a pang, Ellis knew he would have to tell her the truth. "Yes, Lily. I'm sure of it. Now would you like me to drive you home? And I don't mean the farm."

Softly, she murmured, "Oh, Ellis, I always seem to be saying the same thing to you. You're such a dear friend. What would I do without you?"

# Chapter 29

IT was twilight as Ellis's car rolled over the Triborough Bridge. The lights of the city were just beginning to turn on. Lily, who since Jeremy's death had done everything she could to push thoughts of Harry from her mind, was suddenly obsessed with learning about his emotional state. She was hungry for any information Ellis might give her.

"How has Harry been? Has he been working? Oh Ellis—tell me."

For a moment, he thought of Valerie. Then he recalled the way Harry had looked just yesterday, how low he'd sunk. "He's been writing. But lately, I think he's slowed down a bit. It's been hard for him"—Ellis hesitated—"with you gone."

When they pulled up in front of Lily's building, Ellis carried her bags inside for her. "I imagine it would be best for you to go up alone."

"Yes," she said slowly. Then, turning, she embraced him and the warmth of her kiss lingered on his cheek as she looked into his eyes. "Thank you . . . for everything."

Harry was in the middle of his third Scotch when he heard the key in the lock. Angrily he thought, Valerie again. Several times in the past few days she had come over uninvited, and each time he had sent her away. But it seemed she couldn't take the hint. Harry cursed himself for ever having become involved with her. Hearing footsteps click on the parquet floor, he rose rather unsteadily and shouted, "Go away!" But speech left him the second he saw Lily framed in the archway.

At the sight of him, she almost gasped. My God, she thought, he looks dreadful. A five-day growth of beard dotted his chin;

his eyes were bloodshot and ringed by dark circles. His clothes looked as if he had slept in them and hung loosely, revealing how much weight he'd lost in the past few weeks. A choking pall of cigarette smoke hung over the room.

Even without the empty bottles littering the coffee table Lily would have known that he had been drinking heavily.

As he stared at her mutely, Lily thought in anguish, *What have I done to cause this?*

"Harry?" she began uncertainly, "I've come home. . . ."

Without a word, he staggered over to her, flung his arms around her, and began to cry.

She couldn't understand the fierce, inarticulate things he was mumbling—but she knew what he was trying to convey. Tears coursed down her own cheeks—tears of love, of guilt, of gladness to be in his arms once again.

Finally, raising his head, he looked at her with burning eyes. "Is it really you or am I hallucinating?"

"It's me, Harry."

"Oh God, I've missed you so!"

Drawing her down onto the sofa, Harry swept her into his arms once again, stroking her hair and kissing her hungrily.

"Harry, I want to explain—"

"Lily, I don't want to know why you went away," he interrupted, "or why you stayed away so long. All I care about is that you're back."

# Chapter 30

TEN months had passed since Jeremy's death, and though Lily and Harry had reconciled, their guilt surrounding that death still plagued them. In some ways little had changed, for all their mutual pledges.

At first, sensing that Harry didn't want to talk about him, Lily was careful to avoid all mention of Jeremy. Later, she found it only natural to reminisce about his childhood, about his early years. But Harry seemed to want to blot out all memory of the boy. He cringed every time Lily spoke his name.

For however much Harry tried not to react, and however much Lily tried not to bring up Jeremy, the two of them couldn't help but gravitate to very different ways to handle their grief.

And so, despite all the trials and heartaches they had weathered, and despite Harry's promises to change, Lily found herself back in their Sutton Place apartment as isolated and as aimless as she had been when they first moved to the city.

Harry turned to his writing with renewed dedication while Lily grew more unsure of herself than ever. She questioned everything about herself—her abilities and her own worth. There were many days when she was almost afraid to go out of her own apartment. The prospect of moving into a career the way Ellis had proposed so long ago seemed daunting.

Deep down, Lily knew she must turn her energies somewhere, lest she slip back into the severe depression that had overcome her after Jeremy's death. And she knew she had to carve a niche for herself if she were to survive Harry's withdrawal.

Yet every time Ellis called with new suggestions as to what to do, she was overcome by anxiety and demurred. "I don't think I'm really qualified . . . perhaps something else."

Aware that she was crippled by self-doubts, Ellis determined to force her hand gently. Finally, he hit upon the idea of calling his friend Joan Lawrence. "There is a woman I'm very anxious for you to meet. She's Harry Kohle's wife. She'd like to get involved in some volunteer work. I think she'd be terribly good in the Opera Guild. She lost her oldest son last year, so she has had a rough time recently. What I thought I'd do is have a dinner party for, oh, about ten people, so that you can meet. I think she needs a little push to get herself started again. Are you and George busy Wednesday night?"

"No we're not, and we'd love to come. I'll look forward to meeting her."

As he went down his guest list, he hesitated. He was somehow loath to ask any of the women he dated. It was a quirk he couldn't explain, but somehow he didn't want Lily to sit at the same table with anyone with whom he'd been involved.

For his own dinner partner he chose Judith Gold, his associate for some dozen years. Everyone knew their relationship had always been strictly platonic.

The evening was a great success, as Ellis held court at his usual table at "21," but best of all, Lily seemed to be enjoying herself. He knew that she and Harry almost never went out. Over the years, Harry had become almost a recluse when it came to restaurants; he hated being interrupted to sign autographs for fawning fans. But tonight it was obvious that Lily loved being out on the town for a change. She and Joan took to each other immediately. Before the evening was over, much to Ellis's delight, Lily had become a patron of the Opera Guild.

Lily was soon pleased to be involved and not long after that propitious evening, she also began to work as a volunteer for the March of Dimes, for which Ellis was a trustee.

But she was far from prepared when one evening Joan called. "Lily, how would you like to be chairman of the Spring Ball?"

"Oh, no!" she exclaimed. "I couldn't handle anything like that!" The ball was the biggest fund-raiser of the year.

"Well, Ellis seems to feel that you're eminently qualified."

"He does? Oh no, Joan, please find someone else."

"Well, from what I know of you, I think you'd be fabulous too. You are so good with people, Lily, so good at getting them all to work together."

Joan elicited a reluctant promise from Lily that she would think about it. As soon as Lily hung up, she dialed Ellis.

"How could you? The biggest social event of the year and you're trying to put me in charge?"

"Why not?"

"You know that I've never done anything in my life like this before!"

"Neither had Lindbergh before his solo flight across the Atlantic," came the calm reply.

There was a long pause before she asked again, "You really think that I could do it?"

"You bet."

What she didn't know was that he was going to back her up with more committee support and more money than any chairman had ever had.

He added quietly, "I have every confidence in you."

It was Ellis's unshakable faith that finally swayed her decision. She accepted with trepidation, but the choice proved to be the right thing. After leading such an isolated life, Lily found the challenge exhilarating. She discovered she had talents she little suspected she possessed. What's more, her activities kept her too busy to think about Harry, who was more wrapped up in his work than ever before. Much as she worried and fretted over every detail, this undertaking was a godsend.

Long before the big event, Lily began to wonder what she would do with herself once the ball was over. She dismissed her apprehensions. Something else would turn up, she knew. And to think, weeks ago she'd dreaded even taking this on! Suddenly she had a reason to wake up in the morning, something to occupy her days. More important, she had friends. But most of all, she had what every woman needed: a confidante.

And strangely, that bosom buddy was not one of her newfound friends, but Harry's secretary, Valerie. It was almost a relief that she was not a part of the social scene but was instead like a member of their own family.

Harry's feelings about this budding friendship were apprehensive at best. There was something unseemly about one's wife becoming so friendly with one's discarded mistress, not that Lily could have known.

He wondered if he had made a mistake upon Lily's return in allowing Valerie to stay on. He had fully intended to give her severance pay and a glowing recommendation, but when he'd begun with, "Now that Lily is back, I realize that it would be an untenable situation for you . . . ," she had replied sweetly, "But Harry, there's no reason that we can't continue to work together. I was just happy that I was there when you needed someone. But I love working for you, and you know how important *The Genesis* is to me." Harry was taken aback, but Valerie was insistent. And besides, she was a damned good secretary. She would be tough to replace.

And so it was that one evening, after Lily had invited Valerie to stay for dinner, the two women sat in the drawing room over their coffee. Valerie's expression was sweetly concerned. Lily failed to see the watchfulness in her eyes. Why would she? Lily had never forgotten Valerie's supportiveness, how she had taken over after Jeremy's death.

"Lily, darling, what's wrong? You look so sad tonight."

In truth, she did feel a little disappointed. She had just scored a great coup over arrangements for the ball, and there hadn't been one opportunity yet to tell Harry. He had talked about the novel all through their meal and hadn't even bothered to ask about her day.

"Oh, nothing really . . ."

But Valerie prodded her.

"Well," Lily replied, "it's just that something wonderful happened, and I wanted to tell Harry, but he's so involved with the new work that I didn't have a chance."

"What was it?"

"Oh, I got Benny Goodman for the ball. I guess I just wanted to preen a little bit. It's really a coup."

Valerie feigned sympathy. "I suppose it's difficult to be the wife of a famous author. You must feel rather left out a great deal when Harry and I are talking shop."

"Oh, no—it's just . . . I don't know. . . ."

"Look, Lily, I practically live here and I see what goes on. You don't need to put on a false front. Harry works all day and half the night in the study, and you're lonely."

Lily was startled. "Is it that obvious?"

"Only to me. I'm sure that Harry doesn't realize it. Maybe it takes a woman to know another woman."

"If only once in a while Harry would discuss something else . . . ask me about what *I'm* doing. I know I shouldn't complain, and I'm glad that the work seems to be going so well, but—"

Gently Valerie touched Lily's hand. "It's hard on a woman when a man's whole life is his work. I like and admire Harry, but sometimes I do think that he overdoes it. He really ought to try to spend more time with you . . . not that it's any of my business."

In reality, Valerie did everything she could to promote Harry's obsession with *The Genesis*—not that he needed that much encouragement. She was always there early in the morning and never too tired to work with him late into the night.

On occasion he would say, "Listen, Valerie, we're going to knock off early. I want to take Lily out to dinner tonight; I've made reservations at the club."

But Valerie would reply, "Does she know about it? She told me that she was going to be so busy this evening with her telephoning, she wouldn't have a second to spare. You know, you don't realize how busy she is—she almost has more of a career than you do. She really seems to have found her métier with this charity ball. I've never seen her so happy."

Shrugging, he said, "Well, why don't you call and cancel, then," and turned back to his writing. At least Lily was happy.

But Valerie was not. Harry had not slept with her again since Lily's return. Secretly she longed to know if he was sleeping with his wife. What kind of love life could they have? she asked herself. Harry often didn't go to bed until very late, and he was up and about early in the morning. That didn't leave much time to romance his wife.

But still, she had to know positively, and once again Valerie turned to Lily—sweet, kindhearted, seemingly without guile.

"I loved my ex-husband, Ken, so much," Valerie said, with a little sad smile, "but he simply couldn't live without other women. And when our marriage finally broke up, I just couldn't think about falling in love again. I was too deeply hurt."

Then, almost idly, she said, "Funny, isn't it, how women

can get along quite contentedly without a love life for a long, long time. I know that I have, but men can't seem to survive more than a day or two without."

"I don't know about that. Harry seems to survive," Lily said wryly.

Secretly Valerie rejoiced. If Harry and Lily were not making love, that could spell doom for their marriage.

"Don't you ever get frustrated, having a husband who is married to his work?"

"Between the two of us, I do."

As time passed, Valerie continued to feed Lily's discontent—and ironically, Lily always ended with the greatest of accolades. "Oh, Valerie, you're so understanding. You're just an angel. . . . I don't know what I would do if I didn't have you to talk to."

Valerie smiled. She was still determined to snare Harry. Cottoning up to Lily was all part of her plan. She sensed how disturbed Lily was about the subject of lovemaking. She determined to make the most of it.

The subject had troubled Lily long before she and Valerie discussed it. Lily and Harry never made love anymore. During the years of their marriage, there had been many periods when they had not made love frequently, for one reason or another—but infrequency had never lapsed into abstention such as this.

In ways, Jeremy's suicide and its aftermath remained the irreconcilable barrier between them. She had never truly forgiven Harry for his role in Jeremy's self-destruction, and he had never forgiven her for abandoning him. They still had the other children to think of, though Drew seldom came home, even for vacations. Even Randy and Melissa kept themselves scarce.

Now, between the charity work which kept her so busy and Harry's novel, they had little in common to talk about. While they both did their best to remain amicable, each of them was harboring grudges that would only fester with time.

Valerie was the one to work at the chinks in the armor they'd worked so hard to construct around their tender selves. Yet even Valerie could not have contrived the master stroke Harry himself delivered.

One evening as the three sat over dinner, Harry said quite

matter-of-factly, "Lily, there's something I've been meaning to tell you. I've got to go to Israel to do some research."

"Oh? How long will it take?"

He hesitated. "Well, six months to a year, anyway."

"A year?" she repeated. "And when do you have to go?"

"I'd like to be over there by the beginning of next week."

"Harry, I have the ball to think of. I'm committed—you know that!"

"Well, my dear, I'm committed also, and I think that my work is more important, frankly, than some social event."

Lily was infuriated by Harry's casual dismissal of her work. And once again, he was informing her of a major decision concerning them, announcing it as fait accompli. In her head she replayed the long-ago conversation: "I bought this property yesterday, Lily." "Without even asking me?"

She had given in then and had even apologized for resenting his high-handedness. But once again, Harry had failed to consult her. He hadn't even taken her into his confidence about a major change in their lives. He hadn't so much as hinted to her what he was planning, even though it meant pulling up stakes and disrupting every facet of their existence.

Of course, he expected her to give in—and she could; she could probably even get someone else to fill in for her as chairman, and the children would not be home for vacation for some time. But a little rebellious voice whispered, "Why should I always have to be the one who gives in?"

All through her married life, she had given in and smoothed things over even when she knew that she was in the right. But she too had needs, maybe as important as his. Perhaps her work was not as significant, but it was significant to her, if only for the sense of accomplishment it gave her.

And suddenly, she knew that for once she would hold her ground. She wouldn't give in. Not this time . . .

Her voice carefully modulated, with no trace of bitterness, she said, "Of course, Harry, your work is the most important thing. I'm not denying that. But it's only a few months until the ball—couldn't the research wait that long? It would mean a great deal to me and that way we could take the children too."

"Look, Lily, I'm not going to alter all my arrangements because you're involved with this ball. You don't understand that the creative process can't be put on hold. Rafi and Tony are leaving next week, and Valerie's following the next day."

Valerie knew already . . . her dearest friend, and she hadn't said one word?

But she had to swallow the hurt. "Harry, I've undertaken a commitment—and frankly, I don't feel that I can just walk away from it."

"Oh come on, Lily," he said with mounting irritation, "I don't mean to offend you, but no one is indispensable."

Not that Harry wouldn't apply the term to himself. With a growing sense of irony, she heard him add, "There must be a lot of women with time on their hands who'd jump at the chance to take over your position."

With rising anger, she realized how trivial Harry considered her work. But dammit, it wasn't to her. "Harry, what you say may be true, but I'm simply going to have to stay here until the ball is over. That way I can make arrangements for Randy and Melissa. Maybe they'll want to join me, but if not I'll need to settle them at camp."

But all Harry said was, "You're not going with me. Well, that's more or less par for the course, isn't it?"

"Harry, you just don't understand! I'd been looking for something worthwhile to do for so long. Then this came up, and now you're asking me to abandon it halfway through."

Coldly, Harry inquired, "Being my wife isn't something worthwhile? You're tired of that role?"

"No, of course not!" Lily cried. "I just want to accomplish something—do something I can point to, something to be proud of!"

"Well, that's all very well and good, but the fact of the matter is that I have to go to Israel now, not in six weeks' time."

"I'm not asking you to give up your work. I'm just asking you to put off this particular trip, so that I can go with you!"

Harry threw down his napkin, pushed back his chair, and snapped, "I'm not going to argue with you about this; if you're not in a position to come along, or not of a mind to, then don't. It's your decision; I've gotten used to your leaving me!"

When he had gone and she and Valerie were left alone, Lily asked quietly, "Valerie, why didn't you tell me about this?"

Reaching out and taking her hand, Valerie exclaimed, "Oh,

Lily, I only just found out about it myself. You know how Harry is. He's so impulsive when it comes to *The Genesis.* He told me yesterday. I really thought it was his place to tell you. To be honest, I thought he'd discussed it with you first. . . ." Her voice trailed off.

"And the way he told me when he finally did. He virtually commanded me to come along," mourned Lily. "If only he had said that he *wanted* me, and asked me to please give up the chairmanship. That's all he would have had to say, and I would have been happy to do it. He makes me feel so trivial—everything I am, everything I do."

Squeezing her hand, Valerie murmured, "Men just don't understand, do they?"

Lily sighed. "Well, regardless, it's my duty to go with him, he is my husband. And I can come home when the kids get out of school."

As Valerie saw Lily begin to waver, she knew she had to intercede. "Oh, I don't know. I think it's time for you to make your declaration of independence. Stay and finish up, wait for Randy and Melissa, and then come out to Israel. Show Harry you really care about the things you do."

Lily hesitated uncertainly. "I just wish he'd think of me for a change."

"Well, that's what every woman wants, Lily. But more than that, Harry just doesn't realize what an enormous responsibility the chairmanship is. And it's not so unimportant. This ball raises hundreds of thousands of dollars. Can you, in good conscience, leave them in the lurch?"

Lily hesitated. "Well, I don't know if I'm all that indispensable, but at this stage it would be difficult for someone else to step in."

"Well then, what choice do you really have? Stay here and let Harry miss you for a little while. I hate to say it, but Harry just assumes he'll always get his way."

"I don't know, Valerie. . . . I'm just so confused. . . ."

Sensing Lily weaken, Valerie cannily unleashed her ultimate weapon. "And had you thought about Ellis, Lily? How would he feel if you abandon the ball, when he went out on a limb to get you the chairmanship?"

"I hadn't even thought of that."

"Well?"

It was Ellis who decided her. "You're right. I can't do that to him. And a couple of months is not really such a long time."

Valerie could hardly hide her sense of triumph as she bid Lily good night. Once home, she gloated. Her plans were working out beautifully, beyond her wildest dreams. She and Harry would be alone in Israel for almost two months! And out there, with the desert moon overhead, and the soft breezes wafting in from the Mediterranean . . .

Meanwhile, Harry and Lily lay side by side in hostile silence. Finally Lily spoke. "Harry, I've come to a decision."

"Yes?"

"Since I have undertaken a responsibility to the March of Dimes, I don't feel that I can drop it. I'll come over as soon as the ball is over and I know what the children are doing for the summer."

"Whatever you like," he said coolly, though he felt a smoldering rage.

She was abandoning him once again! It had been less than a year that she had left him after Jeremy's death and now she was willing to part from him again.

Guilt and anger washed over him. He couldn't shake the feeling that all this had something to do with Jeremy. Lily wouldn't really stay for a ball. Abruptly Harry got out of bed, went to the study, and poured himself a stiff drink. He wound up sleeping on the sofa. He just couldn't stand to be in the same bed with Lily that night.

# Chapter 31

THE next week, Lily and Harry walked into the El Al waiting room at Idlewild and were greeted by the most extraordinary sight they had ever seen. It was a kaleidoscope of color, sound, and smells, as a dizzying array of humanity jostled for space in the huge waiting room. It was February of 1951, and the tide of immigration to Israel was rising as never before, accompanied by enormous fund-raising efforts for the newly formed state.

There were scores of middle-aged Jewish women from New York on a mission for Hadassah who spoke rapid, broken English interspersed with Yiddish.

And there were Baptist ministers and their wives, all with thick southern accents. Twenty-five Italians from Chicago were going to the Holy Land to make a novena.

Most alien of all were the Hasidim, whose long earlocks fell from under wide-brimmed hats. The little Hasidic boys were exact miniature replicas of their fathers, minus the beards. The wives sat in close ranks, so much alike in their identical brown wigs and ill-fitting black dresses, it would have been impossible to tell them apart. Each woman guarded a mammoth brown paper bag bulging with kosher foods, emanating pungent odors of herring and kosher pickles.

The Hasidim could not be too safe, it seemed, or too cautious. Even the kosher food served aboard El Al was suspect; no Hasid ever traveled without his own supply.

Lily noted with surprise that there was even a small contingent of Japanese, huddled together with their canvas bags. It seemed that Israel, among other things, represented a potential market, and the Japanese, attempting to rebound from the economic devastation of the war, were leaving no stone unturned in pursuit of new markets.

In sharp contrast to the colorful ethnic assemblage, there were several elegantly dressed ladies representing the United Jewish Appeal. Their mission was to absorb inspiration from Israel's enormous need, then return to the United States to impart to others the urgency of supporting Israel.

As the time approached for boarding, Lily steeled herself for the moment when Harry and she would say their good-byes. The last week things had been strained between them. She was hoping that somehow she would find the right words so they might part on a positive note.

Now that he was actually leaving, she had a sudden panicky feeling that she had made the wrong decision, that she should be waiting, bags packed, to board with him.

But the waiting room provided distraction. It had become more and more crowded as the departure time approached, and the air was so thick with the scents of perfume, perspiration, and delicatessen that Lily began to hope they'd soon board.

But a full five hours after the scheduled departure time, no boarding announcement had come. Harry had gone up and inquired several times, but was given the same evasive reply each time: As soon as the plane was ready, the announcement would be made to board.

Then, quite suddenly, a young Israeli materialized and picked up the microphone. An expectant stir ran through the crowd.

"Ladies and gentlemen," she announced calmly. "There will be a delay in the departure of flight number 638. Please feel free to visit the duty-free shops, but stay within the El Al boarding area in order to hear any further announcements. Thank you for your cooperation."

She repeated the announcement in Hebrew and French.

Lily and Harry exchanged impatient looks. Five hours late, and that was all El Al had to say? All around them, there was evidence of other travelers' restlessness and discontent.

The only ones who appeared calm and unflurried were the Hasidim. Nonchalantly, the wives opened their brown paper bags and passed out mammoth corned-beef sandwiches on dark Russian rye, along with kosher dills and paper cups of cream soda. The elegant ladies representing Israeli bonds looked on in disgust. They clucked their tongues in disapproving criticism. But Harry watched with increasing fascination. He was only too glad for something to take his mind off his perhaps not so imminent departure.

Ever since he had broken the news of his trip to Lily, he had been unable to concentrate on the work that lay ahead of him. However hard he tried to deny it to himself, her refusal to accompany him had troubled him deeply. Over and over he asked himself why, but rational analysis seemed beyond him. He could only be overwhelmed by bitterness. Once again, she was deserting him at a critical juncture.

All week there had been an uneasy truce between them as he assembled the material he would need for his prolonged stay, while she vainly tried to proceed with the ball preparations as though everything were normal. Nevertheless, it had been a very silent ride this morning to the airport.

Now, however, as he watched the Hasidim, he began to forget his anger. He was strangely drawn to these people with their air of being set apart. They seemed somehow like the Patriarchs of old, the mortar that held Judaism together. They, of all Jews, still truly kept the faith, the ancient covenant.

It was quite different from anything he had known. The Kohles had been comfortable in their Judaism, true to their beliefs. Harry had been the only one ever to marry a Gentile. But they had belonged to a Reform congregation and had never observed kosher laws. In fact, they regarded the observance as being antiquated.

However, as he began in *The Genesis* to explore the character of a man who had been the fulcrum of the struggle to bring about the new Israel, he had begun to explore what Judaism really meant.

According to the anthropologists, their race should have been extinct centuries ago. But something had brought them together as a people, through centuries of Diaspora and persecution. There were the beliefs and rituals and holy days of Judaism—but fundamentally, the strength of the Jews seemed to lie in the fact that they simply refused to be beaten. Here they were, alive and thriving in the twentieth century even after the horrifying, horrendous revelations of Buchenwald and Dachau. These were an indomitable people; the roses of

Zion—still blooming through the broken headstones on the Mount of Olives while battle had raged all about them—were an apt emblem.

Standing in the midst of this mass of humanity bound for their Promised Land, Harry was filled with an intense awareness of his heritage as a Jew. He thanked the Lord that he was a writer. For now he was going to the source, where he was going to give birth to *The Genesis,* the novel that would reveal the inner strength and hardiness of his race.

He thought again of Lily, how, as a Gentile, she could ill appreciate the significance of this journey—*she really doesn't understand at all how important this is to me, how The Genesis is not merely a book, but a mission—and how much I need her standing behind me. . . .*

And so they sat with their separate thoughts, close enough to touch each other, but already on opposite sides of an unbridgeable gap.

"Maybe we should inquire again about why there is such a delay," she suggested.

"I doubt they'll tell us anything. I'm sure it has something to do with security."

There was a strained silence, and then he said stiffly, "There's no need for you to stay if you're getting tired."

"Of course I'm staying, until you're safely in the air."

There was no further conversation between them, as Harry took out his briefcase and began leafing through his notes.

Finally a voice came over the loudspeaker. "Ladies and gentlemen, we have received word that El Al flight number 638 was delayed in Tel Aviv due to security problems. It is now in the air and should be in New York in less than three hours. El Al wishes to thank you for your patience."

There was a collective moan. The elegant ladies of the United Jewish Appeal looked positively wilted. There was no question that they would not have scorned the bag lunches of the Hasidim at this point. Only the Japanese bore the same impassive looks as upon their arrival.

Meanwhile the voice continued. "El Al has arranged for a meal to be served at the airport hotel. If you will kindly go to the second landing, there will be buses to take you there. Passes will be issued as you leave. Again, El Al thanks you."

Thankful for the prospect of a break from the now-familiar waiting room, everyone but the Hasidim got up stiffly, stretched, and filed out. There was a bumpy bus ride to the hotel, and then the bedraggled would-be travelers straggled wearily into the dining room.

The hostess said briskly, "All right, those who take kosher, stand to the right, the others to the left."

"Kosher?" inquired a Baptist lady curiously. "What does that mean, Clyde?"

"I believe," drawled her husband, "they got some kinda rule says they can't eat a piece of meat along with their milk at the same time."

"Well, I declare!" she said, staring in wonder at those assembling in the kosher line.

The kitchen staff had geared up for the invasion, and as the meat eaters sat to one side and the dairy to the other, the meals began to arrive.

The meat eaters were given a choice of Mendelbaum lamb or chicken frozen dinners in paper containers. The lamb was tough, while the kasha tasted like glue—but the chicken eaters fared no better. The birds were gamey and stringy. The mashed potatoes were soggy. After one taste, the Baptists shoved them aside and made a meal of their Kaiser rolls, defiantly spreading them with butter. But the dairy group had a feast. Back and forth went platters of lox and whitefish, herring in sour cream, dill pickles, Greek olives, cottage, Swiss cheese and cream cheese, potato salad and cole slaw, along with bagels, rolls, and rye bread. To top it off, they ate luscious apple strudel with a perfect flaky crust while the meat group watched enviously. But before anyone was barely finished, another announcement was made: they had five minutes to assemble in the lobby for the buses to take them back to the El Al terminal.

When they were back in the waiting room once again, the travelers' patience had worn thin. Nine hours, Lily thought, closing her lids wearily over aching eyes. How much longer would they be kept waiting?

The long-awaited announcement finally came. "Ladies and gentlemen, we are now ready to board. El Al thanks you for your patience. Have an enjoyable trip. Shalom."

Lily's fatigue was suddenly replaced by alarm as Harry stood up to go through the line. What could they say to one another as they parted? She didn't want Harry to leave with this rift between them still. But pride prevented her from saying the words she might have said. She would have abandoned the ball, all her obligations, half her life for him. In truth, all she wanted was to be first in his life, to mean more to him than anything else, even his work. And she knew that if Harry were to say, even then, at the very last minute, "Darling, I can't bear to be parted from you. Please come with me!" she would reply, "I'll be on the next plane."

But all he said, after a long, searching look, was, "Take care of yourself, Lily."

"You too." She tried to smile through lips stiff with misery.

If she had only known that in truth Harry longed to say, "Dammit, Lily, I love you! Come with me!" But he too had his pride. If she didn't want to come, he wouldn't beg her. He couldn't bear to have his appeal rejected yet again. But as he turned and handed his ticket to the attendant, his heart ached with a misery he had rarely known. She was being so unfair to him. This latest separation only conjured the horrors of the last one and the awful reason for it. If Harry was pulling away from Lily, it was mainly because her refusal to go with him made him feel all her blame again.

The truth was that he had loved her from the moment he had met her and would love her until the day he died. And that at this moment he was so angry with her that he almost wished he didn't.

And so they stood, imprisoned by unspoken griefs, silenced by their pride. They kissed each other lightly on the lips, then clung to one another for a long moment before Harry turned and mounted the stairs to the plane.

She waved, tears welling up in her eyes as she vainly wished she could have said what was in her heart.

# Chapter 32

HARRY sat by the window, staring out into the darkness, feeling disgruntled and confused. It was almost five in the morning before the propeller-driven plane finally revved up its motors, taxied down the runway, and, after a mercifully brief wait for clearance, took off. From the length and breadth of the plane there was a collective sigh of relief as the giant bird became airborne.

Shortly after the No Smoking sign was turned off, a clipped young Yankee voice came over the intercom. "This is Captain Mordecai Ben Levi speaking."

It seemed an unlikely name, but in truth the captain had grown up in New England as Morton Benjamin and had changed his name when he had emigrated a few years before—against his family's wishes—to join the Israeli air force in its struggle for the new nation.

"On behalf of El Al, I would like to welcome you aboard and apologize for the delay. If all goes according to schedule, and allowing for a fuel stop, we should arrive in Tel Aviv tomorrow morning about six a.m. local time. Shalom."

After repeating the message in Hebrew and French, he switched off the intercom, unbuttoned his shirt at the neck, and relaxed behind the steering gear.

As the head stewardess came up behind him, he turned and asked in fluent Hebrew, "Well, Hava, how is everything up front?"

"Don't ask," she said wryly. "Nothing but complaints. Many of them are threatening never to fly El Al again. I overheard one lady say that it was 'so typically Jewish.' "

Ben Levi frowned and said tightly, "I wish you'd told her it was 'so typically Arab.' It took them most of the night hours to check out that sabotage threat. They were damned decent to tip us off about a nonexistent bomb! Dirty bastards."

Hava nodded sympathetically, then returned to the cabin, where the stewardesses had taken off their jackets and put on aprons to serve a light breakfast. They knew that there was nothing like a snack to soothe frayed nerves, and before the disgruntled passengers could say "Mazel tov," the trays appeared in front of them.

Soon afterward, overhead lights were turned off, seats tilted back, and children and adults alike bedded down under blankets. Soon a light chorus of snores rose above the faint drone of the plane's motors.

As the strains of the long delay were forgotten, even Harry found himself drifting off as the plane sped through the darkness. At sunrise, however, there was a rude awakening. The Hasidim had assembled for the minyan. They stood in the aisles, chanting and rocking back and forth as they began the morning prayer. All around, eyes opened and heads popped up.

Bells rang indignantly, and one of the Hadassah ladies almost hissed, "This is ridiculous! Can't you do something to keep them quiet?"

Apologetically, the stewardesses shrugged. "I am sorry, madam. We have no right to stop them."

"Well, at least they should be put in the back of the plane!"

"I'll make that suggestion. Now, may I perhaps bring you a cup of coffee?"

"Yes, please—and two aspirin."

Hers was not the worst difficulty. The minyan was stationed in front of the lavatories. One man in particular blocked the way. He made no attempt to move, even at the request of a woman whose pregnancy was so far advanced she looked about to deliver.

He continued to sway and chant. No earthly voice must come between him and his ritual. Angrily, the pregnant woman's husband joined her and said menacingly, "My wife urgently needs to use the bathroom. Will you move, sir?"

But the man wouldn't budge, nor would he reply. The

husband was finally forced to steer the Hasid out of the way. The man continued his prayers, not missing a beat.

Harry observed the scene with growing fascination. From the moment he had entered the waiting room at the airport, he had been struck by the clash between East and West, the old customs and the new, even among the Jewish passengers. In some ways these different strains were intertwined and beholden one to another. He was determined to divine the nature of the ancient bond. It was for this reason that Israel drew him, to the source.

After a day and a night of what seemed an eternity, Captain Ben Levi's voice finally crackled over the intercom. "Ladies and gentlemen . . . we are beginning our final descent into Tel Aviv. Please fasten your seat belts and extinguish all cigarettes. On behalf of the crew of El Al flight 638, I would like to thank you for your patience and wish you a joyous stay in Israel. Shalom."

An "ahhhh" ran through the passengers at the thought of the Holy Land. Suddenly, without warning, several voices started to sing the Hatikvah, Israel's national anthem. Other voices joined in.

Craning his neck, Harry caught his first glimpse of Israel's shores, gleaming in the morning light, and a feeling of sudden joy suffused him. The fatigue, the inconvenience, the long wait—even parting from Lily—suddenly seemed insignificant. He was here at last!

The crowd pushed and jostled their way off the plane and then surged toward the luggage carts. The scene was overpoweringly emotional as families, friends, children, and young women cried and hugged, welcomed back their loved ones. As Harry patiently waited for his baggage to emerge, the first thrill of arrival had begun to fade. Suddenly he felt very tired. He didn't have much hope that anyone would be there to meet him.

Then from behind him he heard a voice calling, "Harry! Harry!"

Whirling, he saw Valerie making her way through the crowd. It was good to see a familiar face.

"I'm so glad you're here," he cried.

"I'm glad you finally made it. Christ! Talk about delays! What happened? You must be beat."

"I certainly am. Do we have a car?"

"Outside. Everything is all arranged; you don't have a thing to worry about."

"Great. I think the effort of trying to hire a car and driver at this point would just about finish me off."

"You're going to love the villa I've found in Safed, or Tsefat as the Israelis call it. There's plenty of room for all of us."

"If you picked it out, Valerie, I'm sure that it will be fine."

Suddenly a dark young Israeli materialized beside them. "Your bags have been taken care of, Mr. Kohle."

"Harry, this is Yossi, our driver." She added, "When the Jewish Agency here heard that the famous Harry Kohle was going to write a book set in Israel, they rolled out the red carpet. Be prepared. You're going to be wined and dined."

"I could look forward to that," said Harry, pleased that anyone in Israel would want to make a fuss.

The main road from Tel Aviv to Jerusalem led southeast through the mountains of Judea. To one side was the deep gorge that separated Israel from Jordan. On the horizon were the tower-crowned hills of Micph. The sight was as breathtaking as it was awesome: young trees, pine, eucalyptus, and cedar, had been planted among the ancient boulders.

In the growing glow of the morning sun, Harry could see burned-out trucks nestled among the rocks and trees—a jarring testimony to the thousands of brave men killed in the defense of besieged Jerusalem during the 1948 war of independence. This was the only monument these heroes had.

As they went through the Valley of Ajalon, where Joshua had commanded the sun to stand still, the highway divided. The road approaching the inn at Bab-el-Wed was open only to small vehicles. Buses and heavy trucks had to detour to the left.

As they took the narrower road upward, Harry caught his last glimpse of the Mediterranean. It seemed to him a passage back through the centuries as they made their way past Abu Ghosh with its once majestic Crusader church, near the site of the ancient Gibeonite town of Kiryath-Jearim; and then through the modern farming settlement of Kiryat Anavim.

Finally, they rounded a curve and there it was: Jerusalem.

"Pull over, Yossi," Harry said suddenly. "I want to take a look."

As Harry and Valerie walked together to the crest, Jerusalem stood like a jewel among the surrounding hills, golden as the sun. Harry knew that words would fail him if he tried to convey the myriad feelings the site inspired. No artist could do justice to this view, no poet could capture the image.

Far in the distance lay the old city. Above the ancient wall was the golden Dome of the Rock, the Moslem shrine. Harry could hear the muezzins calling from the minarets while the church bells of the basilica tolled somberly.

To one side lay the Mount of Olives, a gentle incline covered with ancient, twisted trees and beyond, in the distance, was the dusty white limestone line of the Judean hills.

How many millions of lives had been ground into that dust over the centuries? Harry couldn't help but wonder.

The tinkling of a bell brought him out of his reverie. He turned to see an Arab boy leading his donkey down the hill behind them to cross the road.

Taking one last look, he savored these first impressions, committing them to memory. But as he turned away from the sight of the exalted place, his joy began to be tinged with anger and regret. Lily should have been here to share this moment with him.

An hour later, the Mercedes was gliding slowly through the streets toward the King David Hotel. It was magnificent, with high colonnaded arches, smooth stone walls and floors, all befitting the king for whom it was named. In the lobby there were huge urns of fresh flowers. Bunches of people conversed amicably together around low tables.

It was a strange irony that such an oasis of culture and civility could exist, when only twenty feet beyond, Jordanian snipers sat behind turrets above the old walled city with guns pointed toward the Israeli sector, ready to shoot on sight anyone attempting to enter the Damascus gate.

There had been no Jordan before 1918—only a sparse population of Bedouins. But after the First World War, Winston Churchill had sat—perhaps in this very spot—and decreed that Palestine was to have another Arab state.

If the stated aim of the Balfour Declaration, to establish a Jewish homeland in Palestine, ever became a reality, Churchill felt that a buffer state would be needed between the Jews and the Arabs.

In addition, he wanted to repay a favor to his friend Abdullah ibn Hussein for the aid he had given Britain during the war and thus had persuaded Parliament to bestow this strategic piece of real estate upon the Hussein family and allow them to establish a state and a monarchy where none had existed for centuries.

And so, Transjordan had come into existence, and instead of being a buffer, it was the bitterest enemy of the new state of Israel.

As the golden sun climbed to reach its zenith, Harry's mind gradually drifted from the treacheries of twentieth-century politics to the Mosaic world of the first millennium. It was these thoughts he was entertaining when he saw the Wailing Wall for the first time. The Wall was not a place Harry could ever examine up close—it would be death for a Jew to approach it. But as he stared at it from a distance, it seemed to him that he could hear the prayers of the centuries.

He found himself softly repeating the prayer he had learned in that impeccably serene, sedate temple where his family had worshipped when he was a small boy, an echo from the past. "Hear, O Israel, the Lord our God, the Lord is One. Praise be to His name, whose glorious kingdom is forever and ever. Amen."

This wall, the last remnant of Herod's Temple, had endured through the ages. It had stood through the long wars, the Diaspora, the cyclical destructions and rebuildings of the city—in short, millennia of upheaval. Harry trembled at the miracle of it all.

Perhaps he had dreamed of this all his life, without really knowing it. Perhaps the latent feelings of blood loyalty and a vague sense of heritage had driven him to begin *The Genesis*, but until this moment Harry had not truly appreciated what it meant to be a Jew.

And suddenly he felt a great sense of self-reproach—and tremendous, inexpressible sadness. How little he had given his children! They had been taught a basic code of ethics and morals, but they had been given no sense of the spiritual and religious. Was it because of that deprivation that his children seemed so strangely aimless? Did they perhaps need a spiritual reservoir to draw from, beyond their parents' love?

Was it something Jeremy had longed for, however inarticulately? Harry felt a stab of pain as he reflected again that perhaps he was responsible for his boy's death, yet not in the way he'd always assumed. And despite his own childhood training, Harry himself felt spiritually bereft. His own reservoir had run dry years ago.

Standing next to him, Valerie tried to divine the tumble of thoughts behind Harry's troubled face. Spiritual insight was beyond her. She was a woman who lived for today, who would have scornfully dismissed the idea that there was more to life than what she could reach out and grab with her own two hands. But she was shrewd enough to sense that Harry had an extra dimension, one that was being strongly evoked by the dramatic setting of the ancient city of his forebears.

And so when he finally turned around to face her, a look of sadness in his eyes, Valerie said softly, "*The Genesis* can't be written anywhere else but here in Israel, can it?"

Staring at her with wonder, he said, "You understand that, don't you?" Then, with a touch of bitterness, he added, "If only Lily did."

After he and Valerie had gone to their respective rooms, Harry napped for most of the afternoon while Valerie attended to various chores. They had arranged to meet in the dining room at seven o'clock, but Valerie was already seated before Harry arrived.

She glanced up and saw him framed in the doorway. She caught her breath at the sight of him. Valerie had never seen him in evening attire, but tonight he wore a white dinner jacket. With his dark hair and olive skin, he could have passed for an Israeli. He was certainly the most handsome man in the room.

And as he glimpsed her and strode across the room toward her, she felt a thrill of sexuality, remembering how he had felt against her naked, the power in his muscular, sensual body.

Her smile of greeting was demure, but as they ordered their drinks, she couldn't help but think what a fool Lily had been to let Harry go halfway around the world without her. And for what? A charity ball. Clearly Lily didn't appreciate the gravity of her situation. If, by her own admission, she and Harry hadn't made love for such a long time, didn't she understand how vulnerable he'd be, how susceptible he'd be to another woman's charms?

The romantic aura of the city had already begun to work on Harry. It might not happen tonight—and Valerie had the luxury of time—but sooner or later they would become lovers again. And this time it was going to last. Valerie was sure.

Now that she had him all to herself, she was going to make herself indispensable in a way that had been impossible in Manhattan: editing, organizing his research, orchestrating his social life. Soon he would become totally dependent on her.

But above all, he was going to fall in love with her. She was beautiful, charming, irresistible. By the end of it all, by the time the last chapter was written, she was going to be Mrs. Harry Kohle, with all the fame, fortune, and reflected glory that entailed.

When Valerie went over their social schedule for the next week, Harry was staggered by the scope of the entertainment planned for him. No effort was to be spared in making him welcome.

After dinner, as they strolled up King George Street toward the center of town, Valerie described the living arrangements she had made.

"Wait till you see the house I found, Harry. It's incredible. Like something out of *The Arabian Nights*. This big, rambling villa spills down the hillside on three levels. Rafi and Tony have bedrooms on the upper level, I'm in the middle, and your bedroom is adjacent to the study on the lowest level. It will be perfect for your work. The living room and dining room are huge, and beautifully furnished, and although I don't imagine you'll spend much time there, the kitchen and servants' quarters are more than adequate."

But Harry's interest had suddenly dwindled. Before them stood the Mandelbaum Gate. Sentries were posted on either side of it. Beyond the checkpoint was hostile territory. No doubt a thousand enemy eyes stared at them through the night.

Valerie again recognized the faraway look Harry had in his eyes. He'd been the same way at seeing the Wailing Wall. Instinct told her that now was not the time to push. Though she herself did not feel the same tug, she understood the overwhelming effect this country had on Harry. She smiled to herself. In ways, Israel was a tougher rival than Lily. But Valerie knew that if she were patient, this place would prove as good as any to snare Harry Kohle.

For the next week, Harry and his staff were entertained by literary groups and by members of Israeli society. While festivities were lavish throughout the week, the final night proved the most spectacular of all.

They had been warned that the guest list included such figures as David Ben-Gurion, but Harry was nevertheless staggered to find that his dinner partner was to be Golda Meir.

As they talked, he was fascinated by Mrs. Meir's extraordinary knowledge of the country. He eagerly plied her with questions. There was so much he wanted to learn.

Valerie had been paired with Moshe Dayan, the first sabra born on a kibbutz. After dinner, he and Harry became immersed in a discussion of the Israeli soldier. Dayan was so mesmerizing that Harry was shocked to hear the clock strike midnight; he had completely lost track of time.

Apologetically he said, "I hope you'll forgive me for monopolizing you."

Dayan replied, smiling, "Mr. Kohle, it has been my pleasure. And I want to tell you, I am confident that Israel will someday have cause to thank you."

Harry replied, more prophetically than he knew, "I have a strange feeling that someday Israel will be thanking *you*."

# Chapter 33

THE next morning, before the sun rose, Yossi arrived in the van that would be their utility vehicle during their stay. Rafi and Tony were already in the truck and Valerie, dressed in trim khakis, clambered into the back while Harry sat in front with Yossi.

The day soon grew swelteringly hot. Harry realized why Valerie had recommended that they leave so early.

It wasn't until they began wending their way higher into the hills surrounding Safed that they began to feel a gentle cooling breeze blowing in from the Mediterranean.

Primitive cottages dotted the landscape. Sheep grazed on the hills amid whitewashed shrines. The town itself was nestled under the crest of the mountain, an assemblage of low white buildings with angled roofs on which the burning sun danced.

This was the ancient home of the Kabbalists, which Harry wanted to visit. But the others were eager to get to the villa to have a tall, cold drink. So they passed the town without stopping, turning instead onto a dirt road that led to the villa.

Harry emerged from the van and stopped, enchanted. The Judean hills spread themselves before him in dusky magnificence, across a vast valley. What an extraordinary choice Valerie had made! The gentle breeze, scented with juniper and myrtle, felt like velvet on his skin. As he surveyed the picturesque stone villa covered by a gentle riot of roses of Sharon, he smiled at Valerie.

"It's perfect. Even more beautiful than you described."

His satisfaction grew even greater as she showed him around.

The stone walls were so thick that the heat barely penetrated, Persian rugs softened the floors, while the sun filtering through the pierced wood shutters made the rooms soft and welcoming. The villa was owned by a fabulously wealthy Arab who now made his home on the fashionable Avenue Victor Hugo in Paris. His impeccable taste and unstinting purse were largely in evidence here.

Just as Valerie had promised, Harry's bedroom was spacious and perfectly situated, adjoining the study, which she'd already equipped with typewriters and filing cabinets.

As they gathered on the veranda, drinks in hand, Harry complimented her on her efficiency. "On all counts, you couldn't have done better. I don't know what I'd do without you."

Valerie blushed, secretly relishing a smug satisfaction. You're not going to have a chance to find out, Harry Kohle, she thought.

As the pleasant, smiling houseboy replenished their drinks, Rafi, who was a native of Tel Aviv, said, "Well, it's great to be back home."

Holding his glass aloft, Harry said, "Long live Israel!" The four clinked their glasses in toast.

Tony intervened dryly, "We had better drink up now, because tomorrow is my first day at Masada."

The next morning, after the researchers had gone off in the van, Valerie said, "I can't wait to show you Safed. It's absolutely fascinating; you're going to fall in love with it."

They walked into the town as the lightest of breezes was blowing. Under the blazing blue sky, Safed was as much a place of the imagination as something from the palette of Chagall.

Safed had a history that was as intriguing as it was strange. In ancient times the place had been the northernmost spot in Palestine. Huge bonfires were lit there, heralding the new month and announcing holy days. Not much mention of it was made until the time of the Crusades, when a huge castle was built on the mountain looming over the town. It had passed thereafter into the hands of the Knights Templar and later those of Saladin. After his demise, Moslems killed or expelled all the Jews, but by the sixteenth century they had returned, and it had become a center of Jewish learning during the Diaspora.

This was the birthplace of the famous Kabbalists, that strange rabbinical sect devoted to word-by-word study of Holy Writ, who believed that every letter, word, and line of the Five Books of Moses had a higher mystical meaning and offered the key to life.

Later the Jews had been driven out yet again, and by the time of the war of liberation in 1948, the town had become overwhelmingly Arab. It was one of the miracles of the war that fewer than 2,000 Jews had managed to defeat over 12,000 Arabs.

Now, Valerie explained, artists and craftsmen inhabited the quaint old Arab quarter through which they were walking, with its narrow, twisting cobbled streets, whitewashed houses, and wrought-iron balconies, through which they could hear muted Yiddish and Hebrew.

Harry was filled with wonder. These ancient walls, the small pristine whitewashed synagogue, the long-ago rabbis who had studied and kept alive Jewish learning in a hostile land. Again it struck him how little he knew of his heritage. How would he ever take in five thousand years of history in such a short time?

Later, as they stood amid the ruins of the Crusader citadel after a strenuous walk up the steep mountainside, Harry raised his eyes to the horizon and frowned. In the distance was a sparkling blue sea.

"That's not the Mediterranean," he said slowly.

"It's the Sea of Galilee," Valerie told him.

He was speechless for a long moment. They really were in the Promised Land, a place that had always seemed mythical to him. But it was real, and spreading out before his searching, yearning eyes.

Turning north, he saw snow-capped Mount Hermon above Lake Hula, a miniature echo of Galilee at the head of the Jordan River. To the east, across a flat plain, was the darker blue of the Mediterranean. "It's—beautiful," he finally said in awed wonder. "I can hardly wait to get out there and see it all."

"Me too," Valerie said, echoing his enthusiasm. "I know it's going to be a marvelous experience." Only she understood just how marvelous an experience she had in mind.

That evening, as Harry walked out on his balcony and felt the coolness of the stone under his feet, he relished the evening breeze against his silk robe. Then he was startled by the Arab houseboy, who had slipped up behind him on soundless feet. "Yes?" he said, almost sharply.

The boy bowed, then said in heavily accented English, "Would you like anything more tonight?"

"I could use a drink. Bring me—oh, a tall Scotch and soda."

The interruption stirred him to think of the work the morning would bring. Sitting down, he began to sketch out an itinerary. Masada, where the Jewish inhabitants had chosen to cut their throats rather than be enslaved by the Romans, would be first. After that, Atlit, where in the early part of the century the brilliant agricultural pioneer Aaron Aaronsohn had proved the desert could be made to bloom.

Harry knew that that was only the beginning; how long it would all take, or what else he might find valuable, he had no idea. He was sure only that he had to traverse Israel until he found what he was searching for.

Geographically, the country was remarkably small; it could be covered in a weekend—or it could take years. After a few days, it seemed to Valerie that Harry had the latter timeframe in mind.

He spent endless hours at Masada in the intense heat, poring over the ruins and talking to people, the whole while writing voluminous notes and assigning various topics to Rafi or Tony to research further.

More often, however, he would simply wander about, absorbing the aura that still clung to the ancient stones. At this rate, Valerie thought in frustration, they might never get back to Safed. And she could hardly seduce him while they were camped out by the shores of the Dead Sea in a tent.

Still, she cleverly hid her irritation and made a great show of being as fascinated as he. Harry would be charmed by her devotion to the task he increasingly regarded as his mission in life.

However, to her chagrin, Valerie couldn't help but notice that Harry's work was blinding him to her attractions. As the weeks went by and the research continued, she began to wonder if she would ever get her chance.

When they finished at Masada, they traveled northward to the Hula Valley, just below the Golan Heights. Harry was struck by the contrasts in this historic valley. It had been reclaimed by Jewish pioneers in the early part of the century, literally dug out from the swamps. Now every inch of the land was lush farmland. The sprinklers whirred peacefully, a symbol of the human ingenuity which had overcome all nature's obstacles.

But high above the valley in the Golan Heights, Syrian commandos and riflemen lurked, armed with submachine guns to shoot the descendants of those pioneers.

In the kibbutzim, there were children who had slept every night of their lives in concrete bunkers. It seemed incredible to Harry that a people could endure and even flourish, going about the business of daily living, with such a sword of Damocles hanging over them.

The agency had arranged that Harry be invited to the homes of sympathetic Arabs. Over cigarettes and Turkish coffee, Harry was surprised to learn that they did not seek the extermination of the Jews. Many did not advocate violence at all, but even the most educated among them were unanimous on one point: There could never be peace in the Middle East so long as Israel existed. And they clung to this conviction despite the fact that there were Arabs sitting in the Knesset, Arabs who conducted their businesses and lived happily in Israel.

All these facts came as revelations to Harry, but it was just the information that he sought. Names and dates and statistics could be found in the Jewish library in New York. They came alive to Harry only as he walked the streets of the new nation. Nothing could simulate the emotion engendered in him by seeing innocent children under threat of slaughter—and the courageous way they learned to rise above the mere struggle for survival.

*The Genesis* would deal with the base as well as the exalted part of man—humanity in the universal sense. As Harry envisioned it, the novel would wrestle with the ancient notion that man had a choice in his life: He could be only a little lower than the angels, or only a little higher than the beasts. During his first weeks in Israel, Harry began to absorb the mystifying truth that man could be both at the same time.

And though *The Genesis* concerned essentially one man in the twentieth century, choices which had been made throughout five thousand years of history and by civilizations which had long since been ground into dust were still guiding his destiny.

# Chapter 34

AFTER a month in Israel, Harry knew he had only scratched the surface, but he felt he had absorbed enough history to feel initiated. He was anxious to get back to Safed to begin translating his impressions into manuscript while Rafi and Tony continued their research.

Now was the time to make her move, Valerie knew—but she was slightly taken aback when Harry called Lily the night of their return. She was so impatient to know what was being said that when he placed the call, she quietly lifted the receiver in her bedroom and listened.

What she heard reassured her enormously.

"Lily, I'm sorry. I would have called before this, but it has been impossible. We've been to Masada and down to the Dead Sea, and to the Golan Heights. . . . You wouldn't believe what I've seen. This is the most incredible country—the more you learn the less you know. I swear that I could be here ten years and still not know everything."

Foolishly, Lily had hoped that maybe being separated from her for so long now would have impelled him to say, "I miss you so. . . . I wish you were here."

She bit her lip and managed to murmur, "I'm glad that the work is going well."

"We're going to Mount Carmel day after tomorrow," Harry continued, "and I don't know how long that will take. I want to speak to the descendants of the Aaronsohn family who came here from Rumania in, oh, 1867 or so. You know, I mentioned that I was very interested in Aaron Aaronsohn, the agriculturist."

Had that been mentioned during one of those numbing dinner-table conversations where he and Valerie went on and on, nearly ecstatic over their *Genesis*-related research? "That sounds wonderful," Lily said rather blankly.

As he continued, she found herself thinking, Harry hasn't asked once how I am or what I'm doing.

Finally, belatedly, he paused. "How is everything going for you, Lily?"

"Everything's fine."

"I'm glad. Well, I'll be in touch again soon."

"Yes, I'd like that."

Valerie was filled with new confidence as they said their good-byes. There had been no endearments, only a one-sided conversation. Harry could have no idea how neglected Lily must feel.

Harry, on the other hand, had hung up feeling frustrated and misunderstood. Lily had shown little interest and no enthusiasm for his discoveries. He just couldn't share anything with her.

Unconsciously comparing her with Valerie, he thought, What a difference! Valerie had entered into his world fully and completely. She was as thrilled as he about everything that was going on. But what impressed Harry most was that she had an extraordinary feeling for the scope of the work he was attempting.

It had really been tough, with the heat up there in Masada, and Valerie had shown her mettle. She never once complained.

By the time they sat on the terrace the next evening at sunset, he found himself thinking that she seemed different from the image he had always carried of her. She had more depth, more soul, more maturity and insight than he had ever given her credit for.

He had always thought she was beautiful, but somehow out here in the deserts of Israel she had acquired a loveliness of spirit which seemed to shine through in everything she said and did.

One of the servants came out on the terrace and announced dinner. Extending his hand, Harry asked, "Valerie? Shall we?"

It was very quiet. Rafi and Tony were still out in the truck and the houseboy had disappeared.

Valerie shook her head, smiling. "No. Let's have another drink."

As the scent of roses wafted gently through the air, they watched the sun sink in a glory of red, orange, and glowing gold. For a long moment, it seemed to hang suspended in the pink-streaked sky.

God, this country is magnificent! Harry thought.

Standing near his shoulder, Valerie gave voice to his thought. "Isn't it breathtaking?"

He, looking into her eyes, took the glass from her hand and set it down on the table. Harry felt impelled by a deep sense of inevitability as he took Valerie's arm. Although he had refused to recognize it, he realized that he had been fighting this for a long time. He would have liked to be indifferent to Valerie's appeal, but now that seemed impossible. Yesterday's conversation with Lily had left Harry with a brooding resentment and here was Valerie, warm and willing.

Harry fondly recalled those tempestuous nights back in Manhattan. Suddenly he was overwhelmed by the urge to feel her body once again. He bent and kissed her with deliberate sensuality.

Darkness began to fall. The sound of a muezzin could be heard in the distance as Harry turned and led her down the winding steps to his balcony and through the French doors into his bedroom. Moonlight filtered through the slats of the shutters, casting shadows onto the marble floor.

He undressed her slowly, savoring the touch. Then her fingers were on him, unbuttoning first his shirt, then softly working the zipper of his trousers. As the last piece of underclothing was discarded, they clung to each other in an impassioned moment.

Valerie kissed the lobe of his ear, then his cheek; she opened her mouth and gently touched his tongue and then deepened the pressure. The kiss ventured down slowly, unhurriedly, until it reached the place that made Harry moan with ecstasy.

Lifting her up from her knees, Harry brought her to the bed. His world spun as he entered her. Valerie writhed with pleasure under his weight.

Then she was upon him, planting reverent kisses all over his chest and face. Finally, Harry lost all control as he moved urgently within her. Nothing mattered to him except her.

Once it was over, Valerie curled up close to him, content, remembering how she had dreamed of this ever since his first week in Jerusalem. She had lain in her bed in her room just below Harry's at the King David, wanting him so much that it was all she could do to keep from sneaking down the corridor and up the stairs.

But Harry was already beginning to feel the old, nagging regret. He had done exactly what he had vowed he'd never do again.

Lust was not the force that drove Harry. If it had been, he would have been in Valerie's arms long before this. But as he lay there beside her, stroking her hair, he knew he would be sleeping with her again and again.

Still, his last remaining shred of conscience forced him to say, "Valerie, you know I find you very attractive. But I want you to understand that if we have an affair, I still can't promise you anything. Lily and I have our problems—you know that—but I still love her, and eventually I know that we will be able to work things out."

Valerie was tempted to roll her eyes and frown. But exercising restraint, she remained understanding. "Of course, Harry," she told him. "I know that. It's worth it to me just to be with you now."

In spite of his confident speech, Valerie could detect that Harry was trying to convince himself. He was powerfully attracted to her, and his work was drawing them even closer together. Time was on her side.

Breaking the tension of the moment, he ruffled her hair teasingly, brushed a kiss across her forehead, and hopped out of bed.

As he pulled on his robe he ordered, "Out of bed, wench. I'm starved."

Rafi and Tony exchanged a single, significant glance as Harry and Valerie entered the dining room. They had seen this happen before, back in New York, and had guessed it would be only a matter of time before the secretary and the boss climbed back into bed together.

In the ensuing weeks, Harry was happier than he had been in a very long time. Valerie had given him more than just a physical release; she had given him the kind of affection and understanding he'd been starved for, ever since Jeremy's death had torn him from Lily. Yet this time, he found that he was not tortured by guilt because this time, Lily had no good excuse for leaving him.

Valerie was there and Harry was frankly grateful to her for alleviating his loneliness and longing.

His work began to progress better and faster. The physical stimulus of his affair with Valerie seemed to act as a mental stimulus. His work became even more meaningful with her there to share in it.

And Valerie was a tremendous help to him. Harry was rare among authors in that when it came to his work, he was completely objective. His ego was irrelevant; the best idea must carry the day, even if it came from someone else.

He had come to realize that Valerie's opinions were invaluable. She edited his scripts, pointed out foibles in his reasoning, made him see that one idea or scenario didn't work quite as well as another. More and more often he found himself taking her advice.

He treasured the great empathy he found in Valerie—a quality he had always found lacking in Lily. Valerie wanted to take a large role in his writing, while Lily had always shied away from that part of his life.

Often in the early days of their marriage, he had wanted to share a moment of triumph with her, but she had always been too busy. Bath time or feeding time, it was always something. Those occasions had given him a reservoir of injured feelings, a reservoir he now drew on.

Well, you couldn't have everything, Harry reflected, but right now he was a lucky man to have Valerie around.

After another week had passed, the most crucial part of his research began in earnest—exploring the life of Aaron Aaronsohn.

Packing Rafi, Tony, and Valerie into the van, he headed to Zichron, near Mount Carmel in the northern coastal part of Israel, where Aaronsohn had lived as a young boy.

Aaronsohn's story enthralled Harry. He had been unique among Jewish pioneers. Like the Americans who had seen the vast prairies and wanted to tame them, Aaronsohn had a vision that had known no bounds. Despite the neglect of centuries, he knew that Palestine could be a land of milk and honey once again.

Born in Rumania, he had emigrated to the Middle East at

the age of six. His family was not affluent, but as he grew up, his genius was noticed by the Baron Édouard Rothschild, who sent him to study at an agricultural college in France.

He returned to Israel and became recognized as an outstanding agronomist. With grants he received from American universities, he began to write scholarly papers on scientific agriculture. Palestine was then a barren wasteland, but Aaronsohn discovered a primeval strain of drought-resistant wheat which he believed was the key to making the land productive.

In 1910, he established an agricultural experimental station at Atlit in order to test his dry-farming theories. They succeeded brilliantly, but he ran into opposition from other Jewish settlers, Zionists whose outlook was communal and socialistic rather than scientific and individualistic. They condemned his practice of hiring Arabs to work on his farms, rather than relying on Jewish labor alone. But Aaronsohn was an immensely practical man and if Arab workers could help make the desert bloom, so be it.

That would have been enough to base a novel on, but as Harry became caught up in his research, he discovered a man of tremendous strength, extraordinary power and dimension.

With the outbreak of World War I, Aaronsohn became increasingly concerned about the Turkish rule of Palestine. Not only was there a spreading specter of famine, but also the Turks' slaughter of a million Armenians, with their bodies left for carrion, made him fear that the Jews would be next. And so it was that he secretly founded a spy network called NILI with his brothers and sisters and a few other young Palestinians, with the aim of wresting Palestine for the Jews.

Permitted unusual freedom of movement because of his status as a longtime settler and his agricultural work, he began to collect information about Turkish movements which he then fed to the British, even going back and forth behind the lines to Cairo and London to warn of the projected Turkish attack on the Suez Canal.

But in 1917 the spy ring was discovered. The members, including Aaron's sister Sarah, were tortured and executed, and only the imminent capture of Jerusalem saved the Yishuv from mass arrests, hangings, and deportations.

Aaronsohn somehow survived the war, living in Cairo, but

he died in a plane crash a year and a half later while en route to the Paris Peace Conference.

And strangely, the Zionist movement for which he had done so much barely mourned him—for he was not a socialist and he had exposed them to great risk through his espionage.

Aaronsohn's story was one of contrasts—from an unsettled childhood to far-flung triumph and acclaim, from the quiet rhythms of farming to highest drama, from happiness to tragedy and loss.

His only wish had been to try to carve out a civilization for future generations. Knowing that the march of science allied to human effort could bring about his vision of a desert in bloom, he loathed war and other such petty human struggles. Yet, unable to ignore the conflict threatening his new land, he had given up his own desires and risked his life for a better world.

His story was emblematic not only of Israel, but of the human experience itself. Harry could not resist Aaronsohn as a model for his protagonist.

The Aaronsohn farm at Zichron had since been preserved as a shrine. Harry let the sandy earth sift through his fingers. Staring at the magnificent blue Haifa bay, where so many refugees had been smuggled into the Promised Land, he imagined the young Aaron standing on the same spot, dreaming of his vision of Israel.

Later, Harry gazed out at the Mediterranean by moonlight and imagined the British frigate lying offshore, waiting for vital information on troop movements to be brought by Aaron or his sister Sarah.

Valerie divined that a great sense of peace had come over him. She felt he had come to some kind of watershed.

"Happy?" she murmured as he turned away from the ocean.

"Very," he answered, slipping his hand in hers and starting to walk along the beach. "Very happy and content."

"I'm glad."

"You've been just wonderful. I can't tell you how good it has been to have you by my side, how much help you've been."

Her only answer was to squeeze his hand.

"But you know, I think we need to relax a little at this point. I've gotten some wonderful material, but it's been so intense I'm ready for a break. How about if I take you to Caesarea for a few days—just the two of us?"

"Oh, Harry, I'd love it!" she cried. Twining herself around him, she gave him a long, passionate kiss—and he didn't resist.

The next day, leaving Rafi and Tony to do further research at Atlit, they wound down the coast to the ancient Roman sea resort at Caesarea.

Caesarea was a stunning site of antiquity. Established as a port by the Phoenicians in the fourth century B.C., it became the favorite watering-place of the Roman occupiers and was enlarged by Herod into a great maritime city. But as the Roman Empire had disintegrated, the city had fallen into decline, and into the hands of the Byzantines, Persians, and Crusaders, only to be retaken by Saladin.

The place still had an aura about it, no doubt inspired by the historical array of triumphs and defeats which had taken place right there. But now the temples of Rome had fallen to ruins, and the two magnificent huge statues, one in red porphyry and the other in white marble, were merely reminders of past grandeur.

They stayed in an inn which was over two thousand years old and had once housed Roman charioteers. The stable had been converted into a luxury hotel by a New York financier in the twenties. During the war years, it had been used to house refugees, but now it was a hotel again, and Harry and Valerie indulged themselves shamelessly. After the days visiting different desert sites, they were hot and felt permanently dusty, and there was no greater pleasure than to dip into one of the old Roman baths. There was a prescribed succession, from the faintly sulfurous *caldaria,* or hot baths, to the *tepidaria,* to the *frigidaria,* from which Valerie emerged squealing, "How do they get it so cold?"

"It's good for you," teased Harry, pulling her back in beside him and kissing her. He could never remember feeling so carefree. It was the best time in his life. He knew that *The Genesis* was to be his masterwork, and this week, he had fallen in love—with Aaron Aaronsohn.

He realized that in an ideal world he would be sharing this miraculous experience with his wife, not his mistress, but then, he consoled himself, life was too short to waste on vain regrets.

He was here, Valerie was here, and they gave each other great pleasure. They swam, they sunned themselves, they made love on the beach by moonlight. After the intense mental and physical exertions of the preceding month, they reveled in the pleasures of their short vacation.

It was on their last night, as they lay on the bed after making love, that the turning point came. The windows were open to the warm Mediterranean breeze, and there was a scent of oranges in the air. Still feeling the afterglow, Harry lay with his arms around Valerie. She uttered a faint sigh.

"What is it?" he asked idly.

"Oh, Harry. I wish this could go on forever," she blurted out.

He shifted uncomfortably at the fervor in her voice. Deliberately avoiding the point, he said, "What about the book? We can't just leave it to write itself, now can we?"

"You know that's not what I mean."

As she turned to face him, the moonlight suddenly fell across her face, illuminating it.

"I love you, Harry," she whispered.

He stared back at her, not knowing what to say. "Valerie, I—"

"You don't have to say that you love me. I just wanted you to know."

Tremendous guilt washed over Harry. Subconsciously, he had known that this was coming, yet he had avoided even thinking about where they might be headed. But what had he expected? That he could make love to a woman time and again and still tell her each time, "Remember, this is only an affair."

He had done absolutely nothing to discourage her. If anything, he had done the opposite, making love to her night after night, spending every day with her, sharing his every thought. Valerie could hardly be blamed for assuming that this was something more to him than a mere affair.

But now that she had brought him face to face with the issue, he had to deal with it head-on. Valerie was sweet, charming, vastly useful—but she wasn't Lily. It was as simple as that. She had brought him a little oasis of happiness, but his secret soul longed to have that happiness with Lily.

He couldn't encourage Valerie or allow her to hope. And yet, how could he be unkind? "Valerie, I don't know what to say. I care for you very much, you know that. And if I were free, who's to say what might happen between us?"

Valerie listened with rising displeasure. She knew what this was a preamble for. She had taken a risk in displaying her emotions so openly, but she could suppress her feelings no more. And time was at a premium. Once Lily was done with the ball, she would be coming out to Israel to join Harry. It was imperative that Valerie widen the rift between them—and quickly.

Choosing her words shrewdly, she asked with the greatest apparent sincerity, "Harry, can I speak freely with you?"

"Of course you can, Valerie."

"Well, something has been on my mind for a long time. I have tremendous feelings of guilt about saying anything, but in a way, I feel that you're not a good friend if you're not honest."

"Agreed. That goes without saying."

"Oh, Harry, it's just that when you see two people who mean so much to you, and there's a terrible problem in their lives . . ."

"Go on," he said, frowning slightly.

"No . . ." She hesitated. "No, forget that I said anything. I shouldn't have brought it up."

"But Valerie, you have brought it up. Please tell me."

With a great show of reluctance, she began. "Well, Harry, over the past year I've spent a lot of time with Lily, and gradually I've begun to wonder. Do you think she still really and truly is happy being married to you? I mean, if a woman is content with a man she doesn't keep him at arm's length. . . ."

"Wait a minute," Harry interrupted. "Our marriage has gone through an upheaval, there's no denying that, but I don't think that it's anything that, given time, can't be worked out."

"You're probably right, Harry. Just forget that I brought it up."

But something within him wouldn't let it go at that. "Valerie, do you know something I don't? Has Lily actually said anything to you about not being happy?"

She looked at him for a long moment, then averted her eyes.

"Well, is there?" he probed.

Heaving a deep sigh, she finally said, "No, not in so many words. But it's just that when we were talking and I urged her to come to Israel with you, she kept saying . . . well, frankly, what she seemed most concerned about was not letting Ellis down."

"Not letting Ellis down!" Harry exclaimed. "In other words she cares more about pleasing him than pleasing me?"

Valerie's expression was troubled as she replied, "Well, you know, Harry, she and he are very close friends. You know—oh, I shouldn't say this. I've said much too much already."

But Harry said grimly, "Now, there's something you're holding back. I want to hear it."

Swallowing hard, Valerie said gently, "Harry, Ellis is in love with Lily. Don't you know that?"

"No, dammit—I don't!"

She shook her head. "It's so apparent. It's there every time he looks at her, every time he talks to her. You haven't seen it because you haven't wanted to."

"That's ridiculous!" Harry exploded. "He's my agent, and my best friend. He has been for many, many years. There's nothing between him and Lily but honest friendship."

But in spite of his bravado, Valerie's words came as a terrible shock. It seemed impossible—and yet, Lily had refused to come with him. Could that damned ball really have been the entire reason? No, it was absurd. Curtly he told Valerie, "I think you've misinterpreted the situation. Let's not talk about it anymore."

Soothingly she whispered, "Of course, Harry, darling. I'm sorry I brought it up. I'm sure it's better not to think about it."

But inwardly she felt triumphant. His anger was directed not at her, but at the very thought of his wife's being unfaithful. She had planted the seed of doubt and mistrust. She suspected she'd hit upon fertile soil.

Turning to him, Valerie whispered urgently, "Hold me, Harry." As she twisted closer, a fierce desire came over him and he made love to her again, almost savagely.

But the next day, as they drove back to Safed, Valerie sensed a subtle but definite change in him—a certain reserve, a withdrawing from their intimacy, and that afternoon, when they arrived back at Safed, he threw himself back into his work with renewed intensity, as though he might erase the sensual indulgences of Caesarea.

That same night, he called Lily. It was time to forget his pride and beg her to come. Valerie was wrong about Ellis, but somehow he was filled with an intense longing to see his wife, a longing he hadn't felt for some time.

But unexpectedly, as he waited for her to answer the ringing phone, he was overcome by a renewed wave of hurt and anger—and jealousy. Unbidden came the thought of Ellis, in constant contact with her. . . .

And then Lily answered. Over the scratchy connection, he heard, "Harry, I'm so glad to hear your voice! . . . How is the work going?"

Silently, Harry cursed the long distance between them and the barrier of the phone. "Fine, Lily."

"I'm glad, darling."

Forcing himself to sound pleasant, he asked, "How are the preparations for the ball coming along?"

"Oh, it's all going beautifully."

*With Ellis's help*? There was a long moment of silence as he fought with himself, but finally, abandoning his pride, he blurted out, "Lily, I want you to come out now—right away. I need you."

"But Harry, darling . . . ," Lily cried helplessly. "The ball is only two weeks away! And I need to make arrangements for the children's summer camp. It's impossible for me to come now; it really is. I'm sorry, darling, but it won't be long now. . . ."

Rage swelled in him. He'd always held on to the hope that if he really begged her, she'd come. But clearly she planned to stay thousands of miles from him . . . and only blocks from Ellis. It's no wonder, Harry thought to himself, that he'd embarked on this uneasy affair with Valerie. Was it so strange to seek out other company after months of being shut out by your wife?

But at that moment, he didn't think of his adulterous relationship with Valerie; that seemed irrelevant. What was important was that Lily's allegiance to Ellis seemed stronger than her allegiance to him.

"I'll be out just as soon as I can, darling," she added

quickly. "The day after the ball, in fact. But I just can't let Ellis and everybody else down now."

At his utter silence, Lily hesitated, then said, "Harry? I am sorry that I can't come now, and I know that you're unhappy with me . . ."

"Oh, spare me your excuses, Lily!" he suddenly snapped. "If—the ball"—he had almost said Ellis's name—"is more important to you than I am, then so be it. I've told you that I want you, but if you're too busy or not interested, then fine. I'm not going to force you."

Lily clutched the receiver tightly. "Harry, you don't understand. . . . I really would if I could. . . ."

"I think I do understand, Lily—all too well. Listen, have fun with your ball. I'm sure it will be a huge success. Good-bye."

"Harry," she cried. But he had already hung up.

His breathing gradually returning to normal, an odd sense of relief diluted his anger. If he'd had pangs of guilt over sleeping with Valerie, he wasn't troubled by them now.

Lily had chosen once again to place him last on her list of priorities—and the more he thought about it, the more defiant he grew. He could just pick up with Valerie where they'd stopped.

He switched out the light and strode from his study, slamming the door behind him. After a perfunctory tap on Valerie's door, he entered to find her lounging on the bed in a brief satin negligee.

"Tired?" he asked.

A slow, enchanting smile lit her face. "Not a bit." She clarified her statement. "Not now."

And once again, they came passionately together.

# Chapter 35

THE next day in New York, as Lily sat with the members of her committee over lunch, she scarcely heard what anyone was saying. The conversation with Harry haunted her thoughts.

His peremptory demand had been totally unreasonable, but then, what if something had come up? What if he just *had* to see her? Wasn't yesterday's call the one she'd been waiting for? He hadn't begged her really, or said "I love you." But his simple "I need you" spoke for itself.

All night she lay awake berating herself. Her place was with her husband; she should not have allowed anybody to convince her otherwise, even Valerie.

"You're certainly in a fog today," she heard her friend Joan say teasingly.

Smiling, Lily returned quietly, "Will you all excuse me for a moment? I need to make a phone call. There's something I forgot."

Once inside the booth, she dialed a familiar number. "Ellis, this is Lily. Can you come to dinner tonight?"

"Is anything wrong?" he asked with quick perception.

"No, not really. Are you free?"

"For you, my dear, I'd give up a meeting with Hemingway himself."

"How about seven, at my place? I want to cook for you."

She desperately needed to do something, to occupy herself with hard work. She went out and made the rounds of her favorite food shops. She wanted only the best for Ellis.

The butcher found her two of the thickest, tenderest fillets, the fishmonger a dozen fresh Blue Points to be served on the half-shell; the greengrocer, truffles, shallots, and dainty white asparagus flown in from France. While picking up fresh apricots and cream, she decided to bake a French fruit tart, an elegant version of a pie that had been Ellis's favorite from her days on the farm. Finally, she selected a lovely '47 Château Lafite and hurried home to start her preparations. It was so wonderful to have someone to cook for for a change.

Promptly at seven the doorbell rang, and Lily, having just closed the oven door on the tart, glanced at the clock, took off her apron, and ran to the door, smoothing her hair.

There stood Ellis, half hidden by an enormous bouquet. The first spring lilies had just come into bloom, and the fragrance was heady. In his hand were a bottle of Dom Pérignon and a box of elegant Swiss chocolates.

"Oh Ellis! You shouldn't have!"

"I think you deserve a few treats, Lily," he smiled.

"You're too good to me, you know."

Reaching up, she kissed his cheek lightly. "I don't know if I deserve it, but it's sweet of you anyway, Ellis. Now why don't you go in and help yourself to a drink. I'll be right with you."

Lily surveyed the kitchen one last time. The tournedos Rossini were ready to go on; hers would be medium rare but she remembered Ellis liked his rare. The tart would take another thirty minutes.

Returning to the living room, she found Ellis turning from the bar with two glasses. "I took the liberty of making you a martini."

She took one and sipped lightly, then smiled up at him. "Perfect. You do make the most marvelous martini, Ellis."

"Thank you, ma'am." He bowed slightly, accepting the compliment. "After all these years, I think I can mix it to your taste."

Dinner was a masterpiece. Lily had been a little apprehensive, lest her long absence from the kitchen would be evident, but as course succeeded course, she forgot everything except the sheer pleasure of Ellis's company. In the most unobtrusive way, he always made her feel like the most charming woman in the world.

"Lily, the PR has been incredible on the ball. Already the press has been trumpeting what a fabulous job you're doing as chairman. Now that I'm here, you'll have to tell me the truth—how did you persuade Benny Goodman to do it?"

"Bribery," she answered with a straight face.

He laughed. "I'm sure that Benny took one look at you and agreed, with no bribe needed."

"Seriously, Ellis, the committee has been tremendous. They've done most of the work."

How like her to be so modest, he thought. Joan Lawrence had privately confided to him that Lily was the most effective chairman they had ever had. The Goodhue and Kohle names helped, of course, but Lily's particular magic was in being able to mediate between all the various egos involved. In a group of strong-minded women, she somehow had a way of making each one feel that her contribution was invaluable.

"It's extraordinary, Ellis," Joan had told him. "She gets things done, but in the most diplomatic way. No screaming or tantrums or throwing her weight around."

Now, Lily smiled at him. "How about another piece of tart?"

As her eyes met and held his warmly, a queer pang struck him. If only Lily were his wife, and this were his table, and he could be with her every night. . . .

Shaking his head slightly, as though to dispel the illusion, he said, "It's wonderful, but no thanks."

"Shall we have our coffee in the living room, then?"

"How about champagne instead?"

With a little smile she acquiesced.

After settling themselves side by side on the sofa in front of the fire, they picked up their glasses and Ellis said, "Here's to all good things, Lily."

Touching her glass to his, she smiled faintly.

"Well, now," he said lightly. "Did you get me over here simply to ply me with all these good things, or for some other reason?"

"A little of both."

"Okay then, we've had the good things, so now let's get to the other reason."

For a moment she watched the bubbles rise in her glass. Then, taking a deep breath, she began. "Ellis, the truth is that I'm in a real bind."

He nodded judiciously. "Tell me about it."

With a sigh she said, "I spoke to Harry last night and out

of the blue, he demanded that I come over to Israel immediately. He was as adamant as could be."

"And?"

"Well, of course I told him no, that there was no way I could get away before the ball. But I have to admit that I feel terribly torn, and tremendously guilty."

Ellis's mind worked furiously. He knew that Harry had broken off his affair with Valerie after Lily's return, but he also knew, with an absolute certainty, that out there in the Middle Eastern desert, they were sleeping together again.

It was impossible to guess why Harry had suddenly demanded that Lily come—perhaps it was a momentary attack of guilty conscience—but it didn't alter Ellis's deep-seated conviction.

And at long last, his anger overcame his scruples. It overwhelmed any sense of loyalty he felt he owed Harry. The eager, sincere, passionately honest young man he had known years before had long since disappeared. He was lying to Lily, cheating on her, making a fool of her—and she deserved better.

The passing years had been a strange torment for Ellis as he had watched Lily forgive Harry over and over again, even when she blamed him for their son's death, and Ellis told himself that it could be only because she still loved him. Maybe Ellis could have taken advantage of the Kohles' troubles to drive her into his arms, but he would have been haunted by the fact she still loved Harry. Or so he had thought in the past.

But now, somehow, he felt that things were different. When people were at such constant odds with each other, what marriage could there be left to preserve? The truth was, Harry and Lily had stopped living as husband and wife long ago.

They might have fallen in love, but even almost twenty years together and four children did not alter the fact that they were utterly unsuited for one another. Harry needed a wife content to be an adoring admirer of his every move, whereas Lily longed to be adored as only he—Ellis—could adore her.

He didn't pretend to be unselfishly motivated. Ellis loved and wanted Lily desperately, just as he always had.

He drained his glass and set it down on the coffee table and then said abruptly, "Lily, I've got a suggestion. Obviously you want to see Harry. Why don't you fly over now, just for the weekend? Surprise him. The committee can spare you from the preparations for a day or two."

"But Ellis, that's a terribly long trip, just for a few days, isn't it?"

"I'll tell you how to do it: fly from here to London, stay overnight, and then go on to Tel Aviv. It's only five hours from there and you won't be so tired when you arrive."

Lily started to demur. "Oh, it sounds too complicated."

But Ellis went on. "I'll reserve a room for you at Claridge's, and I'll also call Harry's publisher there. He's a very pleasant man—you can have dinner with him."

"That would be lovely, but—"

"No buts. Just do it and don't think about it."

"Shouldn't I even call Harry?"

"Oh no. It will be a fabulous surprise for him. You'll see—he'll be thrilled."

Impulsively, she threw her arms around Ellis and hugged him tightly. "Oh, Ellis, what would I do without you? I knew that you'd have the answer!"

In spite of all his rationalizing, now that he had cast the fatal die, Ellis felt intensely guilty, knowing that he had deliberately urged Lily on a route that might lead to disaster.

The next day Lily was up bright and early. Forgotten were her uneasy parting from Harry and their awkward phone conversations. She bid Ellis good-bye at the airport and promised to call him from London.

At the airport she was met by Harry's British publisher, who drove her to Claridge's. Later, they went to Simpson's in the Strand for the famous roast beef and Yorkshire pudding, but Lily was too excited to notice what she ate.

The knowledge that by this time tomorrow she would be reunited with her husband had put her in a daze. But that night in London, for however distracted she seemed, Lily was the Lily of her Paris youth; she was spontaneous and sparkling, and Harry's publisher, a stout little man in a bowler hat, was plainly entranced by her. As he saw her onto the El Al plane the next morning, he assured her that she must visit again, with or without Harry.

Lily smiled, but her thoughts had already turned to Harry. She barely heard what the kind publisher said.

But in Rome, where the flight had been scheduled for a

twenty-minute stopover, the passengers were forced to disembark and wait for over three hours. Apparently there had been another terrorist scare and the aircraft had to be searched thoroughly before they could take off.

Wearily, Lily sat alone in the bare waiting room, her spirits sagging as the hands on her watch circled slowly once, twice, three times. It would be so late by the time she got into Tel Aviv.

When they were finally cleared for takeoff, she had worked herself into a frenzy of anxiety over what awaited her in Tel Aviv. Suppose the driver Ellis had arranged for her had not waited? She would have to take a taxi to a hotel in the city, then try to make arrangements to get to Safed the next day.

But miraculously, even though it was ten at night, a young Israeli approached her as soon as she came through Customs. "Mrs. Harry Kohle? I am David. Let me take your bags."

"How do you do? I'm sorry to be so late—the plane was delayed."

"Don't apologize, Mrs. Kohle. We live in a country where war and the threat of it delays many things." He shrugged. "It is part of the life here."

"Well, I don't know what to do at this point. I'm supposed to go to Safed, but now perhaps I should just try to get a hotel room here and go on tomorrow."

David shrugged. "If you like, but I am happy to drive you there now. Safed is not so very far."

"Really? What time would we arrive?"

"Twelve-thirty, perhaps."

Lily thought for a moment. Harry was a night owl, and she didn't want to have to search for a hotel and unpack and waste more precious time; she had only two days.

"You really wouldn't mind?"

"My pleasure."

Some fifteen minutes later, they were speeding through the warm Israeli night.

Tel Aviv was nearly dark as they passed by; only a few lights were burning. Lily was overwhelmed by the millions of stars shining more beautifully than she'd ever seen. Moonlight lapped gently over the Mediterranean.

They followed the coastal road north as far as Haifa, taking the same route Harry had several days before. Lily debated on whether to stop to call Harry and let him know she was coming, but then it would be such fun to surprise him. And after all, she was almost there. If she had to wake him, what did it matter? They hadn't seen each other for over two months. And especially in light of their last conversation, he'd be delighted by the surprise.

They wound through the hills of Safed, and then finally David announced, "It's right along here . . . a mile past town, on the left."

A minute later, they pulled to a halt in front of the sprawling stone villa. Moonlight illuminated the roses of Sharon clinging to the walls. The aroma was intoxicating. Lily thrilled at the romantic charm this place held.

The villa itself lay in darkness; plainly its occupants had gone to bed. Lily checked her watch: one o'clock. Asking David to wait with her bags, she mounted the broad stone steps and peered through the filigree of the front door. Then, with a start, she made out the form of an Arab houseboy lying on the floor in front of the door, in the manner of Oriental servants. Softly, she tapped, and a moment later a dark face peered from the door.

"Yes?"

"I am Mrs. Kohle. Could you please tell me where Mr. Kohle's bedroom is?"

The servant stared at her so blankly, Lily thought that he must not understand English. Slowly and clearly, she enunciated, "Master Kohle—your master? Where is his room?"

The boy shrugged his shoulders in a gesture of incomprehension. Lily was sure he couldn't speak English. She pushed the door open in exasperation and began walking toward the back of the house saying, "Master Kohle?"

Shrugging his shoulders again, the houseboy wordlessly pointed toward the staircase leading downward.

At the bottom of the flight of stairs she found the door. Ever so gently, she pushed it open, then stopped short. The room lay in shadows, but there was the sliver of moonlight pouring through the French doors. It fell in a lacy pattern on the naked flesh of two bodies lying tangled among the sheets.

For a moment Lily thought that she must have the wrong room. She stepped back, about to close the door. Then she saw one of the bodies stir slightly, and the face turned just enough for her to recognize her husband. Then she saw the luxuriant chestnut hair and knew that the woman next to him was Valerie. *Valerie!*

A wave of nausea overwhelmed her. She turned and ran up the stairs, passing the gawking houseboy, and stumbled out into the warm Israeli night. There she became violently ill, retching until there was nothing more to come out of her save her own soul. She slumped to her knees as the tears came flooding and sobs of anguish racked her body. How long she remained that way, she didn't know, but gradually she grew calm again. She had to get away. Immediately. She had to escape from this terrible place where her husband had become a man she didn't know.

Mercifully, the car was still there. Seeing her stricken face, David refrained from questioning her. When she said, "I want to go back to Tel Aviv," he merely nodded, saying quietly, "Tel Aviv it is."

For the entire drive, Lily sat numbly. David found her a hotel room and Lily passively allowed herself to be checked in. David phoned El Al and booked her a direct flight home at noon, then said he would pick her up at nine.

Lily smiled wanly in thanks. Then, as the door closed behind him, she sank onto the bed, burying her face in her hands. After one brief glimpse in that darkened bedroom her whole world lay shattered.

*Why, Harry? Why, why, why?*

He always claimed he loved her. If that were true, how could he do this to her? Maybe their sexual relationship had not been steady since Jeremy's death, but was that fact alone enough to justify this?

Marriages went through their bad periods—surely Harry understood that—and the time surrounding Jeremy's death had been one of those periods. Whatever their problems, she had always trusted Harry. The only time she had ever doubted him was that one time when she had seen it in print. But then, after their wonderful "honeymoon" in New York, she had been completely reassured. It had all been malicious gossip. He would never be unfaithful to her. She was his wife, and he was a man of honor.

But nothing seemed as sure and steady as it once had. Not her marriage, not Harry, not Valerie, not even her. Suddenly it seemed her whole life had been built on fantasy. Well, she would be deluded no more. Perhaps there had been something in the Jennifer Quinn episode. Perhaps there had been others as well, over the years. A man capable of having an affair with a woman who was practically part of their household—a woman who was his own wife's best friend—was a man without scruples. He was capable of anything.

Lily chided herself. How naive she had been! How trusting! How stupid! And what a fool Harry had made of her! Humiliation seared through her whole being, and once again she had to choke down nausea.

Lying down sleepless, fully clothed, she couldn't bring herself to prepare for bed although she was bone-tired. It was almost four in the morning, and the hours stretched endlessly before her. It would be a long night before David would collect her to send her home.

Now, she wanted nothing more than to leave Israel as quickly as possible, to exorcise the very thought of this land from her mind forever. To her this would always be a cursed place. New York was her haven, her refuge. If only she could be there in an instant. Right now!

As she lay there, filled with desperate yearning, the image of Ellis flashed through her mind. She wanted nothing more than to hear his deep, calming voice. He was the rock she needed to cling to after this night of hideous revelation.

She sat up abruptly, turned on the bedside lamp, and took the telephone into her lap. A half-hour later, the operator rang her back. "You have a line open?" Lily nearly shouted. "Oh, thank you!"

It seemed like a miracle when, after two rings, Ellis's familiar voice came over the line.

"Lily? My dear, where are you?"

"I'm in Tel Aviv, Ellis, but I'm coming back to New York today. I mean, tomorrow. As soon as possible."

Her voice quavered slightly. Ellis had mixed feelings at hearing her so upset. Clearly she had discovered the truth about Harry and Valerie.

"When will you arrive? I'll meet your plane."

There was a long pause as Lily resisted the urge to tell him everything. If she could confide to anyone in the world, it was Ellis, and she wanted so much to talk to someone, to share the awful truth.

Still, something stopped her. Was it the old habit of loyalty to Harry? Or was it her own pride? She was so confused she didn't know the answer. But she would be seeing Ellis in person in twenty-four hours. That would be soon enough.

She wasn't sure of her arrival time, but she knew the flight number. "El Al number 343, Ellis. You'll have to check about the time."

He could hear the agony she felt, no matter how she tried to hide it. There was no doubt about it, she was devastated. Perhaps as desperate as when she'd learned about Jeremy. Ellis cursed himself for ever sending her on such a damnable mission. He would do his best to make it up to her in the future. For now he just said, "I'll be waiting for you."

"Oh, Ellis," Lily couldn't help but add, "I wish I were there now."

After she hung up, she wondered what to do next. The sun was coming up outside her window, but its beauty was lost on her. She called room service to order black coffee, then paced the small room restlessly until it arrived.

But gradually, as she sat sipping her cup on the tiny balcony overlooking the sea, one thing became clear: She had to confront Harry. But how? A phone call? She could not make such an accusation over the telephone. A letter? Again, it seemed ludicrous. *Dear Harry, When I saw you and Valerie together . . .* But the more she thought about it, the more she realized she couldn't simply slip away. If only to redeem her self-esteem, she was going to face the issue here and now. Lily had always shied away from unpleasant situations, but this was one time she could not let herself dodge. Harry was not going to get off so easily.

She picked up the phone and gave the operator the number of the house at Safed. She was strangely calm when Harry's voice came over the phone. "Harry? It's Lily. I'm here in Tel Aviv. . . . Yes, quite a surprise, I know. . . . You can be here in two hours? Fine, I'll be waiting."

With the same strange calm, she canceled her airplane reservation, then placed a second call to Ellis in New York. She was somewhat relieved that he wasn't home. He must have thought she sounded so strange. She left a message with his housekeeper about her change in plans. At least Ellis wouldn't have to wait for her in vain.

Lily began pacing again but coached herself with every step. *I must be calm when Harry gets here. Calm enough to tell him what I think of him and how much I loathe him.* She began to take deep breaths.

# Chapter 36

IT was just over two hours later when the knock sounded on the door. Lily's heart began to beat faster. "Come in," she called. Harry entered. The sight of him was as good as a physical blow. All she could think of was seeing his naked body entwined with Valerie's.

She steeled herself as best she could as she examined him in the light of day. He was tanned and fit. The days of hiking and digging in the Israeli sun seemed to have made him more attractive. But however appealing his appearance, Lily couldn't get beyond the treachery concealed in the blue eyes she'd always thought seemed so clear and candid.

"Lily, darling, what a wonderful surprise!" he said warmly as he put his arms around her. During the drive down from Safed, he'd not thought once how he was going from his mistress's bed to meet his wife. All he knew was his sense of joy and relief: Lily had given up her ball for him after all. He did love her so. And he felt deeply touched that she had flown in as a surprise.

But just as he tried to embrace her, she pushed him away. "Don't touch me!" she shouted.

Harry stared at her in genuine disbelief. For a moment he thought he hadn't heard correctly. Recovering his self-possession, he dug his hands into his pockets, leaned back against the door frame, and asked in a cool, ironic voice, "What, may I ask, is the problem?"

Lily thought she might scream. Her anger was too great to be suppressed. "The problem? I'll tell you, Harry. I didn't just get here. I arrived last night around ten o'clock and drove up to Safed." She took a deep breath, trying to maintain a civil tone. "I went into the house, to your bedroom, in fact." Lily looked at him coolly. "It seems I wasn't the first to get there."

Harry tried to speak but Lily could contain herself no longer. "Do you have any idea how I felt, seeing you lying there with your arms around her? God, Harry—Valerie! My best friend!"

"Lily, it's not what you think—"

"What was it, then? What else could it possibly be?" The tears began streaming down her cheeks. "My God, Harry, how could you do this? I thought you loved me!"

His philandering finally had caught up with him. This affair—so meaningless, so stupid—had suddenly assumed unthinkable proportions. There was no way he could justify himself to Lily. Seeing her cry so hopelessly was even worse than her recriminations.

Awkwardly, he put his hand on her shoulder. "Please, Lily, don't cry."

But Lily shook off his hand and eyed him sternly through tear-filled eyes. "Don't lie to me, Harry. How long has this been going on?"

Harry knew that he couldn't admit that he had slept with Valerie while Lily was up at the farm still mourning Jeremy's death. Yet, in all conscience, he could not pretend that last night had been the first time. At first, he tried to evade the issue of time.

"What's the difference, Lily? The point is, she doesn't mean a damn to me."

"But last night was not the first time?"

"No, it wasn't." He could not lie.

In her heart of hearts, Lily had hoped that last night had been the first time he had ever succumbed to temptation.

"I think it started a few weeks after we arrived here. I was lonely, and she was there. It really didn't mean anything, Lily."

"So you were just like a pair of animals in heat? And I'm supposed to understand? God, it's so degrading! To think of the two of you doing the same things that we do . . . another woman, touching my husband—"

She broke off, unable to go on.

As she spoke, Harry felt increasingly defensive. It sounded

so bestial, the way she put it. Guilt began to weigh heavily upon him. He could not bear it. Though he thought to check himself, he lashed out, assigning blame to her. "Listen, Lily! You're not exactly blameless in all this, you know! I'm a man, with normal physical needs. You must admit we've been pretty distant lately. And I'm not just talking about my being in Israel and your staying on in New York. Why, ever since—" Harry broke off.

"Since Jeremy's death? Is that what you were about to say? When I'm mourning for our child, I'm supposed to be worrying about your needs?"

"No, Lily, of course not! But it's been a while since that time. All I'm saying is that I'd like some affection—"

"Anywhere you can get it? Come on, Harry. I've never denied you!"

"There's a difference between not denying it and wanting it! This has been going on for years. So many times I've felt pushed aside—times when the children were little and you spent all your time with them, and very little with me."

"That only happened because you got so involved with your work!" Lily stormed.

"I don't think so, Lily," Harry returned coldly. "I'll never forget, years ago, how I tried to share my work with you but you were always so busy with the children . . . always the children!"

"That's a lie, Harry. The children became my substitute for the affection and companionship that you didn't give me! You shut me out of your life, out of that room—I always felt like an intruder."

"Let me refresh your memory. I remember wanting to read an article, the first meaningful thing I had done—and God, I wanted to share it with you. But you weren't there, Lily; you were busy being Jeremy's mother. You always made me feel as if I didn't count, as though I came second, and I did resent it—I admit it."

"The children left home a long time ago, Harry. I didn't see you try to bring me into your confidence then."

"Patterns that have been established over years aren't changed overnight. What was I supposed to do, get on my knees and thank you for finally having time for me?"

Lily was stunned by the rage and bitterness in his voice. Had he been suppressing these thoughts all these years?

Didn't he realize what work it was raising children? How much time they took from your day? Didn't he suspect how isolated she'd felt in their marriage? Harry had always had other outlets—his career, his fame. Who else did she have to turn to besides him? And now, she found, she didn't even have that. But Harry was still ranting.

"And worst of all, you abandoned me when I needed you most! Do you realize what I was reduced to when you made me feel that I was responsible for Jeremy's death? Can you understand how that made me feel? It was bad enough hearing it from Drew, but from you, Lily? You clung to your grief, building such a wall around yourself even I couldn't get through. So now I've gone outside our marriage for affection. Can you blame me?"

There was complete silence in the room. Lily stared at him coldly. "No, Harry. How could I ever blame you?" But for all the sarcasm in her tone, she had to admit there was some truth in what he was telling her.

Maybe Harry sensed her softening. He pushed on. "Can you honestly say I'm totally to blame for this thing with Valerie?" He drew a deep breath. Before she could answer, he said, "Don't get me wrong, Lily. I'm not trying to blame you. This has been a hard time for both of us. But the fact is, in the last few years, I haven't felt that you've been a wife to me."

In a low voice, Lily asked, "So where do we go from here, Harry? I suppose you want a divorce."

"Divorce?" He stared back at her. "What do you mean, I want a divorce?"

"Well, if you've been so unhappy with me . . ."

Harry shook his head. "Lily . . . darling, look at me. I've said a lot of things today that have been bottled up inside me for a long time. But I don't want to lose sight of something far more important." He paused. "Lily, I still love you. I have since the moment I met you, and I will until the day I die. I know I've hurt you, probably too much to ask that you forgive me, but is there any way we could make a fresh start? I—I just can't face the thought of life without you."

His voice trembled slightly as he uttered the last words. In spite of her grief and disillusionment, Lily felt a sudden rush of hope. Perhaps they would survive this storm.

"Lily?" Harry persisted. "Do you—still love me?"

Her look gave him answer.

Gently framing her face with his hands, he looked at her longingly for a moment, then kissed her.

It was a moment fraught with the hope of reconciliation and renewal.

After a long while, Harry spoke again. "Darling, when do you have to be back?"

"Soon. I was only going to be here for two days."

"Well, I know that you have an obligation. I never should have asked you to give it up, but could you just take one or two more days?"

Eyes bright, she nodded.

"Wonderful. We're going to Paris, darling." Kissing her again, he murmured softly. "Paris is for lovers."

It was a glorious three days. They stayed at the Ritz, and Lily discovered a whole new Harry—or, rather, one who had been lost for a long time.

By night, they went to Maxim's and the Tour d'Argent, the Folies-Bergère and the Club Américain. By day, they shopped at Dior and Chanel and at all the elegant little salons of the Rue du Faubourg-St.-Honoré.

Harry insisted on buying Lily an entire wardrobe, down to new hats and new shoes. On their last day there, he took her to Cartier and bought her a magnificent emerald necklace.

By some unspoken agreement, they avoided discussing Israel and Valerie, but as they stood at the airport waiting for their respective planes, Harry brought up the awkward subject.

"Lily, the minute I get back to Safed I'm going to tell Valerie that she has to go."

"Immediately?"

"Yes—of course, darling."

Taking her into his arms, he whispered, "It was a mistake, Lily. A huge mistake, and I'm sorry. Am I forgiven?"

"Yes," she whispered back. "I love you, Harry."

When they heard Lily's boarding call come over the loudspeaker, Harry took her into his arms and held her very close. There was a gentleness in the gesture which left Lily feeling that this was the beginning of a new life—a new love—for both of them. She no longer needed words to reassure her.

"I'll call every day, Lily. I can hardly wait until you can come and join me. I want you back in my arms."

Their flights were scheduled closely together. No sooner was Lily airborne than Harry heard his own boarding call.

Half an hour later, the silver TWA plane was winging its way over the Mediterranean toward Tel Aviv. Harry sat rehearsing what he would say to Valerie once he arrived.

Discarding a mistress wasn't easy. And Harry did have some fondness for Valerie. That he could not deny. She had given so generously of herself—in and out of bed. She had provided such solace to him just when Lily was neglecting him most. He owed her much for these last few months.

Harry felt a twinge of guilt when he recalled Valerie's frank declaration of love at Caesarea. To ease his sense of culpability, he reminded himself that she had known from the outset that there was no hope of anything permanent between them. He'd been up front from the start. And in truth, she'd be better off without him. After the breakup she would be free to move on to a relationship with a real future.

But despite his rationalizing, he was pained by the sight of her rushing to greet him at the gate. She gave him a kiss hello and cried, "Harry, welcome back! I've missed you so."

Harry broke away from her gently.

Her eyes sparkled. "Oh, Harry, I'm so glad you're back. What made you take it into your head to fly off to Paris, anyway?" Not waiting for an answer, she kissed him again and said, "How about instead of going back to Safed tonight, we stay here in Tel Aviv? I know a great hotel. It would be such fun, Harry!" She gave him a suggestive look.

It was difficult for him to meet her gaze. He was tempted to put off the confrontation. But his reconciliation had left him strongly imbued with new resolve.

"Valerie," he said simply, "we need to talk."

"About what?" She was suddenly curious—and concerned.

He hesitated. An airport terminal was no place to discuss this.

"Listen, I'm hungry. How about if I take you to dinner and we'll talk then?"

"You sound so serious, Harry. Can you give me a hint?"

Valerie's mind worked fast. She could sense Harry's reserve. Something had happened. He was a changed man.

Maybe he met someone in Paris? Why had he gone there in the first place? Valerie had been completely taken aback by his spur-of-the-moment trip. He'd slipped away without so much as a word to her.

Having steamed open Lily's letters to him, she knew they had no immediate plans to meet; those letters contained nothing but a recital of her dull charity activities, polite inquiries after his welfare, and a restrained "Love, Lily." Nothing there to throw a monkey wrench into her schemes.

Harry seemed withdrawn through their dinner. Whatever he'd had to discuss so urgently did not seem so pressing now. Valerie kept her mood and looks wistful. The little-girl-lost look was one of her specialties. She thought it might appeal to Harry's protective side.

But for once Valerie was not the architect of Harry's thoughts, for however much she'd baited him in the past. As they sat there he was secretly comparing her to Lily as she looked the night before in Paris. And there was no comparison.

Truth be told, he would miss Valerie most for her assistance with his book. But Harry well understood he'd have to incur the inconvenience. There was no way he could continue to associate with her—not in any capacity. Lily had given no ultimatums, but she didn't have to. Harry well knew Valerie would have to go. If only he'd released her from service when Lily first returned to Sutton Place from the farm.

Tonight Valerie seemed especially sweet and vulnerable. Harry cursed himself for what he had to say.

He swallowed his last sip of coffee, cleared his throat, and began. "Valerie, it won't do any good to beat around the bush. Lily has found out about us."

Her worst fear had come true. She was not ready for Lily to know about them—not yet. "But how?" she stammered. "Who told her?"

"Nobody told her. She flew in Friday night to surprise me, drove up to Safed around midnight, and—well, I'm afraid she actually saw us in bed together."

Lily must have been stunned—and furious. The reason for the Paris trip suddenly became clear: Harry had taken Lily there in hopes of patching things up between them. But Valerie still had reason to hope; Lily had not returned to Israel with Harry. Perhaps he would be free even sooner than she'd planned.

"So what did you decide to do?" she asked.

"Obviously, Lily was very upset, but we had a long talk, then the trip. We're going to work this out." Harry paused. "I guess you know this means we're going to have to stop seeing each other."

"Stop seeing each other?" she cried. "Just like that?" Valerie could hardly believe it.

"You know there's no way we can continue working together, not after all this."

"You mean you're firing me?" She had thought it only a matter of weeks—days—before he realized that he was in love with her. My God, she had made herself indispensable. She had been there for him when Lily never was. How could she lose him like this? Valerie knew that if she wanted to buy more time, she'd have to take a pragmatic approach. "Why, we're in the middle of the first draft! I can't leave. Does Lily understand how closely we work together?"

"Yes," Harry replied. "Lily understands exactly how closely we've been working together—that's the whole point."

Valerie could not believe that at the very least Harry would not keep her on in her secretarial capacity just as he had before.

"Okay, Harry," she said in a calm, reasonable voice. "So you and I have had an affair. But the book—doesn't it mean anything to her at all? She must know the importance of what you're doing. Is she going to let petty jealousy keep you from the kind of secretary you need?"

"Look, Valerie, the subject is not open to debate. Frankly, at this point, Lily wouldn't care if I put the entire manuscript of *The Genesis* in the fire, if it meant getting rid of you."

Valerie's blood began to boil. "Getting rid of me? As if I'm some old shoe?"

"Valerie, I know this seems abrupt. But from the start I've made it clear I couldn't promise you anything. And you can imagine how Lily feels. She's angry, and very hurt. I can't say I blame her."

"She's angry and hurt? Really? And you can't blame her for that? Or for Ellis Knox, or anything else?"

"Now, wait just a minute, Valerie. You can't compare yourself to Ellis. Nothing has ever gone on between them. What you and I did was wrong. There's no way around it."

She let out a bitter laugh. "So now you're going to get moralistic on me? You certainly didn't have many scruples that night on the terrace when you whisked me off my feet. Or back in New York last year either, for that matter."

Harry shifted uncomfortably in his chair. Valerie was well within her rights. "Look, Valerie, I'm not trying to say that I'm blameless—far from it. I'm just saying that we've let this go too far already, and it's time to break it off. I wish that we could go on working together, but we can't. It's as simple as that."

"Simple?" Valerie shrilled. "You mean you're going to just dump me?"

"Valerie, for God's sake, I'm married—you knew that! Right from the very start, I told you that there was no future for us. I didn't promise you anything."

"Really? Well, you might have said that there was no future in it, but you sure didn't act like it that weekend in Caesarea! In fact, you acted as if you were madly in love with me! A woman has intuition, Harry. Are you trying to tell me that you were thinking about Lily when you were screwing me?"

"Valerie, keep your voice down," he said, flushing.

"I won't!" she screamed. "You liked me well enough when I was doing all those things to you! The things your wife—the frigid bitch—is too much of a lady to do!"

Harry was stunned to see sweet, schoolgirlish Valerie shrieking like a harridan and cursing as well. Recovering slightly, he flushed with anger and muttered through clenched teeth, "How dare you talk like that about Lily! She considered you her best friend."

"So now she's the angel, and I'm the bitch?"

Harry was grim. "Yes. And maybe I've been a fool for not seeing that from the start."

But Valerie was nearly too hysterical to hear. "You can't do this to me, you rotten bastard, you son of a bitch!"

Harry glanced around the restaurant nervously. He prayed that no one would recognize him. What a story this would make if it reached the press.

Without a word he grabbed Valerie by the arm and dragged her outside. But Valerie would not be led. With her free arm, she began battering him, screaming every unprintable name in the book. Harry had never heard such language from a woman, and seldom from a man.

He tried to catch her arm, but she evaded him and managed to land a blow to his jaw. Without a moment's hesitation, he slapped her across the face. "Stop! Valerie, stop!"

The unexpected retaliation quieted her. She stood wild-eyed and breathing hard. Harry looked at her as though they'd just met. Only this time he saw her for what she really was. He wasn't deluded by her outward charms.

"I'll have your things sent to the King David, along with two months' severance pay."

Taking out several large bills, he held them out to her. "And then I never want to see or hear from you again. In fact, I want to forget I ever knew you."

After her taxi drove off, he walked slowly back to his car. What a nightmare this had been!

Harry couldn't help but wonder, had that vulgarity always been in Valerie? How could he never have sensed it? How could he not have known? For all of his supposed insight into the emotions and sensitivities of his fictional creations, Harry could hardly believe how blind he sometimes was to real people's character and motivation. He had made the same mistake with his children and his wife. Now he'd been equally stupid with Valerie. Oh, not that tonight's scorned woman was the real one either. In truth, she represented the kind of intertwining of good and evil which was the leitmotif of *The Genesis*.

But Harry couldn't think of his novel. Not then. Instead, he tried to focus on Lily. How beautiful she had looked as they strolled along the Champs-Élysées. Wonderful Lily, waiting faithfully for him in New York. How lucky he was that she hadn't left him, that she had been able to forgive.

Meanwhile, back in New York, Lily had just arrived at the airport; Ellis was waiting for her at the gate. He had nearly died of curiosity and apprehension since he received Lily's message. What had made her cancel that earlier flight? Then, when she called from Paris, he had wondered whether—no, hoped—she had gone there to console herself. He had expected sadness, resignation, a brave front on her misery. But as she descended from the plane, there was a lilt in her step, a smile on her lips. For whatever might have happened on her arrival in Israel, Harry had managed to persuade Lily to forgive him. It figured, he thought bitterly. No doubt a man as creative and imaginative as Harry invented a story to pacify her.

Yet her face was radiant as she waved to him over the crowd. "Ellis, how wonderful to see you!" Suddenly Ellis felt that she and Harry were really going to make it "happily ever after," and he didn't have the heart to wish them anything but good.

If Harry was what Lily wanted, then he would just have to conquer his own longings, and try to be happy for her.

# Chapter 37

AFTER all of Lily's work and worry, the night of nights had finally arrived. She felt as though destiny was taking her by the hand and leading her into a new dimension.

As she sat at her dressing table the evening of the ball, clipping on her diamond earrings, Ellis stood by the windows in the drawing room, looking incredibly distinguished in his white tie and tails, gazing down at the glittering lights of Manhattan. He sipped his martini thoughtfully. He was the most successful man in his field, yet none of it meant anything to him compared to the woman he'd loved for what seemed a lifetime: Lily.

"Ellis?"

Whirling around, he saw her framed in the doorway. She was like a fairy-tale princess. Her rippling auburn hair was swept up in a French twist. Her skin had never looked so pure, her eyes so green and sparkling. She was dripping with diamonds. Her gown was mint-green and encrusted with shimmering crystals. The low-cut bodice showed off her figure, which was still gorgeous, even after four children and so many years.

"My dear, you are absolutely ravishing."

"Am I really?" she asked, almost shyly.

"Exquisite," he answered. Then, fearing that his emotions were showing too plainly, he turned away and asked over his shoulder, "Martini? Or would you prefer a sherry?"

The ballroom of the Waldorf-Astoria was a wonderland. The ceiling had been tented in palest green and festooned with silvery streamers. Huge tubs of pink and white rhododendrons backed by giant ferns banked the walls. Extravagant bouquets of orchids, roses, and garlands of smilax gave the room the appearance of an enchanted garden.

It was Lily's night of triumph, and from the moment she entered the room on Ellis's arm, she was engulfed by praise.

"Lily, darling, this room is fabulous. It's just divine, my dear. . . . How did you manage to snag Benny Goodman? . . . Just look at the crush tonight. . . . It's by far the biggest success we've ever had. . . . A real tribute to you, Lily. . . ."

Laughingly she denied full credit, but inwardly she was filled with a mixture of elation and bewilderment at all the accolades. Until tonight, it had all been preparation and work. The scope of her accomplishment hadn't really hit her. But now, from the way everyone was talking, she realized she had really done something to be proud of. They had raised over $500,000, John had told her this afternoon—the most ever.

Many were curious about Harry. "Where is your famous husband? We just adore his books!" But tonight, she was the star—in her own right—and it felt good.

Seeing her so surrounded, Ellis finally intervened. "I'm sorry, ladies and gentlemen, but you can't monopolize Lily any longer. In a few minutes she has to make a speech."

The music was in full swing. The ballroom hummed to the rhythms of Benny Goodman's band as Ellis guided Lily through the crowd toward the stage. As they reached it, the music swung to a close. There was a brief lull. A quiver of nervousness ran through Lily as she looked at the podium. Sensing her qualms, Ellis turned to her and said quietly, "Listen to me, Lily. There's nothing to be afraid of. Just be yourself, and they'll love you." And then a drum roll shattered the lull as the spotlight sought them out.

Ellis straightened his tie, stepped into the circle of light, and strode to the podium, as thunderous applause rose from the audience. He addressed them with an easy confidence. "Good evening. The annual Spring Ball is, as you know, one of our principal sources of funding. I am happy to announce that this year's is the most successful ever. And the credit for that—and for this gala evening—must be given to this year's ball committee chairman. Ladies and gentlemen, may I present: Lily Goodhue Kohle!"

As she stepped forward into the spotlight, Ellis kissed her cheek and presented her with a great sheaf of pink roses which seemed to materialize out of thin air.

As he stepped back and she turned to the microphone, the applause began to swell tumultuously. There were whistles and cheers, even foot stamping, as the crowd demonstrated their appreciation not only of the beauty of this titian-haired woman in the mint-green gown, but of the job she had done so spectacularly.

"Thank you, all . . . thank you." As the applause began to die down, Ellis held his breath, afraid for a moment that Lily would be overwhelmed. But as her voice came over the public address system, it was clear and composed. He let out a sigh of relief, smiling as he stood unobtrusively in the shadows.

"Ladies and gentlemen, I thank you," she began. "By being here tonight, you have made a contribution to a very important cause—one which is very close to my heart, as a mother. We must defeat this cruel disease, the crippler and killer of children. That triumph may become possible through the research made possible by your generosity. . . . Again, thank you all so very much."

As she finished, the applause rose even more thunderously than before. When the music finally started up again and Lily rejoined Ellis, her eyes were sparkling. She could have been the younger woman he had first fallen in love with.

"I did it! It wasn't hard at all," she said enthusiastically. "Now, can we dance?" Without a word, he swept her away to the strains of "Stardust."

The evening was like an enchanted dream for Ellis. It was the wee hours of the morning before he finally collected his topcoat and Lily's sable, then called for a taxi.

Lily was elated. "Wasn't it just marvelous? I can't believe that everything turned out so well! When I think of how I worried and fretted . . ."

On and on she went, not noticing how unusually silent Ellis had become.

As the taxi swung in front of her building, she asked, "Will you come up for a nightcap?"

"I don't think so, Lily."

His tone was light, but for the first time she caught a note of constraint.

"Oh. Well, I suppose it is a bit late. It's just that I've had such a good time tonight. I guess I don't want it to end."

He gazed down at her, trying to keep the longing from his eyes. It was so hard to leave her. Tonight, as he had circled the room with her in his arms, he had imagined that she was his wife after all—that at the end of the evening he would be able to claim a husband's privilege of taking her home and making love to her all night.

But now, standing outside the door, he reminded himself that Lily was Harry's wife. It seemed that nothing would ever change that.

He steeled himself and softly bade Lily good night. With a curt nod, he turned and strode off.

A little of her elation seemed to vanish with him. In spite of the mildness of the spring night and the warmth of her sable, she suddenly shivered.

The next morning Harry called, eager to hear the details of the ball. But first he was apologetic. "I wanted to send you flowers, Lily. I spent hours trying to get a connection to a New York florist, but our lines were down here." Then he begged her to tell him how it had gone.

After she had described it modestly, he exclaimed, "You'll never be the one to tell me, Lily, but even long-distance I can tell this was a total triumph for you. It wouldn't have happened if it weren't for you. I only wish I could have been there to share in it."

"Oh, I would have loved that. But darling, now that I'm free, I'm planning to take the next available plane. Drew is traveling and Randy and Melissa will be at camp next month so I feel totally carefree."

Harry hesitated. Deep down, he feared that Lily could never be happy in Israel in the wake of what had happened to her there. Could she ever feel comfortable again, with those memories haunting her? The midnight drive, the discovery of him with Valerie? No, she could never enter that house in Safed again, never sleep in that ill-fated bed.

As they spoke, Harry firmed his decision. "Lily, I have a surprise for you. I'm going to be able to wind the research up out here much more quickly than I had thought. I'll be home in a few weeks. There's really no need for you to come out."

Lily was relieved to hear it. She suspected that Harry had

sensed her antipathy to the country in light of that fateful visit. And he was right, she dreaded the place, even more than he knew.

But she was equally determined not to let her insecurities in any way inhibit Harry's work on *The Genesis*. Neither Valerie's ghost nor the specter of Israel would have her keep Harry from that most important project of his life.

"Harry, please don't compromise what you're doing for my sake. The ball is over. There's no reason in the world why I can't leave tomorrow."

"No, Lily. I've already gotten exactly what I came for. Anything else would simply be frosting on the cake."

"Then why do I feel like you're going out of your way for me?"

"I'm not, darling. It's just that now I realize there's nothing more important to me than being with you. And I want to be with you there, in our own home."

"Oh God, Harry. I love you so much!"

"The feeling's mutual, darling. I love you more than I can say. I'll call you every day to keep you posted on my plans." He paused, then added casually, "Incidentally, I've hired a young Israeli secretary named Avi. He'll be coming back with me."

And so the weeks passed. Finally, the long-awaited phone call came. "The research is finished, darling. I'm going to leave Rafi and Tony to wind up. I'll be home day after tomorrow."

Lily was thrown into a frenzy of anticipation. She ordered all kinds of delicacies, filled the apartment with flowers, and bought herself a new suit to wear to the airport.

Meanwhile, for Harry the leavetaking was poignant. As the plane soared up over the dry, golden land of his forebears, he felt a new spiritual oneness with his heritage. His roots would always be in this ancient land.

But however much the weight of his responsibilities regarding his novel pressed on him, Harry's preeminent concern was to make things right with Lily. Before he could do anything else, he had to reaffirm his commitment to her.

Lily was waiting for him at the gate. As soon as he caught sight of her, he ran over and swept her into his arms, kissing her with an almost savage need.

"Darling, darling, darling," he whispered. "I love you."

Their reunion was sweet and passionate, no doubt inspired by the difficulties they had so recently overcome. Their marriage had been tested again and again, and they had come through. Now they were going to find a new peace together. Their love had survived trials that—even separately—would have torn most couples apart. They could take that bond for granted no more than they ever had; yet as they faced the future, both Harry and Lily felt their love had grown, tempered by trouble and time, and would keep them together for the rest of their years.

Months passed before the final manuscript of *The Genesis* was finished, but for the first time, writing did not consume Harry's life. He confined his work to certain hours; he delegated much to his trusty help.

Avi, who had a degree in literature from Trinity College, Cambridge, turned out to be a treasure. The two researchers were a wealth of Judaica. Harry had the leisure to become the romantic figure Lily had fallen in love with. He was the Harry of their first days together: buying her flowers and candy and indulging her every whim.

By the time Harry finally turned in his novel, he was relieved as never before. Now he would be free to concentrate on Lily; they were really going to live. He wanted to take her somewhere; they had never been free to do that since their marriage. He told Ellis, "I'll call you once a week and you can talk to me about business, but that's all. We're going on a long-delayed honeymoon."

Without any real destination in mind, they drove up the coast to Woods Hole and took the ferry to Martha's Vineyard. There, Lily fell in love with an eighteenth-century house near Edgartown Harbor. Harry promptly took a three-month lease.

This truly was the honeymoon they had never had. They would stay in bed until noon, then have a leisurely brunch. Afterward they would stroll hand in hand through the quaint village or out for miles along the shore.

For the first time in many years, there were none of the demands of child-rearing or publishers' deadlines to pull them apart. It was just the two of them—the first time they'd been alone together since the nine months before Jeremy's birth.

The only interruption was a brief ten days in Manhattan while Randy and Melissa were between camp and school.

After their return to the island, they took one excursion to see the magnificent fall foliage in New England, another to visit Boston, but in the main they were content simply to rediscover each other in the pleasant confines of the Vineyard.

But as the days grew cooler, the few remaining visitors left. Harry and Lily reluctantly turned over the key to the house and headed back to Manhattan.

In no time at all the two found themselves setting off for The Meadows for the Christmas holidays. Drew had announced his intention of not coming home. Both Harry and Lily secretly heaved a guilty sigh of relief. It always seemed that he and Harry ended up fighting; they were pleased to be avoiding that this year.

When he called up to say he'd like to go skiing at Vail instead, Lily felt he was doing it as much to stay away from Harry as he was for the skiing itself. And so there were two empty places at the Christmas table, but Randy and Melissa, Randolph and Ellis, helped make the place seem cozy even in the absence of their two boys.

Harry and Lily behaved like newlyweds. It was impossible to miss the happy glow that emanated from them this holiday. The tender glances they exchanged, the way he touched her hand, the new harmony of minds and spirits—all were tokens of their rekindled flame.

It was exquisite agony for Ellis. He could hardly bear the love pats and glances. It was all he could do to keep from leaving. *She was never yours, Ellis,* he told himself. *She never will be. Accept it like a man.* And so, he did his best to smile and play the role of old family friend, while inwardly he still longed for Lily.

After the packages had been opened on Christmas Day, he cornered Harry and dragged him off to the study. Closing the door behind them, Ellis said without preamble, "Listen, Harry, it's about time we had a little talk. You know, the publication date for *The Genesis* is only two weeks off."

"I know, I know."

He didn't know why they couldn't have held off until summer.

"Well, what the hell do they want from me? Tell them to go sell the book."

"You know damned well what they want. Interviews, book signings, parties. And Renaud's is talking about a big nationwide tour. They love the book, you know."

Harry had never appreciated this aspect of the publishing business. He didn't see why the book couldn't just sell itself. He'd put off making a firm tour commitment, and now he had plans of his own.

"Well, the great American public is going to have to wait this time. I'm taking Lily to Bermuda."

Ellis sighed wearily. "When? And for how long?"

"We're leaving Monday and we'll be gone for as long as I damned well please."

"Harry, you can't! It's the worst possible time—they're going to be clamoring for you the second the book hits the shelves. And in fairness, you do owe it to Renaud's. They've put a hell of a lot of money into pre-publication advertising. You can't just abandon them. They're counting on you to live up to your end of the deal."

"Okay, Ellis, listen to me. For years, I've been living my life according to what you or Renaud's or the public dictates, and it almost succeeded in ruining my marriage. Lily comes first from now on. It's cold and gloomy here, and Bermuda is warm and beautiful. So we're going, and to hell with everything else."

"I wish you'd reconsider—put the trip off, for a few months at least."

"Sorry," Harry returned flippantly. "You can forward my checks, care of the Bermuda Bay Hotel."

The following Monday he and Lily boarded their plane as planned.

Bermuda was the island paradise of their dreams: a small coral jewel in the middle of the ocean, dusted with fine pink sand, fringed by swaying palms. More than ever, Lily and Harry felt like a pair of young lovers.

Martha's Vineyard had been charming, but in Bermuda something wild and primeval beckoned. They found themselves doing things they had never done before, even in their youth: dancing all night, sleeping all day, shedding their clothes in a secluded cove.

One explosive night, with a full silver moon overhead, they

made passionate love on the beach. The waves lapped gently at their feet as they became one.

The next day, as they sat over a late-morning breakfast, Lily sipped her iced mimosa, then closed her eyes for a moment, remembering the magic of the night before. Opening them, she looked at Harry relaxing in the sun and smiled slightly. How she loved him. It seemed impossible that they could ever have been estranged.

Then a white-jacketed native waiter interrupted with a telephone. "Mr. Kohle? Telephone call from New York."

Harry frowned. "I suppose it's Ellis. I forgot to call him yesterday."

Sighing, he lifted the receiver. "Harry Kohle here . . . Hello . . . Yes? . . . Well . . . Okay, I'm sorry, I was busy . . . So sue me, I just plain forgot . . . What was that? . . . *What?*"

Then he sat listening for a long time while Lily watched curiously.

"Yes, of course," Harry said finally. "But dammit, Ellis, can't we put it off?"

Lily could now hear Ellis's voice nearly shouting from the other end of the line: ". . . Has the sun gone to your head or something? You simply can't tell them to wait on your convenience; you have to let them know. What are you going to do?"

"I don't know," Harry finally snapped. "Now, Ellis, don't push me on this. I'll think about it and call you back. . . . Right . . . Good-bye."

For as good as the news was, Harry resented the intrusion from the outside world. Harry had finally discovered what was most important to him, and the answer wasn't success or fame or fortune or any combination of the three. What mattered was his life with Lily. He would do nothing to jeopardize their newly found happiness. But back in New York, it was as if there were a conspiracy forming against his hard-won peace of mind.

Though she didn't quite know what had been said, Lily felt apprehensive. It wasn't like Harry to react so moodily. She wondered what Ellis's news could be.

"Problems?" she asked tentatively, almost frightened to find out.

Harry chuckled. "Well, no—not exactly. Ah, Lily, at

one time, I would have sold my soul for news like this."

"What, Harry? Tell me!"

"Well, for one thing, Ellis just heard that next week we'll be number one on *The New York Times* bestseller list."

"So soon after publication? Harry, that's absolutely marvelous!" she cried. "I'm ecstatic!"

"You and Ellis both," he returned briefly. "But there's something else, Lily. He wants me to fly back to New York right away. Apparently *Time* magazine wants to do a cover story on me."

For a moment Lily couldn't speak. The cover of *Time*! She threw her arms around him and kissed him. "Congratulations, darling!"

But Harry just sat there, frowning slightly.

"What's wrong, Harry? What's the problem?"

"The problem is that I've finally taken some time to do all the things we always dreamed of doing and never had the time to do. And we've been so happy here, I don't ever want to leave."

"Darling, can't we go and do the interview and then come back? It's only a few hours' flying time; we don't even have to give up our suite."

"No, Lily, it's not that simple. Once I get back, I'll be deluged. There will be other interviews, and Renaud's will be insisting on my doing that tour. I was kind of hoping I could avoid all that this time. But now . . ."

"Look, darling, even if we have to leave home, we'll be together. We'll still have each other."

"Lily, you're the most wonderful woman in the world to be so understanding. But as soon as this is over, we'll go off together to a deserted island somewhere. And I mean it—no calls, no publisher's demands, no newspapers. I'm not even sure I'll even write another book."

"Well, we'll see." Lily smiled at the thought.

"Don't laugh, Lily. I really mean it."

# Chapter 38

BACK in New York, they instantly realized that *The Genesis* was not just a book, but a phenomenon. It had surpassed everyone's wildest expectations and seemed destined to reign on the bestseller list week after week. And the critical accolades were pouring in faster than they could be pasted into scrapbooks.

"Harry Kohle's masterpiece" was the consensus. A few critics even went so far as to speculate about a Pulitzer Prize.

Like *The Wars of Archie Sanger*, the new book had a universality which touched people of all backgrounds, but it also had a poignancy which stirred the deepest emotions. The research Harry had done in Israel had laid the groundwork for a vision of a point in history that had never been so eloquently and grippingly conveyed.

Lily could only rejoice for Harry as he basked in the commercial and critical acclaim. He needed this validation; he needed to know that his instincts about *The Genesis* had been exactly right.

Yet after the first few weeks it became evident that Harry's current success was on a much vaster scale than that of his earlier works. There were pyramids of books in the store windows on Fifth Avenue—Scribner's and Doubleday—with Harry's larger-than-life image hanging behind them. Hollywood was already negotiating for the rights and promising him total creative control, dangling the carrot of the new star Marlon Brando for the male lead and Anna Magnani for the female.

And then the *Time* cover story came out, with a striking,

enigmatic photograph of Harry, and his fortune was sealed.

He couldn't go anywhere in public without being mobbed. There was no way to avoid the media's probing glare. Harry was hounded. His time was booked for weeks. In February, he was honored at a black-tie gala given by the Literary Critics Circle, which had just awarded him its annual fiction prize. The vast ballroom of the Waldorf-Astoria was filled to capacity. Lily sat at the head table with him while speaker after speaker lauded his book.

But when Harry finally rose, he said, "I thank you for all the kind words and appreciate the honor you have awarded me. But I wish to make it perfectly clear to everyone present that none of this could have happened without my lovely wife, Lily, who has supported, sustained, and inspired me through the years, and who inspires me still. Lily?"

Lily could hardly believe her eyes. This thanks was so unexpected. But Harry was clapping and motioning for her to take a bow. The crowd applauded enthusiastically. Lily rose gracefully, murmured "Thank you," then took her seat again, gratified that Harry should choose so public a forum in which to acknowledge his love.

Later that evening, she agreed readily when Harry told her about the short publicity tour planned for him. "San Diego, Los Angeles, San Francisco. A few book signings, some interviews, maybe a radio show or two. Do you mind, darling?"

"Oh, no, Harry. It sounds wonderful—I've never seen most of those places before."

At first Lily was aglow to see the enormous response that greeted *The Genesis*. She was thrilled to see Harry bask in the glory. Wherever they went—sometimes to as many as several cities a day—the crowds were always overwhelming. But as Renaud's began adding more and more stops to the itinerary and the pace became more and more hectic, Lily again began to find herself pushed aside in the whirl. And there was little Harry could do to help her.

And it wasn't only that. Something had happened to Harry. At first, he had taken a detached, almost ironic view of his publicity. But now, it was as if he had begun to believe his own press. He began to lap up the praise, becoming even boastful of his triumph.

Harry had lived with acclaim ever since his *Archie Sanger* days, but he had never felt the effect of that fame beyond the perimeter of New York City. Intellectually, he understood that people across the country treasured his work, but he'd never before come in contact with the adoring hordes. No one could have remained unaffected by the nationwide hubbub, but Lily was unhappy to see Harry's ego affected so dramatically.

As she sat in the back of the limousine, waiting for Harry to break free of the crowd in front of the civic auditorium in Portland, where he'd just given a reading from his book, Lily couldn't help but fear that he was slipping away from her yet again.

Orchestrating this whirlwind tour were Kate Hathaway, the publicist from Renaud's, and Roy Flatt, the tour manager. They took care of everything: planes, trains, hotels. Lily didn't even have to pack or unpack a suitcase for either herself or Harry, so extensive was their control. As the days went by, she found herself feeling more and more superfluous.

It was becoming almost embarrassing the way Harry made a big point of bringing her forward to give her credit. The initial thrill of hearing him introduce her as "my wonderful wife, Lily" was gone. She well understood that no one in the crowd could care less about her.

For a while Lily feared she was becoming jealous of her own husband's success. But after an honest examination of her own mind, she knew that there was much lacking in Harry's behavior of late, for all the praise he gave her.

Suddenly Harry didn't seem to mind the fanfare and the thrill of being in public demand. As the days passed, he neglected Lily more and more, speaking little of the trip he'd spoken of so fondly.

And the gulf between them widened.

The four of them sat together at the bar at Ernie's in San Francisco: Kate, Roy, Lily, and Harry. Kate had arranged for Harry's picture to be taken with Victor Gatti, the proprietor. She busily directed the photographer while Lily gazed about her, admiring the crimson damask walls and velvet banquettes and the warm glow of the Baccarat chandeliers.

Then she suddenly heard a woman tourist behind her exclaim, "Look, George! That's Harry Kohle. Maybe we can get his autograph."

After a brief wait they found themselves settled at the

banquette laid with gold and white Limoges china and heavy silver. The conversation resumed.

"I heard from Renaud's today," Roy began. "They're very anxious that you expand the tour to the Midwest."

"What would that entail?"

"Kansas City, Chicago, Detroit, Indianapolis, points in between."

Lily listened with a growing sense of tension as they discussed the plan. Now the Midwest. How she'd been counting the days until their final stop in Seattle. The prospect of more weeks looming before them was too daunting. Suddenly, all she wanted to do was lie down.

As soon as dessert was served, she rose. "If you'll all excuse me, I think I'll go back to the hotel."

"Lily, darling, are you feeling all right?" Harry asked, concerned.

"Yes, of course, dear. I just have a slight headache."

Back in their suite at the St. Francis, Lily put on her dressing gown, but instead of lying down, she went to the window and looked out at Union Square.

Again she considered those idyllic months when Harry had deliberately put Lily first. She had been so sure they had conquered the forces pulling them apart. But now there was no use fighting it: Her husband belonged to the world, and she was going to have to recognize that inevitable fact.

Before, she might have blamed him, but even she could see the seductive appeal of fame. The months they'd shared after his return from Israel had been more precious than ever in retrospect. Lily consoled herself with that knowledge that all the clamor would at least subside. In the meantime, she knew what she must do. Just as during that time long ago in Hollywood, she was not needed now. If she stayed, the rift between them was bound to grow. The only way she could keep him was to let him go. He must be free to see the tour through to the end without worrying about her. She would wait for his return at home.

When Harry came in an hour and a half later, he found her still awake. "How are you feeling, darling? Is your headache still bothering you?"

"No, thank you, dear. I'm feeling better."

"I'm glad. I would have come back earlier, but I didn't want to disturb you in case you were trying to sleep."

"That was sweet of you. Actually, I've been doing some thinking."

"Mmmm?"

"About us, Harry." She paused, then continued slowly. "Harry, you don't need me around to worry about on this tour; you barely have enough time to sleep and eat as it is. Frankly, I'm just in the way."

"What are you saying, Lily?" Anger flashed in his eyes.

"I'm saying that I think that perhaps the time has come for me to go back to New York."

Harry struggled to suppress his rage. How could she even suggest leaving? Everything was going beautifully. The tour was a smash success, the arrangements superb. What could she possibly object to? He had thought she was enjoying herself. For his part, he loved having her by his side—but obviously, the feeling wasn't mutual.

She told him she felt superfluous. What the hell did that mean? Lily did not tell Harry that she felt he was becoming swept up by his own publicity. But Harry sensed it in her resolve to return now. Well, he was through with feeling guilty, about Lily or anyone else. And much as he wanted her to stay, he wasn't going to beg her. Not again.

"If that's what you want, Lily."

"Well, it's not really what I want. But I think it would be for the best. And it will only be for a few weeks."

"You're right," he said curtly. "You're absolutely right."

And on that cold note, they went to bed.

# Chapter 39

WHEN she arrived in New York, no one was there to meet her. Ellis was out of town for the day and Mary and Joe were down at The Meadows, supervising some renovations.

The apartment was dark and quiet as she entered, and despite all her brave resolutions, Lily felt forlorn. She kicked off her shoes and went to the living room. She started a fire, then poured herself a stiff brandy and curled up under an afghan. She took a long swallow, then cradled the glass in her hand musingly and gazed at the shimmering reflection of firelight on the amber liquid.

The room was still, save for the hiss of the logs on the grate. For weeks she had been lonely in the middle of a crowd. Now she was lonely on her own, suddenly questioning the wisdom of her plan. She had been so convinced that this course would be best for their marriage, but now . . .

At last she fell into a troubled slumber, but she woke the next morning feeling refreshed, full of certainty in her plan. She had done the best thing for them both, she was convinced. She was filled with an energy and happiness she hadn't felt since they left Bermuda. She was going to get on with her life. And the person to help her do that was Ellis. She picked up the phone and dialed his office.

"Lily!" came his surprised voice a minute later. "Where are you?"

"I'm back in town, Ellis."

"When did you get in?"

"Last night, late."

"Nothing wrong, I hope?" he asked tentatively.

"Oh no—not at all. But there are a few things I'd like to talk to you about. Are you free for lunch?"

"For you I am," he replied, mentally making a note to cancel two appointments. "Say, '21' at twelve-thirty?"

Lily was looking forward to seeing him. She felt a warm glow as he rose from his table to greet her. Until this moment, she hadn't realized how she had missed him.

He kissed her cheek. "It's wonderful to see you, my dear. It seems as if you've been gone forever."

Lily smiled ruefully. "It seems like that to me, too."

"How is Harry doing?"

"He's fine."

"From all reports, the tour has been like the Second Coming."

"It certainly has."

"Why did you decide to come back?"

She hesitated, hating to lie to Ellis, but she couldn't be disloyal to Harry. Finally she said, "Well, Harry wanted me to stay—begged me to stay—but when it developed that the tour was going on to the Midwest, I decided that the time had come for me to get on with some of my own activities."

"Did you enjoy being on the road?"

Lily remained evasive. "Oh, yes and no. The crowds were terrific, and it was fun to see Harry being such a star, but there wasn't much for me to do and, frankly, I began to feel a little as if I were in the way."

He nodded. "Well, I think perhaps you're wise to let him have his day. Meanwhile, what do you have in mind for yourself?"

"I was hoping that you might have some suggestions."

"Actually, I do. I thought of you the minute I heard about this the other day. The Manhattan Historical Landmarks Society has an annual auction of art and antiques and they need someone dynamic to organize it. Would you be interested?"

Knowing that the Landmarks Society was one of Ellis's particular pet projects—he detested modern art and architecture almost as much as she did—Lily was flattered by his offer.

But still, she demurred. "Of course I'm interested, but I don't know if I'm really capable of anything that demanding."

His brows drew together in a frown. "What do you mean, capable? What has happened to your self-confidence? You'd be fabulous, just as you were with the Spring Ball."

What *had* happened to her confidence? Was its loss simply the result of weeks of feeling like a nonentity on the fringe of her husband's fame?

"Look, Lily," Ellis said, seeing her hesitate. "I wouldn't ever propose something that you weren't comfortable with and that wasn't well within your capabilities."

She smiled wryly. "I know that, Ellis. It's just that I think you have a much higher opinion of me than I deserve."

"That's impossible," he returned lightly.

He always made her feel wonderful. And eventually she found herself acquiescing.

Lily found checking and cataloguing the furniture and art donated for the auction unexpectedly fascinating, and she gradually became caught up in it.

When she talked to Harry, however, she didn't dwell on the details. Instead, she turned the conversation around to him. Were the crowds as boisterous as ever? How had the radio program gone?

The tour was going well, it seemed. The show had been a huge success. There was to be a big interview in the *Chicago Tribune*. Oh, and they had added a swing through Texas. He wasn't going to be able to fly home for some time.

Lily couldn't get over how stilted their conversations had become. What had happened to the intimacy which had developed since their reconciliation? Harry never seemed to say "I love you" anymore, or any of the other little things she longed to hear. When she ventured, "I miss you, darling. I can hardly wait until you come back," his response was simply, "I'm afraid it will be a while yet."

Lily hung up feeling unhappy and frustrated. But all she could do was try to fill up her time while she waited. Little did she know then that it would be almost five weeks before Harry finally returned.

At the airport, she instantly detected the new air about him. He was every inch the media swell. The glittering soirees, the jammed lecture halls, the radio and newspaper interviews, the fawning praise from provincial critics had all left their mark. Lily could feel his ego pulsing even before he spoke.

"Hello, Lily. I've missed you," he said. He kissed her briefly.

"I've missed you too, darling," she said, putting her arms around him. "It seems like forever that you've been gone."

The scene was flat. It was as though they were dutifully repeating the lines expected of them.

"Did you have a good flight?"

"Oh, it was so-so."

Just then Roy Flatt and Kate Hathaway joined them.

"Hi, Lily, how have you been?" Roy greeted her genially.

"Oh, hello. I didn't realize you were all on the same flight . . . but of course, you would be."

"Can we give you a lift?" Harry asked. "Lily has the car."

Lily drove in silence as the rest of them talked shop. Apparently the last reading had been a comedy of errors. The microphone didn't work, the fire alarm had gone off as Harry began to speak. Lily felt utterly left out of their intimate trio.

Harry helped them with their luggage when they were each dropped off at their apartments.

"Sounds as though you had a good time," she said dryly when they were finally alone in the car.

"Oh, not bad," he returned casually.

"It's nice to have you back."

He stretched and yawned. "It will be good to be home. I need a rest."

And that was all. No protestations of love, no impassioned embraces. That night, Lily had planned a gourmet meal to celebrate his homecoming, but Ellis dropped by for a drink in the late afternoon, and as the dinner hour approached, Harry asked, "We'd love to have you for dinner—can you stay?" There was nothing Lily could do but second the invitation, and Ellis promptly accepted, saying only, "Of course, I don't want to intrude on your first night back. . . ."

"Oh, no, no," returned Harry heartily. "No problem. There are quite a few things I need to talk to you about."

The dinner conversation revolved around *The Genesis* and the pending question of movie rights. The elegant meal—fresh Maine lobster, imported *petits pois*, and beautiful *croquembouche*—was disposed of without ceremony while the men debated the issue.

Finally, after Mary had poured the coffee, Ellis settled back in his chair and said, "Lily, we've certainly neglected you thus far this evening. Harry, has she told you much about this big auction she has been whipping into shape?"

"Oh, yes. It's for the—the—"

"Historical Landmarks Society," Lily sullenly prompted him.

"That's right—of course. Well, it should be interesting. What is it that they do again?"

"They work for the preservation of our architectural and cultural heritage," Ellis said, adding humorously, "Something a Philistine like you wouldn't understand."

"Sure, I understand it," Harry said jokingly. "Seems to me that my father got a nice tax break last year when the Kohle Mercantile Bank building was reclassified as a landmark. I guess that this society isn't such a bad thing after all."

They all laughed, but Ellis glanced swiftly at Lily, fearing that Harry's indifference had hurt her. But as always, she remained smiling and gracious under his gaze. "Shall we have a little more champagne? This is a celebration, you know."

"I'd love it," Ellis replied. "But after that, I'm going to leave the two of you to yourselves."

"No need," said Harry, yawning. "You know, all of a sudden I'm so tired I'm ready to drop. It must be the long flight catching up with me. If you'll both excuse me. . . ."

There was an awkward silence after he departed in the direction of the bedroom. That his mind was not on a romantic reunion was painfully obvious.

What had happened to the attentiveness, the loving attitude Harry had displayed toward Lily at Christmastime? Ellis wondered. He seemed a changed man.

Lily tried bravely to summon up a smile. "He's tired. . . ."

"Well, now your life will settle back to normal a little bit."

But this time his words proved not to be prophetic.

Early the next morning, Harry got a phone call from Renaud's. Apparently, an extemporaneous lecture he had given after a reading at the University of Oklahoma had been such a resounding success that Kate and Roy had proposed a lengthy lecture tour of colleges and universities.

"Are you going to do it, Harry?" Lily asked, her heart sinking.

"I think so," he said decidedly. "They seem very anxious

to have me, and I enjoy the prospect of dealing with students."

"Oh," Lily answered flatly. Not one word about missing her, or being sorry to leave her again. Two days later he was gone, and Lily threw herself back into her auction committee. Try as she might, she couldn't understand what was wrong. It was as if Harry were angry with her, though he showed no sign of irritation. He was calm, cool—and indifferent.

# Chapter 40

WEEKS passed, and the auction came and went. It was a complete success, but Lily accepted the congratulations wearily. When Ellis proposed another committee for her, she told him, "Thanks, but no thanks. I don't think I have the energy left for anything else right now."

As time passed, Ellis became more concerned. Lily seemed strangely listless. She lacked her usual sparkle. "Are you feeling well, Lily?" he asked her one evening.

She shrugged. "Oh, I'm healthy enough."

"Well, you look as though you could use a night out. How about dinner? Anywhere you'd like."

"Thank you, Ellis, but I think I'll just go home and try to get a good night's sleep."

Tonight more than ever, the silent phone mocked her, and when she finally turned the light out, she lay staring into the darkness.

In the morning, having slept only two or three hours, she dragged herself out of bed, slipped on her bathrobe, and went into the kitchen for a cup of coffee.

Mary was there, putting away the morning's marketing. "My, my," she said, greeting her employer, "you look tired this morning. Here, have some coffee and one of these cinnamon rolls."

"I am a little tired, Mary—but I think I'll just have coffee right now."

She took her cup out to the terrace, letting the pale sunshine bathe her face. Sitting there sipping her coffee, she felt like an old lady at a sanatorium, wheeled out into the garden by the attendant for some fresh air.

Wearily, she went into her mirrored dressing room, intending to change. Instead, she pushed back the shutters, flooding the room with harsh daylight, and allowed her robe to slip onto the floor. Rarely did she spend a lot of time looking at herself in the mirror. Most of the time her toilette consisted of pulling on a dress or suit, brushing her hair, and perhaps dabbing on a little lipstick.

She was far from being a vain woman; in fact, the memory of her childhood, when she had heard her red hair so constantly disparaged, had left her with an inferiority complex about her looks.

Still, from the time in Paris when she had become an overnight social success, she had grown accustomed to thinking of herself as at least reasonably attractive. But now, looking at herself in the mirror, she thought: I'm past forty now, middle-aged.

Her auburn hair still showed no signs of graying, but it hung loosely about her shoulders in no particular style. She had never regained the weight she had lost after Jeremy's death and her face looked drawn and tired, her complexion dull. The tiny crow's-feet around her eyes suddenly looked like cavernous furrows, especially today. No wonder Harry was no longer interested in her. She was aging, plain, a hausfrau. She was, worst of all, ordinary. And, God only knew, her husband was no ordinary man. He was still virile and handsome, his few lines and the silver at his temples only serving to enhance his appeal.

In truth, she was fighting not another woman, but a much greater adversary: celebrity. It was a seduction in itself, beyond mere looks and wealth. She couldn't dazzle the way the glowing, glittering sphere of fame could, and now she didn't even have beauty to offer Harry.

In her despair, Lily had lost all perspective. She'd convinced herself that her looks were the source of the problem. Somehow it suddenly seemed that nothing else mattered except regaining her lost beauty.

But the solution came to her with unexpected swiftness, even though she had never thought of it before: Switzerland. Even in her convent-school youth, women had come to the spas for rejuvenation, and now there were the world's best plastic surgeons.

She would have a face-lift, and then recuperate at one of the famous spas. Perhaps even put on a little weight. Then she would go to Paris and get herself a smashing new wardrobe. Harry was always telling her to spend money. Well, for once she would. The whole thing would take no more than a month and she could even be back before Harry returned from his lecture circuit.

When she called him that evening she told him, "Darling, since you're away, I've decided to take a little vacation in Europe. I've been feeling a bit run-down, and I want to have a little rest in Switzerland, maybe get in touch with my old friend Colette in Paris. Just a few weeks—I'll be back before you finish your tour."

"Fine, Lily," he said flatly. "I think you should. Sounds wonderful."

When he hung up, he gave a short, cynical laugh. She couldn't be bothered to travel with him, claiming that she felt superfluous, but now she was going off to Europe to see a girlfriend. That said it all, as far as he was concerned. Lily had her own life and was best off living it—without him.

A week later, Lily was operated on by the most eminent plastic surgeon at the Clinique Lassalle in Geneva. She had vaguely thought that the procedure entailed little more discomfort than a trip to the beauty salon, but soon she realized how naive she had been. For two weeks afterward, as she sat in her room and looked out through the pale, clear air at the Alps, her face was swathed in bandages. The pain was excruciating.

Even worse was the mental torture of knowing that she might have made a great mistake. There would be no improvement. Indeed, she would be lucky if she weren't horribly scarred and unnatural-looking. Harry would hate it. . . .

But after the bandages were removed and the swelling and bruising receded, she was the Lily of old once again. As soon as she realized that the operation had been a success, she found herself enjoying being in Switzerland again. She walked in Alpine meadows, sailed across Lake Geneva, ate *glacés* in tiny cafés, and was carried back to the long-ago days of boarding school.

How unhappy she had been as a child, how utterly friendless. A shadow of that unhappiness had always hovered over her. She had never really stopped being that miserable, lonely little girl who knew herself to be unloved.

Whether she realized it or not, this sense of being unloved was the root of why she had come here for this operation. Harry's strange aloofness had conjured up all the old feelings of low self-worth.

As the days passed, the clear air and mineral baths and exercise brought fresh color to her complexion, sparkle to her eyes, and a spring to her step. By the time she left, she felt like a new woman.

Yet the second phase of her transformation awaited. It seemed exactly like the first time Colette had taken her to Paris. She was massaged and pampered; her nails were manicured and her hair was cut and curled.

Then she went to the Rue du Faubourg St.-Honoré, the heart of Paris couture, and ordered an entire new wardrobe from Lanvin. They assured her that all would be complete within ten days, and they proved as good as their word.

As Lily stood in front of the mirror for her last fitting, she thought, I may look like a new woman, but all I want is to be the woman Harry fell in love with over twenty years ago.

Filled with renewed confidence, she found herself impatient to go home. Upon her arrival back in Manhattan, she was startled to hear that Harry would be flying in at six o'clock that evening, earlier than expected.

"Oh, Mary, I've got so much to do!" she cried. "I want dinner at home tonight."

"I'll take care of the marketing, Mrs. Kohle. Just make a list of what you want."

"Fine—fine," she said distractedly. "I have to call Elizabeth Arden."

At the salon, the attendants secretly thought that seldom had anyone needed beauty treatments less. Lily's skin glowed, her hair shone—she was the picture of youth and loveliness.

Hurrying home, oblivious to the admiring stares, she checked with Mary to make sure that preparations for dinner were well under way, then she flipped through her mail. Invitations, thank-you notes, committee business, nothing that couldn't wait.

She called Ellis. "I'm back—and I feel like a million. This trip was simply marvelous."

"I'm glad. I was a little worried about you before you left."

"No need to worry about me," she laughed. "Everything's just fine now. I'll see you soon."

After hanging up, she glanced at the clock. Good heavens, it was five-thirty. Harry would be home in less than an hour. Thank God he had told Mary that he would get a lift home with the people from Renaud's.

Dashing into the bedroom, she surveyed the closet where Mary had already carefully hung up her lovely new Paris clothes. There were so many stunning dresses from which to choose. Which would Harry like best?

Finally she chose a gown of the softest flowing chiffon. Its clear spring shades were reminiscent of a Monet garden.

Donning her luxurious new silk lingerie and a cloud of French scent, she stepped into the dress, drew on a pearl-and-diamond necklace and matching earrings, then went to the living room to add the finishing touches to the huge bouquet on the mantel.

A minute later, she stood back and surveyed the scene. Satisfied, she was about to turn away when she caught a glimpse of herself in the huge Venetian mirror. Even to her own critical eyes, she looked beautiful, her skin flawless. In the subdued light, she could have been twenty years old again.

And then, suddenly, came the sound of a key in the front door. Harry was early.

Lily took a deep breath and went into the front hall. He was just hanging his coat in the closet and putting his hat on the shelf.

"Harry?" she said softly. "Welcome back."

Turning, he saw her and stopped short. A flash of shock registered on his face. "What have you done to yourself, Lily?"

She was so stunned, she couldn't speak. How she had dreamed of this moment, of how he would look at her, incredulous delight in his eyes, and then, overcome by her beauty, sweep her up in his arms. Instead, his words pierced her to the core.

"What do you mean?" she finally managed through stiff lips.

"You've had a face-lift, haven't you?"

Tears formed in her eyes. "Does it look artificial? Is it that dreadful?"

"No, but there was nothing wrong with your face the way it was." He shrugged. "I hope you didn't do this for me."

It was all Lily could do to keep from bursting into tears. Instead, she managed to hold herself together with her usual poise. "I know you must be tired after your flight. Perhaps you'd like to change before we have dinner?"

But when he had left the room, she sank onto the sofa and cried. All the hopes and dreams that had buoyed her up for the long weeks she and Harry had been apart had been laid waste in these few moments.

Dinner was a silent affair, the conversation stilted. Lily made no protest when Harry finally said, "I'm really not hungry, Lily. I'm totally beat. Would you mind if I just went to bed?"

As he walked into the bedroom, he yanked off his tie, a bitter expression crossing his face. He had barely been able to restrain his anger. Instead of touring with him, she had dashed off to Switzerland and had her face done. It was the biggest insult she had ever offered him, as well as the most unnecessary. But he would not utter one word of reproach. The thought of more fruitless discussions, more failures of communication, daunted him.

God only knew, Lily was a beautiful woman and always would be; their problems had nothing whatsoever to do with her looks.

# Chapter 41

NOT having been in New York for so long, Harry had a host of people to see: his publisher, his attorney, Ellis. Lily didn't see him until dinnertime.

The next evening, he was honored at a dinner given by the American Booksellers Association, and although Lily would have preferred not to go, she dutifully put on one of her new gowns and went with him. The drinks flowed, the food was superb, and the accolades lavish. In spite of herself, she began to relax and have a good time.

Harry was elated by the praise and stimulated by the champagne. On the way home, he became much more talkative than he had been since his return. She too was feeling the effects of the champagne, and found herself thinking that maybe she had misinterpreted Harry's coldness and indifference. He had simply been tired. That was all.

Still exhilarated, she donned her new French peignoir while Harry fell a little unsteadily onto his side of the bed.

Lily slipped into bed next to him, turned off the light, and put her arms around him. But a minute later she realized that Harry was already asleep. She kissed him and waited for a response, but instead he groaned and turned away from her. Wearily, she told herself that he had simply had too much to drink, but the nights that followed were no different.

A gloomy depression settled over Lily. Why was he trying to punish her? For what reason? Finally she decided she was going to confront him.

And then came the telegram that drove every other thought from her mind.

Harry was in his study on the telephone. When she rapped at the door, she heard him call, "I'm on the phone."

But Lily couldn't wait. Telegrams were imperative, demanding attention; the yellow envelope was a harbinger of good news or disaster. A terrible dread crept over her. She'd feared sudden news ever since she had received that phone call concerning Jeremy.

She entered abruptly and waved it at Harry, who muttered briefly, "I'll have to call you back," and hung up.

"Open it, Harry! Please hurry!"

Harry grew silent after he ripped the envelope open and read the cable.

"What is it?" Lily cried.

But Harry was speechless. She seized it from him. It read: "On behalf of Columbia University I am pleased to inform you that you have been named the recipient of the 1954 Pulitzer Prize for Fiction," and carried the name of the president of Columbia.

"Harry!" she breathed, raising her eyes to meet his. "I can't believe it!"

Finally, he found his voice. "I can't either! A Pulitzer Prize!" Leaping up, he gave her a fierce hug. It was the first thaw in his coldness. Yet somehow it didn't feel like a shared triumph, for however much he'd credited her on the road. Just as quickly, he let go of her. "My God, what a coup! I've got to call Ellis."

It was impossible for her not to be both awed and moved as she sat at the presentation ceremony and heard the speaker address the vast crowd in the ballroom of the Waldorf-Astoria talking about the establishment of the prize and the fact that it recognized and rewarded the highest achievements of humanity. Her husband had achieved much: He had written a work that would last forever, a work of significance beyond its time.

She was brimming with pride. For all their recent trouble, for all the struggle and Harry's relentless drive, this recognition made it all endurable. Lily just had to admire Harry, looking as distinguished as he did in his black suit.

Afterward, as the crush of friends and well-wishers surrounded them, it was almost impossible to move. The most glamorous of all the Pulitzer recipients, Harry received the lion's share of media attention. Fighting their way through the crowd, the group from Renaud's reached him.

Clapping him on the back, Joe Constantine, his editor, exclaimed, "Harry, you old son of a gun, you knocked 'em dead!"

"Wonderful speech, Harry! I hope you have a copy of it," Roy Flatt said.

"Thanks, everyone," Harry said, thoroughly exhilarated.

Lily found herself watching with a strange sense of detachment as the mob edged her off to the side. Harry gave off an aura of excitement which was almost palpable. Everyone wanted to reach out and touch him in some way, as if his magic would somehow brush off on them.

And then, with sudden clarity, she saw Kate Hathaway standing next to Harry. She was saying nothing, only gently smiling at him—but suddenly Lily *knew*. She knew, with dead certainty, that Kate and Harry were having an affair. Before tonight, she had never paid any particular attention to the woman. If anything, she had a vague idea that Kate and Roy were an item. But now she looked at Kate with fresh eyes.

There was no denying it, Kate was beautiful. She had wheat-blond hair, fair skin, and clear blue eyes. She was as slender as a reed. There was nothing suggestive about her appearance per se, and she made no gesture, spoke no word that was at all intimate or personal, but by some mysterious channel, Lily sensed the vital connection between her and Harry.

She had an urge to seize Kate and scream, right at the gala, but Lily Goodhue was not one for public scenes.

Lily swallowed hard and tried to keep from trembling as she stared first at Kate, then at Harry. It was simply too much to bear. She turned away with a quiet moan and literally ran into Ellis.

"Hello, Lily!" he greeted her. "I've been trying to get to you for ten minutes. The ceremony went beautifully, don't you think?"

She stared at him with wide, pain-filled eyes.

"What is it, my dear?" he asked more quietly. "Is all this too much for you?"

Blindly, she shook her head. "Yes . . . no . . . I don't know."

Ellis looked past her to Harry with Kate Hathaway next

to him. Keenly sensitive, he picked up what was on Lily's mind.

He was about to say something but just then someone called, "Would the recipients and their spouses please gather up here for a few pictures." Lily closed her eyes for a long moment. Ellis feared she might faint. Then she took a deep breath and turned back to the stage.

The photo session seemed endless. Lily kept a smile frozen on her face while Harry could have been a stone statue next to her; she steeled herself against his touch.

Then, just as she felt she could bear the pose no longer, the media people finally said, "That's all. Thank you very much."

By now, the crowd had thinned out considerably, and the only ones left standing near Lily and Harry were Ellis, Roy, Kate, and Joe Constantine.

"How about going out for a drink?" Joe asked. "A little Dom Pérignon—on Renaud's?"

"Great," Harry said enthusiastically.

Lily felt as though she were living through a nightmare. Harry and Kate were so nonchalant, so offhand with each other, yet Lily was sure. And clearly neither one had any idea that she had fathomed their secret.

For as calm as Lily appeared, she knew that if she had to sit at the same table with them, pretending to celebrate, her self-control would disintegrate. Already it had been strained too far. As quietly as she could manage, she said, "I'm afraid I'll have to take a rain check. I have a bit of a headache."

Everyone fell silent. Harry was obviously torn. He wanted to go out and celebrate. But at the same time, how could he simply put Lily in a cab and send her home?

Slowly, he said, "Well, perhaps we had better all take a rain check. I know it's early, but it has been a long evening for Lily."

The others nodded, the party atmosphere fading perceptibly as they turned toward the exit.

"I'll stop by the office tomorrow," Harry called after the group from Renaud's. "We'll have to see how all this comes out in the press."

"See you tomorrow, Harry," Ellis said quietly, giving him a long, level gaze before turning away.

Lily and Harry rode home in absolute silence. Lily could

barely speak; Harry seemed absorbed by his own thoughts.

When they reached home, Harry headed for the bar. More than a little annoyed with her, he poured himself a drink. Walking into the library without ceremony, she picked up the Scotch decanter. "I'll take this, thank you."

Without another word, she walked out of the room and down the hall to her dressing room, shutting the door behind her. She threw her new Lanvin on the floor and kicked her shoes into a corner as she headed toward the bathroom and began running a hot tub. She scrubbed her face clean of makeup, then lowered herself slowly into the fragrant bubbles, setting the decanter on the ledge next to the bathroom glass.

Lily stayed there a long time, draining several glasses and staring off into space. Much later, when she finally emerged, she slipped on a delicate-pink chiffon dress and high-heeled shoes. She felt cleansed, as if she had shed all the false poses she had assumed in hopes of pleasing Harry. Bolstered by that thought, she felt a bud of self-respect. Now she realized that she could not live with herself until she told Harry just exactly what she knew—and what she thought of him.

After a perfunctory knock, she entered Harry's study and confronted him. "Harry, I'm going to ask you a question, and I want the truth. A simple yes or no: Are you having an affair with Kate Hathaway?"

For a long moment, he sat stunned. So that was it—she knew. But how? He would have sworn that everything was normal when they set out for the awards ceremony. How could she have found out? Kate would never, by word or gesture, reveal a thing. She had far too much presence, and too much skill in handling people. He couldn't imagine how Lily had discovered the truth, but now that she knew, he felt a queer sense of relief.

Wearily, he said, "What do you want me to say, Lily?"

No attempt at denial? Lily's heart sank. "Are you in love with her?" she asked curtly.

Harry hated having to look Lily in the face as he answered. Once, not so very long ago, he would have sworn that he would never fall in love with another woman, that Lily was the only one who would ever touch his heart. Yet it seemed as if a curtain had fallen on the stage, as if suddenly their scene together was played out. After all the ups and downs and travails of some twenty years, their love had simply worn itself out.

He had so recently thought his marriage was invincible, but already he knew it was not.

And then there was Kate, bright and clever. With her, there were no recriminations, no memories of old quarrels and past problems. He could be joyous and exuberant again, and suddenly the shared years with Lily didn't seem to count for anything.

Yes, he was in love with Kate now, and not with Lily, but it was hard to summon up the courage to say it aloud. For how little he loved her, he still couldn't bear to see her hurt.

"That's a complicated question."

"It's not complicated at all, dammit! Yes or no—are you in love with her?"

Softly he said, "Yes. But—"

Not waiting to hear the rest, she raised her hand and slapped him across the face, crying, "God damn you, Harry! When I found out about Valerie Kirk, you swore to me that it was all a mistake and promised that it would never happen again! And I forgave you! Now you tell me that there is yet another woman!"

Lily was wild with hurt and rage. "I stuck with you through thick and thin . . . and this is how you repay me? Harry, I never want to see you again. I want you out of this apartment—tonight! Do you hear me? I can't bear to be under the same roof with you!"

Turning, she started to leave, but Harry leapt to block her.

"Get out of my way, Harry!" she screamed.

"Wait a minute, Lily! Please listen—"

But Lily ran down the hall. She paused only to grab a wrap from the hall closet, then slammed the front door in his face.

She hit the elevator button three times, fighting vainly for self-control. Sobbing, she stumbled toward the stairs. She did not want to face the curious eyes of the doorman, so she let herself out the back door. She fled unsteadily through the dimly lit alley full of garbage cans, her vision blurred by tears.

How could Harry have betrayed her so? And after she had so quickly forgiven him for his affair with Valerie? Most important of all, why had his love for her evaporated?

This was as bad as having caught Harry in bed with Valerie

in the villa at Safed. No, this was worse. What a fool she had been to take him back. Bitterness overcame her at the thought of her naiveté. She had been an idiot, a trusting simpleton.

Lily felt so overwhelmed by misery, she sank onto a doorstep, buried her face in her hands, and wept. She had been cursed from the day of her birth. Never in her life had she had a true, enduring, sustaining love. Not from her parents, not from Harry, not from her children.

Her parents had detested her, she'd always known that. Harry was the first human being to love her wholly and unconditionally. That was why she had never begrudged her lost inheritance, the hard work, or the poverty of their early years. To her, the struggles were nothing compared with what he had given her.

When success came, their life together had seemed to come apart, yet as recently as last fall it had seemed that they were going to make it. Their love was stronger than ever before. But apparently it had been merely the last flicker of a dying fire.

"Anything I can do for you, lady?" said a kindly though peremptory voice.

Seeing the blue of a policeman's uniform, she quickly brushed away her tears with the back of her hand and shook her head.

"In that case, you have better not sit here. It's not safe, this time of night."

Mutely, she nodded, then rose uncertainly to her feet.

She had no idea how many blocks she had come or where she was; she had stumbled aimlessly through the streets, oblivious to her surroundings.

All at once, she recognized the familiar façade of Ellis's building. Without consciously meaning to, she had walked almost directly there. Clad in a dressing gown, he answered the bell. When he saw her ravaged face, he registered pure shock.

Ellis collected himself quickly and drew her inside, asking, "What is it? What on earth is wrong, Lily?"

"I've left Harry."

"Why?"

He drew her into his library, poured her a brandy, settled her into the loveseat near the fire. "What happened?"

"Harry told me tonight that he is in love with Kate Hathaway. He's been having an affair with her; I imagine it's no news to you."

He made no comment, and she continued almost incoherently.

"I tried everything, Ellis. I really did. I supported him and encouraged him all these years—and believe me, sometimes it was as hard for me as it was for him—and Harry took it all for granted. But what hurts me most is that I thought that this past year was the best of our lives. It seemed as if we had worked it all out, that we'd conquered all our problems. Obviously I was wrong. Harry doesn't love me. Maybe he never did."

"Lily, that's ridiculous!"

"No, I don't think so. If Harry loved me, he wouldn't have treated me like this. He couldn't have."

Ellis had never seen her look so unhappy. "I even went to Switzerland for a face-lift to please him. But I could have saved myself the pain. He was already sleeping with Kate Hathaway."

"Maybe it's just a passing fling, Lily."

She shook her head. "I don't want him under those conditions, Ellis. I don't want a man who is capable of being unfaithful to me. And besides, he admitted that he is in love with her."

What torture it must be for her to say those words, Ellis thought.

"My marriage meant everything to me. It was my life. And now I don't care what happens to me. I don't care about anything. I know that sounds melodramatic, but I just don't feel as if I've got anything to live for."

"Don't say that, Lily. You've got someone very important to live for!"

"Who?"

"Yourself, dammit! If only you could see what a magnificent human being you are, Lily. You're worth ten of Harry Kohle—a hundred!"

She shrugged, obviously unconvinced. "Harry apparently does not think so. Or is it just that all men grow tired of their wives?"

Pausing for a long moment, she asked suddenly, "Do you mind if I ask you a rather personal question? When you were married, were you completely faithful to your wife?"

Reluctantly he admitted, "Well, as a matter of fact, I was."

"Why?"

He shrugged. "I guess that for me it had something to do with those vows."

They fell silent.

Then, abruptly, Ellis stood up. "Lily, did you eat at all at the dinner? Let me fix you something."

She shook her head. "No, thanks. I'm not hungry. But if you have some, I'd love a glass of champagne."

He disappeared and returned a moment later with a bottle and two crystal champagne glasses. As he filled a glass and handed it to Lily, he asked, "Now, what are we going to drink to? This doesn't quite seem like an occasion to celebrate."

"On the contrary," she said evenly. "If you say that I'm worth something on my own, that I have to go on living, I guess we can toast my new life—without Harry."

With stern deliberation, she clinked her glass against Ellis's.

"Here's to you, Lily. Still the last princess in town."

"Thank you, Ellis. You're the best friend I have in the world."

Lily found relief in the sudden lightheadedness brought on by the champagne. Ellis's solicitude made her feel cozy and snug. As Ellis drained the last of the bottle, barely filling Lily's glass, she cried petulantly, "Oh, don't we have more?"

"Of course."

Barely halfway through the second bottle, Lily set down her glass with a snap and tried to stand. She lurched unsteadily. Ellis sprang to his feet and caught her. Lily looked up at him and blinked to put him in focus. Huskily, she whispered, "Make love to me, Ellis."

This was the moment Ellis had dared to dream of. His gaze slid down her ivory throat to the seductive curves of her body. Her lips were so close to his, so tempting. Ellis looked in her emerald eyes. They were still beautiful, though clearly fogged by alcohol.

Ellis abruptly regained his self-control. He longed for Lily, but this was not the way he would have her.

Gently, he disengaged himself from her embrace. "I don't think it would be a good idea, Lily."

"Because of Harry? He's not worth your scruples."

"It has nothing to do with him. It has to do with you and me."

"So you don't find me desirable, either."

"That's not it, Lily! But I don't want to sleep with you for revenge."

"But Ellis, that's not the reason. I love you."

Almost angrily, he turned on her. "Lily, we're not children. Why should we pretend? I have always loved you, can you not have known? There is nothing I want more than to hear you say those words to me. But when you say it tonight, I know that you don't mean what I want—that you're *in* love with me. I long to take you to bed, God knows! But not like this."

It was as if the words were torn from him. Lily stared at him. "Ellis . . . I never thought . . . you never told me. . . ."

"I never told you because you were married to Harry. What purpose would it have served?"

"But you didn't tell me about Valerie or Kate, even though you knew."

"I'm not as noble as you believe, Lily. Think back. I deliberately encouraged you to go to Israel, knowing that you would probably find out about Valerie. And you did, but after you forgave Harry for that, I figured you loved him so much that you would forgive him anything."

This was too great a revelation to take in all at once. Reeling from the shock as well as the champagne, Lily cried, "Ellis, you don't understand! I want you because I love you. . . . I do. . . . I really do. . . ."

Tears began to roll down her cheeks. She felt woozy. Suddenly she felt him lift her and carry her across the threshold into his bedroom, just before everything went black.

# Chapter 42

THE next morning, Lily woke up in Ellis's four-poster. For a moment she couldn't recall where she was. She sat up and felt the first stab of a piercing headache. She knew then she must have drunk far more than she realized the previous night.

Gradually, memory of those hours came back to her. Ellis and she? What had she said to him? And what had they done? She glanced at the other side of the bed. The sheet and spread were still smooth and neatly arranged. The pillow was undented. She'd spent the night alone. With a sense of wonder, she remembered Ellis's words: He loved her.

In the clearer light of morning, she reflected on what had passed between them. How could she not have realized how Ellis felt about her? They had always been close, that much she had known. But now that friendship had changed suddenly.

As for Lily, she was not ready to love any man at this time in her life. In fact, she doubted that she ever could or would again. But if she could not return Ellis's affection, where did that leave her? Lily knew the answer: alone.

Another woman, especially a woman her age, might have jumped at the opportunity. After all, Ellis—so handsome and successful—was a man with special appeal. He was a catch, by anyone's estimation. He was everything a man should be. If Lily were smart, she'd gladly accept him. Yet she knew that she could not—not now. And after all that had happened, it seemed impossible they could simply be friends again.

Bereft of a husband and now a best friend, Lily had not felt lonelier since the time she'd lost Jeremy.

Her future seemed bleak, a grim wasteland. But her immediate problem was still Harry. Reaching for the bedside phone, she dialed her own number, heart pounding, praying that Mary would answer.

When she did, Lily's pulse slowed. "Mary, is Mr. Kohle there?"

"No ma'am. He wasn't here when I got up this morning."

No doubt he was already in the arms of Kate Hathaway.

Remorseless, Lily calmly told Mary, "Mr. Kohle has moved out. I want you to call the locksmith and have all the locks changed."

"Yes, Mrs. Kohle. I'll do that immediately."

If Mary was surprised, she didn't sound it, but then servants always knew their masters' intimacies. However diligently the Kohles had tried to keep the more personal part of their lives hidden, Lily realized that she had probably known all about Harry's affair with Kate, just as she'd known of Valerie. The humiliation was overwhelming. Well, they said the wife was always the last to know.

After hanging up, Lily looked around Ellis's room. She must go. After dressing quickly, she sat at his leather-topped desk and wrote on a piece of his stationery, "Dear Ellis . . ." Then she stopped. What could she say? *I wish I hadn't thrown myself at you. . . . I wish you hadn't told me that you loved me. . . .* Or simply, *Thank you for all the gifts of friendship you have given me through the years. They are the only things which have kept me going . . . and they will remain in my treasure chest as my only souvenirs.*

Instead she wrote, "Thank you for listening to me last night. I apologize for burdening you, and hope all will be well with you. All my best—Lily."

Half an hour later, Ellis found the envelope propped up on the console table in the hall.

He tore it open and read the few words Lily had written. She had fled, and this note seemed to him a eulogy to their friendship. He had gone for a walk this morning to give Lily a chance to compose herself, in hopes of overcoming any awkwardness that might have lingered from the things they had said and done last night. But instead of waiting for him, she had run away—as though he were as untrustworthy as

Harry. He cursed himself for the night before. The mistake he had made was in timing. It was wrong for a declaration of love. But it was Lily herself who had tempted him. In a flash, he regretted not having taken her up on her offer. He should have carried her off to bed and made passionate love to her. Wasn't that what she wanted? Not his ill-put declaration of love. She had already decided to leave Harry. He wasn't even coaxing her along. Maybe last night's scenario was not the one he'd envisioned, but since when had life ever worked out as one hoped? He should have gratefully embraced the opportunity. Instead, he'd as good as thrown it away.

But in truth, his reluctance wasn't purely a matter of scruples. Dammit, he thought, he hadn't wanted to catch her on the rebound, he wanted her to come to him out of love, not hurt.

When Mary opened the door to Lily, her face was sympathetic. "Here, let me take your things. How about a cup of tea?"

Numbly, Lily obeyed, and as Mary disappeared into the kitchen, she stood for a moment in the foyer, listening to the deafening silence. Their home seemed so vacant—not that it was still "theirs." She could hardly believe it. Harry had walked out, and for the last time.

She wondered if he could have forgotten the way he had pinned the pink baby roses on her shoulder the day of their wedding, forgotten those cherished times when the children were young and the world seemed so new, forgotten the shared triumph of *Archie Sanger* after the long years of struggle, but most of all, forgotten the last year, in which they'd shared the richest renewal of their love.

Lily almost cried aloud, "What happened to all our dreams, Harry?"

Mary reappeared from the kitchen. "Here's your tea, Mrs. Kohle."

But Lily shook her head. "No, thanks. I've changed my mind, I don't want it."

She went to her room, fell down on the bed, and wept. Harry was gone, the children were gone, and her whole life lay in ruins. Once her tears had subsided, she got up and wandered about aimlessly, but the apartment's emptiness seemed a reproach. The master bedroom with its big bed, empty, the closed door of Harry's study, the living room where they had argued.

Lily couldn't bear it anymore. She could still hear the echoes of her reproaches. No, she could not stay here, she would go to the farm. Strange how whenever trouble came, that was the only place she'd ever feel better.

That afternoon, when Lily drove up, Mrs. Gallagher was tactful enough not to inquire as to the reason for the unannounced visit, but the blank despair in Lily's eyes wrung her heart.

And as the days went by, Lily took long walks, read a little, ate almost nothing, and spent a great deal of time sitting in the kitchen watching Mrs. Gallagher make preserves.

Once, she turned to ask Lily a question and was surprised to see a tear rolling down her cheek. Impulsively putting an arm about the younger woman's shoulders, she asked, "Now, now, what's wrong, lovely?"

But Lily merely blinked back the tears and shrugged, trying to smile. "Oh, nothing—just reminds me of old times, that's all."

Lily tried to comfort herself with memories of the old days, but those idyllic times seemed so long past, they were of little consolation.

Now she didn't even have Ellis to turn to. She was still embarrassed by the way she'd behaved that fateful evening. Imagine, begging someone to take her to bed!

Over and over she replayed that scene. Had Ellis truly said he loved her? It seemed unbelievable.

It was not that the idea of falling in love with Ellis was unthinkable; succumbing to love again was the issue that couldn't be brooked. In her life it seemed that loving someone simply led to infinite pain and sorrow. For Harry, forgiveness was out of the question. The very thought of Kate Hathaway chilled her. She hoped that their affair would lead to nothing but misery for them both.

But they were in love. Harry had said so. What unhappiness could await them?

Meanwhile, Harry had been badly shaken by Lily's rage. He knew the saying "Hell hath no fury like a woman scorned," but never would he have thought his gentle wife capable of such deep and lasting anger.

Somehow, he had thought she would be calm, almost indifferent, when she found out. She didn't really love him anyway, so what would she care if he was in love with someone else?

When Lily slammed the door, he had remained in stunned shock for a long while, almost unable to grasp what had happened. Finally, unable to stand the silence, he had seized his hat and coat and gone to Kate's apartment. Dressed in her robe, she answered the door, and when she saw him her face lit up.

"Hello, sweetheart! I didn't expect you tonight—"

But quickly, she saw the grim expression on his face, and her tone changed. "What's wrong? Come and tell me about it."

Even before Harry spoke, Kate sensed what was coming. He and Lily had had a confrontation. Nothing else could have changed Harry so.

As Harry sat down and accepted a Scotch, Kate looked at him, seeing for the first time the graying at his temples, the lines around his eyes. He seemed to have aged overnight.

Leaning back heavily against the couch, he lit a cigarette with a trembling hand. Then, with a quick, angry gesture, he tilted back his head and drained his drink.

Kate allowed a full minute to pass while she poured him another. Then she said softly, "Tell me what happened."

Harry stubbed out his cigarette and said flatly, "Lily knows about us. She's left me. That's all there is to it."

"But isn't that what you wanted? I mean, we don't want to go on like this forever, sneaking around and hiding."

He sighed. "No . . ."

"This isn't just a casual affair, Harry," Kate went on, her eyes troubled. "I love you and you say you love me. This had to happen sooner or later. We'll be happier being honest with each other and the world."

He said nothing and she probed, a trifle anxiously. "You do love me, don't you?"

"Yes, of course I do, Kate."

She moved over and put her arms around him; he turned to embrace her. "I'm sorry. I knew that she wouldn't take it lightly. She's not that kind of woman and it was so obvious we'd drifted apart; I didn't think she would take it so hard.

If anything, I thought she might be relieved. I guess it just goes to show you how thick a man can be. She said that she hated me, and that was a terrible thing to hear. I don't hate her. . . . Our marriage just went stale somehow. . . . Oh, damn, I don't know what I'm saying."

Kate kissed him. "Don't think about it, sweetheart. It won't do any good. She'll get over it."

"I know. But tonight . . ."

Kate could feel him stirring restlessly in his sleep and once, toward daybreak, she woke to see him sitting on the edge of the bed, smoking.

They stayed in bed until noon. Subconsciously, Harry wanted to put off the crucial encounter with Lily. Would she still be as angry, or would a night's reflection have calmed her?

But finally he got out of bed, saying heavily, "I'm going to have to go home to pack a few things. Lily said she wanted me out."

"You can move in here, you know, darling. I'd love to have us sharing a roof at last."

He hesitated. "Let me see what happens when I talk to Lily."

But when he arrived home, Mary told him that Lily had packed her things and gone to the farm. Cursing himself for not having been there to see her, he asked, "Did she leave any message for me?"

"No. I'm sorry, Mr. Kohle."

Reluctantly Harry packed his things and moved them to Kate's, but as the days passed, she sensed his restlessness and inner turmoil. He still felt as if he and Lily had unfinished business between them, no matter how final she had sounded that night. But a week went by with no word from her. Finally he called the farm.

Mrs. Gallagher answered. "I'm sorry, Mr. Kohle. Mrs. Kohle is out."

Several more tries elicited the same answer, and gradually he realized that she was not going to talk to him. He found himself at a standstill, with no idea of what to do next.

But then, something happened that made him question his behavior even more than before. The children had been alerted about their parents' separation. Lily wanted to be sure that they could always be reached. Harry assumed they would accept the news as a matter of course until he found out from Randy that Drew had dropped out of Harvard.

The next day, he went to the address in Greenwich Village which Randy had given him. By the time Harry stepped over passed-out winos to get to the door, he had worked himself into a rage. When Drew opened the door, Harry went inside, took one look at the filthy room, and thundered. "What the hell do you think you're doing?"

Drew just glared at him. "You bastard. Leaving my mother for some whore—"

Harry slapped Drew across his face. "How dare you? Who do you think you are?"

Though staggered by the blow, Drew managed to keep his balance. "It's not who I am, it's who you are! You're not worthy of her; you never have been. And now you'd like to destroy her, just as you destroyed Jeremy! Wasn't it enough that you killed him? Do you have to kill her, too?"

Harry was speechless. After all these years, he'd managed to push the awful guilt out of his mind, only to hear the old accusation on his son's lips again.

His urge to punch Drew ebbed away. It was no use. They were strangers now; they would never have anything more to say to each other. Harry turned without another word and let himself out.

As Drew watched his father go, he began to shake with emotion. It was all his father's fault—all of it! Mom, Jeremy, the breakup of their home, their life as a family, even the emptiness of his own existence. But suddenly he found little joy in the bare, gritty room he'd taken in hopes of avenging his mother. He had girded himself for a pitched battle with his father, but instead of fighting, Harry had deprived him of his victory by leaving. When Harry had turned to the door, Drew noticed the slumping shoulders, the graying hair. Was his father, the shining god, the indestructible one, vulnerable? Drew regretted his harsh words. He had blamed his father for so many years, but now in the very act of making the accusation, he had begun to realize his unfairness. No one could be ultimately responsible for another's self-destruction. The truth was that Jeremy had been flawed, no matter how much Drew loved him.

And in that moment, Drew realized that he had now also

lost his father forever—and for all the losses, he cried bitter tears.

Meanwhile, to Harry it seemed that his entire family had deserted him. Two days after seeing Drew, he received a call from Melissa's school which bothered him even more deeply. Melissa had been caught sneaking back into her dormitory at two in the morning with alcohol on her breath. She'd confessed to an assignation with a young man. The school warned that one more such incident would bring expulsion.

She had been wholly unrepentant when he'd gone up to Miss Parker's School to talk to her.

"Don't preach, Daddy. So I had a date. At least I'm not committing adultery."

Harry could barely find his voice. "That's no way to talk to me, young lady! I'm your father and you owe me respect, dammit! I didn't come up here to discuss my actions with you."

Melissa had refrained from echoing Drew's angry accusations, but her tone remained caustic. "Sure, Dad. Whatever you say."

As he drove away, Harry gripped the steering wheel in sheer frustration. Fatherhood seemed a heavier burden than ever before. His children seemed to him an array of unpleasant strangers. At the same time, he saw with new clarity how deeply he had failed them. All he had done was sire those children. Somehow, he felt a new sense of responsibility. Perhaps it was too late, but he was going to try to be a real father to the three he had left. All these years the burden had fallen on Lily's shoulders, but now, despite their estrangement, he felt a new urge to take on his share of the load.

Harry's car caught Lily by surprise. She had been walking through the field when it pulled up in the drive. The sight of him walking toward her made her stomach knot.

Summoning her pride, Lily reminded herself to remain calm and dignified. The two went inside to the living room to talk about the children. After Harry briefed her on his latest encounters with them, Lily said, "I hadn't heard about Melissa's problem, but I knew about Drew. He came to tell me about his decision. I don't agree with it, but he is his own person now. There's no way we can force him to do anything he doesn't want to do."

"I suppose not," Harry sighed. "But we still have control over Melissa. We have to do something. This incident at school sounds awful. They don't seem to be able to control the girls and it worries me. And I didn't like the way she looked. Too much damned makeup, and too damned sophisticated for a young girl. She didn't even pretend to be remorseful about what she had done."

Lily shrugged. "Well, in our last conversation, all she said to me was that she wanted to drop out of school and become a model."

"But she can't do that without our permission. It's time that we took a firm stand with her, before it's too late."

Lily looked past him. "I did the best I could with our children, tried to be the best mother I was capable of being. I told myself that if I made mistakes, they would at least be born of love, and that the children would grow to be fine, happy adults. Obviously, that was wrong thinking. Randy doesn't seem to care much about us. Melissa is lazy and terribly self-centered, and Drew is unhappy and rebellious, and clearly not living up to his potential. I guess I left something out of the equation—the discipline they needed. But it's too late, Harry. There's nothing we can do to remedy the mistakes we've made with them."

Harry was shocked by the bitter resignation in Lily's voice. Never had she been so brutally frank in her estimation of the children—always, to hear her talk, they had been perfect.

Now he said in a voice quickened with alarm, "Lily, don't say that! It's not too late. We can't force Drew back to Harvard, but we can certainly cut off his allowance and see if that sends him a message. And we still have jurisdiction over Melissa. I feel that perhaps Miss Parker's is too lenient for her—how would you feel about sending her to a Swiss finishing school?"

"I thought that you were so anxious that she go to college."

"Well, we have to face reality. She has barely scraped through Miss Parker's, and if she's talking about dropping out to become a model, college can't be in her plans. At least a Swiss school will keep her out of trouble for another year or two, and by then maybe she will have acquired a little maturity."

Lily closed her eyes. If they could salvage something from the wreck of their marriage, it must be their children. She and Harry would have to stick together on that. This was probably the last chance they had to influence Melissa. Harry was probably right, the lure of a Swiss finishing school would appeal to her. Perhaps it would exert a moderating effect on her vibrant, reckless nature.

Opening her eyes, she nodded. "I think you're probably right. It would be a good idea."

"Would you like me to take care of it?"

Lily stared at him in surprise. Harry? Taking the responsibility for something like this?

He continued. "I thought I could call your old school. They might be willing to grant late admission for Melissa since she's the daughter of an alumna."

"You'll take care of it?" she asked in wonder.

"Of course," said Harry. "Don't tell me, I know. I've never been very involved as a father. This is too little, too late."

"I wasn't being critical. Believe me, I don't consider myself an ideal parent either."

After a long moment's silence, she asked, "Would you like some more coffee?"

They could have been a pair of polite strangers, Harry thought. There was neither warmth nor coldness nor anger. What emotion she had was clearly reserved for the children.

But here, in the cozy little living room where the first act of their life together had been played out, Harry could not keep the vivid memories from flooding over him. Suddenly he wished for nothing more than a second chance, the opportunity to do it all over again. He realized deep down that he would only make the same mistakes all over again. It was impossible for him to defy his nature, the burning ambition that was inextricably a part of his being. He had been so driven, so relentless, so determined to show his family.

*Be careful of what you wish for—you just might get it.* Ah God, the price had been terrible.

# Chapter 43

HAUNTING images stayed with Harry as he drove back to Manhattan that afternoon, and they stayed with him for weeks to come. As time passed, he began to feel a lonely ache he had never felt before. Gradually he came to see the truth that should have been obvious to him all along: The reason he had resented Lily's seeming neglect was simply that he loved her so much.

And so Harry found himself in a terrible dilemma. He had thought he had fallen deeply in love with Kate; she had been a breath of fresh air, a relief from his problems with Lily, and most of all, she reveled in the literary world over which he reigned.

But in truth, their affair had been born of his anger. There was love between them, of a kind—but it was not the kind of feeling that shook him to the core of his being. It was impossible for him to explain. Lily was simply a part of him.

And as he began to long for her more and more, he became uncomfortably aware that he was cheating Kate, for he could no longer speak the words of love she expected. It was impossible to tell her, but it was equally impossible to hide from her his mental torment.

One night, after he had tried to make love to her and failed, she sat up abruptly and announced, "We are never going to make it, Harry, until we get Lily out of our bed."

Harry flung back the covers, got out of bed, and paced the room, smoking a cigarette. "God damn it, Kate! Do you think it's that easy to give up a marriage?"

"Then why did you leave her if you care so much about her?"

"Because she deserves better," he said bitterly.

"Is that why? Funny, I thought that it was because you loved me."

The edge in her voice suddenly penetrated his self-absorption, and he turned to her repentantly. "I'm sorry, Kate, darling. I do care for you, I do."

She held out her arms. "Then come back to bed, darling, and let me love you."

But it was a difficult coming together, which left neither of them satisfied. The two of them lay awake the rest of the night.

The next morning they sat at breakfast without speaking. Finally Harry broke the silence. "Kate—there's something I have to tell you, and it's not easy—"

"Don't," she said, putting a finger to his lips. "Don't."

Her eyes were bright with unshed tears. "I already know—I knew last night. It's not going to happen for us, is it?"

"No," he said quietly. "I'm sorry—so very sorry."

Kate turned away, fighting back the tears. Six months was all it had lasted, and she had planned for a lifetime.

That day he moved his things to a hotel, cursing himself for the sadness he saw in Kate's eyes, but confident his decision was the right one.

For the next week, he underwent a soul-searching such as he had never known, going back over the entire course of his life with Lily—and the more he pondered it, the more he came to see their marriage through her eyes. He had been blind and selfish. He could have restrained his ambition, tempered it with a deeper commitment to the woman he professed to love. How unfair he had been, expecting her to applaud his writer's life when it was the very thing that took virtually all of his time. He had lost sight of her needs, forgotten that the forlorn child who still dwelt inside the woman needed his love and deserved it.

It was a chastened man who sat in his hotel room, looking out at the streets below and seeing his failure as a family man. Night after night, the level of the Scotch in the bottle sank while he smoked cigarette after cigarette, desperately casting about for some magic way to turn back the clock.

But in the end it all came down to Lily. He knew that she had been deeply hurt by his betrayal. Her love for him seemed to have evaporated. Could he have expected anything less? If Lily had seemed distant, it was he who had pushed her away. Her calm was almost unnatural. He would even have preferred to see her angry. If she was angry, it would have proved she still cared.

But despite his misgivings, he had to make an attempt to bridge the gulf between them before they became irrevocably split.

He called Lily early one morning. After the preliminary hellos, he gathered his courage and asked, "Lily, do you think I might come up to the farm and see you again?"

"I don't know, Harry," came the discouraging reply. "What would be the point?"

"I'd just like to spend some time with you, that's all."

"I don't think so, Harry. We had over twenty years together. I think all we had to say to each other has already been said."

In desperation, he cried, "Lily, can't we try once again? I made a lot of mistakes in our marriage, and our problems have been mainly due to me—I see that now. Can't you find it in your heart to forgive me? I'll do my best—"

"It's not a question of forgiveness, Harry. There's just nothing between us anymore. No love, no affection, not even respect."

"How can you say that, Lily, after all the years we had together?"

"Yes, well, you had all those years to make it work and it didn't. Now it's just too late."

"Lily, I've given up Kate Hathaway. It was all a mistake, and I'm never going to see her again."

But the mention of Kate only made Lily's voice grow colder. "You needn't have given her up for me."

Harry tried to speak, but she cut him off. "Harry, I don't want to talk about it. The issue is closed."

After he hung up, he buried his face in his hands and wept.

Meanwhile, another man was thinking about Lily, wondering what was in her heart. The morning she'd left his apartment, Ellis had called and learned from Mary that Lily had gone back to the farm.

It awakened a strange sense of déjà vu in him. He remembered all too well Lily's previous sojourn there, after Jeremy's death, when she had sunk so low. But he hoped that this time would be different. Somehow divorce was not as tragic as the death of a child. Perhaps Lily would soon bounce back.

For some weeks, he indulged the hope that she would call and ask to see him. But finally he began to realize that with her brief note she truly did intend to cut off contact.

It pained him to consider Lily's rejection, but he tried to put himself in her shoes. She had just undergone the humiliation of finding her husband unfaithful. The injury to her self-esteem would hardly put her in a position to open up to any man again, let alone fall in love.

One Sunday morning, some two months after Lily had left the city, Ellis sat on his terrace, moodily sipping the coffee his valet had brought out along with the Sunday *Times*. It was a while before he realized he had read the same headlines six times without taking in the sense of them.

It was no use pretending. Lily preyed upon his mind during virtually all his waking and sleeping hours. He could not escape a gnawing sense of regret over how he'd handled things between them—and how he was handling them now. Ellis had let his pride keep him from her these months. Lily needed a friend now more than ever. How could he keep himself away simply because he couldn't fit into her life the way he would have liked? Whom did she have to turn to, save him?

Ellis had decided: He couldn't go on nursing this sense of injury. Lily needed him, and he was going to help her—whether she wanted it or not. That very morning, he showered, shaved, and dressed, and within half an hour he was on the familiar road to the farm.

He saw Lily from a distance in the orchard. She was standing near an apricot tree. Advancing quietly, he stopped some distance behind her and spoke her name softly. "Lily?"

Lily spun around. "Ellis? Is it you?"

"Yes, I'm not a ghost."

No, he was no ghost, but the minute he saw her, he feared Lily was. She was as skeletal as she had been just after Jeremy's death. She looked so fragile, more vulnerable than she'd ever seemed before.

He had to fight the urge to run to her and gather her in his arms. She would never permit it; he could sense her reserve.

Instead, he said as calmly as he could manage, "It's good to see you."

She nodded hesitantly. Ellis could tell she'd not gotten over the revelations of their last meeting. He felt he should address her apprehension.

"Lily, I'm not going to bring up what happened that night. We were both emotional, for obvious reasons, and perhaps said some things we didn't intend to. Can we just pretend that none of it happened, and go back to being the friends we were?"

Lily flushed, but she nodded. She was silently grateful he had spoken so directly.

"Okay," he continued, "that's settled. Now, tell me how you've been feeling."

"Oh, not good, not bad. Just kind of nothing."

Ellis frowned, glancing around the orchard. "I think that a change might do you good. How about if we go for a picnic?"

Lily was clearly startled by the suggestion.

"I know—we went for a picnic once before. And it did you wonders, didn't it?"

"Yes, I guess so," she mused, "but then again, all that happened was that I went back to Harry, and look how that turned out."

Ellis said nothing. Lily added, "It's nice of you to try to cheer me up, Ellis, but I just don't feel up to anything. But thank you for coming."

"That sounds like a dismissal."

"I'm sorry," she said, rubbing her forehead. "I really am . . . I'm just so tired. . . ."

Ellis hesitated, then tried once more. "Are you too tired to give me a cup of coffee before I start back to the city?"

She managed a weak smile. "Of course not. Come on into the house."

Secretly, Ellis was elated. At least she was losing her sense of awkwardness around him. That was a step in the right direction.

Mrs. Gallagher had gone to the village to do the marketing, so Lily made the coffee and found some freshly baked coffee cake.

As they sat in the living room, Ellis tried again to find out what Lily had been up to. "So tell me, how do you amuse yourself out here?"

"I feed the chickens, listen to the radio, help Mrs. Gallagher in the kitchen sometimes."

The flat, expressionless words stirred Ellis's anger. For a woman like Lily to be reduced to this state!

"And that's it? That's how Lily Goodhue Kohle, former toast of Paris and New York, fills her days?"

Ellis's sarcasm offended Lily. What business was it of his—or anyone else's—how she spent her time? She was through with having others always telling her what she should do, how she should think or feel. Jumping to her feet, she blazed angrily, "It's none of your damned business! Why don't you just leave me alone?"

Inwardly Ellis rejoiced at her response. Anything was better than that terrible blankness.

Deliberately, he goaded her. "Why are you sore, Lily? Is your way of life out here so wonderful that you simply can't explain it to anyone else?"

"Yes!" she cried defiantly. "Yes, it's just fine."

"Is that why you have those dark circles under your eyes, from all this wonderful country air? Tell me, how many hours do you sleep at night?"

The question staggered her. Ellis had hit upon the thing which tortured her most: Sleep eluded her. Nights, she would walk and walk, hoping the exercise would tire her. But it never seemed to help. Every night found her agonizing over past events—some long ago, others recent—which had so changed her life.

Tears began to stream down her face. "Go away, Ellis!" she sobbed. "Please—just go away."

Ellis could control himself no longer. He gathered her into his arms and stroked her gently while her body shook with sobs. He said nothing, knowing that this storm of emotion was long overdue.

Lily soon regained control of herself.

"Here," said Ellis, handing her his handkerchief. "Dry your eyes."

She stared at him numbly. "I just don't know what to do. I built my entire world around Harry. Now, with him gone, I feel so alone. And I don't have the slightest idea in the world what I'm going to do with the rest of my life."

"Lily, are you trying to tell me that Harry Kohle was your entire reason for being? That without him you're nothing? That's absurd, and you know it. You're just frightened and not, I must say, with particularly good reason."

"You're right—everything does seem frightening to me at this point. But it's more than that. It's just that I feel no one in the world needs me. And it's true, Ellis. No one does."

"Lots of people need you, if you only knew it. I need you." Ellis's voice became husky. He sighed. "Lily, listen. We have to get this straight between us. That night when I told you how I felt about you, I did mean it, every word of it. You don't know how tempted I was by your offer. But the circumstances were just so hopelessly wrong. I know that we both did the right thing by drawing back, but I refuse to let you turn me away. I need your friendship, your companionship in my life as much as—I think—you need mine. There are no strings on my love for you. I love you unconditionally. I always will. And I want you to know it. I don't expect any return from you—especially now. But I'll always be there for you. I've been a fool to stay away."

Tears welled anew in Lily's eyes. At that moment she felt a wave of love for Ellis which went beyond anything she had ever felt for Harry.

"Thank you," she whispered. "Thank you for that. You don't know how much it means to me. I've been so alone—"

Ellis was overwhelmed by her confession. But steeling himself, he said, "Now, listen to me. I want you to come back to Manhattan."

"But—"

"No buts. Pack your bags. You know that the farm is just a step into the past, and however wonderful that past might be, you can't live your life there. Look at you—thin and pale and miserable. You're not solving your problems out here. If anything, you'll create more."

The wisdom of Ellis's words was not lost on her. She decided in an instant. "Can you wait for me while I pack my bags?"

He held out his arms and pulled her into a comforting embrace, murmuring to the top of her head, "I have all the time in the world for you, Lily."

# Chapter 44

UPON hearing that Lily had moved back into the apartment, hope sprang up in Harry. Perhaps she had reconsidered. But she quickly disabused him of his illusions. "This has nothing to do with us, Harry. The reason I've come back is to try to salvage some kind of sense of myself—but I'm going to do it by myself. I'm sorry."

Harry finally realized that she meant what she said. Their marriage was over. In flat-out despair, he turned back to the only solace he knew—his writing. For once, he was devoid of ideas. The first day he sat down to his typewriter again, he stared at it as though it had brought him all the unhappiness he had ever known. But after an hour of gazing blankly at the white paper in the carriage and smoking an endless chain of Camels, he finally found himself typing out the words "Chapter One." It was a time of sheer agony. Never had writing been such a process of grinding it out. But finally an idea began to take shape. This time his story was set in Ireland, the green and lovely land torn by three hundred years of Irish passion and British arrogance.

As the familiar routine of research and writing began to reestablish itself, he began to find, if not solace, at least a measure of forgetfulness.

The year that followed was a strange one for Lily. She had expected to be lonely, unhappy, without a sense of purpose. But surprisingly, her new life began to give her both peace and fulfillment. Harry stopped his pleading calls, so she was spared that torment. Drew still refused to go back to Harvard, but he had found a job as copyboy on a newspaper. Lily didn't object, thinking he would do well to have a little experience of the real world. Melissa, on the other hand, had ignored her parents' counsel. She had dropped out of her Swiss school in the middle of the year to move to Paris. "I've had enough of school; I'm going to be a model," she announced flatly.

"But darling," Lily said. "You're much too young to live on your own."

"I'm going and you can't stop me!" she had returned defiantly—and they had been forced to admit she was right.

If Melissa was determined to have it her way, Lily was equally determined to see that she fared well. Lily flew to Switzerland and helped Melissa move to Paris, even going so far as to help her find a room in a respectable pension on the Left Bank. Before bidding her daughter farewell, Lily dropped in on her old friend Colette, who agreed to keep an eye on young Melissa.

Upon her return, Lily threw herself into volunteer work with renewed vigor, thanks largely to Ellis's gentle prodding. She helped at the March of Dimes and at Ellis's pet organization, the Historical Landmarks Society. Soon Lily branched out to a few special areas—she volunteered at a home for unwed mothers, she read to the blind.

Lily was back in the thick of things. She had blossomed again, just as Ellis had hoped. Even more important, she became a crucial figure in the groups in which she became involved. It should have come as little surprise when, over lunch with Joan and some of her other friends, Joan broached the subject of the upcoming Spring Ball.

"Lily, there's something we want to ask you. The Spring Ball has never been so successful as the year you were in charge. Is there any chance you'd sign on as chairman again?"

Lily instantly demurred. "Oh, Joan, you flatter me."

But Joan persisted. "Now, Lily, you know perfectly well that Alicia made a perfect botch of last year's affair. We're really looking for someone to revive our success. Please at least consider it."

"Yes, Lily, do," the rest of them chorused, and she held up her hands in mock dismay.

"Okay, okay, I'll think about it."

That afternoon, she called Ellis to invite him for dinner. They had slipped into the old relationship, an easygoing friendship, and saw each other several times a week, for lunch or dinner, an occasional theater production, or the ballet.

Ellis was once again her best friend and confidant, and tonight, after they had finished their dinner and adjourned to the living room for their coffee, she asked his thoughts on the chairmanship.

"What do you think? They really seem anxious to have me."

He looked at her, thinking what a difference so little time could make. Last time this subject had come up, he had practically had to browbeat her into accepting. Now she seemed to require only his gentle nod.

Soon her divorce from Harry would be final. At that point, maybe she would at last be ready to close that chapter in her life.

Ellis, as ever, cheered her on. "I think that you would be magnificent, my dear. It's true what they said, the Spring Ball was never more successful than the year you were in charge."

She smiled at the memory of it. "So you think I should accept?"

"Absolutely."

She took a deep breath and said, "Okay, then, I'll do it."

Leaning forward, he kissed her lightly on the cheek. "Wonderful."

For once he truly felt things would be, and not just for Lily alone, but for the two of them.

# Chapter 45

LILY threw herself into her job as chairman to the exclusion of all else. She wanted this Spring Ball to be even better than the one she had chaired before. Soon everyone was marveling at the miracles she began to accomplish. The champagne was to be the finest, and the door prizes were being donated from establishments including Tiffany, Cartier, and Maximilian Furs.

But the real coup was snagging Frank Sinatra as the star entertainer. The skinny singer had engineered one of the most spectacular comebacks in show business history through his performance in *From Here to Eternity*, and even now no one could have been a hotter draw. It didn't hurt that his tempestuous relationship with Ava Gardner was still making headlines. When it was announced that he would be the headliner, tickets began to sell at an unprecedented rate.

As further icing on the cake, Skitch Henderson's band was to perform, and Robert Merrill agreed to sing an aria from *Rigoletto*. When he suggested that he and Sinatra sing "Some Enchanted Evening" as a duet, Lily thought she would faint.

She had arranged for hundreds of potted palms, anthuriums, and hibiscus to be flown in from Hawaii. Set designers were busy at work on a Tahitian theme. In the sketches, the colors were magnificent. The entire ballroom would be transformed into a scene by Gauguin.

It seemed that the Spring Ball might prove to be the event of the year, if not the decade.

As the date grew nearer, Lily became increasingly obsessed with the plans. She drove herself relentlessly. Late into the night she sat up checking her lists and organizational charts. Even after finally turning in, she would often switch on the light and hop out of bed because she had remembered something else.

She seemed to exist on no sleep at all, dropping off at one only to rise at five. By seven in the morning, she was already on the phone, attending to the myriad details.

The Spring Ball was a tremendous responsibility, yet she found herself thriving on it all. She loved the feeling of being needed, of being involved. And finally, after all the hours of work, the headaches, the skipped meals, and the agonizing, it was the day of the ball.

The weather could not have been better. The sky was blue and cloudless, the flowers were in bloom. Lily felt newly born. Ellis had been so right. She was a fool not to have come down to the city sooner. Finally it was just a matter of checking last-minute details. Her sandwich sat untouched as she remembered "just one more thing" a hundred times.

At two o'clock in the afternoon she gave up. Whatever was done was done. She slipped into a pair of trousers, a silk shirt, and a sweater and left Mary to answer the phone.

Once outside, she hailed a cab.

"Elizabeth Arden, please," she told the driver. Two hours later, Lily was a new woman. She emerged from the salon feeling radiantly alive. She had been coiffed and made up and manicured and now there was nothing to do but look forward to the wonderful evening ahead. She almost skipped as she walked up Fifth Avenue to Fifty-eighth, crossed the street and entered Bergdorf's to pick up her gown in the Fine Dress Salon.

Back at the apartment, she went to her dressing room, ripped off the tissue paper, and exclaimed with delight. Monsieur Givenchy had certainly outdone himself. This was indubitably the most glorious dress ever to come from his magic hands.

A seeming cloud of white chiffon billowed out from the tiny waist. The bodice was encrusted with pearls and crystal beads that shimmered in the light.

Lily laughed out loud; she was as excited as a young girl going to her first party.

She shed her street clothes and picked up the white satin chemise from the chaise, admiring its thick border of Alençon lace. It felt satiny against her skin as she slipped it on. She shivered slightly, feeling as radiant as she looked. She pulled up sheer silk stockings and slipped into a pair of dainty silver evening pumps. Then she put on the gown.

Standing in front of the three-way mirror, she gave herself the once-over. Even under her own unforgiving scrutiny, she had to admit, she almost looked twenty-one again, standing in the hall the night of her engagement to Roger Humphreys.

Funny, she hadn't thought of him in a million years. Poor Roger. His had been a strange and tragic story, which his family had tried to suppress. But inevitably it had leaked out. He had moved to Paris shortly after their broken engagement. The word had been that he was pursuing an artistic career. But the truth was that he had moved there with his lover, the former chauffeur on his father's estate. Apparently, the two of them had found happiness together for a time, for Paris was tolerant of such relationships.

But when Hitler's troops had rolled in, they were rounded up along with numerous other homosexuals and taken to concentration camps; Hitler's mania for extermination had extended to homosexuals as well as Jews. Roger had not survived the camps. His bones were presumed buried somewhere in Poland, along with those of his lover. Lily shuddered at the thought. She almost wished that Randolph had not told her.

Next her thoughts turned to Harry. It was still strange not to have him in his own dressing room, struggling into his tails and asking for help with his cuff links. Old habits died hard, she told herself. But different though it was, she found herself thrilled to hear the doorbell ring and then Ellis's deep voice in the foyer saying, "I'll show myself in. Please tell Mrs. Kohle that I'm here." Maybe the best way to break old ways was to develop new ones.

Tonight, for the first time, it felt as if she and Ellis were truly going out as a couple. The thought made her stomach go to butterflies.

She resolved not to dwell on the notion. Time to put on the last touches of makeup—a dab more rouge, a bit more lipstick. Then, after clipping on her emerald-and-diamond earrings, she drew the matching necklace about her throat. As she was fumbling with the clasp, the phone rang.

"Mary, will you get it?" she called.

But it rang and rang again. In exasperation, Lily dropped the necklace and picked up the receiver. "Hello?"

There was a burst of static on the line, and then a foreign voice said, "Allo?"

Puzzled, Lily said, "Hello? Who is this?"

"Allo, allo," the male voice repeated, amid another crackle of static.

"I can't hear you," Lily said again.

She heard the voice say, *"Je voudrais parler avec la mère de Mademoiselle Melissa Kohle, s'il vous plaît."*

Anxiously Lily cried, *"C'est moi. Je suis sa mère. Qu'est-que c'est?"*

Suddenly the line cleared and the voice on the other end began speaking, now in heavily accented English.

"This is the American Hospital at Neuilly. Your daughter was admitted here this morning. She has given birth to an infant and she is gravely ill. We found this number in her handbag; there appears to be no one else to call."

Melissa? Given birth to a baby? But that was impossible! Melissa wasn't even married! She was modeling, and her last letter had said that she was getting lots of assignments. How could she be pregnant?

But the voice on the other end had a ring of certainty to it. And how else would they have gotten Melissa's name, and her number?

Feebly she cried, "Melissa Kohle? A short, dark-haired girl?"

*"Oui, madame.* There is no mistake."

Lily's knees almost buckled under her. She sank dizzily into her dressing-table chair. Somehow she managed to speak. "Thank you so much for calling me. I will be there as soon as I can get on a plane."

As soon as she hung up, she picked up the phone and dialed Harry's number with a trembling hand. Harry's butler answered. "Mr. Kohle's residence."

"This is Mrs. Kohle," she cried. "Where is Mr. Kohle?"

"Mr. Kohle is in Palm Beach, madam. He doesn't wish the number given to anyone."

"Now you listen to me!" Lily almost screamed into the receiver. "This is an emergency, concerning our daughter, who is deathly ill! I'm telling you that you're going to give me that number this minute!" The butler instantly acquiesced.

"I beg your pardon, madam. I will find the number for you."

As Lily waited for the call to be put through to Palm Beach, she couldn't keep from shaking. Ever since that terrible day when the call had come about Jeremy, she had feared that another day would come when something would threaten another of her children. Now her worst nightmare had come true.

For a moment Lily was afraid that Harry wouldn't be there. It would be so typical, she thought angrily. Harry was never there when the children needed him most. But suddenly she heard the crackle as the operator said, "Go ahead, please."

"Harry?" she cried.

"No, madam," came another voice. It must be Harry's valet, Lily thought.

Trying to speak calmly, she asked, "This is Mrs. Kohle. Is Mr. Kohle there?"

"He can't come to the phone, I'm afraid. He's taking a nap."

"Wake him up," Lily said, nearly hysterical. "Wake him up, this minute. This is an emergency!"

Harry was surprised when the man timidly came out onto the terrace. He had left strict instructions not to be disturbed. He had heard the phone ring, but no one he knew had this number. He hadn't even told Ellis or his publisher that he was coming down.

The truth was that for the past several months he had been plagued by a nasty cough and had finally decided to go to a warmer climate to see if the sea air would do some good.

But once here, his bronchitis had turned into pneumonia. His had been a long, slow recovery. If only he could lay off those damned cigarettes! But his three-pack-a-day habit was a hard one to break, and he was sick of all those doctors drawing a long face over him.

After all, he was only forty-seven. As soon as he shook off this illness, he'd be good for another twenty years at least. And if he wasn't, who cared? Life didn't seem to hold as much as he had once thought, after all.

And there was certainly no one he cared to speak to. But before he could snap at Jenkins, he saw the worried expression on the man's face.

"It's Mrs. Kohle, sir. She says it's about your daughter—an emergency."

Those words struck him like a death knell. He, too, remembered the day of that terrible phone call from the dean. Harry threw off his blanket and shakily tried to rise from his chair, but Jenkins stopped him. "I'll bring a phone to you out here, sir."

"Lily?" he cried hoarsely into the receiver as soon as Jenkins brought it. "What's the matter?"

"Melissa is desperately ill in Paris. She's just given birth. She's in the American Hospital at Neuilly. I'm flying there tonight and I thought you'd want to also."

Harry listened with horror. "Oh God, Lily! How sick is she?"

"I don't know exactly; they wouldn't tell me over the phone. But the doctor said for us to come immediately."

Harry knew that he wasn't fit to travel. The doctor had told him that to strain his lungs at this point might be fatal. That didn't weigh in the balance if Melissa was gravely ill, but could he even get himself to the airport and onto a plane? He was using a humidifier round the clock.

He shook his head in frustration. "God, Lily—I don't know what to say. I've been sick—"

"Sick? Even if you're dying, I don't know how you can even think of not coming! Melissa needs us! And—and there's also a baby—our grandchild. Well, if you want to or not, it's up to you. Good-bye." The line went dead, leaving Harry looking at a silent receiver.

Lily, for her part, wanted to scream. Sick? She didn't believe that for a moment. Then, suddenly, she remembered that Ellis was in the living room. She ran to him and cried, "Oh God, Ellis—it's Melissa!"

"Not—"

"No, not dead, but almost as bad."

Between sobs, she choked out the story.

Instantly Ellis took command. "Now don't go to pieces, Lily. Of course it's bad news, but Melissa is young and healthy. I have a feeling that she will pull through this just fine. But you have to be strong now, for her sake. You get your things ready while I call the airport. We'll charter a plane if necessary. We'll be with Melissa before you know it."

The contrast between his reaction and Harry's was so stunning, she almost couldn't take it in. "You mean, you'll go with me?"

"Go with you?" he repeated blankly. "For God's sake, Lily, you don't think that I would consider letting you go through this alone, do you?"

Tears brimming in her eyes, she said chokingly, "Oh, Ellis. I love you so much. I just don't know what I'd do without you!"

"Okay, now go and change and throw a few things in a bag. I'll get Mary to help you."

Mary packed a suitcase while Lily slipped into a simple dress and coat. Ellis took her bag and ushered her to the elevators. As they waited for the car to come, he held her in a tender embrace.

"Don't worry, Lily, dear," he whispered softly. "Melissa is going to be all right."

Somehow, with Ellis next to her, Lily was able to keep going. She could keep at bay the terrifying visions of what might be happening to her daughter.

# Chapter 46

WHEN they were at last airborne, heading toward Paris, she stared out the window and said emptily, "I just don't understand. I know we've been distant. But how could this have happened, Ellis? How?"

"Well, now, she has been living in Paris, hasn't she? On her own . . ."

"That's true. And of course she didn't come home for Christmas." They both knew what that meant. She was already pregnant and starting to show.

"But I just got a letter from her last week and she said everything was fine." Lily said this as if by saying all was well she could make it so. "She said that she was modeling all the time."

Gently Ellis suggested, "She was probably trying to spare you the pain."

Lily nodded. Her appearance was calm but her thoughts were frantic. "She's not married, of course. Oh, Ellis, a *baby*. And my own child didn't trust me."

Ellis could only hold her hand and try to cheer her.

At long last they landed. Their taxi speeded along the road from Orly to the Parisian suburb of Neuilly.

Lily ran into the reception area ahead of Ellis and demanded in her still-fluent French, *"Où est Mademoiselle Kohle? Vite, vite, s'il vous plaît."*

*"Le troisième—trois cent quarante-deux."*

*"Merci."*

Lily walked swiftly down the corridor and into the elevator. Ellis was at her side when the doors closed on them. When they reached the floor, she ran the length of the hall, her heels tapping loudly on the marble floors.

It was a shock to see the pale figure lying so still. It wasn't until Lily stood at the edge of the bed that she could be sure it was her own daughter lying there.

All color and life seemed to have fled from her. Even her shining dark hair lay lank and lifeless. She was so emaciated that Lily flinched at the sight of her bony arm lying on top of the green sheet.

"Melissa, darling?" Lily whispered.

The eyelids flickered feebly, then closed again.

Oh God, Lily thought. She looks as though she's dying.

She turned away as tears flooded her eyes, and stumbled out into the corridor and pressed her forehead against the wall. She was almost unaware of Ellis's presence until he put his arms around her.

Lily wept unchecked for a few minutes. Then, as she began to collect herself, she and Ellis saw a doctor approaching Melissa's door.

Lily looked up, saying, "Doctor? I am Mrs. Kohle, Melissa's mother."

"Dr. Langlois," he replied tersely.

"How is she?"

"Very weak. There was a great deal of blood lost in the delivery."

"But she's so thin and ill-looking!"

He gave a very Gallic shrug. "That has nothing to do with the baby. We have no idea why she was allowed to get into such a condition; she obviously has not had proper nutrition during her pregnancy. She had no strength whatsoever to draw on; we had to deliver the baby by Cesarean section."

His look was one of censure, as if Lily had deliberately arranged for this to happen to Melissa.

"The baby is premature, and weighs under five pounds."

Lily's and Ellis's eyes met. In their concern for Melissa, they had forgotten about the baby.

"How is the child? May we see it?"

"The baby is fighting for survival, *madame*. Its tiny lungs are not developed. It is being given oxygen in an incubator, but its chances are not good."

Lily had cried so much that there were no tears left. She

swallowed the lump in her throat and whispered, "Is it a boy or a girl?"

"A girl, *madame*."

When Lily saw the tiny child lying behind the glass of the incubator, she heard again the echo of the doctor's words: too small, too young to survive.

This unwanted baby girl was her own flesh and blood. In spite of herself, she loved her; it was as simple as that.

"Live," she whispered against the glass that separated them. "Live, little one!" She felt Ellis's arm slip around her as they gazed together at the fragile form, breath barely stirring its tiny chest.

Turning to him, she looked into his eyes and said, "Pray for her, Ellis."

"I am," he answered quietly. "I already am."

Harry arrived the next morning. He came to the hospital room to find Lily and Ellis already there. He expressed no surprise at finding his agent there. All his thoughts were concentrated on his daughter.

Melissa was semi-comatose, but somehow, even in her sedated state, she seemed to recognize her father. "Daddy?" she murmured woozily. "Oh, Daddy?"

"I'm here, darling," he said, taking her hand. "Your mother's here, too."

But Ellis and Lily slipped out once it became clear that Melissa wanted to speak to her father. When Harry emerged some time later, he looked ashen and shaken.

"What the hell happened to her?" he demanded angrily. "Does anyone know?" A fit of coughing overtook him, and Lily frowned. Harry didn't look at all well. Maybe his story about being ill wasn't a complete fabrication. Recovering his composure, he went on, "Where is the man responsible for all this?"

"All we know is that she was brought by ambulance. Obviously, she hasn't been able to answer any questions. We can't press her until she gets her strength back. How do you think she is?"

"What do you think I think?" Harry cried hoarsely. "She looks like a corpse. There isn't an ounce of flesh on her bones! All I know is, I'm going to kill the bloody bastard, but where the hell is he?"

• • •

At that very moment, the man whom they were discussing was poised on skis at the top of a mountain at Val-d'Isère, straining to burst from the starting gate at the sound of the pistol shot.

The shot went off and the skier exploded from the gate. His lean, taut figure sliced down the giant slalom course, whipping past the poles and carving turns with effortless grace. All the other skiers made the run look like a battle against treacherous icy turns, but this one's timing had such magic, he appeared to be gliding with perfect ease.

At last he was snapping past the final gate, tucking his head down, and speeding past the finish line. It had been a spectacular run. The crowd watching gave a roar as his time flashed on the board—a full five seconds better than any of the preceding times.

Bronzed and muscular, he stood in the brilliant sunshine some minutes later, nonchalantly receiving congratulations for yet another unbelievable performance. Golden-haired and majestic, he was like a god amid mere mortals. No one watching him would ever have guessed that Jean-Paul Duval had ever traveled in anything but the jet-set circles he now negotiated as comfortably as he did the slalom course.

But Duval had been born in a rat-infested hovel in Marseilles, son of a fishmonger and his slovenly wife. There had been beatings and scoldings and constant financial turmoil. It came almost as a relief to him when, at the tender age of ten, he had been thrown out into the streets to fend for himself. Forced to subsist on his wits, he had scavenged through garbage cans and stolen anything he could lay his hands on.

He quickly learned the ways of survival, but it had been a lonely, uncertain existence. Eventually, like so many in that port city, he was drawn back to the waterfront of his birth.

He began hanging around the magnificent yachts which rode at anchor beyond the humble fishing vessels. One day, as luck would have it, he was spotted by a captain in such urgent need of a new cabin boy that he was willing to overlook Jean-Paul's obvious deficiencies of dress and manner. The twenty-eight-meter yacht which became his new home was owned by an Italian count and contessa, who took immense pride in the fact that the only larger boat in the harbor at the moment belonged to the Greek shipping magnate Ari Onassis.

The style of living aboard was opulent, to say the least. The count and contessa had spared no expense for themselves and their guests.

Jean-Paul's lot was a cramped berth in a gloomy forward cabin, where he discovered that he was unfortunately prone to violent seasickness. But after the first few weeks his nausea subsided and he began to look around himself with keen interest. At last he was close to the fabled rich people he had looked at so long from afar. He promptly decided that it was his destiny to be equally wealthy, by hook or crook.

Not six weeks after he came aboard, the contessa discovered him. She thought him a handsome, charming little street urchin and decided to befriend him. The contessa took pleasure in rewarding him for some small task or another and soon became inordinately attached to him. When the Italian couple left the yacht to go back to their own home, she managed to persuade the count to take him along with them. And so young Duval began to take in the most chic, most expensive resorts in Europe.

It was at Chamonix, from his small servant's room high up in the attic, that he first saw people skiing. He longed to know the exhilaration of gliding down snowy mountains at such speed. It must feel like flying. Almost immediately, Jean-Paul noticed a group of skiers who were subtly but unmistakably set apart. Another servant told him that they were World Cup racers. To Jean-Paul they were like gods as they schussed down the mountains effortlessly; up close, they were even more fascinating, with their muscular physiques and bronzed, glowing good looks.

He was too impatient to bide his time. Hiding behind the ski chalet, he saw a large party of people tilting their skis against the side of the building and going inside. As soon as they had disappeared to sit by the fire and boast of the day's exploits, Jean-Paul was gone with a pair of skis and poles.

Possessing no ticket and no money to buy one, he crowded onto the gondola with all the others and sidled up to a couple who looked old enough to be his parents.

At the top, he was the first one off, dragging the long skis to an open space. He watched the others to understand the technique, then strapped the skis to his stolen boots as best he could. Duval felt a surge of self-confidence. He could do this!

He dug in his poles and launched himself. As he felt the wind whip against his face and the snow surprisingly firm under his skis, he almost laughed aloud. It *was* like flying!

But the heady sensation lasted only a long, glorious moment before abruptly he knew something was wrong. He was going too fast. . . . He couldn't seem to turn his skis. . . .

A tree suddenly loomed up ahead of him, and he swerved with a sure, catlike instinct, but in the process he caught his edge in a rough spot and tumbled head over heels in a spectacular cartwheel. When he had finally come to a halt, half-buried in a drift, he felt as if he were choking on snow. His skis had come off in his headlong fall, and as he struggled to his feet and looked around, he saw them lying broken behind him.

Well, he thought philosophically, he could always steal another pair.

Leaving them where they lay, he decided to walk down the hill, but he found that his ankle burned with pain every time he put his weight on it. He wanted to cry, but stoically he gritted his teeth and began limping toward the chalet.

The next day, the contessa sent for her little page and was startled when he limped in heavily.

"What is wrong, *bambino?*"

"I fell on the ice outside, Contessa, and twisted my ankle."

The contessa exclaimed when she examined the boy's ankle; it was swollen to twice its normal size.

"You should not be walking on this, *bambino!* Go up to bed now, and I will send the doctor to you."

"Thank you, Contessa." He smiled up at her winsomely. "Your kindness is all I need to recover."

Trying to hide her smile, the contessa replied, "Nevertheless, I will send the doctor. Now go!" As he disappeared, she looked after him with a fond twinkle. The little devil. He knew just how to get around her.

The doctor's report was encouraging. No bones broken, but he would have to stay off the ankle for a week. Jean-Paul shrugged philosophically. In a week they would be gone from Chamonix, but next winter they would come here again. And the next time he was on a pair of skis, he was going to be a little less cocky—and a lot better. Despite his first fiasco, he remained enchanted by this new world of skiing. He determined to make it his own.

They spent the warm, balmy summer sailing on the Adriatic, while Jean-Paul dreamed of skiing. By the fall, he had developed a new plan for the tactics he would employ to become not just proficient but expert.

He realized it would not be enough to steal a pair of skis and struggle along by himself. He took advantage of the count's absence—he was away on business—to put his plan into action. Jean-Paul waited until an afternoon when the contessa had gone to the village and would not be returning until dusk; he lit a single birthday candle and placed it in his window, knowing that when the contessa returned she would see it. His birthday had actually been a month before, but she would not know that, and he was sure that when she saw the candle she would come by to wish him a happy birthday.

Watching intently, he finally saw her come into the courtyard. She looked up, hesitated, looked back, and then started toward his wing.

Inwardly he exulted. It was going to work! Her interest in him thus far had been maternal; he guessed shrewdly that one of the true sorrows of her life was the fact that she had no children of her own. But the time had come to effect a change in that attitude.

The contessa knocked, then opened his door—and stopped short. Jean-Paul was completely nude. He appeared to have been changing from his day clothes to the suit he wore to serve at the table. Simulating confusion and embarrassment, he clutched his shirt to him, but not before he had made sure that the contessa had had a good look at him.

The contessa blushed as she stared at him. Her cute little Jean-Paul was almost a man. In spite of herself, she felt a stirring of desire.

Turning away, trying to hide her burning cheeks, she murmured, "I'm sorry—I had no idea. . . . I didn't mean to disturb you."

"It's all right," he said with feigned shyness.

"Yes, well—come to see me as soon as you've changed, please."

After that episode, their relationship underwent a subtle

transformation. They never spoke of it, of course, but once or twice Jean-Paul caught her giving him the eye. And she had stopped calling him *bambino*.

As he had hoped, just before they started for Chamonix the contessa was easily persuaded to give him an old pair of skis they had in the storeroom. Once there, it soon became taken for granted that whenever he was not needed by the contessa, Jean-Paul was free to go skiing.

This time he started on the gentler slopes, but with his natural athletic ability he rapidly improved. By December he skied from the summit for the first time.

Duval was apprehensive as he surveyed the long, steep slope from the mountaintop. But through iron will, natural confidence, and determination, he barely paused before pushing off.

He took one bad fall that day, but luckily his slender hickory skis didn't crack. He picked himself up, took a deep breath, and went on with renewed abandon.

When he finally skidded to a halt in front of the chalet, he tore off his cap and shook his head, laughing in exultation. He had done it: conquered the highest peak at Chamonix!

Now it was time to impress the contessa. Catching sight of her, he hid himself at the top of the gondola. Then, as she took off down the slope, he followed. After skiing behind her for a minute or two, he increased his speed and drew up alongside her, then dropped back, then came forward again, weaving in and out, carving the arcs at which he was fast becoming proficient.

The contessa didn't know who the graceful boy was and Jean-Paul played up the mystery, allowing her just a glimpse of him on one side before veering off to the other.

At the bottom he waited for her as she skied up and stopped in front of him. Then he ripped off his sunglasses and smiled at the shock reflected in her face.

"Jean-Paul! It can't be! How on earth did you learn to ski like that?"

And in truth it was not just his extraordinary ability that stunned the contessa. The hours of skiing were quickly developing his physique. He had acquired a tan, which well complemented his blond locks and only enhanced his powerful sensuality.

Ever since that day she had seen him nude, the contessa

had not allowed herself to think about the way his body had looked in the candlelight, but at this moment the memory came back.

"You must have the finest instructors," she said finally, still staring at him. "You could be a champion, you know."

"With your inspiration, Contessa," he said, summoning up all the precocious sexuality of his Mediterranean heritage.

More than once, he had let his gaze wander appraisingly over the contessa's full bosom and the rounded bottom so appealingly revealed by her clinging ski pants. It was impossible for her to be in love with the count; he was old and fat and balding.

As a young boy in the streets of Marseilles, he had witnessed the act that went on between women and men, and he knew that he was ready. Indeed, he had been from that day when he had felt the contessa's eyes on his nude body.

When they went back to the villa in Tuscany, Jean-Paul was given a room in the family quarters, just down the hall from the contessa's own suite. The count never even thought twice about it; his contessa must have her little whims. Even though there was a thirty-year difference between his age and that of his wife, he never imagined that she would look elsewhere—and certainly not to a boy of barely fourteen.

The contessa herself could not have explained her compulsion. To take a lover was one thing, but a mere child . . . yet somehow Jean-Paul had never been a child.

The first time he came to her room, she looked into his eyes wonderingly, for they were experienced eyes, wise far beyond his years. When they made love it was extraordinary. She had had lovers before, but never one with Jean-Paul's innate sexual knowledge. It seemed to spring from an endless inner source, as he showed her things she had never experienced before.

He broke through all the barriers and somehow, despite the guilt that plagued her, she could not bring herself to break off their affair.

Meanwhile, she saw to it that he had unlimited funds for his lessons and equipment. Under the top Swiss and French instructors, he was rapidly climbing the ladder of junior racing.

Then, abruptly, at eighteen, he vaulted to the top. He entered his first big-time race—one of the more important on the European circuit—and won. It was one of the most stunning upsets in ski racing history, and the contessa rejoiced for him.

But that night, as she saw him surrounded by a knot of adoring young girls, she knew despair, for she suddenly realized that she had lost him. He was no longer a poor young boy, but a grown man. And as the newest star in the skiing world, he would have women—hundreds of them. Young, beautiful, unencumbered.

The only reason he had stayed with her so long was that he had needed her financial support. That suddenly became clear. But now that he could earn his own way through prize money, he would no longer be beholden to her largesse. She could only bow out of this inauspicious affair as gracefully as possible.

The World Cup circuit was not to be conquered overnight, but by the time Jean-Paul was twenty, he was a figure to be reckoned with, both on and off the mountain. He had already forgotten how many women had offered him their hotel-room keys, and then themselves, and how many of those he had accepted.

At twenty-four, he reached the pinnacle: He won the World Cup. Wealth and fame—the destiny he had dreamed of so long ago on the yacht in Marseilles—were no longer dreams, but reality. He was the darling of fate—until the day he almost literally stumbled across a pretty young girl on the slopes of St. Moritz.

His first reaction was irritation, but as he began to berate her, he was wrenched to a halt. Gazing up at him from where she had fallen was a petite brunette with the most intriguing violet eyes he had ever seen.

"Sorry," she announced. "But you should have looked where you were going."

And with such an unpromising introduction began an affair that would blossom into one of a passion and intensity that neither of them had known.

Jean-Paul was the most handsome man Melissa had ever seen, but he, for his part, couldn't quite fathom the instant attraction he felt toward her. After all, he had known some of the most extraordinary beauties of Europe.

But something about her piquant little face—a certain untouched quality, a youthful arrogance—filled him with an irresistible urge to make her his.

"You're right, I should have," he replied, smiling down at her. "Come on, let me help you up."

As Jean-Paul skied alongside Melissa toward the bottom of the hill, he couldn't help but imagine her trim, petite figure under the ski clothes. Jaded though he had become from his many dalliances, he felt a sudden thrill of anticipation as he watched her. It had been a while since the last time a woman had affected him so.

At the foot of the hill, he turned to her and smiled. "Are you ready to quit for the day? Shall we go into the chalet and have a Pernod?"

He listened with half an ear as she talked. She was a model, she explained, from New York by way of Switzerland. She was sharing an apartment in Paris with two other girls.

Despite her attempts to sound sophisticated, her ingenuous chatter suddenly made him wonder. "How old are you?" he asked.

Unruffled, Melissa lied calmly, "Almost twenty-one."

Jean-Paul relaxed. No fear of the *flics* coming to haul him away for seducing a child.

"And your family?" he asked casually. Better to be certain they were not nearby, poised to interfere.

"My father is Harry Kohle, the novelist."

"Interesting," he mused. "I've read a few of his novels."

No need to tell her that Harry Kohle bored him stiff—too little sex in his fiction. Jean-Paul infinitely preferred Henry Miller to writers like Kohle.

"What did you say your name was?" Melissa asked him. "I feel as if I've seen you before."

"My name is Jean-Paul Duval."

"Jean-Paul Duval—the skier! Of course!" she exclaimed excitedly. "No wonder you look familiar! You were on the cover of *Paris Match* last month."

He shrugged deprecatingly. *"C'est moi."*

Melissa's face was glowing. "I can't believe it! Wow!"

He laughed aloud. She was amusing, this little American girl. He was surer than ever that she would be more than amusing in bed.

Unfortunately, he was not going to be able to pursue this

quarry immediately. He and the rest of the French team were leaving at four-thirty for Val-d'Isère for three days of racing. Her face fell when he finally told her that he would have to be going. "Oh, no! I was hoping we could see each other tonight."

*"Je suis désolé, mademoiselle,"* he said, shrugging slightly. Deliberately tantalizing her, he drew out his wallet and idly leafed through it. Then, lazily, he took out his card, scribbled a number across the back, and tossed it across the table with a flick of his wrist. "This is my private number in Paris. Call me there next week." He leaned over unexpectedly, brushing his lips across hers in a lingering caress, and was gone.

Melissa just sat there, at first stunned, then wistful. She touched her lips, almost unable to believe that he had kissed her. None of her various escapades had ever given her even a hint of this kind of thrill—not even the affair with the music teacher at Miss Parker's, whom she had lured into the cloakroom and made her first lover. Melissa giggled at the memory. The poor man had been so nervous, thinking that they would be discovered at any moment.

Jean-Paul Duval! He was as good as a movie star! She would hardly be able to bear the wait until next week.

When the seven seemingly endless days had passed, she dialed his number, which she'd already committed to memory. But the phone buzzed over and over and no one answered. Finally she hung up in disappointment.

For the next three days, she called Jean-Paul's number constantly, night and day. Finally, just as she was sure that he must have given her a wrong number, she made one last try, at eight o'clock in the morning, and someone answered.

*"Allo? Qui est-ce?"* came a sleepy, irritated voice.

"This is Melissa Kohle," she ventured uncertainly. "We met at St. Moritz, don't you remember?"

In truth, he had almost forgotten the incident. St. Moritz seemed like a long time ago, and at this moment he could barely recall what this Melissa Kohle looked like. While she had been anxiously counting the days, he had been racing and then wining, dining, and bedding Brigitte, the tall, luscious blonde ski bunny he had met at Val-d'Isère and cavorted with at Biarritz for the past five days.

Still, if he had given her his number, she must have been game worth the chase. Duval decided to stall for time. "Can

I call you back? I'm a little tired . . . just got in a few hours ago . . ."

"I thought that perhaps if you were free tonight—"

Rubbing his eyes wearily, he said, *"Oui, oui.* At eight o'clock?"

"Yes, yes—where?" she exclaimed eagerly.

"The Coq d'Or, on the Left Bank? Do you know it?"

"Just off the Boulevard St.-Michel? I'll be there at eight."

As she hung up, Melissa thought she'd burst with excitement. God, what would she wear? And her hair—up or down? Did he prefer a sultry look like Simone Signoret's or an Audrey Hepburn-ish gamine? She almost wished that she hadn't made the date for that very evening, but after doing her hair in a French twist and slipping into the figure-hugging halter dress she had decided upon, she looked in the mirror with satisfaction. Her self-assurance began to come back.

She *was* pretty—everyone said so. Her dark hair was shiny and curled in beautiful ringlets, and her violet eyes were such an unusual color, they always drew attention.

After all, she told herself, she had already made quite a hit with the male sex so far. Now that she was liberated from those stuffy old schools, it was time to spread her wings and live a little. A whole new world was opening up to her, and she intended to make the most of it.

But her self-confidence took an abrupt dive when she walked into the Coq d'Or that evening and Jean-Paul wasn't there. For fifteen agonizing minutes, she waited none too patiently. Then, at last, she saw his tall, bronzed figure saunter through the door. Melissa felt a wave of relief.

Duval was taller than she had remembered, tanner now and more glamorous than ever. Flashing her a devastating smile, he said, "I hope I haven't kept you waiting."

"Oh, no—not at all. That is, just a few minutes."

"Ah," he said, eyeing her with evident pleasure. "You look *ravissante, chérie.* But isn't that dress a little low-cut for a mere child like you?"

Melissa took a deep breath, reminding herself not to seem as excessively eager as she had at their first meeting. She had sounded like a gushing ingenue, and Jean-Paul was too much a man of the world to be interested in those. Maintaining her poise, she smiled provocatively and ignored his question, returning it instead with one of her own. "Isn't it a little unusual for a mere ski bum to know the name of a novelist like Harry Kohle?"

The remark took Duval off guard. He began to feel that in Melissa he'd found a worthy opponent, not an empty-headed coquette. "We're not all total Philistines, you know."

The conversation drifted from one topic to another, and Jean-Paul found himself intrigued in spite of himself. She was certainly pretty, and the contrast between her kittenish face and her provocative way of talking once again made him wonder what she would be like in bed.

He filled her glass over and over with *vin ordinaire*. Melissa didn't even realize how much she was drinking; she was already heady with the excitement of this daring new flirtation.

Finally Jean-Paul decided that the time was ripe. Leaning over, he whispered softly, tickling her ear, "Come on, *chérie*—the night awaits us."

Melissa let him lead her out to his sporty Alfa Romeo. There she paused, turned, and wrapped herself around him, kissing him with abandon. The night was young, she was young. That he returned her kisses with equal ardor was more than she'd dared hope.

They zoomed through the narrow streets along the Seine. The breeze yanked at Melissa's careful French twist. She pulled out the combs, tossing them to the wind. Her hair fluttered loose and free.

They passed Notre Dame, gently illuminated on the Ile de la Cité. Then they circled the Eiffel Tower, turned and roared north over a bridge to the Right Bank, finally skidding to a halt in the courtyard of a magnificent old building on the Avenue Foch.

Melissa was breathless as she gazed up at the wrought-iron balconies gleaming in the moonlight.

"You live here?" she asked wonderingly.

But Jean-Paul was no longer in the mood to talk. Covering her mouth in a long, sensual kiss, he led her up the twisting staircase to his apartment on the top floor.

Once inside, Melissa glanced around curiously. Duval had a magnificent nineteenth-century apartment, with intricate floors of rose and sienna marble, a stunning carved mantelpiece topped by an enormous trumeau mirror, and a glittering Baccarat chandelier. Seeing the evident opulence and antiquity of the room itself, Melissa was surprised to find the furnishings stark and modern and scattered haphazardly about the room. The single couch was piled high with ski clothes and underwear. Skis and boots were stacked against the walls.

But Melissa and Jean-Paul did not long linger in the living room. He slipped off his black leather jacket as he walked her to the bedroom.

Their coming together was more tempestuous than even he had imagined. This *petite poupée* was better in bed than any woman of the world, and he couldn't get enough of her. She stayed the next day and the next, and the lovemaking was as wild as he had ever experienced.

At first he was content, for Melissa was engaging enough to keep him interested even when they got out of bed. But as the weeks turned to months, he began to discover all the ways in which she had deceived him.

Her so-called modeling career was a fantasy; though she had a pretty face, her petite curvaceous figure was wrong for the fashion ideals of the time. Every modeling agency in Paris had told her so. She was also much younger than she had led Jean-Paul to believe; she had not yet reached her eighteenth birthday.

But worst of all was that for all her pretended sophistication, she was utterly ignorant of methods of preventing pregnancy. A mere three months after they had started their liaison, she could no longer conceal it: She was *enceinte*.

Jean-Paul was furious. Marriage and a family were the last things he had in mind; he loved his freedom far too much. He reveled in being one of the most sought-after bachelors of the World Cup circuit. He wasn't about to give it up for any woman, to say nothing of a child he didn't want.

In his own way, he did care for Melissa; she had a coquettish femininity which appealed to his masculinity, and beneath her pretty face a steel will and barbed wit drew him almost against his will. But now that will was making life difficult for him, and he reacted violently.

"*C'est impossible,* Melissa! You must do something about this *bébé, et tout de suite!* It was your responsibility to prevent this!"

"No, it wasn't!" Melissa retorted. "You were there too, you know. You had as much pleasure as I did!"

"That has nothing to do with *bébés*. You must get rid of it!"

"I tried!" she stormed. "I took some pills that Michelle promised would do the trick, but they didn't work! It was too late—I only realized that I was pregnant two weeks ago."

"And you're three months pregnant? How can that be?"

"How was I supposed to know? My cycle's never been regular. I didn't think to worry until this past month."

"I'm not going to marry you," Duval said evenly.

"You want your baby to be a bastard?"

He shrugged. "You're the one who is going to have it! As far as I'm concerned, it's your problem."

And with that, he grabbed his jacket. "I'm leaving."

"Where are you going?" Melissa cried, suddenly fearful.

But he had already slammed the door.

Melissa sank onto the couch. Morning-sick and now abandoned, her fierceness softened. She began to cry.

It was three hours later that she heard a key in the door. She sprang up, hardly daring to hope that it would be Jean-Paul. He stood in the doorway, eyeing her sharply. But instead of embracing her, telling her he still loved her, he said grudgingly, "All right, you can have the baby, but you'll have to stay out of sight when you begin to show, and as soon as it's born, you must put it up for adoption."

"Oh, Jean-Paul! Of course," she cried, throwing her arms around him. "Thank you, darling. I love you."

He was the thing she lived for. She would never again be so foolish as to risk losing him through her defiance.

As the months passed, Jean-Paul was as good as his word. He refused to be seen with her, or let anyone know that she was pregnant. Sitting at home by herself while he was skiing or partying, Melissa cursed her thickening waist. She hated being pregnant—the nausea, the ungainliness, the extra weight.

Realizing that her changed body actually physically repulsed him, she starved herself in an effort to hide her condition a little longer, but there was no way to keep her belly from protruding, even as her arms and legs grew thin as twigs.

As the months passed, she and Jean-Paul began to snap at each other. He spent more and more time away.

One afternoon, while she was in her seventh month, she reclined on the bed as Jean-Paul packed for yet another ski race.

"Please don't stay away so long this time," she pleaded sulkily. "I need you."

"You don't need anyone, *petite,*" he returned harshly, as he snapped the suitcases shut. "You are indestructible."

But that pearl of wisdom had proved to be mere verbiage, for even as he launched himself on the final run of the downhill, Melissa was being raced to the American Hospital at Neuilly.

Had it not been for the concierge with the sharp ears in the ground-floor flat who heard her feeble cries, she would have bled to death amid the tangle of paraphernalia littering the bedroom.

As Duval daringly mastered a giant slalom course, Melissa was wheeled into the operating room, fighting for her life.

While he sat in the chalet, flirting with a lovely skier from the Belgian women's ski team, the tiny baby he and Melissa had so carelessly created came into the world.

And as he finished another practice run and raised his arms to the cheers of the crowd, three people cursed him silently in Paris.

# Chapter 47

FOR forty-eight more hours, Harry, Lily, and Ellis kept up their vigil over the two lives that had been so cavalierly treated—and then they heard the words they had prayed for.

"Your daughter is awake. The fever has broken. You may go in for a minute and see her."

Lily went in first. "Melissa, darling," she murmured softly.

The pale girl on the bed could hardly meet her mother's eyes. The two remained silent for what seemed to each like a very long time.

"What are you doing here, Mother?" said Melissa finally.

"I guess you don't remember. I've been here for several days, darling. The hospital called me."

"You know, then—about the baby."

"Yes."

Tears welled up in Melissa's eyes, and she turned away to hide them.

Instinctively, Lily leaned over and put her arms around her daughter, her heart aching for her.

"Darling, you don't have to talk about it now. Just rest and try to get better. We'll work something out."

A grim look came over Melissa. Her mouth straightened to a thin line.

"I've already taken care of that, Mother."

"What do you mean, dear?"

"I'm putting the baby up for adoption."

Lily could barely speak. "Giving the baby away? How on earth . . . ? Melissa, your own child?"

"I don't even want to talk about the baby, Mother. I don't want it, and Jean-Paul doesn't want it either."

"Jean-Paul—that's the baby's father?"

"Yes. He's very famous. Jean-Paul Duval, the skier—surely you've heard of him?"

"Yes, I guess so. . . . He's your—"

"Lover. He's my lover."

Lily flinched at the bald words, and Melissa said impatiently, "Now don't start moralizing. I love Jean-Paul and he loves me. Marriage is so bourgeois, anyway."

"But when there's a child to consider—"

"Ingrid Bergman didn't bother to get married when she ran away with Roberto Rossellini."

"And look what everyone said about her and her son!"

"Well, that's another good argument for giving up this baby! Look, Mother, I've made up my mind. There's no use discussing it."

Lily could barely believe it. Could this be the daughter she had given birth to? She seemed a stranger, speaking so callously about giving away her own baby. But then, why was she so shocked? Melissa was simply her grandmother Violet all over again, in character as well as appearance. Lily herself had been every bit as unwanted as this baby. Violet had been too conscious of appearances actually to abandon her, but in truth she had been as disdainful of motherhood as Melissa now was.

For a moment Lily wondered if it really was the best thing for the baby for Melissa to keep her. She shuddered to think what life might be like for the child, with Melissa feeling the way she did and this Jean-Paul apparently no better, if not worse. At least her own parents had had some sense of responsibility.

Looking back at her daughter, she quickly made allowances. Melissa simply *couldn't* be as monstrously self-centered as she then seemed. After all, she told herself, she had just been through great trauma; she was very young and scared. It was too much to expect much emotional maturity from her.

Lily tried one last time. "Melissa, please believe me. You'll feel differently once you've seen this baby—your baby. She's so tiny, so helpless in that incubator. The doctor says it's still touch and go, but she's doing miraculously well. If she gets through the next few days, they'll begin to hope that she'll have a chance."

"It would be better for everyone if it died," Melissa said, turning away. Couldn't her mother understand? She didn't *want* that baby!

Lily wanted to scream, to slap her, to threaten. Instead, controlling her temper, she got up and walked out of the room. She leaned her head against the smooth, cool wall of the corridor, tears streaming down her face, while Harry and Ellis looked on, stunned.

"Lily, what is it?" Harry finally managed. "What's wrong?"

"She doesn't want the baby, Harry. She wishes that it would die."

She broke into sobs. Harry gathered her against him, saying nothing, simply stroking her hair while she wept. Finally, as she grew calmer, he said softly, "Shall we go to see the baby, Lily?"

Ellis followed them silently. It was not for him to intrude on their shared moment of anguish.

Down the hall at the neonatal unit, the three of them stood gazing through the glass at the infant. Lily longed to hold her, to cradle her in her arms. That little unwanted baby in the incubator had somehow become herself.

Ellis put a hand on her shoulder. "It won't be long, Lily. She's going to live. That baby is going to make it. I just know she will."

"Oh God, I hope so! I hope so."

Ellis's prediction came true. Even as Melissa regained the strength sapped by her pregnancy and her poor diet, so the baby gained weight and strength.

After Melissa told Lily Jean-Paul's name, Ellis set in motion inquiries as to his whereabouts. Well-known though he was, there was some confusion about his itinerary. The message telling him about Melissa and the baby didn't reach him until he arrived in Gstaad.

Duval sat on the edge of his hotel-room bed and ripped open the telegram. Reading it, he grew very still. The baby had already arrived. God, and it wasn't due for another two months! He was genuinely upset to learn that Melissa was so gravely ill. He felt as though he'd deserted her, though who could have known she would deliver so soon? Like Melissa, he was sorry the baby had survived and was expected to live.

But he wasn't a monster, it was just that everything would have been so much easier if it had simply died.

Sighing, he crumpled the telegram and tossed it in the wastebasket. He might as well go ahead with tomorrow's practice before flying back to Paris; the whole thing was over, in any case, and it was too late for him to hold Melissa's hand.

He did wire her a huge bouquet of flowers, along with a telegram which read, "Sorry I couldn't be there. Hope all is well. Returning to Paris two days. Love Jean-Paul."

Melissa was thrilled by the sight of the flowers the nurse brought in. She ripped open the accompanying telegram, her hands trembling with excitement.

"What does he say, darling?" Lily asked her.

"He says he'll be back in two days!"

"That's wonderful, Melissa. Anything else—about the baby?"

"No, Mother, don't be ridiculous. We already decided all that, long ago."

"I know, darling, but why don't you wait to make your decision until Jean-Paul has actually seen the baby? It might make a difference in his thinking."

"Mother, forget it! There's no way on earth we'll change our minds. And I don't want you to start trying to convince him, either. It will just annoy him."

Lily held her tongue. She just couldn't get over it—what a stranger her daughter had become. As calmly as possible, she announced the intention she had been harboring since she learned her daughter planned to abandon her child. "In that case, Melissa, I'm thinking about adopting the baby myself."

Melissa laughed contemptuously. "You, Mother? You're too old."

"Hardly, darling. I'm quite young enough to run around after a child."

Melissa heard the firm resolve in her mother's tone. Clearly, she realized with dismay, her mother spoke in dead earnest. Sitting up, she stared at Lily unbelievingly. "What are you trying to do? Is this some kind of plan to trick me into taking it?"

"No," Lily replied steadily. "It has nothing to do with you. It's quite simple, really. I love this baby."

"Mother, you can't do this to me. I want to forget this ever happened. If you take the baby, I'll never see you again!"

"The truth is that you don't bother to see me much as it is, do you? Let me tell you, Melissa, if you're going to force me to choose between you and your baby, I will. And once I've adopted her, I will never let you take her back." She paused, then went on calmly but deliberately. "Obviously I made a lot of mistakes somewhere along the line with you children. Well, maybe I've learned a thing or two since then. And I know only too well what it's like to be abandoned. I won't sit by and see my own grandchild passed off to strangers."

"All right, then. Take the damned baby! See if I care! I don't care what you think of me, anyway. I have Jean-Paul and I love him."

"Well, I hope that you'll be happy. But let me give you one piece of advice. A man who wasn't with you at the birth of your child, who doesn't want that child, a man who doesn't return as soon as he knows how ill you have been, a man who won't marry you, is not a very good prospect as far as I'm concerned."

"Oh, and you're a great judge of men, aren't you, Mother? Look where your good judgment's gotten you."

"I won't go into that with you, Melissa," Lily said. "Anything between your father and me is just that: between us."

"Fine. And everything between Jean-Paul and me is between us. I won't hear another word against him. Why don't you just mind your own business."

Lily looked grim. "You are my child. You *are* my business. I can't sit by while this man abuses you. Make no mistake, Melissa. Abusing you is exactly what this Jean-Paul is doing. His attitude toward your baby is reprehensible. That he watched on while you let yourself get so thin is even worse. And now that he knows you and the baby—his baby—are in the hospital, what does he do? Goes and skis for two more days."

Tears welled in Melissa's eyes. "You don't understand!" she said hoarsely.

Lily sighed. "Melissa, darling, listen. I don't want to say things that will hurt you. You're my daughter and I love you; nothing could ever change that. Maybe I've said more than I meant to say. But if you abandon that baby, I am taking her. Are you very sure you want to do that?"

"I won't give up Jean-Paul."

"Well then," Lily said, "you've made your decision." She

leaned over and kissed Melissa's forehead. "I wish you well. Good-bye, darling."

Lily's heart ached as she took one last look at Melissa's pale, resolute face. This, after all, was her own child.

Back in her suite at the George V, Lily was overcome by a throbbing migraine. She pulled the drapes closed and took two aspirin and lay down on the bed with a dampened cloth on her forehead. Thinking of Melissa only made her feel worse. Even animals in the jungle fought for their own young, but Melissa could give up her baby with no more thought than if it were a stray cat. I must have failed terribly as a mother, thought Lily, to have raised such a selfish, heartless child.

Meanwhile, Harry and Ellis had been out to lunch. There was more than a trace of awkwardness between them. Harry had not gotten over the shock of finding Ellis with Lily in Paris. Now he sat chain-smoking as they waited for their meal to be brought. Conversation was an effort.

"How's the work been going?" Ellis asked casually.

Harry shrugged. "I haven't really been able to get going on anything since I sent in *The Sod.*"

Taking a drag on his cigarette, he let out a hacking cough. Ellis's brows drew together in a frown. "That doesn't sound good, Harry."

"Well, I've just been under the weather."

"That's what Lily said. I know you've had bronchitis for some time, but it sounds worse. Have you seen a doctor?"

Shrugging, Harry said, "Actually, I've been in a hospital for the last couple of weeks with pneumonia, but I'm recovering now. That's why I took the place down there in Palm Beach, for the warm climate and the sea air."

Harry seemed wearier than Ellis had ever seen him. The agent thought back to the young man who had presented himself in his office so many years go. He had been so eager, so passionate about his work, so vital and young. But today he looked pale and tired. Almost overnight, it seemed the years had taken their toll. It had been several months since Ellis had seen him, and the change in Harry was startling.

Harry added, "Please don't say anything about it to Lily. She has enough to worry about."

Ellis changed the subject. "I'm glad Melissa is doing so well, and the baby is better every day."

The ghost of a smile touched Harry's lips. "Lily always did love babies."

"She seems to have become totally wrapped up in this one. Did you see all the things she bought yesterday? There must not be a bootie or an embroidered baby gown left in Paris."

Harry frowned. "I hope it won't be too tough on her when she has to leave it."

"Do you think there's any possibility that Melissa will bring the baby back to New York?"

"No. She's serious about putting her up for adoption. She claims to be totally devoted to this goddamned skier—the one who hasn't troubled himself to come see her yet—and he wants no part of her if it means having a kid. Son of a bitch!" A sudden cough racked his body, anger gripped his heart. He felt so frustrated and powerless. If only he could talk to Melissa about this bastard, set her straight. But then, such things were really Lily's province.

And Drew's words still haunted him. Who was he to preach to Melissa? In ways, he was as much of a cad as this Jean-Paul Duval character. Although he wished it otherwise, it was simply too late for him to play the role of concerned father. For all his children, far too late.

Lily lay in her darkened room at the George V. Her head still throbbed but she was determined to develop a plan. A strange tingle had run through her when Melissa had announced, "Go ahead, take the baby." Horrified as she was at her daughter's carelessness, she was secretly thrilled at the prospect of making that baby her own. Another chance for her to be a mother, another child to be loved.

She *must* have that baby—but that meant marriage, for no agency, government or private, would allow a divorced single woman to adopt. She must find a man. Oddly enough, the first candidate to spring to her mind was Ellis. He would marry her, she was sure, and love the child as his own. Ellis had always loved children. But was that really fair to him? He had said that he was in love with her, but the marriage she had in mind was one of convenience. Would he take her on any terms? If he did, could she let him? Would that be fair of her? She had never allowed Ellis to come close to her since that fateful night she had left Harry, but her woman's intuition told her that his feelings were unchanged. She still shied away from examining her own emotions. As wonderful as Ellis was, she could not allow herself to fall in love ever again.

No, he would marry her, without question, without any demands, but he was too fine a man to be condemned to a loveless union. Lily would do much for the sake of this precious baby, but she would not do that.

That left only Harry. Barely a month ago, she would have sworn that it was an impossibility that they would ever be friendly enough even to discuss such a thing. She would have sworn that their paths would never converge again. But the agonizing worry over Melissa and the baby had somehow smoothed the raw edges of anger and recrimination. The crisis had drawn them together. They were still far from love, but somehow concern for their child revived an old bond. Surely Harry would agree to go through a ceremony for appearance's sake.

With a start, she remembered: The divorce was not actually final yet! They had long since worked out the property settlement and alimony, but she had not yet signed the final decree. The papers from her attorney had been sitting on her desk for almost two weeks, and she had been avoiding them, subconsciously putting off severing the tie. Now she blessed her procrastination. All they had to do was tear up those papers, and in the eyes of the law, she and Harry would still be man and wife. And who would be a more appropriate party to adopt the child than her own grandparents?

Glancing over at the chaise, she saw the dozen or more baby clothes she had bought the day before. Lily felt a sense of relief she had not known since her arrival. Tonight, she would broach the subject with Harry. Soon the baby would be in her arms.

She went to the bath and turned the gold taps to fill the tub.

After lunch, Ellis and Harry had gone back to the hospital. It was almost six o'clock when they gathered in Lily's suite.

"Are you hungry?" Harry asked.

"Yes," Lily answered. "But first, I'd like a drink—a nice tall one."

She was clad in a new dove-gray gown, her hair burnished and glowing. Ellis instantly noticed the change in her mood.

As Harry dialed room service, he told her, "You look lovely, my dear."

"Thank you." She smiled. "I just decided to pick up my spirits a little, have my hair done. . . ."

"I'm glad you're feeling better."

After the waiter brought the drink trolley, Ellis mixed martinis, then handed them around. "Here's to Melissa's recovery—and the baby's."

"We can't just keep calling it 'the baby,' " Harry said. "Hasn't Melissa decided on a name for her yet?"

"She doesn't want to name her," said Lily. She took a deep breath and went on. "As a matter of fact, that's something I wanted to talk to you about. Melissa and I had a talk. She has decided to give the baby up for adoption."

The room was utterly still. Then, Harry erupted. "It's that man, that Jean-Paul Duval! He should be shot—"

Lily held up her hand. "Just a minute, Harry. The truth of the matter is that Melissa herself doesn't want the baby. I know it's unbelievable, but she says that she has no maternal feelings about her at all."

"She's very young, of course," Ellis tactfully hastened to say. "I'm sure it would be different if she were older."

"Well, be that as it may, she's absolutely determined."

"So what are we going to do?" Harry cried. "Isn't there any way we can force her to take it?"

"Would that really be the best for the baby? A mother who doesn't want her?"

"But we can't allow her to be given away, Lily!"

"I know." She hesitated, then blurted out, all in a rush, "The truth is that I want to adopt her myself."

"What? Lily, that's insanity!"

"I'm not letting that baby go," she said, determination in every word. "There's no way on earth I'll give my granddaughter away to strangers."

"You're going to raise a child all by yourself—at your age?"

"I'm not that old, Harry. And I'm perfectly able—"

"But we're divorced! No court is going to give you custody."

Lily's eyes narrowed. "Well, that's what I'm getting around to. I was wondering if you would consider putting off our divorce until I've gotten legal custody. The divorce papers aren't final yet." She looked away. "I haven't signed them."

Ellis, watching silently, had to bite his lip to keep from

crying out in protest. He had waited so many years for Lily to be free from Harry, and now this.

But Harry and even Lily seemed oblivious of his inner turmoil. And through the years they'd come to rely on Ellis on every major decision. It seemed only natural that they turn to him for counsel.

"Do you think it will do the trick, Ellis?" Lily asked.

Startled, Ellis said, "You mean concerning the custody question?"

"Yes, of course."

Frowning, he shrugged. "I really can't say. One thing you need to bear in mind is that Jean-Paul Duval is French. The courts here may be a little reluctant to give a child born to a French father on French soil to a pair of Americans."

"Oh, no!" Lily cried. "I hadn't thought of that!" Turning to Harry, she appealed, "What are we going to do?"

Harry's brow furrowed. Suddenly he said, "I have an idea! Lily, what if we pretended that this baby is our child? If we could only get her back to America somehow and keep you out of sight for a bit, we could tell people that we've reconciled and are expecting a child. Then, in a few months, we could announce the birth of a baby girl."

Ellis was stunned. This was the wildest scenario he had ever heard, wilder than anything that had ever come out of Harry's pen. But Lily, though a little taken aback, quickly turned pragmatic.

"Do you really think it would work?"

"Why not?" Harry asked, eyes suddenly ablaze. "It would solve all our problems. The baby would be with us, it would be legitimate in the eyes of the world—and there's something else. Lily, that baby looks so much like you, especially with her red hair, no one will ever doubt you'd given birth to her . . ."

His voice trailed off, but Ellis could have finished the sentence. ". . . and you and I will be together again."

Ellis turned away to hide the bitterness he was sure was evident in his eyes. It was as if the gods were conspiring against him. Just when he thought that he was about to triumph, Harry had once again pulled a rabbit out of a hat. A baby—the one thing Lily couldn't resist. How was he to compete with that? It seemed he and Lily were doomed never to be together.

"Ellis?" she asked. "What do you think?"

Ellis shrugged. He knew when he was beaten. "It doesn't matter what I think. But you'll have a heck of a time getting the baby out of the country without a passport."

"They can be had, for a price," Harry said flatly. "We'll get hold of one."

The rest of the evening was hell for Ellis, as he was forced to sit silently, listening to Harry develop his plans. He could barely be civil. As soon as they had eaten, he claimed he had work to attend to and excused himself.

Back in his suite, he didn't turn on the light. Instead, he walked to the window and looked down at the Seine. At that moment he would have liked to wring Harry's neck. His anger was the closest thing to pure hatred he had ever felt. The thought of losing Lily yet again made him sick with rage—and despair.

# Chapter 48

THE next morning Ellis flew home. Lily no longer needed him. And with the way he was feeling, it would not be good for either of them if he stayed. Meanwhile, through one of Lily's French cousins, Harry got the address of a swarthy little man who knew the ins and outs of document forgery. By the end of the week, Harry was in possession of a false birth certificate and American passport for a Miss Susan Kelly of Baltimore. He hired a French girl to fly the baby to the States; there could be no connection between the infant and Harry and Lily Kohle.

Upon the baby's arrival in America, the bogus documents would be burned and the mysterious Susan Kelly would disappear forever.

After all was ready, Harry went back to New York. He had never told Lily about his hospitalization, but it was obvious to her that his lungs were not what they once were. When it became clear he wasn't getting better, Lily grew concerned.

"Go see a doctor, Harry. See if he can't give you something to get rid of that terrible cough."

Making light of it, he shrugged. "I may drop in on Doc Simon once we get back. But I know what he'll say. 'Cut down on the smoking.' "

"It wouldn't be a bad idea," was her reply.

After his departure, Lily moved from the George V to a charming, light-filled pension just off the Avenue Victor Hugo. It was walking distance from the hospital. She was able to visit Melissa several times a day.

Conversations with her daughter were strained. They avoided talking about the baby and about Jean-Paul. Duval had apparently come to see Melissa and had then gone off to ski again. Melissa said little about his visit.

Lily was glad that her path had not crossed his; she knew that if she had seen him she would not have been able to control herself.

The baby, by contrast, was pure joy, fostering happy daydreams of the time when she would take her home.

In the long hours away from the hospital, she began to rediscover the Paris of her youth. Her old friend Colette came in from Lyon, where she lived with her banker husband and three teenaged children. Colette was as lighthearted and entertaining as ever, and as they lunched and shopped, chattering away about old times, Lily felt the warmth of their old friendship even more than she had in the past.

Several days later, she regretfully bid Colette adieu at the Gare de Lyon. Lily realized how much she had missed having a close girlfriend over the years. Much as she knew Colette had her family to go back to, she wished she could return with her to the States, if only for a time. Then again, Lily reflected, she herself had a family to think of now, too.

Finally the long-awaited day came. The baby was released from the incubator and Lily held her in her arms for the first time. Tears flowed down her cheeks, but they were tears of joy. Never had she felt anything quite like this, even for her own children.

"Cadeau," she whispered softly. "I'm going to name you Cadeau. In French, that means 'gift'—and that's what you are—my gift from God."

It was another two weeks until tiny Cadeau was released from the hospital. The plan went into action then.

They had anticipated no problems at Orly, as the nursemaid boarded holding the baby, but throughout the long flight over the Atlantic, Lily couldn't help but worry. What would happen if the baby's passport were questioned? Suddenly, it seemed so many things could go wrong.

But the first thing she saw as she stepped off the plane, with Françoise and Cadeau three or four people behind her, was the two men in her life, Harry and Ellis, standing together and waving. Her spine stiffened with resolve. She would carry this off—she *would!*

At Customs, Lily answered their question, "Do you have anything to declare?" with outward calm, though she felt dangerously close to hysteria. If only they knew!

She turned and saw Françoise surrendering her passport and the baby's for inspection. Her heart beat faster as she looked on. But the moment passed with incredible swiftness as she saw the official glance cursorily at the documents, stamp them, and hand them back.

When Françoise joined them in the waiting car, Lily reached out for the baby. "Cadeau, darling Cadeau," she cried breathlessly as she cradled the baby in her arms. "I love you, my sweet baby."

Harry reached over and stroked the baby's downy head with gentle fingers. He had never felt such an overwhelming sense of joy. He, Lily, the baby . . . on their way to The Meadows to start a new life together. No scene could have held greater joy for him than this.

Both Kohles smiled involuntarily as Cadeau opened her rosebud mouth in a tiny yawn.

At the wheel, Ellis was aware of a feeling of bitter irony. From the disaster of Cadeau's unwanted birth, all, it seemed, had achieved their heart's desire—all except him.

# Chapter 49

NOT a newspaper in the country, from Boston to San Francisco, failed to print the item Ellis had circulated to the effect that a reconciliation had occurred between Mr. and Mrs. Harry Kohle. It was rumored that they were enjoying a second honeymoon at their country estate, The Meadows.

But the next news to hit the columns was even more of a sensation: Mrs. Harry Kohle was expecting a baby. Although she was middle-aged, with a nearly grown-up daughter, such miracles had been known to happen before. They had given the servants, except for Mary and Joe, the month off and had arranged for them to leave before Lily's arrival with the baby. They simply told their friends Lily was confined to bed rest. It seemed their secret would be safe.

Lily hadn't known quite what to expect from Harry—how they would deal with each other after the long separation—but they settled into their lives at The Meadows with surprisingly little difficulty. It was almost as if they had just been apart for the weekend and now were back together again, so settled was the routine they soon found themselves in.

The only difference was that they had separate bedrooms now. And also this: Despite the long years together, and despite the fact they now shared the same roof over their heads, the two had little emotional involvement. It seemed as if they were polite acquaintances. And Lily was determined to keep it that way.

Harry was not writing. He'd finished *The Sod* six months before, but had not started another project since. His lung problems seemed to improve along with the weather, but he seemed content to do nothing except sit in the warm sunshine playing with Cadeau as Lily spaded in the garden.

From time to time, she would look over and smile. It was wonderful to see him holding the baby, shaking the silver rattle at her or talking to her in his own bumbling version of baby talk.

Much as the scene moved her, she couldn't help thinking, *Why couldn't he have been like this for our own children?* They had needed his love and attention every bit as much as Cadeau. If only he'd taken a more active role in fathering them. But Harry simply hadn't known how to be close to them. When his own children were little, they had simply gotten on his nerves.

Now, Harry was a changed man. This was the Harry she had always wanted—a companion and friend, a devoted father. Ruefully, Lily thought, If he had always been like this, there never would have been the resentment, the quarrels, the estrangement.

But if he had subjugated himself to her needs so totally, would he have become a world-famous writer? Or would he still be struggling along in poverty and obscurity? Or worse yet, cursing her for limiting his potential?

Strangely, she could view the question dispassionately. For now she still felt detached from matters which should have troubled her deeply. The hard shell she had built around her heart in the wake of the separation still remained. The intense love she had felt for him throughout their long marriage seemed to have gone forever, and Lily neither mourned it nor wished for its return. Her only wish was for these peaceful days to continue. Then she would be content.

As the time came closer for Cadeau's "birth" to be announced, Lily began to breathe more easily. The deception that they were perpetrating on the world still troubled her a little. It would be easier for her to accept once she could drop the charade of being pregnant. The "birth" announcement would bring relief.

Then, the bombshell broke: Edward R. Murrow, host of a famous television show, one of the most popular shows in the country, had called Ellis. He wanted to come to The Meadows to interview the Kohles as they awaited the birth of their fifth child.

"No, Harry! Absolutely not!" Lily was adamant. "I'm not

going on camera in a live interview with a pillow tied around my middle!"

"Lily, don't you see?" Harry expostulated. "It's our golden opportunity! Who will question the date of Cadeau's birth when they have seen you, obviously pregnant, on TV?"

"Oh, Harry!" she cried helplessly. "How far can this deception go?"

"It's for Cadeau's sake, Lily. Isn't that worth a little deception?"

Lily had to give in. "Of course. When you put it like that, anything is worth it."

Still, she was nervous beyond words the day the crews arrived and began bustling around the vast drawing room, setting up their cameras and dollies. Meanwhile, Edward R. Murrow and Harry sat together chatting, entirely at ease as they each lit one cigarette after another.

And then, suddenly, they were in position. The director said, "Lights—camera—action!" and the cameras were rolling as Murrow began. "I am here at the beautiful estate of Mr. and Mrs. Harry Kohle. He is, as you all know, the world-famous Pulitzer Prize–winning author of *The Wars of Archie Sanger, The Genesis,* and the soon-to-be-published *The Sod.* Now I take you to their drawing room. Hello, Mr. and Mrs. Kohle!"

Heart pounding, Lily tried to move her lips to respond, "Hello, Mr. Murrow," but no sound came forth.

As Harry answered for them, "Hello, Edward," he glanced at Lily and almost chuckled. She sat with her hands primly folded underneath her false front, for fear that the pillow would move.

"How do you feel, Mrs. Kohle?" asked Murrow.

Lily was caught off guard. She had thought that the first questions would be directed to Harry. As she struggled for the right words, she saw the red eye on the camera blinking. Her mind went totally blank.

"How do you feel, darling?" Harry repeated, hoping she would recover.

Haltingly, Lily managed to reply, "Fine . . ."

"Was it a surprise when you discovered that you were expecting your fifth child?" continued Murrow.

"Oh," she said, "no. I mean, it was a surprise, but a wonderful one." Lily sat rigid, eyes staring straight ahead while Harry carried the ball, laughing and chatting amiably.

Yes, they were thrilled—overjoyed. . . . Of course they had told the other children. . . . Did they want a boy or girl? . . . Does it matter to you, darling? . . . No, they just wanted a healthy baby. . . .

Lily hadn't realized how overwhelming and terrifying it would be to lie before the whole country. Françoise had been instructed to take Cadeau out in the carriage, but Lily still kept imagining she heard a baby's cry.

At long last the ordeal was over. As the grips efficiently packed up their gear and carried it out to the truck, Murrow said, "Thank you, Mr. and Mrs. Kohle. You were superb—and congratulations on the new addition to your family."

This had been the worst strain Lily had ever known—but suddenly, unexpectedly, as she closed the door after Murrow and his crew, she doubled over in laughter. How ridiculous she must have looked, so stiff, unable to speak.

Harry laughed too. "You were wonderful, darling. The picture of the perfect pregnant woman. But you had better not take the pillow out yet, just in case one of them has forgotten something and comes back."

"If they do, we won't let them in," she called gaily, running down the hall and pulling the pillow out from under her dress at the same time. An hour later, Françoise was back with the peacefully happy baby.

"Wake up, sleepyhead," Lily said, going to pick her up.

Cadeau yawned. How fragile she looked! Lily lifted her and cradled her in her arms.

"Oh, the lies I tell for you, Cadeau," she said, stroking the soft little head. "But you're worth it." Behind her, Harry watched the scene. His love for her overwhelmed him. Not even in the beginning, with their passionate lovemaking, had he been so wholly and completely in love with her.

In the past year he had come to know that his life had no meaning without Lily. Like so many men, he hadn't realized how much his wife meant to him until he lost her—until after he had strayed into the beds of other women for motives which, in retrospect, seemed ludicrously thin.

For months now, he had barely been able to function. He had written *The Sod,* but he knew that it was a minor work, not on the scale of *The Genesis,* or even *The Mountains Roared.* For in reality, Lily had always been his inspiration. She had been the most sustaining force behind him. He was unable even to think of other women now; Lily was all he wanted, now and forever.

This coming together over Cadeau had presented him with a ray of hope, but as the weeks and months had passed, he had almost despaired. Lily was pleasant, but distant. It seemed there was an impassable barrier between them. Sometimes, broodingly, he would wonder, Was it even a question of forgiveness? Once, he had mistakenly thought that his love for her had simply burned out. Could it be now that the tables were turned, that her feeling for him had evaporated?

Harry knew he had to face facts. Lily had been anything but eager for this reconciliation. Cadeau's adoption was the only thing that prompted it. Unlike Harry, Lily had no ulterior motive to promote. Looking at her as she bent over the crib, laying the baby down, her face aglow with a gentle radiance, Harry thought that she looked like an angel. And his heart overcame his better judgment. As she turned toward him, he reached out and took her in his arms. Tears glistening in his eyes, he whispered, "Lily, don't you think that maybe we could start over again? I love you so much. . . ."

Lily felt a sudden stirring she hadn't felt in a long, long time. There was hope and joy and the thrill of Harry's nearness. But almost as suddenly, there was the old mistrust and doubt. She wanted so much to believe, after all the long, lonely nights, lying in her bed alone. It was like a glimpse of heaven to have Harry's arms around her again, whispering words of love. Deep down, she always knew that she would love him until death did them part.

Yet she didn't want to let herself love him again. It would give him the power to hurt her once more, and she couldn't bear to be betrayed as she had been before. It seemed as if Harry had changed—she wanted to believe it—but it had seemed to her he had reformed one or two times before. Was she trying to make herself believe in him again simply because she so much wanted to believe? On the other hand, did she want to wind up a lonely old woman, all because of pride and apprehension?

Finally Harry broke the silence. "You still don't trust me, do you?"

"I want to trust you," she whispered back. "But I just can't. . . ."

Just then, Cadeau stirred and Harry gently drew Lily out of the room and down the hall to her own bedroom, closing the door behind them.

Taking her into his arms once again, he said, "When I said 'I love you' in the past, I never thought enough about what it entailed. Not just romance and passion, but living for each other, intertwining our lives and becoming one. That is what I realized when I lost you—that in my self-centeredness I had missed out on a very wonderful part of life, the most important part." Harry swallowed hard. "If you'll give me just one chance, I swear to you—I swear—that I will devote the rest of my life to you and Cadeau. I will be entirely faithful to you—always. For whatever I'm worth, will you accept me?"

Lily now had tears in her eyes, too. She had never heard such heartfelt sincerity in a human voice in her life. There was nothing left to say except, softly, "Yes, Harry."

Harry pulled her into his arms and kissed her. "Oh God," he murmured. "Oh God, Lily, I love you so."

Their lips still pressed together, he fumbled at the buttons of her dress. Drawing her down onto the bed, he felt her satiny flesh against him. How he'd longed for this. He kissed her like a man who had been starved for affection for a long time. Her lips, her breasts, her arms around him, he couldn't get enough of the feel of her, her lovely fragrance. . . .

Lily was intensely aroused by Harry's touch, his nearness after all the lonely months. She wanted him as never before. Then, as he entered her, she moaned softly. *Oh God . . .*

In the final moment before the culmination, he whispered brokenly, "Don't ever leave me. You belong here, with me."

Lying in his arms afterward, spent and exhilarated at the same time, she was content not to talk. Suddenly, it was as though they had no past, only a future . . . and Lily longed to reach out to it.

# Chapter 50

IN the aftermath of the Murrow show, the cards and letters and gifts had poured in for the coming baby. Exactly five months from the date of the Murrow show, the Kohles heralded the birth of a darling baby girl: Cadeau Kohle. In reality, Cadeau was now six months old, but she had been two months premature. She was still very small. Within a few weeks, when they began to receive callers, it was impossible to tell that she had not been a newborn. She was simply a baby, an unusually pretty, alert baby, with a little fuzz of silky red hair and perfect, rosy little lips.

"Isn't she just like a little rosebud!" cooed their guests, as Harry and Lily, looking on, nearly burst with pride.

The weather was now growing cool and so, as soon as Lily was "recovered" from the rigors of her confinement, they closed The Meadows for the season and went back to Manhattan.

The tiny "gift" was put down in a Directoire cradle padded in white satin and tufted with tiny pink roses. A graceful swan held aloft a drift of sheer white organdy tied with an enormous pink bow, from which cascaded slender ribbons.

On the day of Cadeau's naming ceremony, Lily was filled with excitement as she dressed. Before, the ceremonies for the children had somehow been so forlorn, with Harry still a pariah from his family; the elder Kohles attended but seemed distant and grim. The wound of her parents' loss had still been new then, and despite their neglect she had felt intense sadness that they were not there to see their grandchildren.

But this day she felt wholly joyous. When Harry walked

into her dressing room and saw her standing in front of the mirror, he stopped short, overcome. She wore a stunning green silk suit which brought out the color of her eyes, and a small satin toque adorned with violets. A delicate veil hung from the brim.

Holding her at arm's length, he said, "Lily, you look magnificent."

Then he took a box from his inner pocket and opened it, revealing a shimmering double strand of pearls with a diamond clasp whose facets caught and splintered the early-morning light.

"Darling, how lovely!" Lily cried. "They're exquisite!"

"Not as exquisite as you are, Lily." Taking her into his arms, he said softly, "Nothing is too good for you." They held each other for a long moment before going out to greet Harry's parents.

Benjamin and Elise Kohle had been overjoyed at the news of a new grandchild and felt this to be an extra blessing bestowed upon them in their advanced years.

They looked very distinguished today. Benjamin was slightly bent with age, but his silver mane was still magnificent, and his dark suit, though of an old-fashioned cut, impeccable. Elise looked regal in a blush-rose silk dress, along with matching accessories and her heirloom pearl-and-diamond jewelry. A small cloche hat covered with egret feathers set off her snow-white hair and a sable coat protected her against the cold.

Françoise brought in Cadeau, clad in the same silk and lace robes Harry himself had worn. The naming ceremony was not private, as those of Jeremy, Drew, Randy, and Melissa had been. It was held at the cathedral-like Temple Ben Israel, with its beautiful stained-glass windows and mahogany pews, where generations of Kohles had worshipped.

There were myriad guests, but somehow the ceremony itself remained touching and intimate. As Lily stood with the baby, she could not help but offer up a silent prayer of thanks to Melissa. At the same time, she felt an intense sadness—her daughter had deprived herself of the pure joy of this baby.

As quickly as they came to her, she dismissed those thoughts. This was a day to rejoice and be glad.

The reception overflowed the Kohle home, and what Harry and Lily felt was indeed for the world to see.

They were so busy accepting congratulations and best wishes that there was little time for them to talk, but in the late afternoon there came a moment when they found themselves together in a quiet corner. Looking at her with love in his eyes, Harry clinked his champagne glass with her. "To you, darling. The greatest gift God ever sent me."

Standing nearby, Ellis observed the scene. His expression remained unchanged, though his heart was pained. He could not hear Harry's words, but it didn't matter. The way Harry looked down at Lily, the gesture of homage, their obvious closeness said it all. Their new intimacy had little to do with any pretense they had concocted for Cadeau's sake.

Ellis didn't know why this new turn in the Kohles' relationship surprised him; after all, he had seen this coming all along. Lily's deep sense of loyalty was easy to revive, it seemed. After all, he thought bitterly, this was the second time Harry had strayed, only to beg forgiveness, and be forgiven.

The advent of Cadeau seemed to seal the Kohles' fate. Ellis's chance to have Lily to love and cherish was probably forever gone.

You're a bloody fool, Ellis Knox, he thought bitterly. The only chance you had was when Harry and Lily were living apart. And what the hell did you do with that opportunity? You bided your time; you didn't romance her; you were a chivalrous goddamned gentleman—and look where that chivalry has gotten you!

Harry Kohle had the devil's own luck; he had needed no magic wand. This baby who just appeared at the critical moment without Harry's having to lift a finger. No, all Harry had done was come up with his zany plan. And even then, Ellis had done absolutely nothing to intercede.

Unable to bear the sight of the two of them together any longer, he turned away, flagged a passing waiter, and said curtly, "Bring me a double Scotch—straight up."

After Cadeau's momentous "birth" into the world, Harry and Lily's lives began to settle into a new pattern. For the first time ever, they were completely one. Harry began work on a new novel, but he felt no great urgency or passion about it. Meanwhile, Lily continued with her charity work, and although it kept her busy, she was not nearly as involved as she had been at the times of the Spring Balls she had chaired before. More than anything, she devoted herself to Harry and little Cadeau.

Harry and Lily did not try to recapture their old relationship; instead, they forged a new companionship tempered by mutual respect as well as love. At the same time, in the back of their minds dwelt the memory of their past mistakes. They trod softly in reminiscing. As well as joy, there was still much pain in their past. But one thing—if unspoken—remained clear: Nothing was more important than what they now had—not a book or a prize or a lecture tour or a committee. And neither would go anywhere without the other.

It seemed that finally there was no blight on their happiness, no fatal flaw that would doom them when they felt more sure. Having come through all the hills and valleys, Lily would never have believed that life could reach such a blissful mode.

They talked of Cadeau's future. They would enroll her in a girls' school in New York—she was not to be sent to boarding school. They would take her to see the lions at the zoo. If she liked them, perhaps they would take her on a safari in Africa once she was a little older. She seemed musically inclined—they must find a piano teacher for her.

And they went on and on, dreaming their happy dreams, little suspecting the next turn in their fortunes.

Harry's cough had improved slightly after his return from Paris, and he had decided not to see Dr. Simon after all. Summer had come and the warmth had helped him breathe more easily. By the next winter, when he had begun to hack again, he told Lily that it was just his chronic bronchitis. But the next summer had brought little relief. Harry had taken to drinking bottle after bottle of cough syrup to quell the persistent sound. In the fall, however, the violence of the paroxysms was such that he could no longer hide them from Lily.

"See the doctor, Harry!" she commanded. "You sound terrible—surely there's something he can prescribe."

"Don't worry about it, Lily. I know that it sounds bad, but there's nothing really wrong."

Once in a while, he wondered if that was true, or whether he simply disliked the thought of the stern lecture he would certainly get from Doc Simon. Three years ago, the doctor had flatly ordered him to give up smoking, but he certainly wasn't going to give it up, no matter what. He had simply smoked for too long. The truth was that these medicos loved to give orders. No one had ever proved that smoking was bad for you.

But one night, long after Lily had fallen asleep next to him, he was overcome by such a fit of coughing that he got up and lurched into the bathroom so as not to disturb her. And there it was that he stared in disbelief into the basin, where bright red blood and sputum spattered the porcelain. Hanging on to the rim, hardly able to catch his breath, he squeezed his eyes shut as the implications hit home: cancer.

Beads of perspiration rolled down his back. Lung cancer—inoperable, incurable, the wasting away, the helplessness, the intolerable pain at the end. And the timing, so incredibly bad.

When he had lost Lily before, he would have said that life was hardly worth living—but now, when he was on top of the world, he wanted to live more than ever before.

God damn it! Why now? he raged. And how on earth was he going to break the news to Lily?

Harry didn't sleep anymore that night, and by nine o'clock the next morning, he was in Nate Simon's office.

By noon, after his battery of exams, he was dressed again and was sitting in Nate's well-appointed office, smoking one cigarette after another.

"Well?" Harry blurted out anxiously, as the other man seated himself behind his desk.

Nate Simon took off his horn-rimmed glasses, folded them onto his desk, and looked at Harry. It was always difficult to tell a patient news like this, even harder when it was a man you had known all your life. But there was no way around the harsh truth: There probably wasn't one damned thing he could do to save Harry's life. Harry was his age, not even fifty, with everything to live for: beautiful wife, new baby, all the success anyone could dream of.

Clearing his throat, he said, "Harry, I think you already know what I have to say."

Harry nodded.

"I'm going to schedule you for surgery tomorrow morning at seven-thirty. I've got a top man in thoracic surgery to operate."

"How bad is it, Doc? Give it to me straight."

But Harry knew even before Nate Simon spoke by the way

he shook his head. "It's bad, Harry, I won't lie to you. There's a large mass on the chest X ray in the left lung."

"And my chances?" Harry asked, knuckles white as he braced himself, clutching the chair.

Nate hesitated. "Well, they won't know for sure until they go in, but it's right at the base of the lobe. It looks as if it has invaded the mediastinum. We'll know more tomorrow."

But if it was, he was going to die.

Even though Harry had thought he was prepared for the worst, Nate's words were a blow. Harry realized that for however much he'd steeled himself for the worst, he had still been hoping against hope that he didn't have cancer.

"God, Nate," he asked unsteadily, "how am I going to tell Lily? Everything's going so well, we have a new baby. Things are better than they have been in years."

"Do you want me to tell her?"

"No—no . . . I'd better do it."

After he had left Nate's office, he walked aimlessly until he finally came to Central Park. He sank onto a bench and looked around him. The Great Lawn was so green, the first crocuses and daffodils were in bloom. Harry ruefully thought of the opening words of *The Redemption of Archie Sanger:* "If I could know the day before I die . . ."

All his life, he had been a winner. With few exceptions, his had been a charmed life. Not only had he been blessed with a host of natural talents, he'd been lucky enough to be blessed with such people in his life as Lily and Ellis. Grudgingly, he had to acknowledge he was even lucky to have had the parents he had.

The only tragedy that had ever made him think he had lost God's favor was Jeremy's death. As the years had passed, time had helped heal the wounding memories, and the advent of Cadeau had somehow given him a new chance.

What a fool he had been to think that he had gotten away with it all; gotten away with betraying Lily, believing that despite his terrible breach of faith he had a second chance for a wonderful life with her.

Now he knew that his sins had not been forgiven; they had been saved up to chastise him in one shattering blow—now, when he had the most to lose. Six months from this moment, all the things around him, everything he could see from this bench, would still be here, but he would not.

Cadeau would grow into girlhood, then young womanhood. And he would miss it all.

Almost instinctively, he fumbled in his pocket for his Pall Malls, struck a match, and lit a cigarette. He drew in deeply, then exhaled in a sigh as he looked out over the expanse of green, his mind seemingly blank. Then, quite suddenly, he was racked by sobs. Passersby glanced curiously at him as he cried on, not even trying to gain control of himself.

But finally, exhausted, he could cry no more. Sitting up slowly, he took out a handkerchief, wiped his eyes, and blew his nose. Somehow the tears themselves had helped purge him of his fears. He returned to Sutton Place shaken and resigned.

Late that afternoon, he sat with Lily in the lengthening shadows of their magnificent salon. It had all been said. More tears had fallen—Lily's this time, not his—and the disbelieving protests had been spoken.

Lily looked about her at all the beautiful things they had acquired over the years, at all the hard-won bits and pieces of wood and silk and canvas. What happiness could they bring now if Harry couldn't be there to share them with her? Just when it seemed they had hit upon the happiness that had eluded them for so long, it was being snatched away. But still there was hope. Harry was young, he had been in robust health before the recent troubles. And medical science these days would work miracles. The prognosis couldn't be as grim as Harry had said. She couldn't believe it.

But from the very moment he had said the dread word "cancer," she became afraid. And now, as she looked at him, silhouetted in his chair, he suddenly seemed very frail. Harry could die. Already she felt the terrible loss looming. She was afflicted by the same knot in her stomach that she had felt in Jeremy's room at Exeter that awful day. The haunting memories came back.

*Oh, Jeremy,* she thought, *if you sit at the right hand of God, please pray for your father.*

But in spite of her own grief and torment, she knew she must be strong for her husband as he faced his time of trial. He had to be admitted to the hospital that evening. As soon as he had packed his things, they clung together in a long embrace, as though by holding on to each other they might somehow put off the inevitable.

Lily went to the stereo and put on a record. A moment later Harry heard the strains of "My Blue Heaven." A reminiscent smile crossed his lips.

"You always loved this, didn't you?"

"I suppose it's a little corny," she murmured.

"No, it's beautiful," he said, curving his arm about her. "It reminds me of our first date. Would you like to dance?"

They circled for a moment, silently remembering that time when they had been so young, so willing to toss all to the wind for each other. But even dancing seemed too much of a strain. Lily suggested he sit down, she would make them drinks.

Over the years, Lily had acquired Ellis's taste for bone-dry martinis. Standing at the bar cart, she kept her back to Harry as she tried to hide the tears fighting to be shed. She mixed a pitcher with unconscious precision. Plunking two olives into the glasses, she took a deep breath, fixed a calm expression on her face, and brought the tray over to the coffee table. Harry took a sip, leaned over and kissed her, and said, "Perfect—like everything you do."

They sipped slowly, making a staunch effort to pretend that everything would be all right. They each blotted out the thought of what the morrow would bring.

Harry said, "I'm going to take my two best girls to the Bahamas for Christmas this year. Would you like that?"

"Sounds wonderful," Lily replied, trying to keep her chin from quivering.

"I can just see Cadeau running on that beach. Do you think she'll have freckles, Lily?"

"I have a feeling she will. We'll have to get her a hat."

"Matching ones for the two of you."

Then, in an altered voice, he suddenly cried, "Oh, Lily—just hold me."

She held him tightly as he murmured brokenly, "It's not even so much dying, Lily, it's the thought of losing you. God, I love you so!"

But then it was time to drive to the hospital.

# Chapter 51

THE next morning Lily sat in the surgery waiting room, surrounded by Ellis, Drew, and Randy, waiting for news of Harry.

Drew was ashen and silent. He had not laid eyes on his father once since that terrible day when they had had their confrontation in his seedy apartment. In the past two years, he had ignored all of Lily's pleas to reconcile with his father, saying defiantly that he didn't care if he never saw him again. He came to see Cadeau from time to time, but he had resolutely avoided contact with Harry.

But the night before, when Ellis had come and told him about his father's illness, Drew had been devastated. Harry, dying? It couldn't be. His father, the all-powerful, the invincible?

But as the truth of Ellis's words penetrated, Drew knew one thing—he must go to him, no matter how serious their rift had been.

In truth, Drew had never fully recovered from the loss of Jeremy. He still thought about him, still mourned him, and blamed himself for leaving him unprotected. But now Drew knew that he had been wrong. Deep down, his family was as dear to him as Lily was. Now the thought of losing his father devastated him. But his face must not have given away his thoughts, for Ellis's voice was suddenly rough and peremptory.

"Grow up, Drew! Your father is facing life-threatening surgery tomorrow. I know that you and he have had your differences, but you're going to have to set them aside, if for no other reason than that your mother needs you."

The two of them had always had a friendly camaraderie; Drew had never minded Ellis's calm, avuncular tone, the way he'd resented Harry's easily roused fury. He hastened to explain himself to the older man.

"No, of course! You're absolutely right, Ellis. I wouldn't dream of staying away at a time like this."

Ellis nodded, then briefly put his hand on Drew's shoulder. "I knew I couldn't be wrong about you, Drew. You're a good man."

Now, Drew sat silently, thinking over and over again about the angry words he and his father had once exchanged. Were those to be the last they would ever speak to each other? If only Harry survived this operation, Drew would beg his forgiveness and tell him how much he loved him.

Next to him, Randy gazed broodingly at his coffee. Always less mercurial than his brother, he appeared relatively calm. Only the tiny lines around his eyes and the slight furrow of his brow betrayed how deeply worried he was.

Lily sat biting her lip. It had been a tremendous solace to her to see her two tall sons this morning and feel their comforting embraces, but at this moment she longed to have Cadeau in her lap.

If she could only bury her face in her silky red curls, hug her fiercely, it might distract Lily from the thought of the scalpel cutting and probing into Harry somewhere beyond the closed doors.

Next to her, Ellis watched, pained to see her white knuckles, her sodden handkerchief. He reached out silently and took her hand. Tears glistened in Lily's eyes again as she whispered, "Thanks."

In every crisis of their lives, Ellis had been there, an abiding friend. He had so often been their life raft into better times. And time and again they had turned to him. Sometimes Lily felt that he was the greatest fruit of Harry's writing career. And now, she wondered, had they really been fair to Ellis? Their friendship had always been so natural and easy. But whether she wanted to admit it to herself or not, that fateful night when she had offered herself to him had changed everything forever.

She had felt myriad emotions once he had said he loved her, but she had shied from ever examining those feelings again, either his or her own.

At times it seemed almost unbelievable that the entire evening had actually occurred. Neither she nor Ellis had made any effort to talk about it since that day he had driven up to see her at the farm. If he were in love with her still, he was a master at hiding it.

Suddenly her thoughts were interrupted as the door opened to admit Benjamin and Elise Kohle. Lily had wanted to spare them, but Dr. Simon had said that the surgery itself carried a significant risk. She felt she had to break the news to them. On the eve of Harry's surgery, the Kohles had gone to the hospital to talk to their son.

Now, after greeting Ellis and embracing Lily and their grandsons, they sat down. Their grief was evident on their faces.

God, they looked old, Ellis thought a little sadly. Benjamin Kohle looked shrunken where he had once seemed so resilient and strong, and Mrs. Kohle was now a frail little old lady.

For six hours they kept their sad vigil. Finally the surgery doors flew open and Nate Simon emerged, looking weary.

Jumping up from her chair, Lily cried, "How is Harry, Doctor? Tell me."

Simon took her aside. "He came through the surgery fine, and is beginning to come out of the anesthetic. They'll keep him in the recovery room for a little while, and then you'll be able to see him."

"Oh, thank God! What did they find?"

"Well, the tumor had invaded both lobes, so the surgeon went ahead and removed the entire left lung." But his manner was hesitant, and Lily demanded quickly, "What else? What aren't you telling me?"

Reluctantly, he admitted, "It appeared, I'm afraid, that there may have been some encroachment into the aorta. We'll know more when we get the lab report."

In conveying the doctor's report to the rest of the family, Lily emphasized the positive. Harry had come through the surgery, that was the first hurdle. As for the rest, they would know more later.

Harry drifted in and out of consciousness for the rest of

the day, opening his eyes only long enough to recognize the boys and Lily. Once, she was holding Cadeau. Harry tried to smile and say, "Hi, sweetheart." But the stabbing pain in his left side and back was intolerable; it grew worse when he tried to speak. He didn't know how many hours had passed when he finally came to consciousness and saw Nate Simon standing next to his bed.

"How are you feeling?"

With difficulty, Harry grunted, "How . . . do you think? As though I've . . . been hit by a Mack truck."

"Glad you're feeling a little feisty. That's a good sign."

"What's . . . the verdict?"

Nate cleared his throat. He tried to put it gently. "We had to remove the whole lung, Harry. There was a large mass, as we saw on the X ray."

"Was there . . . metastasis?"

"We don't know for sure, but there were some signs. I'm sorry."

"Am I . . . going to die?"

"It's impossible to make that prediction, Harry."

"Nate, don't . . . give me that . . . bullshit!"

"All right. I'm recommending you for radiation therapy."

Harry sank back against his pillow, dangerously near tears. He knew what that meant. It was one of the side effects of being a writer, to know a little about a lot of things. Radiation was a last-ditch measure; Nate might as well have advised him to get a price from the funeral home.

"What are the odds?"

"Harry, you know that there are no guarantees—"

"Weeks . . . months? What . . . are you saying?"

Nate hesitated. Then, almost under his breath, he said, "Months—maybe."

"Forget it, Nate. I know about . . . radiation therapy. Sick . . . all the time, hair falls out. I won't . . . put Lily through that."

Nate had to admire Harry's courage. Most patients couldn't face the truth.

"It's your decision—and I don't know that I don't agree with you."

"The only thing . . . don't tell Lily . . . how bad it is. I'll tell her . . . myself."

It was tougher than he thought to tell Lily the grim news—the cancer was a fast-growing cell type, there were already lesions on his liver and pancreas.

She clung to him, weeping. "There must be something they can do, Harry! Why won't you have radiation?"

"Lily, dammit! There's cancer all through my body! What good is it going to do to irradiate my liver when it's in my bloodstream and my bones, and very possibly my other lung already?"

"But if it will give you any kind of chance—"

"It won't," he said flatly. "I've got to face it, Lily. I'm dying. And I'm going to ask you to just let me live out the rest of my life with you as if it were going to go on forever."

"But Harry—" she cried, but he pressed a finger to her lips. She saw then that his face was wet with tears.

"Lily, please pretend—for my sake? Because if I have to face the thought of leaving you, I . . . I just can't bear it."

Harry returned home, and Lily refused to give up hope until she had spoken to Nate Simon herself. Nate only confirmed Harry's words. The cancer was so widespread that radiation therapy would be a fruitless gesture—one which would make his last months needlessly agonizing.

Lily felt almost sick with grief. "Thank you, Doctor. Is there anything I can do for Harry?"

The best Nate Simon could tell her was, "Keep him happy."

It seemed an impossible prescription, but she walked all the way home repeating fiercely to herself, "Keep him happy . . . keep him happy." By the time she entered the apartment, she determined to be of good cheer.

"Hello, darling," she greeted Harry. "Shall we go out to dinner, or eat in?"

In the weeks that followed, they resolutely avoided talking about Harry's disease or his prognosis. They picked up their life where they'd left off, not dwelling on the future any more than they did the darker episodes of their past. Never once did Harry complain; he had simply made up his mind to cram a lifetime of happiness with Lily into the few short months that remained to him.

Harry relished every waking moment. It seemed that even dying had its compensations: His senses felt sharpened. He appreciated everything he saw or heard or smelled or ate.

It was Lily who had to struggle to keep from railing aloud

at the cruelty of fate. For Harry's sake she was able to keep up a courageous front. Gradually she came to a state of acceptance.

It was the moments which really counted, she told herself, not the years. Yesterday was a memory, tomorrow a promise. The only moment one ever really had was the here and now.

And so, between them, they created a sort of dream world, filled with a false serenity which ignored the disease that would soon take Harry from her.

They spent almost all of their time together, but one afternoon Lily went out alone for several hours, returning just in time for their usual five-o'clock martinis. There was an air of suppressed excitement about her as they settled down with their drinks.

Harry said, "Okay, I give up. What is it that you bought that you're so excited about?"

"Do I seem excited?" she countered with a smile, taking a sip of her martini. Then, setting it down, she asked casually, "What are you doing about that novel you started last year, Harry? Are you working on it?"

Matter-of-factly he said, "No, I've decided to let it go for a while. I'd rather concentrate on the women in my life. Why do you ask?"

"Guess what I've done."

"What?"

"Booked passage for you, me and Cadeau aboard the *Queen Mary*."

"Really?"

She nodded.

"That's wonderful! You know how I love the sea. Where are we headed, and for how long?"

"Around the world," Lily told him. "We'll be gone three months. I know that we had talked about going to the Bahamas at Christmas, but I think that an ocean cruise will be more relaxing."

Three months . . . They let their thoughts lie unspoken. Harry took the brochure from Lily and began to pore over the pictures of the *Queen Mary*'s pool and the staterooms. Meanwhile, Lily flashed back to her conversation that morning with Nate Simon.

"He can't make it, Lily," the doctor had said flatly. "The metastases are appearing so fast, he probably won't even survive three months." He hesitated, then added more gently, "I'm sorry to have to be so blunt."

"So what if he doesn't survive?" Lily returned, her eyes very bright. "If he has to die, I want it to be in the midst of life and living, not in a darkened hospital room."

Nate Simon weakened. "But he's going to be in a lot of pain near the end, Lily. He really should be near a hospital."

"How about if I hire a nurse? If he needs some painkiller, she can administer it. Can't you see, Dr. Simon? This is something I have to do for Harry."

"Okay," he said. "You win. I can prescribe morphine and send it along with the nurse."

Now Harry recognized Lily's gesture as one of defiance against the odds. He loved her all the more dearly for it. God, he was the luckiest man in the world, he thought humbly. Lucky to have found such a woman, lucky to have won her heart, and triply lucky to have been given a second chance with her—however brief.

Ignoring the stabbing pain in his chest, he took Lily into his arms and kissed her, warmly and lingeringly.

# Chapter 52

IN the quiet of the paneled Oak Room at the Plaza the next day, Lily broke the news to Ellis.

"Harry and I are leaving next week on a three-month cruise."

Startled, Ellis asked, "Have you talked to the doctor about it, Lily? I hate to say this, but Harry is getting worse all the time."

"I know, Ellis," she said, her voice flat. "His appetite is gone, he's thinner than ever, and in the morning he's very weak, but maybe this will make him feel better. We're taking along a nurse, and of course Françoise for Cadeau."

Quietly Ellis reached out and covered her hand with his own. The kindness in that gesture completely disarmed her. Bursting into tears, she buried her face in her hands and wept. The months of keeping up the terrible pretense that nothing was wrong had been a desperate strain. Suddenly she couldn't stop crying. After a few minutes Ellis said softly, "Lily, don't cry, dear. It's all right."

Raising a tear-streaked face, Lily choked out, "Ellis, do you know how terrible it is to watch someone you love dying before your very eyes? I feel so helpless, so angry—and I can't show any of it in front of Harry. He's being so brave, and he's doing it for me, Ellis!"

Ellis listened. His heart went out to her, even though all her thoughts still ran to Harry, never to him. There were times during this ordeal that he had allowed himself to wonder what would happen between them after Harry was gone. Would she turn to him? Over the years, he had sensed an undeniable spark of attraction between them. But it had never been nurtured, not even been recognized really, because Harry always came first.

Now, after his death, would Lily revere Harry all the more? Would no man ever rival him? Ellis lay awake at night wondering.

But none of these thoughts were in his mind at this moment. As he looked at her sorrowful face, he could not think of any advantage to be gained, but only of how he might help her through these grim events.

Taking her hand again, he said softly, "I understand how hard it is. You've been wonderfully strong for Harry. You've kept him going."

"But I don't *feel* strong, Ellis! I feel like breaking down and crying, all the time."

"But the important thing is that you don't. You keep going, and that makes it possible for Harry to keep going, too. Nothing's changed in that respect, Lily. You've always been his greatest source of strength."

Lily managed to smile. "Thank you for telling me that. I needed to hear it."

Smiling into her eyes, he said again those words he'd said so many times throughout the years. "You are a princess, Lily dear. The last princess . . ."

The following week, as Lily and Harry stood at the rail of the *Queen Mary,* they could see their boys far below, standing on either side of Benjamin and Elise, with Randolph and Ellis not far behind.

"Look Harry," Lily murmured. "It's our whole family." The only one missing was Melissa. There had been no way to get in touch with her before Harry's surgery, but Ellis had tracked her down afterward. He had arranged for her to fly to see her father.

Françoise had taken the baby away for the day, but it had nevertheless been a brief, awkward visit. Lily could think of little to say to her daughter, much as she still loved her dearly.

When Melissa had seen Harry, she had done nothing but weep and cry over and over, "It can't be true, Daddy—you can't be dying!" in her tactless way, while he tried to soothe her. "The doctors don't know everything, Melissa. We'll see."

Drew and Randy had taken Melissa out to dinner afterward before putting her on the plane back to Paris, but the evening had turned out to be something of a fiasco. The three of them were so different in personality and temperament and had been separated for so long in their respective schools that they felt like strangers to one another.

Melissa started off the argument by repeating for the third time, "I'm just so sad about poor Daddy."

Drew had had it. Throwing down his menu, he blazed, "Oh, Melissa, shut up! That's bullshit! What did you ever care about our father?"

"I did care about Daddy—I do!"

Drew guffawed. "Sure. That's why you haven't been back to America in so long—because you love Mom and Dad so much!"

"But—" Melissa stopped. She had been about to say, "But that's because of the baby." But was that the reason she stayed away? The honest truth was that when she was in France with Jean-Paul, she hardly ever thought about her parents. They were part of another world—one that was dull and confining. All that mattered to her was Jean-Paul and the thrill of being part of his life. He was perfect, she thought, ignoring the memory of the fights, the acrimony, the time she had discovered him with a young blonde skier.

Even so, she tried to defend herself. "I love them as much as you do! Look at how terribly you upset Dad, dropping out of Harvard and going to live like a bum in the Village!"

"I've already told Dad that I'm going back next term," Drew informed her. "I've applied and been readmitted. The *Post* has given me some valuable experience. I plan to major in journalism. And incidentally, you're a fine one to talk about the way I live. I've seen pictures of you and that skier. When is he going to marry you, or are you content to simply be his whore?"

Melissa's eyes filled with tears. Childishly, she wailed, "Randy, Drew's being mean to me."

Randy shrugged. "Look, Melissa, I don't know what this big scene is about. What does it matter to you what we think? You have your own life, we have ours, Mom and Dad have theirs. It's ridiculous to pretend that we're much of a family."

"You always were cold, Randy," accused Melissa in a trembling voice. "I know you don't love Dad. You never did."

Again, Randy shrugged. "He never cared too much for me, either. Let's face it, the only one he really took an interest in was Jeremy, and then only because he was his firstborn son." A trace of bitterness had crept into his voice at the memory of the old hurt. "Frankly, Randolph means more to me than the rest of you put together. He's the only one who really cared for me all these years."

"Even Mom?" Drew asked incredulously.

"No . . . no, I do love Mom," Randy had to admit. "But she was married to Dad, and that made it hard."

The three fell silent as each sat with their separate memories.

Then Drew spoke heavily. "Well, be all that as it may, we're adults now. We can't keep moaning and groaning for their not being perfect parents. And it's funny, they've seemed so different to me since they got back together and had Cadeau."

Melissa stared at her brother's face. Did he know? Had Lily or Harry told him?

Drew continued. "They may have waited a long time for their fifth child, but it was certainly worth it."

Even Randy smiled. "She is a terrific baby, isn't she?"

"And so smart," Drew began eagerly.

Melissa was both curious and repulsed. The baby had seemed like an imaginary figure until now. But it turned out she was real, after all. Clearly Melissa's brothers doted on her. But even so, no trace of maternal feeling sprang up in Melissa. It was Lily's baby, after all, not hers. She listened sullenly as Drew rhapsodized about little Cadeau. If only they knew she was responsible for that charming, bright little baby, and here Mom was taking all the credit.

"Fine, fine. Let's order, shall we?" she finally interrupted. "I have a plane to catch."

That was the only time she had come. Lily tried to make excuses to Harry, but probably neither one of them was deceived. Melissa was someone who would always avoid her responsibilities.

On the ship, Lily merely held Harry's hand, waving with the other as the confetti flew. Then the whistle blew and the huge liner began backing ponderously away from the dock.

Would Harry ever see his sons again, or his parents? Through her tears, Lily glimpsed Ellis holding his arm aloft.

# Chapter 53

THE memory of that farewell had quickly faded. Two weeks into the cruise it seemed that the life on board the *Queen Mary* was the only life they'd known. Harry's health seemed improved, Lily thought with satisfaction. The sea air had taken away the grayish pallor from his complexion. Even his appetite had revived a bit.

She had booked them under the pseudonyms Mr. and Mrs. David Goode, so that Harry would not be harassed by fans. He had changed so much—even since the time of the Murrow show—that he was unlikely to be recognized.

He spent much of his time in a deck chair, reading for a while, then nodding off. When he awoke, it was often to see the face of Cadeau, leaning over him and cooing, "Dada."

Cadeau was now an adorable, curly-headed toddler who ran all over the boat on her tiny legs, smiling and jabbering away unintelligibly to everyone from the captain to the deck boy. In mock desperation, Lily declared that they were going to have to put her on a leash, but the whole ship had fallen in love with her. But Dada was the one she always ran to first. "Pew! Pew, Dada," she begged him this particular afternoon. Before her nap, Harry had taken her for a swim in the heated pool. She clearly wanted a repeat performance, but the effort had exhausted him. Reluctantly, he was forced to say, "No pool now, sweetheart. Dada's tired. Come sit on my lap." And the toddler happily clambered up onto his knees.

Later, as they sat at dinner, Lily could almost close her eyes and pretend that this was the wonderful vacation she had longed to take for twenty years, the vacation where she would have Harry all to herself without the unrelenting demands of his writing career; a vacation where all he wanted was to be with her . . . and the baby.

Why, oh why, couldn't it have been like this before? she began to ask herself. But as she looked at Harry's fine features highlighted by the dining room's candlelight, she fiercely rejected all such recriminations. He was still alive. She would treasure the moments they had remaining.

"Shall we dance?" he asked. His blue eyes gleamed. "They're playing our song." As they circled the floor, she didn't allow herself to think that it might be the last time they danced to that haunting tune.

That night, she made love to him tenderly. Their lovemaking held none of the wild passion of old, but it was touched with a sweetness and poignance that was as compelling. Afterward, they lay close, clinging to each other as though they were two people shipwrecked, whose only hope was in staying together.

And so the days drifted on. Lily wanted to catch each one and wring every moment of happiness possible from it, not so much for herself, but for Harry. But never had time passed so swiftly, she couldn't help notice with chagrin.

She tried not to notice his increasing languor, the episodes when his breathing became harsh and his face twisted with pain, but as the weeks moved on, and the huge ship docked at various ports of call, it became apparent that he was no longer up even to a mild stroll around the different towns.

He seemed happiest when they were at sea. Best of all were the times when he and Lily and Cadeau curled up together under steamer blankets in the deck chairs. Their baby was growing up before their very eyes. They tickled her and played with her, expressed surprise and pleasure over her growing vocabulary, laughed about every funny little thing she did, and admired her shining red curls.

Harry never said anything about pain, but there came a day when Lily entered the cabin to find him doubled over in agony. "Harry, darling—what's wrong?"

When he couldn't speak, she ran and banged on the nurse's stateroom door, then entered unceremoniously. "Miss McFarlane, my husband is in terrible pain. I think that he needs to start having the morphine."

Jane McFarlane's kind, plain face was troubled. "Mrs. Kohle, he's been having it for several weeks now. It's just getting to the point where it's not enough to completely deaden the pain."

Several weeks! Lily listened, stricken. Harry hadn't said a word. And her hopes, which had been irrationally rising during these idyllic weeks, came crashing.

She cried that night, quietly, hopelessly, while Harry lay beside her, but by the next morning she was able to smile bravely when she sat across from him at breakfast.

"Darling, today I think I'd just like to lie in a deck chair and read. How about you?"

"Sounds like a wonderful program, sweetheart."

Still, the decline was not precipitous. As the Eastern ports of call passed like a gently revolving kaleidoscope, they had another happy few weeks.

As the giant ship entered the Panama Canal, and the water began to pour in to raise it, hope began to rise in Lily as steadily as the water rising in the locks. Harry was going to make it all the way home. It was a triumph for both of them. Harry's coughing fits had reached such a point that at his insistence she had reluctantly agreed to sleep in her own stateroom at night. What woke her that awful night was the terrible retching sound from the bathroom.

She raced to the door and knocked. "Harry? Harry, are you all right in there?"

Hearing no answer, she burst in, then stopped short. "Oh, no," she said, almost under her breath. "No!"

Turning, she screamed, "Nurse! Nurse, come here!"

The basin was red with bloody sputum, while Harry lay still on the floor, blood trickling from the corner of his mouth.

Jane McFarlane came in quickly, still pulling her dressing gown about her. She knelt over him while Lily watched helplessly, her heart pounding, tears streaming down her cheeks.

A moment later, she looked up with a frightened look in her eyes. "Call the ship's doctor, Mrs. Kohle—stat!"

Together, Jane and the doctor worked intently as Lily looked on. Dread engulfed her. Was this it? Here, now, in this tiny bathroom?

But Harry's time had not yet run out. Several minutes later, he was removed to the infirmary, where he was examined more thoroughly. Finally the doctor came out to where Lily sat tensely and spoke to her. "Mrs. Kohle?" He made no pretense of addressing her as Mrs. David Goode.

"Mrs. Kohle, your husband is very sick. Apparently the cancer has spread very rapidly. His liver is badly affected, and now his remaining lung is being literally suffocated by the metastases."

"What should I do, Doctor?" Lily whispered hoarsely.

"The only thing you can do is get him off this ship and fly him to a big medical facility, where they can make his last days a lot less painful. It was foolhardy to bring him on this long cruise."

Numbly, Lily nodded. She knew that reason and rationality were on the doctor's side, but he didn't understand.

"I've sent a message to the captain, and it's been arranged for the ship to stop briefly off Panama City. From there, you should be able to arrange a flight back to the States."

"Thank you, Doctor."

He hesitated, looking down at the bowed head. "I'm sorry, Mrs. Kohle. The whole world admires Harry Kohle. I know how hard this must have been for you."

With the help of the ship's crew, she chartered a plane from Panama City and sent a telegram to Ellis in New York to alert the hospital and have an ambulance waiting at the airport.

Harry was conscious, but very sleepy from the increased doses of morphine. As they sped down the runway and took off, she held his hand very tightly. "Hang on, Harry," she said, choking back tears. "We'll be home soon, darling."

His only answer was a feeble squeeze of her hand.

Soon the rugged mountains of Central America receded into the distance as they flew out over the blueness of the Gulf of Mexico. Its bleak expanse seemed to reflect the emptiness of Lily's mental landscape as she prayed fervently, "Just let Harry make it home. . . . Please, God."

But God didn't heed her pleas. They had passed over the U.S. border and were somewhere over Mississippi when Harry convulsed, coughed one last time, and fell forward.

Jane McFarlane had just finished checking his vital signs. Now she sprang forward to catch him. She took out her stethoscope and pressed it to his chest. But after a minute or two she looked at Lily and shook her head.

Lily pushed her away and seized Harry, drawing his head

down to cradle it against her breast. "Harry, Harry, darling . . . I love you. I love you!" she cried. "Harry, speak to me!"

But it was too late. Harry was gone, and as she cradled him his heart had already gone silent.

The plane suddenly seemed very still as Lily sat rocking back and forth, her husband's body in her arms.

Cadeau slept peacefully in her seat, oblivious to what was happening, as Jane quietly told Françoise that Mr. Kohle had passed away. Then, without a glance at Lily, she went forward and asked the crew to radio ahead to New York. "Have them get in touch with Mr. Ellis Knox and tell him of Mr. Kohle's death en route—he'll make all the necessary arrangements."

Meanwhile, Lily clung to her husband's body.

She had thought about how she would react when the final moment came. Would she be prepared? Would she be calm and stoical? Hysterical? As it happened, she sat very still, without sobbing, the tears rolling silently down her cheeks.

*Oh darling, I did love you so,* she thought. *I'm sorry that we wasted so many years, but what we had, in the end, was something that couldn't be measured in time.*

Ellis met the plane, and as Lily stepped off the stair, supported by Jane McFarlane, she saw that he was flanked on either side by Drew and Randy. At the sight of them, she almost broke down. Drew rushed forward and embraced her, holding her for a long moment in shared grief. In his arms, she felt very fragile. He remembered how, when he was a child, she had seemed so very strong. Now, he towered over her and was the one to give her strength and comfort. "I love you, Mom," he murmured.

As he released her, she turned to Randy, and he put his arms around her. Even his usual undemonstrative mien seemed to have cracked. Lily saw a tear glisten in his eye as he said huskily, "I'm sorry, Mother, so sorry."

Meanwhile, Ellis had supervised the removal of Harry's body to the waiting hearse, and then gathered together Cadeau, Françoise and Jane McFarlane.

Lily saw him now as she hadn't seen him before. The expression in his eyes somehow held the comfort and sympathy that Lily knew then had been her mainstay all these years.

"Are you ready to go, Lily?" he asked quietly.

Drawing a deep breath, she said, "Yes."

Back at the apartment, they discussed funeral arrangements. They had all expected Lily to be so grief-stricken that matters would have to be placed in others' hands. But Lily spoke calmly. Harry would have wanted to be buried in the Kohle family crypt, next to Jeremy.

Randy offered to go down to the Sinai Chapel and pick out a coffin, but Lily demurred. "No, I think I'd like to do that myself," she said steadily.

As Ellis looked at her, he marveled at her composure. Where, in all the course of her miserable childhood and youth, had she gotten that inner strength which sustained her? Her courage was so remarkable that he almost feared for her. Could this calm be a thin façade? He prayed that it would not shatter, leaving her exposed and vulnerable.

Ellis knew Lily well enough to know she was devastated. Whatever Harry had been and whatever his shortcomings as a human being or husband were now irrelevant. Whether or not their rapprochement would have lasted, whether he would have remained a faithful, devoted husband were points that had been forever made moot by his passing.

For all the times he had felt intense anger against Harry the man, for all the times he had almost hated him for his cavalier treatment of Lily, now he too felt only a deep sadness, for the loss of Harry, his best friend.

# Chapter 54

THE death of Harry Kohle made the front page of every newspaper in the country. The editorials were grave, almost reverent in tone, as they lauded the contribution Harry had made not just to literature, but to humanity as well.

"He is gone, but his words will live forever. . . ."

Cards, letters and floral arrangements of all sizes flooded in from all over the world. On the day of the funeral, the Temple Ben Israel was overflowing.

Lily, flanked by Drew and Randy, with Melissa to Randy's left, sat through the services like a statue, letting the events swirl around her, barely hearing the eulogy the rabbi delivered. There were no tears to be shed today. Instead, she wrapped herself in the comforting veil of her memories: all the joy and happiness she and Harry had had together. That was what people were supposed to remember at the end—only the good.

Gazing around herself absently, she suddenly became aware of Benjamin Kohle, sitting next to Elise. Tears were running silently down the old man's cheeks as he sat, his massive shoulders hunched. He looked utterly defeated by this blow. Her heart suddenly ached for her father-in-law, for she of all people knew what it was like to lose a son. The feeling transcended sorrow and grief; it was such a grim reversal of the natural patterns of life.

The rabbi's eulogy went on for a few more minutes, and then it was Drew's turn. On an impulse, he had asked the rabbi earlier if he could speak; but when he looked out at the vast assembly before him, Drew was momentarily speechless, and not because of the crowds before him. There was so much to say. How could he begin?

Obliterated from his memory were all the harsh words that had come between them, the accusations and reproaches. Drew was already creating a memory of his father in a new, more benign image. And suddenly, the words he wanted to say came forth readily, as though sprung from a source deep within him.

"My father was a man who made a great contribution to us all. He touched millions through his writing, all over the world. But what I want everyone here to be aware of is that there was another side to Harry Kohle. He left not only a vast public, but a family to mourn him.

"As a writer, he possessed the power to evoke the deepest of human emotions: love and hate, pity and revenge, elation and despair. But within the bosom of his family, there was only love—the steadfast and abiding love he had for his wife and children.

"It is truly remarkable that even with all the demands and pressure of being a famous author, he always made his home the center of his existence. His children will remember him as a kind and affectionate man, a man of infinite compassion and understanding. I only pray that wherever he is, he knows how much we love him and miss him.

"I loved you, Father."

As Drew took his seat again next to Lily, she wordlessly took his hand. It didn't matter to her that Drew had gotten up and told not quite the truth about Harry; the thought that her son had reconciled himself to his father, even posthumously, was of great solace to her.

And then it was time to go to the cemetery. The bronze doors opened slowly, then all too quickly they were swung shut.

Harry and Jeremy would lie side by side in that cold crypt for the rest of time. At that thought, she turned away from the crypt and stumbled some few feet. The grief she had kept at bay suddenly engulfed her.

Who could possibly have foreseen that this was the way their lives together would end? What two young people in love ever thought ahead to the end, to old age and death and loss? That night at the opera, they had been so young and carefree. . . .

But why couldn't they have grown old together? How blessed Benjamin and Elise had been, despite today's sorrow, in sharing the golden years of their lives.

If God had only decreed that it should always be so—that people who loved one another would live out their prescribed span together, and then die peacefully, in each other's arms.

As a sob broke from her, Drew came up and took her arm, saying gently, "Mother? Come on, it's time to go back to the house."

There had been one the day of Jeremy's funeral, but today there was to be no huge reception. Back at The Meadows, only Harry's very closest friends and associates gathered along with his family. They quietly reminisced about him as they sat around the drawing room. Lily could barely stand to hear the loving eulogies and remembered anecdotes. Her head throbbed.

She went down the hall to her bathroom. Maybe an aspirin would quell the headache that had been coming on since this morning. Swallowing two, she wearily smoothed her hair, went back into the bedroom, and stopped short. Facing her—at once nervous and defiant—was Melissa.

"Mother, I have something to talk to you about," she announced.

Unbeknownst to Lily, in the time since she had given up Cadeau, Melissa had experienced some disconcerting reversals.

For a long time she had clung to the belief that eventually Jean-Paul would marry her, but then she began to realize that as the novelty had worn off, his initial passion had waned. He no longer took her with him on the ski tour, and when he was in Paris he quite openly flirted with other women.

The first time she had caught him in a bedroom at a party with the young blonde skier had been a rude shock, but at least that time he had apologized and explained that he was a little drunk.

But just three nights ago, when she had discovered him with another woman in their very own bed, all he had said was, "This is my apartment, and my bed, and I'll sleep with any woman I want to. If you don't like it, you can move out."

And so the telegram bringing word of her father's death had offered a welcome temporary escape from her troubles.

Sitting on the plane, she had found herself feeling an unexpected longing for the baby she had given up.

Suddenly she wanted something of her own, someone to love *her*, and her only. After all, she had nothing else . . . her father was dead, her brothers were indifferent, and Jean-Paul didn't seem to love her anymore.

Yes, she'd decided, she wanted to see her baby. A cute, adorable child to hug and kiss might relieve the loneliness and boredom of her own life.

"I want to see my baby, Mother. And don't look so blank. I am the one who brought her into the world, after all."

Lily felt a stab of fear. Cadeau. She had never considered the possibility that Melissa might someday demand to see her baby. The only other time Melissa had visited, she hadn't so much as inquired about her. Instantly Lily knew that that meeting must be prevented at all costs. It was one thing for Melissa to give up a nameless baby she had never laid eyes on, and quite another to renounce a bright, adorable, precious child like Cadeau.

What if Melissa decided to file suit to recover custody? It was Lily's worst fear, her recurrent nightmare. After all, there were doctors in France who could testify to the true facts of Cadeau's birth . . . her birth certificate was forged. Lily was on shaky ground, she knew, and she was all alone now, without Harry to help her fight back. She couldn't go on living without Cadeau.

But Cadeau was not lost yet, Lily told herself fiercely, and if she played her cards right, she wouldn't be.

Her mind working furiously, she calculated. Before the funeral, Ellis had taken Cadeau and Françoise to the apartment in Manhattan. They would stay there until she came for them. Even if her daughter guessed that they were at the apartment, Lily would have time to call and arrange for them to be spirited away before she could get there.

But as she considered her alternatives, Melissa coolly demanded, "Mother, where is the baby?"

Drawing on every ounce of courage she possessed, Lily answered calmly, "The baby is not here."

"When do I get to see her?"

"What do you mean, Melissa? You said that you never wanted to see her. Not ever."

"That was then, Mother—this is now. I'm here, and I'd like to see her. After all, she's my child."

"She's not your child!" Lily suddenly blazed unexpectedly. "You may have given birth to her, but you didn't want her and I took her. She's my child now!"

Melissa faced her defiantly. "Oh yeah? You know, I could take you to court and prove that she's mine. I could really fight you on this thing."

"Why, Melissa? Why—out of love? Do you really *want* the baby? Are you suddenly feeling maternal? You want to play mother day in and day out?"

For a moment Melissa felt taken aback. "Mother" sounded downright depressing, so staid and sober. She hadn't gone quite that far in her thinking. After all, how could she take care of a baby in Paris? When she returned, she wasn't even sure Jean-Paul would take her back. And it was certain he wouldn't take in the baby.

But as she stared at her mother's pale, set face, Melissa felt a sudden surge of rebellion. Her mother was always telling her what to do, always trying to control her. Falling back on her earlier cant, she repeated defiantly, "It's my baby. You have no right to tell me I can't see it."

Lily felt as though her knees were about to buckle under her. She tried to sound authoritative. "It doesn't even make sense, Melissa. You said that Jean-Paul won't marry you. He dislikes children. What would he say if you brought the baby back to live in your apartment?"

The painful reminder of Jean-Paul made Melissa suddenly flare up. "It doesn't matter what he thinks!"

"But it does, Melissa! Because it has to do with the kind of life you could give this baby. Let me ask you something. If he hated the baby, how long would your newfound maternal instinct last?"

"Don't you talk to me like that! How devoted were you when you gave us to nannies and governesses, and then shipped us off to boarding school so young?"

Lily stared at her daughter in disbelief. This was what she had sacrificed her life for? Yes, she had sent the children to boarding schools, but what about all the years before, when her life had been devoted to them completely? What about all the picnics and taffy pulls and coloring at the kitchen table?

Had none of that made any impression on the children? Had she really been such a bad mother?

Looking at Melissa now, she thought how their family had really been. It pained her to have Melissa before her now, complaining and bitter. Had she truly forgotten all their good times?

Well, it was too late for the rest of them—Harry was gone, Jeremy was gone, Randy was a stranger to her, and Melissa was the most incomprehensible of all—but it was not too late for Cadeau. Lily was never going to give her up—never!

With renewed vigor, she said flatly, "Melissa, I explained all of this to you while I was in Paris. You will never be able to take this baby back. And there's no chance in all the world I'll give her to you. You listen to me, and listen carefully. I went through a great deal to get this baby. I lied to the world, and perpetrated a great hoax so that the baby would be legitimate. You're not even thinking about what would happen to her if her true parentage were revealed. The truth is that you are an incredibly selfish, ruthless, self-centered person."

"You're a fine one to call me ruthless!" Melissa burst into tears. "Taking away my baby! Well, I'll fight you—"

"With what?" Lily asked coldly. It was as if a different person were talking, so severe was her tone. Lily would never have believed she would speak this way to one of her children. "It takes a lot of money to file suit, particularly when it involves international issues. Where are you planning to get the money?"

"I will have money from Daddy—"

"No, you won't," Lily corrected her. "He left every penny to me. It's all at my absolute discretion. And if you fight me, I'll see to it that you get nothing, ever. A baby, and no money. Is that what you want, Melissa?"

"You have everything," she accused her bitterly. "Everything. All the money, all this grandeur, my baby—"

Suddenly, Lily was crying and shaking. "Damn you, Melissa! Damn you! I've just lost your father. We've just come from putting him into his grave, and you tell me that I have everything! I have nothing—nothing except the baby! And just because of some foolish passing whim, you hit me with this today, of all days!"

Stunned by the violence of her mother's words, Melissa stepped back uncertainly. Suddenly the whole thing seemed to have been blown entirely out of proportion. She didn't really want to be tied to a baby, after all.

"I'm sorry," she mumbled. "Forget I said anything."

As the door closed behind her daughter, Lily indulged in a burst of tears. The scene shouldn't have surprised her. Melissa was a Goodhue, through and through. Violet, only with a touch of Charles's ruthlessness. She would step on anyone to get what she wanted.

But Melissa would not have Cadeau to treat as a toy, then toss aside when she had tired of her. At that thought, Lily felt a great sense of relief. She returned to the bathroom, splashed her face with cold water, then went out to rejoin her guests.

Half an hour later, Melissa appeared at the doorway and announced, "I have a reservation for a flight back to Paris this afternoon. Can anyone take me to the airport?"

"I will," Ellis promptly volunteered, and Lily threw him a look of gratitude.

After that, people began to drift away; by the time he came back Lily was alone with Mary.

When she heard the roar of his Bentley in the courtyard, she flew to the door and ran out to the car. Just emerging was Françoise, holding a sleeping Cadeau. "Cadeau, darling, darling!"

Sleepily, Cadeau's eyes fluttered open. "Mommy," she murmured happily, holding out her arms to Lily, and Lily buried her face in her baby's hair, her heart too full for words.

A short time later, Ellis came and found Lily sitting by herself in the dark in Cadeau's room.

"Is she asleep?" he asked quietly.

When Lily nodded, he asked, "In that case, can you leave her for just a few minutes? Drew and Randy are leaving and want to see you."

Drew was going back to Harvard, Randy to his job at Goodhue Rubber. Each gave her a swift, comforting embrace. "We'll be back to see you soon, Mother. . . . Call us. . . . We love you. . . ."

As the car rolled down the hill out of sight, Lily and Ellis turned away inside, and Ellis said, "How about a drink, and something to eat? You look as though you're at the end of your rope."

Wearily, she shrugged. After he had filled a plate with a

few things he thought might tempt her, she allowed him to lead her into the now quiet study.

He poured her a brandy and lit a fire, then came to sit across from her.

After watching her for a few moments, Ellis said quietly, "You've shown so much courage today, Lily. You've been magnificent."

Raising her eyes to meet his, she shook her head and said slowly, "I'm not brave, Ellis. But I have Cadeau to think about. She's lost her father now, and she can't lose her mother too."

Her voice quavered and he asked, "What is it, Lily? Something happened today with Melissa, didn't it?"

"Oh, Ellis, it was dreadful. She said that she wanted Cadeau back."

"Oh, Lily, Melissa doesn't want that baby. I'm sure it was just a whim. Today a baby, tomorrow a dress. She's as unstable as could be."

"But Ellis, she threatened to take me to court! And what if she and this Jean-Paul decide to get married? Surely the courts would award the baby to its own married parents, not its widowed grandmother!" Her shoulders began to shake and the tears to stream down her face as she thought of the dreadful prospect.

"Listen, Lily, I have to confess something. From time to time, whenever I've been in Paris, I've checked up on Melissa and her skier friend. And I can assure you that there's absolutely no possibility that they're going to get married. I've talked to the young man, and he has no intention of ever tying himself down to any one woman, let alone one with a child."

Ellis's words brought overwhelming relief, but Lily was too ravaged by the day's events. He drew her into his arms to comfort her, but that only made her break down completely.

Finally, he said gently, "Lily, dear, this is just the accumulated strain of having been so strong for so long. You need rest, more than anything else."

He carried her to her room, where he found a mild sedative and made her take it. "Come on, now. Get some sleep. Things will look better in the morning. I'll be here if you need anything."

After watching him retire to the nearby wing chair, she finally began to relax and shortly thereafter fell into an exhausted sleep. As soon as she stirred the next morning, Ellis woke from his uncomfortable position in the chair and went to summon Mary.

After asking her to bring Lily a tray, he returned to find her awake.

Sleepily, she asked, "What time is it?"

"Six-thirty."

"When did you come back?"

"I've been here all night."

"You seem to shoulder all my troubles, don't you?"

"My shoulders are broad enough to stand it. Now, Mary's bringing you some coffee."

Weakly, she sipped the strong, hot brew. In the light of a new day, things seemed much clearer. The nightmares had receded somewhat.

The dreadful truth—that Harry was dead—was still with her, but that was a fact she was slowly beginning to accept.

Ellis spent the day with her, not pressing her to talk about her plans, but simply waiting. And then it came.

"Ellis, about six months ago, I came to a decision. I knew that when Harry was gone, I would not want to live here in the city any longer. I want to go back to the farm. I know that before when I've gone back, it has been for the wrong reasons, but this time I don't feel as if it's an escape; it's simply the place that reaches out to me. All of my hopes and dreams were born there. That's where I want to raise Cadeau.

"I don't know, maybe it's because I feel as if I failed with the other children and this is a second chance, a chance to redeem myself. There's nothing here in Manhattan for me anymore. The only thing that matters is Cadeau."

Ellis tried not to feel hurt at her words: "There's nothing here in Manhattan for me. . . ." At this moment, she wasn't thinking of him. Right now, all her love and longing were centered on the child. And he wondered: Would she ever want romantic love to come into her life again, or would she retreat into the fulfillment of being a mother?

This retreat to the farm seemed to give him his answer, but trying to quell his ever devoted heart, he smiled down at her. "Would you like me to drive you?"

. . .

At long last, spring had come. Harry had been gone nine months, and Lily's acute bereavement had softened into a duller sorrow. The grief she had felt at his death was not the stab it had once been. She could think of Harry without pain. She was grateful for their last year together. It had been their best one.

She and Cadeau were gathering wildflowers in the meadow. Lily almost laughed aloud when she looked at her. Her baby was now almost two and a half, and she was a sight to behold. Her burnished red hair shone in the sunlight. Her eyes were as green as the emeralds Harry had bought for Lily in Paris. The tiniest, most diminutive freckles were scattered across the bridge of her nose.

To Lily, she looked like a child from a Renoir—simply an enchanting creature. Lily laughed at the sight of her capering through the knee-high grass.

Lily picked her up and lifted her high above her head, all twenty-five pounds of her. Cadeau shrieked with delight.

"You look so delicious, I could eat you!" Lily said.

"No, Mommy, don't!"

"I said I could, but I won't." Lily laughed, kissing her rosy cheek. "Now let's pick flowers."

As they gathered them, Cadeau peppered Lily with questions. "What's this one, Mommy?"

"That's Queen Anne's lace—like the lace on your petticoat."

"And what's this one?" Cadeau asked, as she added another to her bunch.

"That's a . . ." But Lily didn't finish the sentence. When she looked beyond the sycamores to the clearing, silhouetted against the sky stood a man. As he began walking toward her, she stopped short. She would have recognized that walk anywhere.

She ran through the meadow, her skirts billowing out in the soft breeze, with Cadeau behind her. And just before she reached him, Lily dropped the armload of wildflowers, opened her arms, and ran into his extended ones.

"Oh, Ellis, I'm so happy that you came!"